T0270067

THE WAGES OF SIN

THE WAGES OF SIN

Harry Turtledove

CAEZIK
SF & FANTASY
ARC MANOR
ROCKVILLE, MARYLAND

SHAHID MAHMUD
PUBLISHER

www.caeziksf.com

ISBN: 978-1-64710-092-6

First Edition. December 2023
2 3 4 5 6 7 8 9 10

An imprint of Arc Manor LLC

www.CaezikSF.com

Contents

I

IN THE BEGINNING: 1509

Filipe Sousa and Pedro Alves squelched through the muddy streets of Boma. The trading village—the biggest one this side of the rapids that kept boats from going very far up the Congo—was claimed by Portugal, but no one took that seriously. Dutch and English slave dealers and other merchants also operated here.

White men had been trading in these parts for almost thirty years now. The Africans in Boma had come to take them for granted, which wasn't true everywhere. Blacks who'd never seen a man from Europe before often took him for a ghost—how else could he be so pale?

"*Bom dia!*" called a bare-breasted woman with a big pot and a wooden dipper. "You want some banana wine?" The question was a mishmash of Portuguese, Dutch, and two or three of the local languages.

"No, thanks, sweetheart. Not now." Sousa's answer came from the same stew of tongues. Nobody would ever write poetry in the trade lingo. As long as the natives and the strangers from across the sea could tell each other what they wanted and how much they'd give for it, they were content.

"Mother of God, but that's horrible swill," Alves said, pitching his voice low so the hawker couldn't hear. "Drink a couple of dippers and you'll wish your head would fall off."

"How do you know?" Sousa grinned at his bosun.

The stocky little man grinned back. "Same way you do, *Senhor*."

A man with a missing front tooth used a stick to stir a big iron pot mounted above a fire. "Bushmeat stew?" he asked. He poked something with the stick and held it up so the Portuguese traders could see it: a hand as big as a man's, but with longer fingers and a shorter thumb. "Special good—got shimpanse in it."

Not trusting himself to speak, Sousa shook his head and walked on. He'd seen live shimpanses. They looked too much like people for him to want to eat them. The Africans saw things differently. Cattle and sheep and horses couldn't live in these parts. They died of tropical sicknesses even faster than Europeans did, which was saying something. Without domestic animals, you got your meat from whatever you could catch.

A half-grown boy displayed skewered grubs on a wide, bright green leaf. "I think I'd sooner eat those than shimpanse," Sousa said.

Alves shuddered. "I don't want the bugs, and I don't want the critter, either."

"Remind me why you came to Africa," Sousa said with a chuckle.

"Same reason you come here—to see if maybe I can get rich."

"Fair enough." The merchant-adventurer paused and pointed. "There's Njoya's compound. Whatever he has in his pot, we'll eat it and we'll make like we like it."

"I know." By Alves' face, the knowledge did not overjoy him.

A guard with an iron-tipped spear stood outside Njoya's hut. He wasn't just for show; people here, like people anywhere, would steal anything not nailed down. Sousa's rowers guarded the boat they'd hauled out of the Congo and up onto the riverbank. They wore morions on their heads and swords on their belts, which impressed the locals. And they had arquebuses, which frightened the Africans. The natives had swords of their own, and they could see how helmets worked. But firearms seemed like magic to them.

The guard ducked into the hut. A moment later, Njoya came out with him. The African trader was in his mid-forties, with

2

broad shoulders and a big, firm belly that said he'd eaten well for a long time. Portly men were no more common here than in Europe. You had to be smart or lucky or—usually—both to get that far ahead of hunger.

Njoya folded first Sousa and then Alves into a sweaty embrace. "Filipe! Pedro! Good to see you both!" he boomed in pretty good Portuguese: no *lingua franca* for him. He could also get along in English and Dutch and several of the local languages. He even knew some Arabic.

"Good to see you, too, you old thief," Sousa said. Njoya held that big, firm belly in both hands and laughed out loud, for all the world as if the white man were kidding. Dryly, Sousa continued, "What'll you try and palm off on us today?"

Njoya looked so wounded, he could have been a bad actor. "I don't need to palm nothing off on you, *Senhor* Filipe." His Portuguese was good, but not perfect. "I got a cousin who come here from up the Songha River with a good bunch of people his folk capture."

Cousin, here, probably meant something like *somebody I've done business with before*. Sousa had heard of the Songha. It was one of the rivers that flowed into the Congo somewhere beyond the rapids. He thought it ran down from the north, but he wasn't sure. No white man had ever seen it.

"Well, you and your cousin can show them to us if you want to," he said. You never seemed too eager. Bargaining rules among blacks differed not a copper's worth from those among whites.

"In a while, in a while." Njoya acted as if the slaves didn't matter to him, either. "You can come inside first. You meet my cousin. We eat, we drink, we talk. Then you can look at those stupid people. Must be stupid, hey? Otherwise, they don't get catched."

"That's about the size of it," Sousa agreed. Africans of the not-stupid variety sold slaves to the European traders who came to these parts in ever greater numbers. The market was taking off like a flushed partridge now that Spain and Portugal had found those new lands beyond the Atlantic. And the Africans who wound up on the wrong side of a war or a raid? That was their hard luck.

He and Alves ducked into Njoya's hut. One of the black man's wives was tending a stewpot. She smiled at the whites. She wasn't pretty, not to Sousa's eyes, but she was as well fed as her husband. A centipede as long as a man's middle finger scuttled under some junk. The merchant-adventurer suppressed a grimace. Africa was hell for bugs.

Another woman—a girl, really—dipped out cups of banana wine and shyly offered them to the two Portuguese and to Njoya. A tall, scrawny, very black man of about thirty came in from the back. "This is my cousin. He calls himself Maigari," Njoya said. He switched to an African language to introduce Sousa and Alves to the newcomer.

The girl gave Maigari banana wine, too. He coughed a couple of times as he dipped his head to the merchant-adventurer and the bosun. "Good to meet you, friends," he said in the mixed-up trade lingo they spoke in Boma. He used more native words and fewer from Europe than some who lived here would have, but he managed. The way he stared at Sousa and Alves argued he hadn't seen many white men till now.

"You eat," Njoya's wife said, and filled bowls from the pot. The spoons were made of wood. Sousa ate. Christ only knew what the meat was—no shimpanse hands, anyway. Some of the vegetables were squashes. One was okra, which was seedy and slimy but tasted all right. Sousa didn't know the names of the rest, or of the spices that went into the stew. He emptied the bowl anyhow, washing down the food with sips of the too-sweet banana wine.

Emptying your bowl was good manners. Alves followed suit. Njoya smacked his lips as he made his stew disappear. Maigari ate more slowly, slowly enough to make Njoya's wife frown. "You don't like?" she asked.

"No, no. Is good, is good," said the skinny man from up the Songha. "Just not big"—he ran out of words and patted his belly to show he meant something like *appetite*—"lately."

Sousa wondered if he was well. The way he coughed, the way his eyes bulged, made the Portuguese doubt it. But what could you do except go on? Doctors in Europe talked a much better game than they played. It was bound to work the same way here.

However sweet the banana wine was, it packed a punch. By the time Sousa got to the bottom of his third cup, the tip of his long,

4

pointed nose went numb—a sure sign he'd had his share and then some. Alves, Njoya, and Njoya's wife wore glassy-eyed smiles. Even Maigari looked less afraid he'd fall apart in the next hour or two.

Slapping at a buzzing fly, the Portuguese reminded himself of business. The sooner he bought the slaves, the sooner he took them down the river to Sonho, the sooner the *São Paulo* sailed for Lisbon, the better his chances of not coming down with anything horrible himself. He touched the brim of his hat to Maigari. "Do you want to show me your wares?" he asked. The man from up the Songha didn't follow *wares*. Sousa tried again: "The people you brought here to sell?"

Maigari got that. "Oh, yes. You come with me," he said.

Come with him Sousa did. So did Alves and Njoya. Njoya's wife and the girl who'd served them banana wine—another wife? a daughter? a slave?—got their own bowls of stew then. They'd drunk with the men, but they hadn't eaten with them.

Behind his hut, Njoya had a slave pen: an enclosure whose fence posts were set touching one another, driven deep into the ground, tied together with leather lashings, and sharpened to points on top. The gate had a stout bar—also secured with lashings—and brass hinges that had probably come up the Congo in trade. Sousa wrinkled his nose. Numb or not, it could tell that a lot of people had been pissing and shitting in the pen for a long time.

Njoya nodded to Alves. "You close it behind us and stand watch, hey?"

"*Sim, Senhor,*" the bosun said, drawing his sword.

Into the pen went Njoya, Maigari, and Filipe Sousa. Inside squatted a dozen or so miserable-looking black men and women. Their hands were bound behind them. A long rope noosed around each one's neck held them together. Anybody who tried to break away would choke himself and his partners in captivity.

"Tell them to stand up so I can look them over," Sousa said to Maigari, eking out the words with gestures. The upriver man nodded. He spoke to the captives in a language Sousa didn't know. Catching one another's eyes, they rose in not too ragged unison.

Three or four were men in their prime. One had a half-healed wound in his thigh. *That whoreson did some fighting before they got*

5

him, Sousa thought. *Have to keep an eye on him.* A couple of other men were older, their close-cropped woolly hair going gray. Most of the women seemed pretty ordinary. The last one, though, the one at the end of the line …

Sousa's breath hissed out sharply. The first thing that crossed his mind was the verse from the Song of Solomon: *I am black, but comely.* She was more than comely. Black or not, she was the most stunning woman Sousa had ever seen. That his wife waited an ocean away only made him feel it more strongly.

The African girl was within a year either way of seventeen. Perfect round breasts, a big handful apiece. Narrow waist flaring out to hips made for bearing children. When he walked around in back of her, he found the grabbable behind he'd expected. Her nose might be low and broad, but she had kissable lips, fine white teeth, and gorgeous eyes—frightened now as her head swiveled to watch him.

"Well, well," the merchant-adventurer murmured, and then again: "Well, well!"

Maigari obviously knew what he had. He spoke in another language Sousa couldn't follow. Njoya could. Chuckling, he translated: "He say she cost you plenty, you bet."

"I believe it," Sousa said with resigned regret. Whatever she cost, he'd pay it. He knew he'd make plenty when he got her back to Lisbon. He patted that smooth, warm backside. She flinched, but not too badly. He wouldn't be the first man who'd rested his hand there since her tribe lost its fight. He asked, "Is she as good as she looks?"

He used the trade speech of Boma. Maigari had enough to get his meaning. The skinny man rocked his hips forward and back. Sousa understood some of his answer, but not all of it. Njoya filled him in on the rest: "He screw her every day since he get her, he and his brothers."

"Brothers?" Sousa hadn't heard about them before.

"Three brothers, *sim.* They somewhere in the village, screwing more or getting plastered. They strong, they not smart," Njoya said dismissively. "Maigari here, him you got to watch for. He's no dope."

"Too bad," Sousa said, which made Njoya laugh. He translated for Maigari, who also chuckled and then coughed again. Sousa went on, "So she's broken in to screwing, then?"

"That's right," Maigari said, mostly through Njoya. "Somebody had her before I got her, so my brothers and me, we enjoyed her, too."

Filipe Sousa nodded. "Fair enough." The price he could have got for her if she were a maiden! But there were compensations. Once he bought her, he could take her himself whenever he pleased. Alves would want a taste of that sweetness, too. And he could lend her to Marco Lopes, the *São Paulo*'s skipper, once he got her down to Sonho.

Maigari coughed once more, this time purposefully. "How much you give for her and the rest? I don't like your price, maybe I keep her for myself. I not make so much then, but I smile all the time."

He didn't look like a man who would smile all the time no matter how happy he was. But he did look like a man who meant what he said. Quickly, Njoya said, "What say you settle for the others first? You finish that, then you talk about the girl." He'd get a cut from whatever Sousa paid Maigari. He had an interest in making sure things went smoothly.

"You got manillas?" Maigari asked the Portuguese.

"Oh, yes." Sousa took one out of his belt pouch. The stout copper bracelet weighed nearly a pound. It made up more than three quarters of a circle; the ends flared out. Manillas were the "coins" European traders used all through West Africa. Holding this one so Maigari could inspect it, Sousa added, "Plenty more back at my boat."

Maigari looked a question at Njoya. The local nodded. He set a hand on Sousa's shoulder, as if to say he was an honorable man. "Is good," Maigari said. "We dicker."

"Then you dick her," Njoya said to Sousa, and went into gales of laughter at his own wit. He nudged the merchant-adventurer. "I been in there, too. She the best."

"We'll do the others first, the way you said," Sousa replied. The young, strong men fetched fifty manillas each. Sousa carefully examined the leg wound the one of them bore. It was healing well, and wouldn't leave him crippled. Sousa didn't try to get a break on his price. He bought the older men and the women for thirty to forty manillas apiece. He didn't haggle so hard as he might have; he wanted to keep Maigari as sweet as he could. Pretty soon, only the girl remained unsold. Sousa nodded her way. "How much?"

Maigari held up both hands. He slowly opened and closed them, fingers splayed wide, twenty times. "Two hundred?" Njoya said, awe and alarm in his voice. That was a lot of copper. Well, she was a lot of woman.

"I'll give you half—one hundred," Sousa said.

A brusque shake of the head showed what the man from up the Songha thought of that. "You meet my price or I keep her," he said.

Filipe Sousa studied him. He sounded like a man who meant what he said, too. The Portuguese eyed the girl again. Those tits seemed to smile back at him. Just imagining what she'd be like made his trouser snake stir. He wouldn't get to keep her all that long, but Lord Jesus, he'd have fun while he did! "Maybe you'll take a hundred and fifty?" he asked hopefully.

"Maybe I won't, too," Maigari said.

"Ah, *vai-te foder*," Sousa said without heat. Njoya clicked his tongue between his teeth, but sensibly didn't translate that. Sousa spread his hands, accepting defeat. "Two hundred it is," he agreed. He pointed toward the girl. "Can I try her out now?"

Maigari shook his head. "After you pay." Sousa only shrugged. He'd hoped, but he'd expected no different.

When he came out of the compound, Pedro Alves asked, "How much do we have to bring back from the boat?"

Sousa totted things up on his fingers to make sure he had it all straight. "Six hundred fifty-four manillas," he answered.

"By the Virgin! That's a lot of copper—two trips' worth," the bosun said. "How many?"

"Only a dozen. But one's a girl in ten thousand." Sousa shaped an hourglass with his hands. "Wait till you see her! Worth all I paid and more besides. The gold she'll bring in …"

The two white men hurried back to the boat. Some of the rowers were half drunk on banana wine. Sousa counted out copper bracelets till he had enough. "So many?" an oarsman said. "We'll break our backs lugging all those."

"Got to be done. I'll carry, too." To get his hands on the girl as soon as he could, Sousa dropped his officer's dignity. And if he hauled like an ordinary rower, Alves couldn't very well hang back.

They did make two trips, though; they had to leave some men behind while the rest carried the wooden chests of manillas.

Maigari looked as pleased as he ever did at seeing so much copper all together. Njoya also beamed. They both counted the bracelets. When they were satisfied, Maigari said, "Now you take her."

"Damned right I do." Sousa went into the slave pen again. Lucky the girl was at the end of the line. He cut the rope that joined her to the others and took the free length in his hand so she couldn't get away.

When he brought her out of the pen, Alves' jaw dropped. "Hoo!" he said, devouring her with his eyes. "She's something, all right. I want some of that, too."

"Figured you would. But after me," Sousa said.

He took her around behind the pen. Njoya had other enclosures there, for ducks and chickens. And there was a little bit of open ground that wasn't too muddy. It wasn't a bed, but it would do.

She knew what was about to happen. He saw the fright in her eyes. He didn't want trouble or shrieks; that would make the other slaves restless and dangerous. He jabbed his thumb at his own chest. "I'm Filipe," he said. He pointed at her. "You? Your name?"

"Ada," she said. That wasn't exactly right, but it would do. She'd be Ada from then on.

"Well, Ada ..." Sousa gestured that she should lie down. He didn't choke her with the rope, but he didn't let go of it, either. With a martyr's sigh, she obeyed.

He let her stay on her side and got down in back of her. He would have liked to put her on her back so he could have more fun with those marvelous breasts, but he refrained. With her hands still bound behind her, it would have hurt her without need. He didn't think of himself as a cruel man. He didn't kick a dog or spur a horse for the sport of it.

But Ada was his property now, as much as a dog or a horse was. She was bought and paid for, here to be used. Her folk kept slaves, too. She'd know one of the things men used them for. Now it was her turn. She might not like it, but here it was. If she was as smart as she was pretty, she might even find ways to turn it to her advantage.

9

Because he didn't want to hurt her without need, he smeared spit on himself before he went into her. He had to push hard even so; she was dry as the desert in there. His foreskin got shoved back roughly enough to hurt a little. Things went better after a few shoves, though, and then better yet, and then—quite soon, since he hadn't done it for a long time—as good as they can get for a man this side of heaven.

He took her twice inside a quarter of an hour. He hadn't done anything like that in years. Maybe it was the long abstinence before. More likely, he judged, she was just too lovely for any man not to screw himself silly with her.

After he set his pants to rights, he patted that perfect arse one more time and helped her to her feet. He even brushed mud off her hipbone. His seed was dribbling down the inside of her left thigh. He pulled up some grass and wiped off most of it. No, he was not a cruel man.

Alves, Njoya, and Maigari all grinned as he took her back around slave pen again. "What you think?" Njoya asked after he came out.

"That's top-quality pussy, all right," Sousa answered. All the men laughed goatishly. The Portuguese didn't tell Maigari that he figured he'd bought Ada for a bargain price. What he'd sell her for in Lisbon .... But, like the man who'd brought her down to Boma, he'd be sorry when he couldn't have her any more himself.

"Can I take a crack at her now?" Alves asked.

Part of Sousa bristled, as any man will when another man shows he wants his woman. But that was foolish when you were talking about a slave who'd go up on the block as soon as she got to Portugal. "Why not?" Sousa said easily. "Her crack's there for the taking." Njoya translated that for Maigari. They all laughed some more.

Only a day's journey down the Congo separated Boma from Sonho, but at its end lay the start of another world. Above the palisade, you could see the cross-surmounted bell tower of the church where Portuguese and African converts worshiped. You could also see the tall-masted ships tied up at the quays.

And you could see the vastness of the Atlantic. The rowers had let the river's current do most of the work as they glided downstream.

That way, they could keep a closer watch on the slaves who crowded the boat. Before they set out, Filipe Sousa had used an arquebus to kill a duck that Njoya held out at arm's length. The boom and the smoke and flame impressed the blacks from up the Songha. So did the way the bullet made feathers fly from the luckless duck's carcass. They'd never dreamt of, much less seen, a weapon like that. It made them less inclined to try anything Sousa would regret.

The ocean, when they got to it, was intimidating in the same way. The slaves had no trouble understanding the Congo. It was a greater river than any they'd known before, but the difference was of degree, not of kind. When water filled most of the horizon, though, they stared and stared.

One of them could use a little of the trade talk from Boma. Pointing with his chin to the *São Paulo*, he said "House on water" to Sousa.

Bearers were walking up a gangplank into the ship, some with elephant tusks on their shoulders, others carrying rolled-up lion skins, still others with bundles wrapped and tied so the merchant-adventurer couldn't see what they held. "*Your* house on the water soon," he said. The African didn't get it. Well, he would.

Straight streets and rectangular buildings with red tile roofs also made the slaves gape. Sousa and his men led them to a warehouse and secured them there … all of them but Ada. Her he took aboard the *São Paulo* to show off to Captain Lopes.

Sailors and bearers howled at her like hungry dogs in front of a butcher shop. She shrank against Sousa when they did. He might not be a good choice, but she could tell they would be worse.

"Keep away, you cockproud bastards!" he shouted. "I paid for her!" They gave back the obscenities he'd looked for, but his manner—and his hand on his swordhilt—meant that was all they did.

He and Ada ducked into Lopes' tiny cabin at the stern of the galleon. The *São Paulo*'s skipper looked up from the note he was scribbling. He was past forty, with gray frosting his hair and whiskers, but tough and leathery still. "Ah, Filipe," he said, and then, when he got a glimpse of Ada, "Holy Jesus! What have you got there?"

"I believe it's called a woman, *Senhor*," Sousa answered, deadpan.

Lopes barked laughter. "That's a woman and a half, at least," he said. "Have you tried her out yet?"

"Me and Alves both," Sousa said. "She's got everything she needs, all right."

"She's got everything I need, too. Why don't you leave her here for a while? I'll make sure she doesn't get away"—he paused, considering—"and if she does, I swear by the Father, Son, and Holy Spirit I'll make it good to you."

Sousa made his own calculations. No, the captain probably wouldn't deny the oath. Ada probably wouldn't escape, either. Sousa gave her a gentle push toward Lopes. She looked at him with stricken eyes. "It's all right, dear," he said. "He won't hurt you, I promise." She wouldn't understand the words, but the tone was the one he used to gentle a spooked horse.

She let out a weary sigh as she crossed the cabin. This was all men wanted from her, was it? If she had her wits about her, she'd see she could trade on how much they'd want it. Some women got that right away. Others had trouble realizing just how much men thought with their pricks. Maybe, once Ada learned some Portuguese, he could explain it to her.

The *São Paulo* sailed a week later, making her slow way west across the Gulf of Guinea to get beyond the African bulge so she could swing north toward Portugal and home. All the slaves Sousa had bought were frightened and seasick. Ada, not surprisingly, got better quarters and better food than the other blacks. She also got sicker than any of them, with a real fever, night sweats that soaked her straw pallet, and swollen glands under her arms.

Seeing those made Sousa fear she'd come down with the plague, but she got better after a week or so, though the sweats went on. Then he stopped worrying so much about how she felt, because he came down with much the same thing himself. Wrung out, miserable, and tired all the time, he had to drag through the work of keeping the slaves fed, watered, and not too filthy.

He noted that Pedro Alves seemed listless and out of sorts, too. But, also like him, the bosun did the things he had to do. You weren't going to stay healthy all the time, not if you were a white man in these latitudes—and, by Ada's illness, not if you were a black woman, either. What could you do but go on and hope you got better?

After a while, Sousa did, as Ada had before him. Alves also seemed to have more pep. But, not long after the *São Paulo* turned to starboard and started north, Captain Lopes complained, "I wish this grippe I've got would let up. I feel weak as a wet sheet of paper."

"It's going through the ship, *Senhor*," Sousa said sympathetically. "I've had it, too, and I'm not the only one."

Marco Lopes wiped sweat off his forehead with his sleeve. "God's hairy balls, but Africa is a hellhole," he said. "I hope we live to profit from what we're bringing home, that's all."

"Amen!" Filipe Sousa crossed himself. A beat later, the skipper followed suit. Sousa went on, "By all I've heard, the lands that bound the Atlantic on the west are no bargain, either. Didn't the horrible new pox that's spreading all over creation come from there?"

"I've heard that, too. I don't know if it's true, but I've heard it," Lopes said. "That we've both heard it makes it more likely, chances are. This isn't as bad as that, thank the Lord. That kills you quick and ugly. This … I might as well be a cheese with somebody squeezing the whey out of me."

"You have a whey with words, *Senhor*," Sousa said. Lopes pulled a horrible face and made as if to push him out of the cabin. Chuckling, the merchant-adventurer went.

The *São Paulo* put in at Funchal, the biggest town on the island of Madeira, for fresh water and fresh food. Though Madeira had been discovered only a century or so earlier, Funchal was thriving. Farmers outside of town raised fennel and sugar beets and grew wine grapes. The sugar, especially, made them good money back on the mainland. The harbor bustled.

One of the ships in there was a Spanish galleon undergoing repairs. The *Paloma* had been bound for Cuba in the New World when a storm dismasted and almost sank her. She barely made Madeira, limping into Funchal. Her captain, a dour fellow named Diego Jaramillo, grumbled about the cost of stepping in a new mast: "The carpenters here are charging me both arms and a leg. They're nothing but a pack of damned thieves."

He spoke his own language. Sousa followed it well enough. It was a close cousin to Portuguese, and it wasn't as if Sousa'd never dealt with Spaniards before. "What can you do but pay?" he said. "They've got you by the short hairs."

That thought came naturally to him. He was drinking with Jaramillo in a tavern attached to a dockside brothel. He'd had one round there already. When his lance recovered its temper, he'd screw another girl. Ada was terrific, but variety was the life of spice.

Jaramillo's answering smile was sour. "You can joke. Your ship's whole and sound."

"It's all luck. You spend enough time at sea, something bad will happen to you. Of course, you spend enough time ashore and something bad'll happen to you, too," Sousa said. "Maybe it's good you didn't get to Cuba on time. Isn't that the place where the great pox comes from?"

"You mean the French disease? It could be. I've heard that, but I don't know," Jaramillo said.

Sousa hadn't heard that name for the pox. He bought Jaramillo another mug of wine—the stuff the locals made was pretty decent—and picked the Spaniard's brains till he got horny again. Then he went to a cubicle with a swarthy, dark-eyed girl and did what came naturally.

He brought Ada back some fresh-baked bread, some roast mutton, and a little jug of decent wine—all improvements on the *São Paulo*'s fare. She thought the bread was strange but liked it. The mutton she devoured. The wine … "Banana wine gooder," she said. Her Portuguese had no grammar yet, but she was soaking up words like a sponge.

"Nonsense," Sousa said, and swatted her on the fanny. She smiled; she knew it was more friendly than otherwise. He owned her; he could have done anything he chose. He made an easygoing master, at least with a slave he was screwing.

Before the ship sailed, he sold one of the men he'd bought in Boma to a beet planter for loaf sugar and silver. He planned to resell the sugar in Lisbon. He hoped to make more from it in Lisbon than he would have from the black.

Eight more days of sailing brought the galleon to the Portuguese capital. Ada stared and stared. "So much mens. So bigs houses," she

14

said, having no better word for cathedrals and palaces and warehouses. Roustabouts on the piers caught lines from the *São Paulo* and made her fast. As soon as the gangplank thudded down, Sousa took his ambulatory property to the establishment of Jesus Almeida, the most prominent slave dealer in town.

Almeida was a *converso* who still looked like the Jew he'd been born. "My, my," he said, eyeing Ada. "You don't see one this fine every day. I may try her out before I put her up for sale."

"You wouldn't be the first," Sousa said dryly.

"I'd hardly think so. Anyone who sees her would hope to have her," the dealer said. "Do you want to sell me the lot of them straight out, or shall I offer them on consignment and keep a fifth of whatever they bring?"

"Consignment, *Senhor*. I think I'll do better, especially with her. If a couple of men who really want that pussy start bidding against each other ..." He let it drop there, not caring to say he reckoned Almeida much too cold-blooded to pay that way.

"Just as you please, just as you please." The *converso* rubbed his plump, beringed hands together. "Give me a few days to get word out to customers, and to have a little fun myself. What my lady wife doesn't know won't hurt her."

Sousa set a finger by the side of his nose and winked. "I didn't hear a word you said there." His own wife was waiting on their farm—it wasn't quite an estate, though Sousa had hopes along those lines—outside of town. Maria would keep waiting, too, till he found out how his business dealings went.

Instead of going home, he took a bed at a nearby inn. He didn't use it much; beds with warm, friendly company in the joyhouses on either side of the inn were more fun. He drank wine with Pedro Alves at one of the places, and with Marco Lopes at the other. Only when sleep really meant sleep did he go back to the inn.

Jesus Almeida auctioned the slaves six days after Sousa consigned them to him. When the merchant-adventurer walked into the hall, Almeida grinned and licked his lips. Sousa grinned back; he knew what that meant, all right. Ada stood waiting to be sold, naked as the day she was born but much shapelier. The more the bidders saw of her, the higher they'd go.

15

The other blacks brought decent prices, between eight and twelve English pounds each. Times were hard in Europe; silver was scarce. Manuel, the Portuguese king, coined reals in copper these days. Good English coins were welcome. So were Englishmen. Portugal sold them wine and sugar. And she sold them slaves. One of the bidders was a tall, pale Englishman with a bright red chin beard. He bought one of the older men Sousa'd acquired in Boma.

At last, after the others were gone, Almeida brought Ada front and center. Just as Sousa and the dealer had hoped, that Englishman and a Portuguese grandee both wanted her. So did others, but they couldn't stay with the bidding. When Almeida finally said, "She is sold to *Senhor* Robinson for forty-seven pounds!" he sounded almost as astonished and delighted as he would have when he laid her. Well, Sousa felt the same way. Even for a slave like Ada, that was a lot of money.

Sousa settled with the slave dealer as soon as the auction ended. As far as he could tell, Almeida didn't even try to cheat him—a sure measure of how delighted the *converso* had to be. Sousa had a spree at the better brothel by his inn. One of the ways you showed you'd done well was by spending some of what you'd made. Then, fucked out, hung over, and happy, he headed home to his lady.

He prospered for a while, and traveled as far as Goa, the Portuguese trading town on the west coast of India. But his health failed him not too many years later. He took one sickness after another, and had ever more trouble fighting them off. When he died, he weighed less than a hundred pounds. People said his ending was a mercy. Nor was he the only one to die like that. He was just one of the first.

II

WHAT CAME OF IT: 1851

Spring had finally come to Salisbury. English spring being what it was, it might dissolve into mist and rain and mud in an hour or two, but for now the sky was bright blue, with only a few puffy clouds drifting from east to west. The sun shone brightly. It was almost warm. A redbreast chirped—"Tic, tic!"—in the old pear tree in front of the surgery. Leaves were sprouting on the gnarled branches, and flower buds with them. Soon the little white blooms would perfume the air.

Viola Williams looked past the pear tree to the spire of Salisbury Cathedral. You could see it from everywhere in town, and for quite a distance out in the countryside. It fairly pierced the sky, towering more than four hundred feet in the air. People said not even London boasted a taller building.

From the women's quarters above the surgery, Viola had a fine view of the cathedral. The white-painted latticework wooden gratings in front of the windows were more generously pierced than most. She could—she told herself she could—see out almost as well as if the gratings weren't there. Yet her father, looking up from near the pear tree, had assured her no prying male gaze could light on her or her younger sisters. When Richard Williams spoke as a physician,

17

he often owned himself baffled. When he spoke as a man, he did so with uncommon certainty. Viola trusted his assurances.

A cart rolled by. Hank South held the reins. He puffed on a clay pipe as he drove. Chickens in wooden cages squawked. They didn't like the jouncing ride. They'd like what happened to them after he sold them even less, but they didn't know that. Viola recognized Hank at once. She even knew the brindled hound trotting along beside the cart was named Tobias. The farmer used her father's services, but, of course, he hadn't set eyes on her since she was a little girl underfoot.

Two boys ran down the street, careless of the mud they kicked up. They were urging on a wooden hoop with sticks, and shouting while they did it. Jealousy stabbed Viola like a knife. Once upon a time, she'd run and played and squealed as freely. They'd be able to stay out in the open air and carry on as long as they liked. She'd had to retreat to the women's rooms when she turned twelve. She'd been secluded, sequestered, for seven years now.

It didn't seem fair. It *wasn't* fair. A furrow briefly corrugated Viola's smooth forehead. She knew what her father would say if she complained about it ... again. He'd say what he said whenever she grumbled about the way things worked.

"Life isn't fair." There. She'd said it herself. Except that her voice was contralto, not baritone, it could have been Richard Williams talking.

As if to prove life wasn't fair, three workmen in shabby breeches and none too clean linen shirts came to the surgery door. Two of them were helping the third along. One of the helpers had a W branded on his forehead. Seeing it made Viola click her tongue between her teeth. It showed just how unfair life was: it meant that, even though he as yet showed no signs of the Wasting himself, he'd given it to someone who did show those signs. The brand warned others not to cohabit with him. Though he seemed fine now, he was living on borrowed time.

His friend seemed anything but fine. The man's face was pale as cottage cheese; he supported his left arm with his right. They had to wait for a moment before Dr. Williams opened the door. The hurt man's eyes rolled up in his head; he started to crumple to the ground. The other two kept him upright till they could get him inside.

He didn't come out again for an hour or so. When he did, a sling held his left arm against his body. "How you doing now, Wilf?" the workman with the W asked.

"Better for the slug of laudanum the sawbones gave me," Wilf said. "Still hurts like a bugger, but not like a mad bugger the way it did before. Lord only know what I'll do, though, not bein' able to work for six, eight weeks. How'm I supposed to put food on the table?"

"It's busted." His other friend pointed out the obvious. "You can't do nothin' with it whilst it's busted."

They were back on the street by then, and heading away. Viola couldn't hear Wilf's reply. She hoped he had kin who'd help keep him and his family going while he healed. Or maybe the monks at the rectory by the cathedral could lend a hand.

Steps on the stairs—her father's steps. Viola hurried away from the window to find out what Richard Williams wanted. Seeing him was almost like peering into a mirror. They shared the same long, thoughtful face, the same pointed chin, the same short nose. His eyes were green; hers, gray. They were both brunets, though his hair was darker than hers. His skin was also darker than hers, but he was a man—he could let the sun fall on it more readily than she could. Her mother insisted she'd been there when Viola was born, but you couldn't prove it by looking.

Right this minute, her father looked uncommonly pleased with himself. "You look uncommonly pleased with yourself," Viola told him.

"I am, as a matter of fact." He puffed clouds—happy clouds, no doubt—of smoke from his cheroot. "I actually did a man some good down there."

"Wilf whatever-his-name-is? I was watching at the window when he went away."

"Wilf Bonney—that's right." Her father nodded. "He fell off a roof and fractured his humerus up near the shoulder. Not a badly displaced break. I didn't have to torment him by setting it. The sling suffices. In a couple of months, as long as his shoulder joint doesn't freeze up, he'll be nearly as good as new. And the laudanum will blunt his pain."

"Good," Viola said. "That's good."

19

"You have no idea—well, perhaps you have some idea, since you've been listening to me for much too long—how good it is," Richard Williams said. "Too much of what I do pits me against sicknesses I can't fight."

"The Wasting. Wilf's friend with the W," Viola said slowly, in a small voice. Whenever you thought of it, you shuddered. You couldn't help shuddering. It killed slowly, cruelly, and irresistibly.

Her father nodded. "That's right. The Wasting and fear of it made our world. They have for more than three hundred years now. And they will, until someone wiser than I'll ever be learns how to hold the disease at bay."

"It may happen," Viola said. "We have inoculation from the Turks, so smallpox is a smaller menace than it was in your grandfather's day." She touched her right upper arm with her left hand. She still carried smallpox scars there from the mild case her father had given her.

He sighed. "Back when inoculation was new in England, before the turn of the century, Charles V ordered some of his physicians in London to rub the blood of people just coming down with the Wasting into scratches on people who, as far as anyone could tell, had it not."

"And?" By his heavy tone, Viola could tell the story wouldn't have a happy ending. "It didn't ward them?"

"Two came down with fevers and night sweats directly, and died of the Wasting in less than five years," he said. "The King did support their families afterwards, I give him that. But no one has tried the experiment since—or, at least, it hasn't got into the medical journals."

"Two, you say? What about the others?"

"I don't know. What about them? The inoculation didn't give them the Wasting, at any rate, not right away. Did it protect them?" Richard Williams shrugged broad shoulders. "I have no way of knowing, not for certain. Nor does anyone else. But, judging by the two luckless ones, I would doubt it."

"All right," Viola said, even if it wasn't. She tried to stay hopeful no matter what. When you thought about the Wasting, hope shriveled and failed.

Someone knocked on the surgery door. Her father quirked an eyebrow. "I'm off," he said, starting back down the stairs. "Now to work another miracle of medicine."

If only he meant it, Viola thought. She went back into her room. The outer world called to her. Oh, she could venture forth in the company of other women, all of them robed into shapelessness and veiled to the eyes. That was how you visited shops. It was, in its way, exciting. But it wasn't what she wanted now. She wanted to run and jump. She wanted to climb that pear tree. She wanted to roll on the burgeoning grass under the tree. She wanted to feel fresh air on her arms, and even on her legs. She wanted to, but she couldn't.

Not a minute later, she was reminded why she couldn't. The man who came out of her father's surgery and shambled down the entry path to the street was a skeleton wrapped in yellowing parchment. As he walked, he swigged from a little bottle. That also had to be laudanum: opium in brandy. It wouldn't do him any good, not the way the sling that immobilized Wilf Bonney's arm did him good, but it might take the edge off his torments.

And torments he assuredly had. He coughed a consumptive's bubbling cough. On the back of his neck and on one wrist were angry purple weals. Viola shivered. Those skin growths were sure marks of the Wasting. Less than a year before, Tom Pickering had been a cabinetmaker whose work her father admired. Now .... Now he was a beached wreck, waiting for waves of sickness to break him to pieces.

She shrugged again. Men and women wanted to come together. God had made them want to come together so the human race could go on. These past three hundred years and more, though, coming together had grown deadly dangerous, in the most literal sense of the word. If the one you came together with had earlier come together with someone who had the Wasting, the poison might be lurking in that person's body, ready to pass to yours.

Keeping men and women rigidly separate till they wed, and separating them through most of life, had let life go on ... after a fashion. Deaths now were fewer and further between than they had been when the Wasting and its handmaiden the great pox first rolled across the world. But people still sometimes took chances. No matter how often the priests thundered that the wages of sin were death, they thundered at people, imperfect people, not angels. The Wasting shadowed every land.

There went poor Tom Pickering. And here came her father, up the stairs again. This time, his footfalls spoke of mourning and defeat. Viola hurried out to give him what comfort she could.

Music flooded from Katherine's fingers. After supper, Viola's sister loved to play the harpsichord. The family enjoyed listening to her just as much. Viola thought she had to be as good as men who made their living at the keyboard. If things were different, she might have gone up on the stage herself, or into the orchestra pit. Things were as they were, though. Her family could hear her. One day, her husband and his family might also. No one else was likely to.

When Katherine finished the piece, Viola clapped her hands. So did her youngest sister, Margaret, who was thirteen. "I wish I could play like that," she said.

"Keep practicing, dear, and sooner or later you will." Jane Williams, the girls' mother, was sure practice fixed everything save perhaps a skinned elbow.

Margaret's curls bounced as she shook her head. "She's better at it than I am. Her fingers know what to do without her telling them."

Viola thought she was right. Kate had taken to the harpsichord the way a butterfly took wing. It didn't come naturally to Margaret. It hadn't to Viola, either. She could play a little, but only a little.

Her father knocked the ash from his cheroot into the mug that had held his beer. Instead of bringing it back to his mouth, he pinched it out and stood up. "Do you mind if I play a piece, sweetheart?" he asked.

"Of course not!" Kate almost jumped off the bench. Richard Williams had often sat down at the harpsichord when the girls were little—Viola remembered that well. These past few years, though, as his middle daughter's talent blossomed, he mostly left the instrument to her.

But now he opened the bench and pawed through the stack of sheet music inside. When he pulled out the score he wanted, Jane

Williams gave a little gasp. "Good heavens, Richard, not that one!" she said.

"After today? Yes, this one," Viola's father said, and set the music for Gesualdo's *Hymn to an Angry God* on the support above the keyboard. As he began to play, Kate stood alongside to turn pages for him.

The music made Viola's hair want to stand on end. It was meant to do that. Carlo Gesualdo had written it in a fit of fury just after he realized he was sick with the Wasting. From everything Viola knew of Gesualdo, he'd been much given to fits of fury. He'd murdered his first wife and her lover in one, for instance, a few years before penning *Hymn to an Angry God*.

Richard Williams didn't have his middle daughter's gift for the harpsichord. Most of the time, his playing was competent and workmanlike, no more. Not now. Now he felt the music in a way he seldom did, and made his family feel it, too. For the first time, Viola understood that the piece should have been called *Hymn from a Man Angry at God*.

After the last outraged chord faded, Viola's father leaned forward and buried his face in his hands. Kate set one of her hands on his shoulder. Viola thought he would shrug it away, but he didn't. Quietly, she said, "Tom Pickering isn't going to get better, is he?"

He straightened up. In the candlelight, harsh lines and shadows scored his face, making him look years older than he was. "No," he said, his voice flat and hard. "He'll die soon. I know it, and he knows it. By the time he does, death will be a relief."

"A blessing," Jane Williams said.

"No," the doctor repeated, and shook his head. "There are no blessings with the Wasting. God cursed mankind when He loosed it amongst us."

"'The judgments of the Lord are true and righteous altogether,'" his wife murmured. "Blessed be the name of the Lord." She crossed herself.

"No," Richard Williams said yet again. "I will not bless Him for that. I've watched too many die of the Wasting, and I expect to watch too many more, and I shan't be able to do even a farthing's worth of good for any one of them. The best advice I might give them would be to set their affairs in order, climb to the top of the cathedral spire, and cast themselves down. Then, at least, everything is over quickly."

"Don't you dare do any such wicked thing," Viola's mother said. "Suicide is a mortal sin, sure to lead to hellfire."

"At the last ecumenical council, twenty years ago, there was talk of relaxing that rule for those with the Wasting." The doctor laughed a sawtoothed laugh. "And I can see how there might have been, when three or four Popes have died of it for all their vows of celibacy. The proposal failed, but I look for them to examine it again whenever the Holy Father next summons all the bishops."

"Unless someone first finds a way to defeat the sickness," Viola said.

"If anyone says he can, don't give him your money—that is the best working policy," her father said. "He is a quack and a charlatan, out to line his pockets on desperate people's hope. Remember what I said of inoculation earlier today."

"I do remember," Viola said. And she did; she had the kind of capacious memory that could have made her a learned professor had she been a man and freely able to go about in public. She dredged something else out of it now: "What of quinine, though? Isn't quinine sovereign against malaria?"

"It is ... said to be," her father answered cautiously. "I've seen only two or three cases, in men returned from tropic lands."

"Well, then," Viola said. "*Something* must do some good."

"Something *may* do some good," Richard Williams answered. "What that is, though, no man knows—no physician in Europe, no Red Indian medicine man, no swami in India, no Chinese apothecary. We have tried every nostrum we could find or concoct, and not a one of them has slowed the Wasting by even a hair's breadth. Willow-bark tea for fever, laudanum for pain .... Oh, if someone has the French pox with it, say, I can feed him quicksilver till his gums bleed and his teeth fall out, but I'm far from sure I'm doing him a favor." He flipped the score for *Hymn to an Angry God* back to the beginning. "Just thinking about it makes me want to play this over again."

"Please don't," his wife said. "Once was enough."

"Once was too much," Margaret added in a small voice. "You can hear the rage boiling from the harpsichord." Viola and Katherine both nodded.

Their father sighed. "All right," he said, though Viola didn't think it was. He got to his feet. "I'm going to have a knock of apple brandy before I go to bed. Does anyone else care for some?"

His wife and daughters didn't admit to wanting any. He pulled the cork from the jug, poured a hefty dollop into a glass, and held it up so he could look at a candle flame through the coppery liquid before bringing it toward his lips. "Aren't you forgetting something, Father?" Viola asked.

"Why, so I am," he said, blinking, and raised the glass on high. "To his Majesty, King Michael III!"

"King Michael III!" the women echoed, though they weren't drinking. Richard Williams was. He took a small sip to savor the apple brandy, then poured down the rest to numb his wounded spirit. Apple brandy was strong stuff; Viola wouldn't have cared to drink it that way. Had her father slugged it back whenever he found himself losing a hard case, he would have been a hopeless drunkard.

But he was a moderate man—in moderation, of course. Even a moderate man sometimes needed help in slowing down the thoughts whirling inside his head so he could sleep.

The Poet's words resounded in Viola's mind:
"Cut is the branch that might have grown full straight,
And buried is Apollo's laurel bough.
Hell hath no limits, nor is circumscribed
In one self place, for where we are is hell,
And where hell is there must we ever be."

She sighed. Christopher Marlowe was the best versifier and playwright the English language had ever spawned. Across two and a half centuries, his words still glowed like burning coals. What might he have done if the Wasting hadn't claimed him before he saw fifty? Who else might have been cut down even younger, so his muse never saw the light of day at all?

"I'm for bed," her father announced, as if someone had claimed he wasn't. He lumbered out of the living room, his head hanging. Jane Williams hurried after him.

Viola, Katherine, and Margaret looked at one another. "That was … worse than usual," Kate said.

"It was, wasn't it?" Margaret sounded worried, even frightened. She was still of an age where she wanted to believe all problems had neat, clean, tidy solutions.

Viola wanted to believe that, too, but she couldn't come close, however hard she tried. She stood up. "We can go to bed, too, that's what," she said. "Maybe things will look better in the morning." She didn't claim they would be better. Sometimes looking better was as much as you could hope for.

Things looked different in the morning, anyhow. The sun of the day before had disappeared, swallowed by a cool, wet, clinging mist. Viola thought she could make out the cathedral spire through it, but she wasn't sure. On the plain north of town, the mystic menhirs of Stonehenge would be all ghostly when you got close enough to see them at all. Then again, the mist wouldn't bother the jackdaws that nested in pits in the ancient stones one bit.

Viola had seen Stonehenge when she was a girl and could still go up and down in the world as she pleased. Druids visited the great circle at solstices and equinoxes, to pray for the favor of the gods who, they hoped, dwelt there. The Church frowned on that, but not enough to forbid it. When Father, Son, and Holy Spirit had turned their backs on the Wasting, what harm in petitioning other Powers to come to agonized mankind's aid?

No harm at all, not that Viola could see. But—also as far as she could see—no help, either. *What's the evidence?* She could hear her father's voice in her head again even before she went down to breakfast. How often had he asked her that since before the words so much as made sense to her? Often enough so he didn't need to do it much any more, that was sure.

Breakfast was bean porridge with salt cod stirred in—the kind of thing that would keep over a banked fire and still be fine when it got heated again the next morning. Viola's mother and father were already eating and sipping their thick, sweet coffee when she came downstairs. Her sisters, though, still lay abed.

"Good morning, dear," Jane Williams said.

"Good morning, Mother," Viola replied. She turned to her father. "How are you?"

"Foggy as the weather," he said with a theatrical yawn. "I'll need an extra cup of restorative to get me through the day."

"Well, we have plenty." Viola got herself a bowl of porridge and a small cup of the strong coffee. She chipped some sugar off the loaf on a plate on the dining-room table, then sat down with her parents. Kate came down a few minutes later, Margaret later still. Margaret loved to sleep late.

"You'd sleep through the crack of doom," her father grumbled when she finally made an appearance.

"I hope so, Father," Margaret answered cheerfully. Richard Williams opened his mouth, then closed it again without saying anything. His youngest had left him without a comeback, which didn't happen every day. Clicking his tongue between his teeth, he got up and fixed the second—or was it third?—cup of coffee he'd promised himself.

After breakfast, the women washed up. It was Viola's turn to do the utensils. Horn spoons were easy. The bigger wooden ladle needed more scrubbing, and she worked hard with a pumice stone to grind rust off a serving spoon and a knife. No matter how carefully you cleaned and dried iron, those little pits and red flakes came back.

"All right?" Viola's father asked. When nobody told him no, he went on, "I'll go outside and take down the shutters, then. And I'll open the surgery for another day of cures."

In another tone of voice, he might have meant that. The way he said it, it sounded more like a confession of helplessness. Jane Williams retreated into the bedroom she shared with her husband. Viola and her sisters hurried upstairs. They would be gossiped about in no good way if they left themselves visible—not that any man was likely to set eyes on them from the street with the mist coming off the river.

That mist left Viola's room gloomier than usual. The light that sifted through the grating was dim and leaden. She didn't want to burn a candle; it seemed so extravagant when the sun, even if shrouded, was in the sky.

She read for a little while, but without the candle it quickly gave her a headache. She started embroidering on a linen towel. Ever since at least her grandmother's time, women in her family had ornamented towels and washcloths and pillowcases with cross-stitch birds or pitchers or fish or whatever else struck their fancy.

Viola wasn't sure that was a good idea—when you slept on an embroidered pillowcase, sometimes you woke up with the pattern of a bird, a pitcher, or a fish imprinted on your cheek. But, good idea or not, it gave her something useful and improving to do for a while. She didn't have to stare as hard at the work as she did with words. Her fingers moved almost of their own accord. Then she pricked herself with the needle. She said a word her mother would have frowned at and stuck the wounded digit in her mouth till she couldn't taste blood any more. That didn't take long. She dried it on her apron—decorated with cross-stitch daffodils—and got back to the embroidery.

When fancywork went well, time slid by without your noticing. Viola looked up and saw to her surprise that the sun had fought through the mist. Her room was about as bright as it ever got. How had that happened? She didn't know, but she was glad it had.

Footsteps on the walk leading to the surgery made her peer out through the grating to see who it was. Her brows came together and a small crease appeared between them when she recognized Alfred Drinkwater. It wasn't that she had anything against the solicitor. She didn't; he'd been her father's particular friend since they were both boys. To this day, Richard Williams would often go on about how he'd heard something or other from good old Alf.

But this made the third or fourth time Drinkwater had called at the surgery in the past month. Viola's father hadn't gone on about anything he'd heard from good old Alf after these visits. That made Viola fear they weren't social calls. If the solicitor was using her father's professional services …

The vertical crease between her eyebrows deepened. That made her look more like her father than ever, even if she didn't know it. When someone started regularly seeing a physician, you had to think something was wrong with him. Viola didn't want to think that about Alfred Drinkwater, whose son and two daughters were more or less the same ages as her sisters and herself.

Most of all, Viola didn't want to think the barrister was seeing her father on account of the Wasting. That would be dreadful for all kinds of reasons. It would mean he wasn't long for this world, which was bound to matter most to him.

And it would mean the solicitor had betrayed his wife (or that she'd betrayed him, although, given how hard it was for a respectable married woman—especially one with children in the household—to manage an illicit affair, that seemed less likely). If Drinkwater *had* caught the Wasting from some loose woman, he might have passed it on to his wife, not even suspecting he had it till much too late. That would be a true tragedy, though hardly a unique one.

Viola knew what went on between men and women in the marriage bed—or, more dangerously, beyond it. Any girl learned that on passing into womanhood: a doctor's daughter more thoroughly than most. Boys whose beards began to sprout got the same kind of lessons. Both sexes learned why they shouldn't join together except in marriage, and how to cool their hot blood by themselves before they wed.

No lessons were perfect, of course. Otherwise, the Wasting would long since have faded away, while in fact it remained a worldwide scourge. Sequestering women made men less liable to give in to temptation. But *less liable* didn't mean *not liable at all*. Some men wanted to find women to take those chances with ... and what men wanted, they commonly got. Some women wanted to take chances with men, too. That was how things had worked, no doubt, since the days of Adam and Eve.

Half an hour after Alfred Drinkwater walked into the surgery, he came out again. From behind as from in front, he looked the same to Viola as he always did: tall, thickset, with a slight swagger in his stride that announced he knew he was somebody. As was his habit, he had the stem of a pipe clenched between his teeth. He didn't gulp opiated brandy the way Tom Pickering had, at least not while Viola could see him.

Her father's footsteps on the stair made her whirl away from the grating-covered window. He had to know she watched the outside world as much as she could, the way a caged linnet surely watched the parlor where its little house of confinement hung. The bird couldn't escape being watched while watching. When Viola could, she did.

As she took a step toward the doorway, she noticed that her father's footfalls seemed less slow and tired and dejected than they had after he saw the cabinetmaker with the Wasting. *Maybe I'm borrowing trouble*, she thought hopefully. *Maybe good old Alf has nothing worse than a carbuncle or a stubborn emerod.*

Richard Williams paused in front of her door. "May I come in?" he asked.

"How can I say no?" Viola returned.

He let out a dry chuckle. "Easily enough, I expect, if you've a mind to. But I thank you for your courtesy."

"And I you for yours." Viola meant that. For as long as she could remember, her father and mother had treated her as much like an adult as they could, or perhaps even a little more than that. Viola stepped aside to make way.

Her father glanced at the embroiderywork she'd left on the bed. He said not a word about it. She might have been imagining things, but she thought his eyebrow's twitch told his opinion of it quite well enough. After clearing his throat, he did say, "You will know good old Alf's been coming by lately."

"Oh, I will, will I?" Viola didn't have to admit how she looked out hungrily on the world beyond the grate, looking out being the only way she could engage with it.

Her father, of course, understood that as well as she did. "Well, you may," he said.

She abandoned her pretense. "I do. Is he well, I hope?"

"As well as any man sliding into middle age is likely to be." Richard Williams suddenly focused on her instead of just looking at her. "I see what you were asking. You feared he was visiting me because I'm a doctor."

"Yes. I did." Viola nodded. "I knew how unhappy that would make you, and it worried me."

"No need for concern there. He hasn't done anything lately he would enjoy for a little while and then rue the rest of his days—or if he has, he got the enjoyment without the ruing. One may, if one's lucky. But I don't think Alf's like that now. He wears braces *and* belt these days. So no indeed, he's had no unfortunate reason for calling. To the contrary, as a matter of fact. Very much to the contrary."

"How do you mean?" Viola had no idea where the conversation was heading.

Her father cleared his throat again. "You may recall from your girlish days out in the town that Alf's son, Peter, is about a year and a half older than you are."

She did remember—after he reminded her. Peter Drinkwater had been loud and obnoxious and overbearing: a *boy*, in other words, and an older boy at that. A year and a half seemed an enormous difference in age when you were six or eight or ten. Somehow, it wasn't so much of a much now. Later, she realized she should have got her father's drift at once. But she didn't; she was too much taken with remembering the vanished days when she could roam as she pleased. And so, foolishly, all she said was, "Yes? What about him?"

"You know Alf and I have been particular friends since we were small," her father said. "You know that to this day our stations in life are not too different, the one of us from the other. And you know that the good Lord has allowed us both to grow to manhood free from the taint of the Wasting and to raise healthy families of our own." He crossed himself to show God he was giving thanks, not boasting, and went on, "All this being so, these past few weeks we have been discussing the possibility of joining our two families together through a marriage alliance between, um, Peter and you."

"*You* have been discussing? Have I nothing to say about this?" Afterwards, by the stricken look on her father's face, Viola realized she must have sounded furious. She was thunderstruck, all right, but more with astonishment than anger. She knew—she couldn't very well help knowing—she was of marriageable age. But having the theoretical come crashing into the real world in the space of a couple of sentences took all the wind from her sails.

"You have everything to say in the matter. If Peter does not suit you, the union will not go forward," Richard Williams replied. "But Alf and I have come to the point where I should like him to bring Peter to the house so the two of you can get acquainted with each other. If he does not suit you or if you do not suit him—though I'd think you would suit any young man marvelously well—then that will be the end of it, and no harm done. On this Alf and I are both agreed."

31

Viola had no idea whether she would suit young men in general or Peter Drinkwater in particular. Even if she did, marriage would turn her whole life upside down and inside out. A new home, new people to get acquainted with and put up with, new people who would have to try to put up with her …. In a very small voice, she asked, "When would the wedding happen, if it happens?"

"Not for some little while." Her father whuffled out air through nearly closed lips, something he did when he was incompletely happy. "Alf wants Peter to follow in his footsteps as a solicitor. To do that, he needs must train at Lincoln's Inn, one of the Inns of Court, in London."

"London!" Viola breathed. The city wasn't just the center of government. It was the lodestone that drew writers and musicians and painters and all manner of other kinds of clever people from all over England. From Salisbury to London was only about ninety miles, but the distance from a quiet provincial town to the country's beating heart seemed longer than that from the earth to the moon.

"London." The name had an entirely different inflection in her father's mouth. He wasn't thinking about the clever people who flocked to London—or he wasn't thinking about them from the neck up. He went on, "London has a great plenty of unattached young men in it. And it has a great plenty of unattached young women to make them happy ... happy for a little while, anyhow. And London has far and away more of the Wasting—both *in toto* and *per capita*—than any other city in the world save Paris, New Amsterdam, and perhaps Constantinople."

"Your particular friend took no harm there. Why should his son?" Viola said.

"Maybe Alf was just fortunate." Richard Williams shrugged. "I pray his son will also be. For his sake and for yours, I pray it. But only God knows beforehand, and God never tells."

III

eter Drinkwater's comb was cut from bone, with very fine teeth. Since his sandy hair was on the wavy side, the comb pulled and tugged more than he would have liked. He used it vigorously even so. He wanted to look his best this evening. You didn't call on a girl you were thinking of marrying every night.

You didn't call on a girl, or have anything to do with a girl, at all. Oh, Peter had plenty to do with Julietta and Joanna, but they were his sisters. They weren't *girls*, not to him. When you saw girls old enough to be sequestered who weren't your sisters, all you saw were bundles of cloth with eyes. You had to imagine what lay under all the wrappings. Peter prided himself on his imagination.

Alfred Drinkwater stuck his head into his older son's bedroom. "Aren't you ready yet?" he asked sharply, as if taking a deposition from a reluctant witness.

"Just about, sir," Peter said, trying to get his part just the way he wanted it. "Am I all right?"

"But for the unfortunate fact that you look like me, you're a handsome young man," his father replied. "Now put on your jacket and let's go."

"I'll do it," Peter said, and he did. His tailcoat was of plain black wool. His father's, of similar cut, had silver threads running through the fabric to show his standing in the legal profession. His father's shoes boasted polished silver buckles, where his own had plain ones of blacked iron. Even his father's breeches had an inch-wide white stripe along the outer seams; the ones he wore, again, lacked the ornamentation.

As Peter and his father headed to the door, his mother stopped them for a moment. "I hope everything goes splendidly," Amanda Drinkwater said. "I expect it will." She had a much sunnier disposition than her husband's. Alfred Drinkwater accounted for that by saying she didn't need to deal with so many habitual liars.

Peter's mother ducked away from the door before he and his father went out through it. As a solicitor's wife should have, she also had a strong sense of propriety. Peter wondered whether Viola Williams did. What he remembered of her was loud and screechy, but he also remembered how young she'd been. People could change as time went by.

Salisbury's gutters ran down the middle of the larger streets. People used them to get rid of garbage and slops, which often left them odorous. Peter and his father stayed as far away from them as they could while walking to the Williams house.

As they walked, Peter's father said, "Of course you'll get your training in London before the ceremony, even if you and Dick's daughter decide you suit each other. You need to put your professional life in order before you worry about personal affairs."

"Yes, Father." Peter had heard that often enough to make him disinclined to argue about it. And he did want to go to London. He'd spend most of his days dealing with wills and contracts and occasional lawsuits here in Salisbury. Wasn't he entitled to at least a taste of the big city's famous fleshpots before he came home to a provincial town where nothing ever happened and most people were glad it didn't?

Maybe he shouldn't have thought about fleshpots. His father seemed to pick the notion right out of his head, saying, "I'm going to tell you one more time, Peter—you have to be careful in London."

"Yes, Father," Peter said again. By his reckoning, this particular *one more time* brought the warnings up to a thousand and twelve. But he might have missed a few when he was just starting to keep count.

As if he hadn't spoken, Alfred Drinkwater went on, "Some of the lads who'll be at Lincoln's Inn won't be careful, sure as sure.

They'll want what they can get right this minute, and devil take to-morrow. I can think of half a dozen who started with me that never saw thirty, one or two of the most promising in our crop amongst 'em. The Wasting is hell on earth, nothing less."

"Yes, Father," Peter said once more. Anybody who didn't know that was blind and imbecilic. But the way you got it would tempt anyone: did tempt everyone. Peter was bored with his hand. A woman, a real woman, was bound to be so much better…

A monk in a brown robe held closed by a rope belt came up the street toward them. "Alms!" he called. "Alms for the poor and the infirm!"

Peter's father took a silver shilling from his pouch and gave it to the man. He was always generous to beggars … and the Church cared for those sick from the Wasting as well as anyone could.

"God bless you, sir," the monk said. "You store up virtue in heaven."

"I hope so," Alfred Drinkwater replied. "We all need as much as we can get."

"How right you are," the monk said, and went on his mendicant way.

The sun was sinking in the west, painting the sky in all the colors of fire. Silhouetted against that glow, Salisbury Cathedral might have been built from shadow rather than stone. "One of these days, a painter should take that view for his subject," Peter said.

"That would be excellent—if he can paint very fast," his father said. Peter nodded. As sunsets do, this one changed second by second. An ancient Greek had said you couldn't step into the same river twice. No more could you see the same sunset twice. If you looked away for an instant, or even if you didn't, it changed.

The Williams family lived in Harnham Road, south of the cathedral on the far side of the Avon. Peter knew where the house was. His father had brought him there to have a sprained ankle bound up, and to be inoculated against smallpox, and for soothing syrup when he was coughing his head off, and a couple of other times for reasons he couldn't remember. That old, old pear tree made him nod to himself. Yes, this was the place.

This time, though, they went up the less-used path, the one that led to the living quarters, not the surgery. Peter and his father scraped mud off the soles of their shoes on a couple of bricks left outside the door for that purpose. "You knock," Peter's father said when they finished. "You're paying the social call. I'm just along to cadge a supper."

He was a solicitor, all right. Stirring so much truth and falsehood together in a couple of sentences might well have been beyond anyone unacquainted with the law and its quillets. Peter almost said so. But if he did, he knew his father would only deny it, using words to obscure his meaning the way an octopus used ink to darken the waters around it. Sometimes nothing was the best thing you could do. Peter did nothing—except knock.

Well-oiled hinges meant the door opened silently. There stood Richard Williams. "Hullo, Alf, you old scoundrel! Hullo, Peter— you're on your way to becoming a young scoundrel, eh? Come in, both of you, come in!" He clasped their hands one after the other, then stood aside to let them walk by.

Neither his wife nor any of his daughters were in evidence. Peter would have been startled if they were; not even a particular friend got to know his particular friend's womenfolk. It wasn't done, except in the direst of emergencies or in courtships like this one.

In fact, some cloth draping that looked newly put up covered a doorway that had to lead into the kitchen. The Williams women would be working in there, but Peter wouldn't set eyes on them while they were.

He would set eyes on Viola, though. He would. He could hardly wait.

But he would have to, at least for a bit. "Something to drink?" her father said. "The apple brandy will put hair on your chest if you haven't got any. Donald Reynolds, the farmer who cooked it up, gave me a jug as part of my fee for lancing a boil on his son's leg and putting a soothing poultice on afterwards. Young Jeremy healed well, too, God be praised, so I even earned what his father paid me."

"Isn't life grand?" Peter's father said. "I've got paid in chickens and in shoats and in beer and once, heaven help me, in a badly printed volume of some of the worst verses ever inflicted on a reader. The worst part of that was, the pages were too stiff and crackly to be used as they deserved."

Laughing, Richard Williams poured apple brandy into three mugs. Then, as if as an afterthought, he poured one more. Peter didn't believe the little delay was spontaneous. Some of the steps here were as formal as those of a gavotte. "Viola!" the doctor called. "Why don't you come out and join us?"

The drapery over the doorway to the kitchen rustled. Out came ... a young woman. When you saw women walking along the street, all you really saw of them was their hands and their eyes. Everything else was loose cloth that hid them and took away their shape. Viola Williams wore the same kind of indoor clothes as Peter's mother and sisters. Her dress, of sky-blue muslin, reached the floor and covered her arms to the wrists, but didn't try to deny that she had a figure.

She had a very pleasant figure, Peter realized. She was nice look-ing, too. If she seemed flustered at the moment, well, Peter felt more than a little flustered himself. If after tonight they both thought they could put up with each other, they would be together for the rest of their lives. How did Matthew go? *What therefore God hath joined together, let no man put asunder*—that was the verse. Yes, they'd both earned the right to some nerves.

"Viola, let me present to you my particular friend, Master Alfred Drinkwater, and his son, Peter." Richard Williams could have been etiquette personified. Only the way one eyebrow rose a little suggested he might not be taking things so seriously as he let on.

"I am very glad to see you both," Viola said. Her voice was smooth and pleasant and not too loud. Peter's sisters often yelled at him. This made a nice change.

"Very pleased to see you, Mistress Viola," Peter said at the same time as his father was saying, "Good to see you, Mistress Williams." Odds were she couldn't understand either one of them very well.

Her father handed out the mugs of apple brandy. He raised his on high. "May the coming union of our families be joyful!" he said.

"May it be so!" Alfred Drinkwater agreed. He sipped at the apple brandy. So did Peter. It was smooth enough to disguise its strength. By the beatific expression on his father's face, the older man also favored it. He said, "I may have to call on Donald Reynolds myself, spend a bit of silver."

Viola turned toward Peter. He wanted to blush; except for his sisters and mother, he wasn't used to a barefaced woman looking straight at him. "You are going to London to study law?" she asked.

"That—that's right." The small stammer made him want to sink through the floorboards. "Uh, what do you like to do?" Not brilliant dialogue, but at least he managed to ask her *something*.

"I cook. I embroider. I clean. I wash. I do the kind of things women do." Viola hesitated, then added, "Oh—and I read."

Everything else she mentioned was as mundane, as ordinary, as could be. That last gave room for another question. "What do you like to read?" Peter asked. This time, he didn't stutter.

"I read medical books—for some reason, there are a lot of them in the house," Viola said.

"Can't imagine why," Richard Williams said. Peter remembered his father remarking on the doctor's sardonic cast of mind. Now he saw that for himself.

"What I really *like*, though, are tales by travelers who've come back from faraway places," Viola went on, ignoring her father. "I know I'll never be able to go to places like that myself, but with books I'm able to picture them in my mind's eye, anyhow."

Peter had never gone farther than a day's travel from Salisbury himself. He looked on the upcoming journey to London with an odd mixture of eagerness and dread. He would be doing strange new things in a strange new place, but all the things he would be doing in the strange new place would be strange and new.

Still, her answer made him smile. "I like reading travelers' stories, too," he said. "There are supposed to be explorers' societies in London. If I have the chance to go to any of their meetings, I could write you what I hear—if you like, I mean."

"That would be wonderful! Thank you," Viola said, so he'd done that right, or near enough.

He thought he had, at any rate, till his father coughed and said, "Unless you aim to hang out your shingle up the Amazon or down the Nile, the first thing you'd best explore is your studies."

Rustlings from the kitchen saved him from having to answer that. Richard Williams ducked in for a moment. When he came out again, he was smiling. "We seem to be about ready. Viola, will you do the honors?" He waved toward the table. "Gentlemen, be seated. It may not be the fatted calf, but I hope you'll enjoy it."

The china in front of Peter came from Delft, like his own family's good service. Dutchmen might be heretics who denied the Pope and half the sacraments, but they were damn good potters. Most of the time, the Drinkwaters ate off English earthenware and turned wood. No doubt the Williamses did, too, but this was a special occasion. Most of the time, the cutlery wouldn't be silver, either.

Viola came out with a large tray. On it lay a roasted fowl surrounded by heaps of vegetables. Her father chuckled as she laid it on the table. "You see, Alf? We've cooked your goose for you."

"Plenty have tried, but no one's done it yet," Alfred Drinkwater said. "How about some more of that excellent apple brandy, though?"

"Help yourself." Viola's father nodded toward the jug. "Forgive me, but I'm going to carve the bird." He did the job with a scalpel ("Yes, I've washed it," he said, answering Peter's question before he could ask it), and with a skill and dexterity that amazed. But then, who would know anatomy—even a goose's anatomy—like a doctor?

Viola went back to the kitchen and came out with fresh-baked bread, butter, and honey. "*Kyrie eleison!*" Alfred Drinkwater exclaimed. "You'll have to roll us home in wheelbarrows—we'll be too stuffed to walk."

"Last time I used our barrow, I brought manure back for the little garden behind the house," Richard Williams said cheerfully. "But you're welcome to ride in it if you like."

"You're too good to me, Dick," Peter's father said.

"I know I am." You couldn't faze the doctor.

Peter's wits were working hard. He didn't want Viola Williams to think him no more than a button on his father's jacket, but he'd never tried talking to a young woman who wasn't his sister. For some little while, he couldn't come up with anything he thought worth saying. Then he did: "If we are wed, Viola, I will care for you as best I know how for the rest of our days."

She stared down at her plate. She was, he realized, even more anxious than he was. After a moment, she seemed to make herself look at him. "That is good," she said in a low but firm voice. "I think it necessary, but it is not sufficient. If we are wed, Peter, will you

39

listen to me, and not treat me as part of the furniture or another house pet?"

He blinked. He didn't know what he'd expected, but that wasn't it. He did know his own father had a way of taking his mother for granted that grated on her. Viola, he could tell at once, was stronger-willed than his mother, and very possibly more clever, too. "If, as I look for you to do, you show me you are worth listening to, you may be sure I will pay particular attention to your every word."

Beside him, his father nodded. He barely noticed; he was paying that particular attention to Viola now. He watched her setting his words and his whole manner in her mental balance and weighing them against … well, what? Against whatever she judged a husband ought to be, he supposed. He also supposed he was doing the same with her. Was she pretty enough? He thought so. Was she clever enough? Definitely. Would they get along together? He could hope, but how could you know till you went ahead and found out?

The small vertical crease between her eyebrows disappeared. She nodded. Something inside Peter that he hadn't even known to be tight unknotted; he'd been weighed in her balance and not found wanting. Viola said, "That is a good answer, or good enough. For my part, I vow to extend you the same courtesy."

Courtesy? Wasn't attention from a wife a man's by right? Would Peter have to earn it? Perhaps he would—unless he turned down the match. But that would damage, perhaps ruin, his father's friendship with the doctor … and Viola intrigued him. There was more to her than he'd guessed there would be.

"Shall we go forward, then?" he asked her. "Go forward as man and wife, I mean?"

Again, she didn't answer right away. He could see why. He would have a life outside the home; she, not. But she nodded once more. "Yes," she said. "I think we shall."

"Very good!" her father said, a broader smile than usual on his face. Alfred Drinkwater's head bobbed up and down. Several small squeaks came from behind the makeshift drapes that screened off the kitchen. Viola's mother and sisters were bound to be eavesdropping there. The noises made Peter think they approved of the match.

He wondered if he did himself. He thought so, but he wasn't sure. How could anyone be sure on the strength of one brief meeting? If this did go forward, Viola was the woman who would bear his children, who would spend the rest of her life with him. The rest of her life, or of his. Henry VIII had thought of instituting divorce in England, even of breaking with Rome as the Germans and Portuguese were doing if he had to, but he'd died of the Wasting before bringing any of that to reality.

What if Viola doesn't suit me? Peter wondered. *What if I don't suit her?* If he didn't suit her, she was probably stuck. Being a man, he wasn't. But he knew the chance you took whenever you lay down with a stranger. You might catch your death—literally. And you might bring it home with you, too.

Richard Williams wasn't worrying about that. Or, if he was, he wasn't showing it. He picked up the jug of apple brandy. By the way it sloshed, they'd already put a good dent in it. He didn't care. He poured fresh slugs into all the mugs.

"To the joining of our families!" he said. "To the happiness of our children! To many healthy grandchildren!"

"So may it be!" Peter's father boomed. Everybody drank.

The trunk was of leather-covered pine, with shiny brass fittings. It was so full, Peter had to push down hard to close it. He secured the latch with a stout iron padlock; the key went into the pouch on his belt.

His mother sent him a worried look. "What will you do, dear, when everything in there gets dirty?" she asked. "We shan't be in London to wash things for you."

Peter smiled. He didn't laugh, which, he told himself, showed how mature and sophisticated he'd become. "I trust they have laundries there, Mama," he said. "I don't plan on running around in filthy rags."

"Oh, I trust they have laundries, too." Amanda Drinkwater sounded anything but reassured. "Laundries, though, they've got *laundresses* in them." By the way she came out with that, laundresses were a danger beside which lions and tigers and bears—to say nothing of floods and blizzards and earthquakes—paled to insignificance.

"It will be all right," Peter said. "I'll give my clothes to the man at the front, that's all, and get them back from him once they're clean."

"London's not a natural place. There may not be any man at the front, just one of those *laundresses*." His mother bore down on the word even harder this time.

"I'll be careful," Peter said, though the thought of a business run by women alone felt perversely exciting.

Ever since he'd started to shave, he'd thought of his mother as foolish, almost simple. Now, though, she read his mind like a stage mountebank. "What do you know about being careful? You're a young man, wild for life, out in the big world for the first time. I'll pray for you and hope it does some good, that's all."

"Thank you, Mama," Peter said, and meant it more than he'd thought he would.

"Are you ready, boy?" Alfred Drinkwater asked.

"I think so," Peter replied, because he knew *no* wasn't an acceptable answer.

"Then say your goodbyes, and you'll be on your way. I'll go with you to the King's Arms, where you'll catch the diligence to London. After that, and whilst you study, you'll be on your own." His father made it sound dreadfully final.

Peter kissed his mother. He hugged his sisters. Joanna, who was sixteen, sniffled; Julietta, who was nineteen, looked almost as jealous as he guessed Viola Williams would have.

He picked up the trunk by the leather-wrapped handle. It was heavy enough to make him grunt. It also made him list to counterbalance its weight, and smacked the side of his leg at every step he took.

Alfred Drinkwater made shooing motions. The women of the household withdrew as he opened the door. "We're off!" he said grandly, and blew smoke from his pipe. He could afford grandeur; he wasn't lugging the blasted trunk.

A procession of two, they made their way east to St. Johns Street along the North Walk at the edge of the cathedral grounds. Peter's father stopped to chat with acquaintances a couple of times. Whenever he did, Peter set the trunk down on the ground. He wondered if his arm would be as long as an African ape's by the time he boarded the diligence.

Three women came toward them, all robed and veiled and hooded against prying male eyes. As was only mannerly, Peter and his father pretended they weren't there. Not all men were mannerly, though. A shabby fellow repairing a stone wall howled like a wolf when they walked by on the far side of the street. One of them stiffened; the other two ignored him altogether. Peter's father sighed, but said nothing.

On the grass in front of the King's Arms sprawled a drunk. The big half-timbered building was the oldest and busiest inn in Salisbury, a natural place for the coach on the way to London to stop. "Wait here, in case it comes," Peter's father told him, and went inside. He came out with a pint pot in one hand and a half-pint in the other. He gave his son the half.

"Why don't I get a proper pint myself?" Peter asked.

"Because old Rufus brews strong ale, and I want you to keep your wits about you, that's why." His father raised his pewter tankard. "His Majesty, King Michael III!"

"His Majesty, the King!" Peter echoed. He poured down the ale.

Clarence Starr came up just then. His father, Chester, was a jeweler. He and Peter had been friends since they were boys; they'd probably stay particular friends the rest of their lives, the way Peter's father and Richard Williams had.

"I came to say goodbye and good luck," he told Peter. "Don't know what I'll do without you till you come home again."

"I'll miss you," Peter said. "By God, I will!" Just then, he was sure he'd miss everything about Salisbury.

"We'll write back and forth," Clarence told him. Peter nodded, wondering whether they would. Alfred Drinkwater went into the inn and came back with a pint for Peter's friend. Clarence wasn't going anywhere; he was learning his father's trade. No miserly half pints for him.

Peter had drunk several miserly halves by the time the diligence finally came in, an hour and a half after it was supposed to. "Zorry 'bout that," the driver said in a buzzing Devon accent. "A bridge rotted out, an' we had to get ferried acrost."

Peter and Clarence heaved the trunk up to the driver, who put it with the others on top of the coach. Alfred Drinkwater squeezed

Peter's hand in both of his. "You'll show them what we're made of out here in the provinces," he said. "If I did it, I know you can."

"I hope so," Peter said, and hugged his father for all he was worth. He blinked several times. He was leaving behind everything he'd ever known. Strangeness loomed ahead of him, all misty and frightening.

Clarence thumped him on the shoulder. "You'll do fine. You'll do better than fine."

"I hope so." Peter had trouble believing it.

"Give me the fare, young zir—two quid an' zix shillings it is—then climb on up," the driver said. Alfred Drinkwater handed him gold and silver. The man from Devon got down, touched the front of his tricorn, and opened the door to the diligence.

Gulping, Peter stepped up and went inside. The door closed behind him. The coach's springs creaked as the driver returned to his place. A priest smoking a pipe made room for Peter to sit beside him. The man in the seat across from them had his nose in a book of horoscopes and hardly seemed to have noticed the diligence had stopped.

The driver released the brake with a squeak from the lever. He cracked his whip above the four-horse team. The diligence swayed as the horses began to walk. Peter's father and his particular friend vanished behind him. So did the King's Arms. Pretty soon, so did the rest of Salisbury.

Cattle and sheep grazed on the meadows outside of town. Fresh green shoots of wheat and barley sprouted from plowed fields. And, speaking of fresh ... Peter had lived his whole life in a town of several thousands. He was so used to the stinks of slops and sweat and smoke that he'd come to take them for granted—until suddenly he didn't smell them any more.

He glanced at the man who was reading. The sharp-faced fellow didn't look friendly. The priest seemed a better bet. "Someone scrubbed the air, Father!" Peter blurted.

"That would be the Lord Himself," the priest replied, making the sign of the cross. Peter imitated him. The men went on, "God's creations are of perfect cleanliness. Dirt and filth and stench come from dirty, filthy, sinful mankind."

Isn't mankind a creation of God's? Peter thought. Saying that struck him as a good way to land in hot water. Since he didn't want to end up starring in a stew, he kept his mouth shut and watched the fields and tiny villages roll by. He tried to doze, but the motion of the diligence defeated him.

They stopped for the night in Andover, a town not much smaller than Salisbury. Peter had come there once before, to watch a horse race; it was as far from home as he'd ever gone till now. Off in the distance stood Beacon Hill and, near it, Highclere Castle, seat of the Earl of Carnarvon, a great landowner in these parts. Peter got only a glimpse of the castle. He was more occupied with wrestling his trunk down from atop the coach and hauling it into the inn where he'd eat and sleep.

The Danebury didn't seem like much to him next to the King's Arms. An overdone duck leg and a mound of mashed turnips and parsnips in gravy cost more than they would have at his hometown inn. The beer, however, was both cheap and good.

He had to share a bed with his fellow traveler who studied horoscopes. He shed his shoes and his belt, no more; his pouch went under his pillow. The other man took similar precautions. The thundermug at the foot of the bed did boast a tight-fitting lid, which made the room a bit more pleasant.

"You snore," the other man said when the morning sun woke them.

"So do you," Peter replied. "You wiggle, too."

They broke their fast on bread and honey, washing them down with thick, sweet coffee. Three more men got into the diligence before they set out, which turned it from comfortable to packed. "Thiz here, thiz ain't nothing," the driver said. "We can ztuff eight or ten in there." Peter didn't want to believe it. The priest's martyred sigh said it was all too likely to be true, though.

Off they went, the horses working harder now because they were pulling more weight. The miles slid by. Every so often, someone asked for a stop so he could ease himself behind a tree or a boulder or a stone fence. Whenever anybody got out, everyone did. Like his close, close, close companions, Peter relished the chance to breathe without his rib cage pushing against somebody else's. Squeezing back into the diligence … that was a different, and less enjoyable, business.

45

They made Oldham by nightfall—with the days stretching out as summer drew closer, the horses could go and go (though the driver did change them for a fresh team at the stable next to the inn there). Oldham was just a hillside village, but someone in the kitchen had turned out the best kidney pie Peter'd ever eaten. He'd had only a little bread since breakfast, so hunger also added its sauce.

There were two beds, none too wide, for the six passengers from the diligence. The driver slept in the stable with his horses, and probably made more comfortable bedding from straw than any of the travelers got. They gave the priest half of one bed, then matched coins to see who got the other half and the other bed. The two losers would sleep on the floor. Peter was one of them. If the boards were harder than a mattress would have been, at least he had room to stretch out as he pleased.

He woke up early the next morning. The light sliding in through the shutter slats went from gray to pink to gold. He could hardly wait to get going. By the end of the day, he'd be in London!

London didn't happen all at once, he discovered. As the sunrise had that morning, it grew and swelled. Houses clustered closer together; open spaces got fewer and smaller. More and more shops appeared, selling more and more kinds of things. More and more people and horses and carts and wagons crowded the street. The town fug Peter'd been long familiar with in Salisbury came back, doubled and redoubled. More and more smoke, from coal and wood, filled the air till he blinked again and again to relieve his stinging eyes. Soot stained planks and brickwork.

Every time he thought he'd reached the city's beating heart, he found himself still on the outskirts. Vaster than he'd imagined, London sprawled for miles. You didn't count the people here by thousands, as you did in Salisbury, or even by tens or hundreds of thousands. London held over a million, and had to spread wide to do it.

Peter was stuck in the middle of a seat, with a man to either side of him, and couldn't see as much as he would have liked. That he'd be living here for some time to come and would be able to explore didn't make it any less frustrating. He wanted to experience everything all at once. He was still very young.

The diligence creaked to a halt a hundred yards from the Tower of London. Peter got out and stretched till his cramped joints creaked. The Thames made its odorous presence known. It was the sewer for London's million and more, and left no one in any doubt of that.

Soldiers in red coats who shouldered newfangled flintlocks marched and countermarched outside the Tower. Peter wondered what sort of heretics and other rebels were mewed up there. He shivered; he didn't really want to find out.

A stooped, gnomelike little man came up to him and said, "'Ello, sir. Where might your honor care to go?"

"Lincoln's Inn. It's one of the Inns of Court," Peter said, not wanting the fellow to think he was only looking for a lodging-house.

"That it is, sir." The short man nodded briskly. "It's not far—not much above a mile. I'll take you there for one and six." He gestured to a little cart drawn by a single thin, swaybacked horse. When Peter didn't answer right away, he frowned and added, "That's the going rate, sir. So 'elp me God, it is. You'll get no one to 'aul you there for only a shilling."

"All right." Peter wasn't sure it was, but he didn't see that he had much choice. Even a shilling would have been a lot for a mile's ride in Salisbury. People talked about how dear London was. Evidently, they knew what they were talking about.

"Obliged, your honor." The gnomelike man knuckled his forehead. Then he picked up the trunk more easily than Peter could have and carried it toward the cart. Over his shoulder, he added, "Come along, if you please." Numbly, Peter came.

His trunk went into the back of the cart. He sat up front, next to the man who drove it. The fellow flicked the reins. When the horse didn't move, he touched its croup with a switch. It wasn't a harsh stroke—more a reminder that he could be harsh if he had to. With a resigned snort, the horse got going.

Pretty soon, the gnomelike man used the switch in earnest, not on his own animal but to fend off other wagons and carts, riders, and a stray dog that dodged through traffic as if it had been doing that for years—and it probably had. The driver also swore at everyone he shared the streets with, loudly and with great vigor.

Peter only half listened. He was staring at the city, at its brawling immensity. No, Salisbury wasn't like this ... although, when they rattled past St. Paul's, he decided he liked the cathedral in his home town better. St. Paul's flat-topped spire felt abridged.

Because of the swarms of people and vehicles, they took most of an hour to make the mile to Lincoln's Inn. The building lay on the east side of a large green square. Used to the country just a short walk from his front door, Peter got the notion he would grow very fond of that park. He also admired the building, which looked to have come from the age of Henry VIII and Mary. Its roof was of weather-faded oak, elaborately carved.

"Good fortune to you, sir," the driver said as Peter paid him, and knuckled his forehead again at a threepenny tip. He heaved the trunk out of the cart. Peter hauled it into Lincoln's Inn.

An old man with a fringe of white hair sitting behind a desk in a corner of the entrance hall waved to Peter as he came in. "Over here, lad," the oldster called. "Let me have your name, and I'll tell you if you have any outstanding fees to settle and to which room upstairs you're assigned."

"I'm Peter Drinkwater, sir."

"Alfred's son?" The old man answered his own question: "Yes, of course. You're his spit and image. I remember him well from years gone by." He checked a ledger. "You're paid in full. I'd expect nothing less from your father. They've put you in room 206. Your roommate's name is ... let me see"—he flipped pages—"Walter Haywood, yes. He came in this morning, so he may well be there. Oh, and supper will be served in the refectory in half an hour's time."

"Thank you, sir," Peter said.

The bursar or whatever he was gave him a room key. Going up two flights of stairs with the trunk was no fun, but Peter did it. He found room 206 and tried the door. It was unlocked; the latch worked under his thumb. In he walked.

Walter Haywood was there, all right. He was a skinny chap of about Peter's age, with frizzy brown hair and bushy side whiskers. Peter noticed that only later. His roommate lay on one of the narrow beds, naked from the waist down. He was frigging himself, his hand greased with goose fat or lard from a little cup beside him. "Hullo, old man!" he said cheerily. "Shut the door, why don't you? I shan't be a minute." And he wasn't. He groaned and spent and, businesslike as you please, set about cleaning himself up.

IV

Peter set his trunk on the floor by the unoccupied bed. "Do you do that all the bloody time?" he asked. Of course you took yourself in hand when you got the urge, but rarely with such matter-of-fact calmness as Walter Haywood showed.

Haywood paused while soaping himself over the basin on the low chest off drawers. He shook his head. "No," he answered. "I got a letch, that's all. Mother Thumb and her four children are better than nothing, and it was too soon before supper to go out and hunt up a woman. I couldn't very well know you'd choose that exact moment to walk in, now could I?"

He sounded very cool and reasonable ... in one way, anyhow. In another, to Peter's way of thinking, he might have been a maniac, fit for nothing better than to be locked up in the Bedlam lunatic asylum. "A woman?" Peter said. "The kind of woman you can find in London, you won't live long enough to sit for your bar examinations."

"I just don't worry about it—not one bit. And you know what else? I'm still here, same as you are," Haywood said, pulling on his trousers. He continued, "The difference between us is, I've had more fun than you. You can frig from now tills doomsday without ever understanding how grand cunt is, and what it's like when a girl quivers under you because she's spending, too. If that's not heaven, there is no such article."

"You're quite mad," Peter told him. If he sounded shocked, that was only because he was. Walter Haywood wasn't talking blasphemy, not exactly, but some people might have reported him to an ecclesiastical court nonetheless. Fornication had always been a serious business, and with the Wasting it became a matter of life and death. Stiffly, Peter added, "I shall enjoy wedded bliss when I go home to my fiancée after finishing my training."

"And you'll waste all the time before that with nothing but your hand to keep you company?" Haywood rolled his eyes. They were a pale gray-blue, and rather protuberant. "I know you're a provincial—by the way you talk, you come from somewhere in the West Country—"

"Salisbury," Peter said automatically.

"Salisbury." In Walter Haywood's mouth, the town's name might have been that of North Tidworth or some other village almost too small to be visible to the naked eye. "In *Salisbury*, then, do they believe in throwing away some of their prime fucking years?"

"Not all of them do," Peter said with a shrug. "My fiancée's father is a physician. He tries to keep alive some of the ones who play the game your way. By what he says, he hasn't much luck. Have you never seen anyone with the Wasting upon him?"

Having buttoned his fly, his roommate fluttered his fingers to show what he thought of that. "Fiddlesticks, I say. I've fucked myself silly more times than I can count, and I'm healthy as Moses."

"Moses is dead," Peter pointed out. "He has been for a long time."

"But he lived a hundred and twenty years," Haywood replied, proving he'd dipped into Scripture after all. "Me, I aim to do the same thing—and to be shot the day after my hundred and twentieth birthday by an outraged husband."

"Do as you please." Peter shrugged again.

"*Fais que ce voudras*—that is the whole of the law at the abbey of Thélème," Haywood said, proving he'd also dipped into books other than the Bible.

One more shrug from Peter. "They say Rabelais perished of the Wasting, too."

"They say all kinds of things. Just because they say them doesn't make them true. You're going to study the law, and you don't know that?"

Peter was a good deal larger than Haywood. It occurred to him that one way to shut his roommate up would be to punch him in the nose. But, before he could convert thought into action, a large, pure-toned bell rang several times. "What's that?" he asked, startled.

"One of the older chaps told me they ring in supper," Haywood said. "Shall we find out?"

They weren't the only ones hurrying downstairs to the refectory. The food was simple but filling: roast pork and potatoes washed down with small beer. Floury apple tarts added a touch of sweetness at the end.

Peter went back to his room after eating. All he wanted to do was sleep. He hadn't got much at either inn on the way to London. Instead of a nightshirt, Walter Haywood put on a coat and headed for the door again. "Where are you going?" Peter said around a yawn.

"Out after cunt—where else?" Haywood said. "It'll be more fun than listening to you saw wood, I promise you that."

"However you like. Just don't make a racket when you come back in." As long as Haywood kept quiet, Peter was too weary to care what else he did.

It was some time in the middle of the night when Haywood returned. Peter's roommate carried a stub of candle to keep from tripping over anything on the floor. The light woke Peter, but he didn't see how he could reasonably complain. Haywood was humming under his breath, also not loud enough to make Peter say anything. He reeked of cheap gin and of rosewater: the scent Peter's mother favored. It smelled nastier on him than it did on her, or so Peter thought. He pulled the sheet up over his eyes and drifted back into slumber.

No bell announced breakfast. Someone came down the hall and banged on the doors one after another. Peter came back to himself three or four doors before the banger reached his. He slid out of bed. "Time to be up and doing," he said—he was used to waking at sunrise.

"I was up and doing a hot little blond bitch last night," Walter Haywood said, his head still on his pillow. "Cost me five bob, but worth every farthing of it. Nothing like a girl with a lively arse."

Peter wouldn't have spent five shillings for sport that was liable to bring his ruination. He didn't think he would have, anyhow.

"Speaking of arses," he said, "will they birch yours if you stay in bed any longer?"

"Not my vice, thanks. I had to turn the other cheek too bloody often at Eton ever to care to do it for sport," Haywood replied ... but he did get up and start dressing.

He and Peter went down to breakfast together. Peter was thoughtful as he forked up sausage where the meat seemed to have been stretched with sawdust and lumpy mashed potatoes (the coffee, though, was first rate). You couldn't catch the Wasting from getting flogged. That might have been one of the things that made the birch popular up and down England. Even in provincial Salisbury, people told dirty jokes about it—and Peter knew a couple of men, respectable fellows his father's age, who were said to enjoy being on the receiving end.

Here, if not in many places, Peter found himself agreeing with Walter Haywood. Pleasure was pleasure, whilst pain was pain. Commingling the two didn't strike him as enjoyable.

After breakfast, the term's new arrivals—there were several dozen of them—trooped into the biggest lecture hall at Lincoln's Inn. A large, imposing man stood on a podium behind a fancy lectern, peering at them through eyeglasses as if he'd just discovered them on the sole of his shoe and was deciding how best to clean them off it.

"I am Stephen Heath," he rumbled when they'd grown more or less quiet. "For my sins, I have the unenviable task of transforming the lot of you into barristers and solicitors. I shall do it, too, or else send you back to the sorry kennels you came from with your tails between your legs. If you study hard and refrain from drunkenness, gambling, and whoring, you may ... possibly ... do well. You seem a most abject set of objects, so you also may not. But if you labor under the delusion that you can at the same time get through your course and enjoy yourselves, then all hope is lost."

Peter glanced at his roommate, who sat to his right. Walter Haywood looked as earnest and attentive as any of the other new scholars ... all of him except for one eyebrow, which twitched in amusement. If he'd really done what he'd boasted of doing, if he kept on doing that instead of poring over law books and lecture notes, what would become of him?

Whatever becomes of him, don't let it happen to you, Peter said to himself, and looked toward Stephen Heath once more.

Viola Williams put on a dark blue robe that touched the floor and had a hood like a monk's habit. Unlike a monk, though, she wore no belt, not even one of rope. A belt would have shouted to the world that she had a waist, and a narrow one to boot. It would have defeated the point of the robe, which was shapelessness.

Before Viola raised the hood, she put on a matching scarf and checked in a mirror to make sure she'd left no lock of hair visible. Then she secured her veil in place. She checked the mirror again. Except for her eyes and a bit of her forehead, everything was cloth. She nodded to herself. She was decently clad to go out in public.

From the ground floor, her mother called, "Are you ready, girls?"

"I am," Viola said, and went downstairs to prove it. Jane Williams' outfit was dark gray rather than dark blue. Otherwise, the two were nearly identical.

Katherine came down a moment later. She'd chosen brown. As with her mother and sister, all you could see of her was her eyes and her hands. "It will be nice to find out what the shops have," she said.

"It will, yes, if Margaret deigns to join us." Her mother raised her voice: "Shall we leave without you, Meg?"

"Don't you dare!" the youngest Williams sister screeched. Viola wasn't surprised Margaret was holding up the works; she often did. She hurried down the stairs in deep purple—along with the colors her mother and sisters were wearing and plain black, a shade reckoned fitting for women out and about.

Margaret tripped on the bottom stair. Viola caught her before she could fall. "Careful, dearie," she said. "You don't want Father splinting your arm, do you?"

"No," Margaret said, and then, fiercely, "I hate these stupid robes! I feel like a sack of beans with eyes whenever I put one on. They're ugly and they're stupid."

"They're necessary," her mother said in a voice that brooked no argument.

Viola had more sympathy for her little sister—who was, now, within an inch of her own five feet four. Up until not long before,

Margaret had been able to go outside wearing whatever she pleased. No more. She was a woman now, and had to be screened away from men's prying eyes. It took some getting used to. Viola remembered how it had for her.

"We're all here now, so shall we go?" Kate said. As usual, she had a knack for smoothing things over. From bits of talk Viola had heard, middle sisters often did.

Jane Williams held the door open so her children could leave before her. Viola breathed in fresh air through her veil. She smiled behind the cloth. Yes, that was what air was supposed to taste like! The town smells were still there, but not with the mustiness so usual inside the house.

And the sun felt warm on her hands and the uncovered strip of skin around her eyes. If she stayed out in it long enough, those exposed parts would darken, as men's hides often did. She remembered how brown she'd got when she was a little girl running around as she pleased. Those days, those years, were gone now.

The outdoors, though, held hazards you didn't need to worry about inside the house. Viola sidestepped quickly to keep from stepping in a big, fresh horse turd in the middle of the road. No matter how quick she was, the hem of her robe brushed it. She felt her face twist into a disgusted expression ... and found one small advantage to wearing the veil: no one could see her look.

With her mother and sisters, she crossed the bridge over the Avon and walked past the greensward in front of the cathedral and the nearby bishop's residence. A priest and a monk walking on the grass nodded gravely in their direction. Margaret nodded back. The older women didn't. The less you did to encourage men, even men who'd taken vows of chastity, the better off you were. Vows might be vows, but men were sure to be men.

Men were men, all right. A carpenter in a leather apron who was repairing a shed next to the bishop's home lowered his hammer and chisel to gape at the Williams women as they went by. He meowed loudly. When they took no notice of him, he dropped his tools, cupped his suntanned hands in front of his mouth, and called, "Hey, pussies! Hey, pussies!"

54

They went right on ignoring him. He laughed and made as if to lift his apron to show them what he had underneath. A quick glance toward the clergymen, though, made him think twice. Laughing still, he went back to work. He'd had his minute of amusement.

"I'd like to give him a kick right there," Margaret said through clenched teeth.

"Dearie, we all would," Viola said. Her mother and Katherine both nodded. Under the robe, Viola's shoulders slumped a little. No matter what she would have liked, things didn't work that way. Luckily, the carpenter wouldn't be able to notice her sag, either.

The women got more filthy catcalls from men as they went up Exeter Street, which turned to St. Johns without warning or any reason Viola knew of. Travelers waiting for the diligence in front of the King's Arms were bad enough to make Jane Williams sigh and say, "This kind of thing is the reason going out is no fun even shrouded as we are."

"They couldn't be much worse if we came out naked as Lady Godiva," Margaret said, which was both deliciously scandalous and the unvarnished truth. Viola imagined walking down the street in nothing but her skin. She imagined the hooting men falling over dead of apoplexies from the shock. *That might almost be worth it*, she thought.

Not many other women showed themselves, even decently robed. Given the kind of reception she and her mother and sisters got, Viola was anything but astonished. No matter how you might long to move about freely, you couldn't, and that was all there was to it.

North of New Street, St. Johns changed its name to Catherine, and then to Queen. The town market bustled on the west side of Queen. More women were in evidence there, examining produce and eggs and ducks and cups and feather dusters and whatever else people were trying to sell. Viola picked up a bolt of woolen cloth. Then she noticed a little sign showing what the fellow selling it hoped to get. He wouldn't get that much from her—she wasn't made of money. She put the bolt down in a hurry.

Her mother brought some caraway seeds, then went into the bookseller's across the street from the market. Viola followed. The smells of paper and ink and mellow leather bindings were old friends to her.

"Good morning, ladies." To his credit, the proprietor, a bespectacled man named Mortimer Blackwell, was scrupulously polite. He peered through the round glass lenses at Viola. "If you are who I believe you to be, I am to wish you good fortune on your engagement."

"Thank you, sir," Viola said. He probably recognized her as much by her outfit as by what he could see of her. However he did it, being treated as a person—or at least as a customer—felt good. She went on, "Have any new travelers' accounts come into your establishment?"

"Why, yes, Miss Williams," Blackwell replied. Her voice—and, no doubt, her taste in reading—confirmed her identity for him. He pulled a volume off a shelf. "This is by a man called Samuel Langhorne, who traveled down the Father of Waters in North America from its confluence with the Ohio to New Orleans on the Aztec Gulf. It speaks of the sights he saw and of his dealings with the natives."

"What do you want for it?" Viola tried to hide her eagerness. America was still the land of wonders, in truth the New World. English and Swedish colonists were pushing past the Appalachians, but few had seen, much less traveled on, the Father of Waters. Most of its length belonged to native chieftains, the rest to France (or, for a few years of dynastic confusion, to Spain).

"Eleven shillings, sixpence." Mortimer Blackwell spoke with admirable precision.

Viola paid no attention to it. "I'll give you eight and six," she said. She was her thrifty father's thrifty daughter.

"You can't jew me down like that!" the bookseller yipped. "I paid nine and tuppence my own self."

"You have infinite riches in your little room. I hold there is no sin but ignorance." Yes, Viola adapted Marlowe at any excuse or none. After Blackwell's gibe, that the verses sprang from *The Jew of Malta* only pleased her more. They haggled amiably and settled at ten and two.

And bringing such an intriguing new book home made—well, it almost made—running the gauntlet of foul-mouthed, dirty-minded men worthwhile.

Peter Drinkwater had thought he understood most of what his father did for a living. Settling last wills and testaments in court, going after people who didn't live up to contracts they made .... All that required attention to detail, certainly, but how complicated could it be?

What he hadn't thought about was where all that detail came from. Case law and precedent ran back to the Norman Conquest, sometimes to Anglo-Saxon days. A working barrister had to have all that detail at his mental fingertips so he could tell in a split second in a courtroom what applied to the situation he was dealing with—and how it applied as well.

The tutors and lecturers at Lincoln's Inn expected him and the other new sufferers to soak everything in like a hotcake soaking in syrup. The sheer amount of what he had to learn made his head want to explode. He felt as if his skull were packed with gunpowder and a sizzling fuse threaded through his ear.

He grudged the time he had to spend eating and sleeping—it cut into his swotting. However much he learned, it seemed like a wood chip floating on the vast Atlantic of what he hadn't covered yet.

Walter Haywood didn't work nearly so hard. How could he, when most of his interest focused on pleasures far from the intellectual? It wasn't that Peter despised those pleasures. He burned as hot as any other twenty-one-year-old man. When he burned too hot to stand it another moment, he took matters into his own hands, so to speak. That was what you were supposed to do, instead of risking your life with some loose woman.

His roommate cared not a ha'penny for what you were supposed to do. "Frigging's hardtack and water, man!" he said. "Fucking's a banquet, a banquet with a new course from every new cunt."

"If you say so," Peter answered. "By what I've seen, you must like hardtack and water pretty well, too, though." As he had back in Salisbury, he tried to be discreet when he played with himself. Haywood hardly cared. The instant he got an urge, he gratified it. And, even for a very young man, he got lots of urges.

He leered now. "When my tack is hard, what else am I going to do?" Having made Peter wince, he went on in more serious tones: "Honest to God, though, you don't know what you're missing."

"I'll find out—on my wedding night," Peter said.

"And disappoint yourself and your lovely bride because you don't know what you're doing or what she needs to do?" Haywood shook his head. "That's no way to go about it. You should get some experience first, is what you should do. Come along with me of a night. Nothing easier in all the world than finding friendly gash in London."

Turning him down didn't make him shut up. Peter might not have had any experience with women, but he'd had too much experience with that. He tried a different slant instead, asking, "How do you think you did on the last examination?"

"Well enough," Haywood answered carelessly. "I'm not worrying about topping the group or any nonsense like that. I just want to get through."

Peter only grunted. He wanted to top the group. He didn't think he would; three or four of his fellow pupils showed an aptitude and a facility for the law that he would never have. But he was no fool, and he owned as much stubborn persistence as any bulldog. He would go as far as hard work could take him, and he'd already found out hard work could take you a long way.

Not to care whether you did very well …. He shrugged. That attitude baffled him. "What would you do if they tossed you out of the Inn?" he asked.

"My pater's the second-biggest tobacco importer here in the city," Haywood said. "Without getting through, I'd have to be his left-hand man instead of his right-, but I'd end up in the family business just the same. He'd pay someone else to get what he wants from me, that's all."

"Oh." Peter left it right there. If he came back to Salisbury as anything but a solicitor, everyone in town would know he'd failed. He'd have trouble holding his head up for the rest of his life. Half the people would feel sorry for him. The other half would snicker behind their hands whenever he walked by. He might have to move away or go to the colonies to live down a disaster like that.

Walter Haywood didn't worry about such things. He had a place in his father's firm whether he passed the bar or not. No wonder he chased women instead of keeping his nose in the law books.

When Peter wrote to Viola, he described his roommate as *rather less a striver than I am* and let it go at that. The less he said about

Haywood's taste in amusements, the better off he thought he'd be. If he mentioned it, she might think he shared it. That would not be good, especially when her father was a doctor.

One Saturday, the first-year pupils squared off against their second-year fellows for a football match in the parkland across Serle Street from Lincoln's Inn. Each side had twenty-five or thirty men. The rules were catch-as-catch-can; football had never been an orderly game. The only thing everyone agreed on was that throwing the ball forward was right out.

The second-year scholars won the match, 24-19. Peter came out of it with a black eye and a wrenched knee that pained him for the next three weeks. He also came out of it with a certain amount of glory, having not merely tackled but knocked cold a second-year man who'd run the ball to within a couple of yards of the goal line.

Haywood got nothing worse than bruised ribs and a swollen ear. Unlike Peter, he'd hung back from the fiercest action. "If you're going to play, you should *play*," Peter told him.

"After that, they should have us studying the laws on felonious assault," Haywood said, a non-answer which was an answer of sorts.

"Oh, rubbish. No one held a dagger to you and made you join in," Peter said.

"No, but I should have seemed the perfect wet blanket if I didn't," his roommate replied. "Taking a few lumps to steer clear of that was worth it … I suppose."

Put that way, Haywood made pretty good sense. Where his cock wasn't involved, he often did. He was no one's fool; he couldn't have kept his head above water studying as little as he did if he were. But when his yard stiffened—which it did at any excuse or none—thought jumped straight out the window.

Before Peter could crack wise about that—and probably spark another quarrel—someone knocked on the door. With a languid wave, the wave a sultan might use to order a fresh wench fetched from the seraglio, Haywood indicated that Peter should open it. Peter's bed *was* closer. But his knee barked at him when he limped to the door and threw it wide.

The tall, skinny fellow in the old-fashioned clothes standing in the hallway was no pupil at the Inn. Peter would have recognized his beanpole build if not his pointy-nosed, nearly chinless face if he were. "Yes?" Peter said, not moving aside for him. If he were a dog, he would have bristled.

"They told me down below this here was Master Haywood's room," the stranger replied, his accent as outdated and barbarous as the cut of his corduroy jacket.

That accent got Walter Haywood off his bed and onto his feet. "And so it is, Eb," he said, coming forward to nudge Peter aside. "You're talking to my partner in misery, Peter Drinkwater. Peter, this is Ebenezer Cooke, one of the leading sot-weed factors from his Majesty's colony of Baltimore."

"Sot-weed?" Peter echoed, in over his head.

"Baccy," Cooke more or less explained, and held out a long-fingered hand. By the time Peter finished shaking it, he'd realized that had to be American dialect for *tobacco*. People said the English used in the colonies was almost another language. Now he had proof they knew what they were talking about.

"I hadn't even heard you were back in the mother country, Eb," Haywood said.

"Well, here I be, Master Haywood, with hogsheads of the finest Chesapeake an' Rappahannock leaf," Cooke said. "Your da, he done told me I should rout you out so you can have yourself a look an' a taste."

"Did he?" Haywood looked as thrilled as he sounded. "A traipse down to the docks wasn't what I had in mind for the evening."

"Your da told me to fetch you," Ebenezer Cooke repeated in tones of doom.

Peter's roommate sighed. "All right, I'll come." Then he brightened. "I know a lupanar by Blackfriars Bridge as fine as any in the city, and cheaper than most."

"You know a what?" Cooke said. It was Greek to him. It was Latin to Peter, but he had the Latin to understand it.

"A bordel. A brothel. A whorehouse. A joyhouse. Is that plain enough, or shall I draw you a picture?" Haywood said. "Maybe we can pay the girls in Rappahannock. Most of them smoke or dip snuff."

The sot-weed factor shaped the sign of the cross. "Reckon you don't want I should tell your da what you just said. Your body, that there's your temple. You shouldn't ought to profane it with sinfulness."

"If God didn't want us fucking, why'd He give us a cock and bal-locks?" Haywood retorted. "Why'd He give women cunts?"

"To reproduce our kind in holy matrimony," Cooke said piously. "You know what happens to them as spills their seed all over cre-ation? The Wasting, is what."

"Not always. Not even very often. I've fucked my socks off more times than I can tell you, and I'm healthy as a hoptoad." Haywood plucked a hat from the tree by the door, set it on his head at a jaunty angle, and left the argument behind with the room. Or did he? As Peter was closing the door, he heard Walter say, "After we finish the tobacco, I'll show you how to worship at my temple. *Ave Maria*, yes I will!"

He didn't hear Ebenezer Cooke's response. All things con-sidered, that might have been just as well. He hobbled back to his bed and tried to massage some of the swelling out of his poor, abused knee.

Things being as they were in the Williams household, Ned Slayback had long since got in the habit of delivering letters to the door of the surgery. Viola remembered the days when Ned's side whiskers were coppery as a new-struck penny. They looked more like snow faintly streaked with rust now. Time marched on everyone, but on some harder than on others.

The postman always knocked twice. Unless very busy with a patient, Viola's father always went straight to the door. Sometimes, after paying the threepence delivery fee, Richard Williams would come upstairs right away. When he did, Viola would meet him on the landing. The odds were, her father was carrying a letter for her from Peter Drinkwater.

Sure enough, this morning he handed her an envelope sealed with green wax stamped with the image of a well: a good signet for someone with her fiancé's surname. Quirking one eyebrow, he remarked, "I ought to charge you for bringing this up here, get back some of what I give old Ned."

"If you like," Viola answered coolly. "Since I get my money from you, though, isn't that like giving with one hand and taking with the other?"

Her father considered. Having done so, he made a wry face. "Now that you mention it," he said, "yes."

"Had you said no, we could have argued," Viola said. "Then you wouldn't have needed to go back down to work quite so soon."

"Things are quiet today. Most of me is glad—no one injured or diseased enough to require my services means less pain in Salisbury than usual," her father said. "On the other hand, it also means no fees coming in. If that keeps up for long, I'll steal a tin cup—I shan't be able to afford to buy one—and take my place with the rest of the mendicants in town."

Viola sniffed. Like any doctor's daughter, she hadn't needed long to learn people didn't always pay their bills. "If they gave you what they owed you, or even half, you could hurry to emergencies in a coach and four, not on shank's mare."

"They always intend to pay."

"And which road is paved with intentions like that?"

Her father spread his hands. "There you have—" Before he could finish the thought, someone banged on the surgery door with great vigor. He started down the stairs, throwing "Maybe we'll eat tonight after all" over his shoulder as he went.

"Yes, Papa. Keep the wolf from the door. By the knocking, he's trying to beat it down." Viola smiled. She got on well with her father. She was more than fond of her sisters. She even liked her mother— Jane Williams owned not a mean bone in her body.

And when she moved away from her household and into Peter Drinkwater's, what then? She'd have to get used to a whole new set of people. Peter himself would top the list, but she'd also keep company with his mother and sisters. She barely knew them. Women led isolated lives. It wasn't fair or just, but she couldn't do anything about that. She had to hope they'd get along.

She popped the seal off the letter with her thumbnail and smiled when it came free in one piece. She was making a little collection of unbroken ones. *With a different cast of mind, I might do something nefarious with them,* she thought, half regretfully, as she opened the envelope and unfolded the letter.

Peter's hand was firm and legible, without many frills, which matched the impression she'd formed of him when they met. *My dear Viola,* he wrote, *I am hobbling about like some ancient mariner, and have been since Harry Elliott tried to tear my leg off in the football match this Saturday* ultimo. *I kicked him in the stomach, but fear he won the exchange nonetheless.*

Viola nodded to herself. Her father hated the football matches that sometimes roiled the meadows outside of town. He claimed they were more riot than sport. He'd reset too many dislocated shoulders and splinted too many broken arms and legs to see the fun in it ... though he'd played as eagerly as anyone else before he started practicing medicine and even for a while afterwards.

Peter went on, *Knowing your interest in distant shores, I should also mention that I have made the acquaintance of one Ebenezer Cooke, a sot-weed factor from the colony of Baltimore. Sot-weed, it appears, is one of the things they call tobacco on the far side of the sea. Cooke is in the employ of Haywood's father, who is amongst the leaders in the tobacco trade.*

She knew Peter shared a room with Walter Haywood. She'd also gathered that Haywood was less interested in the law than he might have been. What he *was* interested in, Peter hadn't really said.

He did have more to say about Cooke: *He is an extraordinary specimen, above six feet high but straw-thin and altogether graceless, moving as if he were a puppet made from badly jointed sticks. His face, I fear, is as homely as his figure and his gait. And, if you can believe it, despite speaking the King's English like the creature from the back of beyond he is, he fancies himself a poet. He will recite his verses on the Baltimorean wilderness at any excuse or none, and each proves worse than the one before. My father talks about the book he received from a local poetaster, but I have trouble crediting that anything in it could outdo the horrors perpetrated by Ebenezer Cooke.*

Slowly, Viola nodded again. Peter could tell a story on paper, sure enough. He made her see the American bumpkin inside her head, though she knew she'd never lay eyes on him in the real world.

Peter went on about his studies. Viola found those less interesting than the Baltimorean, but realized how important they were to her fiancé. She didn't suppose he would be fascinated if she dove into detail about the cross-stitch phoenix, all scarlet and gold, she was working on when she didn't have anything else to do.

And so she resolved not to. As soon as she finished Peter's letter, she inked a quill and began a response. She asked him to tell her more about Ebenezer Cooke and relayed the bits of gossip she'd heard that he might find interesting. About the cross-stitch phoenix she said not a word.

V

Peter studied through the spring. He never stopped being amazed by how much the grizzled barristers and solicitors who taught at Lincoln's Inn expected their pupils to learn—and not just to learn but to know, to know not only so they could bring it out pat but so they could take a piece from here, one from there, and one from somewhere else, then stir them all together into an argument that would sway a judge or a jury.

"Think of yourselves as cooks in a kitchen," Stephen Heath rumbled. "It's all very well when everything you need is on the table or in a pantry. But what do you do when you find out you haven't got any ham ten minutes before your dish goes onto the fire? If you can't think on your feet in this business, you're done for."

To show what he meant, he invited—by which he meant *required*—the first-year pupils to justify the abolition of the trade in African slaves, a trade now forbidden for more than a century and a half, without mentioning the Wasting. In his bull *De libertate humana*, Pope Innocent XI had decreed that, since the deadly disease had come to Christian lands out of Africa, continued traffic in people who might bring it with them was too great a risk to countenance.

Peter struggled with the assignment. He watched Henry Haywood scribble away at the other desk in the room as if he had not a care in the world. "What are you saying?" he asked after a while. "What *can* you say? Everyone in Europe had traded slaves up till

65

Innocent's bull. Without it, everybody would have kept on doing it—it made people money."

"Oh, I'm putting out a bull of my own—a cock and bull," his roommate answered with a laugh. "If you pick your legal citations and your Biblical citations carefully enough, you can make a pretty fair case that selling slaves—any slaves, mind you, not just African slaves—is against God's law and man's."

"Can you?" Peter said tonelessly. Haywood nodded and went on writing. Peter scratched his head. Now that Walter'd pointed it out to him, he could see that that case might be there. But he wouldn't have come up with it himself—he was sure of that. Walter thought on his feet better than he did.

Half an hour later, Haywood set down his pen and stood. "That should be enough to keep the old vultures happy till they find some new way to peck at our livers. I'm going to find some fun. Want to come along and live a little, shake the dust off your shoulders?"

"I wish I could," Peter lied, "but I'm just getting into this. I'll probably have to borrow candles to finish."

"All work and no play is no way to spend your day," Haywood rhymed. Peter only shrugged. With a sigh, the other pupil said, "All right, if you don't want to get your end wet, I can't make you. I'll be back some time or other." Out the door he went, and slammed it behind him, too.

Chances were he'd hoped to make Peter jump and blot his sheet. He failed there; Peter was used to his antics and wrote on, finishing somewhere close to midnight. He didn't think his argument was brilliant, but he hoped it was serviceable. If he hadn't had his room-mate's clever suggestion, it might not even have been that.

He had needed to scrounge a candle from the pupils next door. It was getting down toward the nub when he blew it out and slid into bed. *Coffee in the morning. Lots of coffee in the morning*, he thought as his head hit the goose down in his pillow.

That was the last thing he remembered … till Walter Haywood came in at some heretical hour, singing not nearly soft enough under his breath. Peter had no idea whether he'd found or paid a willing woman, but he'd clearly had plenty to drink and then some.

As if to get rid of what he'd brought aboard, he took a long, loud piss in the pot by his bed, then landed on it in a way more suggestive of falling into it than getting into it. He went to sleep straightaway, but that helped only so much, because he started to snore. Peter thought he'd lie awake forever himself, but forever lasted only about ten minutes.

He jerked awake again when a Lincoln's Inn servant pounded on the door to summon the pupils to breakfast. Light was leaking in through the curtains. Peter got up, splashed his face with cold water, and sloshed a little around in his mouth before spitting it into the chamber pot.

Haywood was still snoring. He lay sprawled diagonally across the mattress, still in all the clothes he'd worn the day before except his shoes. Peter shook him, none too gently. "Get moving, slugabed. That was the breakfast bang."

Walter groaned and put his pillow over his head. "Have you no respect for the dead?" he asked, his voice muffled.

"Not bloody much," Peter said. "Neither will Master Heath, if you don't give him your screed in a couple of hours."

His roommate's suggestion of where Master Heath could stick his screed would not have amused a priest. It did amuse Peter, who might have thought the same thing himself but wouldn't have come out with it. Blaspheming, Walter Haywood crawled out of bed and started to change his outfit.

Both aspiring jurists turned in their work on time. "Thank you, Mummy," Haywood said as they left the lecture hall. Peter told him he could stick that where he'd suggested Master Heath could put his paper. They both laughed.

When the senior master gave back the assignments three days later, he said to Peter, "You and young Haywood share a room, do you not?"

"Yes, sir," Peter said.

"Some of the same elements appear in both your essays," Heath said.

"Yes, sir," Peter repeated. "Walter told me how he was attacking the problem. That seemed a good line to take, so I used it, too, along with other things I thought of."

"Interesting." Heath tapped a front tooth with his fingernail. "Yours is much the better specimen: better organized, better argued, a good deal more thorough."

"Uh, thank you, sir," Peter said. "The idea was his, as I told you."

"It's not always where the idea comes from. What you do with it matters, too," Heath said. "Carry on."

After supper, when he and his roommate went back to their chamber, Haywood thumbed his nose at him and said, "Teacher's pet!"

Peter hadn't asked what Master Heath said to Haywood about his paper. Now he had a good notion. Shrugging, he answered, "I gave you credit for thinking of the line of attack."

"Yes, he said so. He also said being clever usually counted for less in the law than being thorough did." Walter Haywood gave an airy wave of his hand to show what he thought of that. He pulled off his undyed linen shirt and pulled on a fancier one with blue and red stripes.

"Where are you going?" Peter asked.

"Out to find some sport—where else?" Whistling, Haywood ran a comb through his hair. He checked his appearance in the little mirror on the dresser and nodded approval of himself. "Every girl's wild for a sharp-dressed man."

"What about the examination tomorrow?"

"What about it? I'll do well enough. If you want to swot, my dear fellow, swot away to your heart's content. I want pussy." Haywood undid his trousers and picked up the chamber pot. He did have the courtesy to turn his back before he started to piss. He started—and then he stopped, with a hiss of pain. "Oh, bloody fucking hell!"

"What's wrong?" Peter asked. "Did you hurt yourself?"

"Hurt myself? I've got a God-damned dose, is what happened." Peter's silence must have told of his incomprehension, because Walter Haywood set his clothes to rights, put the pot down, and set a hand on his forehead. "The clap, you innocent idiot! My last lady gave me a present. And no girl will let me get near her, not while my pipe is drippy. It'll hurt like blazes for a while when I ease myself, too."

By the way he talked, this wasn't the first time he'd had that happen to him. Peter could think of only one thing: "Pray the clap is all you've got!" Everyone knew women who had the clap or the Spanish pox often had the Wasting, too, even if they didn't show it yet.

But Haywood gave that airy wave again. "Chances are she doesn't. A fine, bouncy, strapping lass." Whether he felt cheerful or not, he sounded that way. "Besides, the game is worth the candle."

"And you call me an idiot? What will you call me when you come down with it?"

"An idiot who chanced to be right, the way a stopped clock is twice a day. But I'll bet I don't. And I want to live my life, not just go through it. Don't you even know what fun is?"

"Of course I do. Why do you think I'm getting married?"

"Married?" Walter Haywood couldn't have looked more disgusted had Peter farted. "How is one woman better than one hand? Variety's what you want in life!"

"A short life but a merry one?"

"A merry one. What else matters? My father's fields of sot-weed across the ocean?" Haywood's derisive laugh said what he thought about that.

"You should visit the dispensary," Peter said.

"If I thought they could cure me, I would. They'll squirt goop up my hose. It'll hurt worse than pissing does now, and I'll still have the gleets when they're done with me. Time will take care of it. Time heals all wounds."

Not the Wasting, Peter thought. All he said, though, was, "Time wounds all heels."

Haywood stopped and studied him for a moment. At last, he answered, "You could be dangerous if you gave yourself the chance."

"I don't want to be dangerous. I don't give a two-penny damn about being dangerous," Peter said irritably. "All I want to do is finish my work here, go home to Salisbury, marry the woman I'm betrothed to, and get on with my life."

By the way Walter Haywood regarded him, he was speaking a dialect of English far stranger and more barbarous than anything that came out of Ebenezer Cooke's mouth. "I don't think I ever met anyone before who wouldn't live in London if he had the chance," he said.

"Well, now you've found something new, then," Peter replied.

Haywood was more subdued than usual for the next couple of weeks—not subdued, but more so than usual. In due course, he announced that his hose had stopped dripping. Even from a roommate, that was more than Peter needed to hear. Haywood went out to celebrate no longer having visible signs of the clap. "Why don't you come along, too?" he asked.

"Thanks, but no thanks," Peter said. Haywood laughed and laughed. Peter wondered whether he'd soon show the horrible night sweats and fevers and weariness that marked the coming of the Wasting.

But he didn't. He went right on roistering and doing not too well but well enough at his studies. *Lucky son of a whore*, Peter thought, and resolved not to play cards or shoot dice against him.

Viola checked the mirror to make sure her headscarf left not a wisp of hair showing. She adjusted her veil and pulled up her hood. Solstice Day was a day when women might leave their home in Salisbury, which meant it was a day when women there did leave their homes. Any chance to get out was a chance to be seized. Viola certainly thought so. Her mother and sisters did, too.

Of course, a woman who went outside was nothing but perambulating eyes and hands. So it was all over England, all over Christendom, all over the civilized world. The exact cut and decoration of the tenting required for people of the female persuasion varied from place to place, but not the brute fact that tenting was required. Even savages who'd learned of the Wasting—to their cost—from civilized men had also learned to cover up their women and hide them away.

Why couldn't the world sequester men instead? Viola knew why only too well—men were bigger and stronger and more insistently lecherous. They also drank in lechery through their eyes more than women did. It all seemed so horribly unfair anyway.

"Are we almost ready?" Jane Williams asked. "It's getting close to four." Four was when the sun rose on Solstice Day, within a minute or two either way.

Viola glanced at herself in the mirror one last time. She almost wasn't there. That meant she looked perfect. "I am, Mother," she said.

"So am I," Kate said.

"Me, too," Margaret chimed in.

"No, you're not," Kate said, and tucked a stray lock of hair back under her younger sister's scarf where it belonged. "You aren't a baby any more. You need to take care of these things for yourself."

"It's all stupid," Margaret said.

"Unless you want trouble all the time—not just for you but for all of us, and for Mother and Father especially—you need to do it anyhow." Viola didn't try to tell Margaret it wasn't stupid; she didn't like to lie. What she said was true: every word of it, worse luck. Whether something was stupid had no connection with whether you had to do it.

Out they went, out into the brightening misty morning. Richard Williams, all bedizened with ribbons and bells, had left before his womenfolk. He was one of the Morris dancers in this year's parade, as he had been for as long as Viola could remember.

With her mother and sisters, Viola crossed the bridge over the Avon. Mist lingered longer and thicker on the river than anywhere else. She heard ducks quacking on the water or on the bank near it, but couldn't see them.

As the Williams women walked past the cathedral, the bells chimed four. The sun scrambled over the horizon, far in the northeast. For the first few minutes after it rose, Viola could look at it through the mist without having to squint. Then it climbed higher and started burning away the vapors, and she couldn't any more.

They got only a few catcalls from passing men while they made their way up to the stretch of Castle Road where the women gathered. Viola looked around for Peter Drinkwater's mother and sisters. They were going to be her family, too, even if she didn't really know them now. She hoped they'd be able to put up with her. She hoped she'd be able to put up with them, too.

Too many sets of eyes and hands, too many tents of dull cloth, packed too close together. Viola couldn't pick out the Drinkwater women. If they were looking for her, they didn't find her, either.

A chant reached her ears from down in the direction of the cathedral. As people heard it, they grew quiet. The parade was starting! Though taller than most of the women around her, Viola stood on tiptoe to see better. That helped less than she wished it would have—everybody close by, and probably everybody along the route, women and men alike, was doing the same thing.

"Here they come!" someone in the front row said in a high, excited voice.

A moment later, Viola got her own glimpse of the Druids. They marched up Castle Road, a dozen men robed all in white. She recognized Mortimer Blackwell, the bookseller, and a couple of others. They went right on chanting in what they said was the language of the ancient Britons before the Romans came.

Viola's father had told her the tongue the Salisbury Druids used was really Cornish, which was still used in the West Country. She'd been around ten then; she remembered asking him why they didn't tell the truth. She was the kind of person for whom the truth mattered a lot.

So was Richard Williams. She remembered the way he'd screwed up his face before answering, "Because they want to connect themselves to the days before the Wasting came, the old, old days of Stonehenge and other marvels. And because, if they make themselves out to be ancient, even fire-eating churchmen are less likely to make life hard for them. It's a ... convenient sort of lie."

"They aren't really ancient, then?" she'd asked.

"That depends on what you mean," he'd said. "There *were* Druids—Celtic wise men and priests—before the Romans came. But the Romans stamped them out, and for a long, long time there weren't any. They started up again here in Salisbury a couple of hundred years ago, and other places around the country, too. I don't know how closely they're connected to the old-time ones. I'm not sure they know, either."

"Why does the Church let them do it?" Even at ten, Viola had known how powerful the Pope was.

"Because they go out to Stonehenge and to other places they call places of power, and they go through their rituals, and they hope those will be enough to free us from the Wasting," Richard Williams had said, and spread his hands. "How could anyone dare stop anything like that?"

And, even at ten, Viola had known that question had no answer. The Wasting's shadow covered the whole world. It would go right on covering the world until people learned to cure it or to keep it from spreading from one person to the next. That hadn't happened in the past three and a half centuries. It didn't look like happening any time soon, either.

Viola looked down at herself—or rather, at her hands, which were all she could see of herself. Because of the Wasting, women lived in tents and in what might as well have been cages. It hadn't always been that way … but it had been for a very long time now.

Behind the Druids, a troupe of seven Morris dancers capered to the music of two flutes. Three of the dancers were dressed as men tricked out with streamers and bells. Her father was one of those. Viola saw his eyes flicking toward the crowd of women again and again, searching for his nearest and dearest. "Here, Father!" she called, and waved to him. His smile said he'd seen her, or at least heard her.

One Morris man danced in fool's motley, with a seven-horned cap with a bell at the end of each horn. King Michael III didn't have a fool, or Viola didn't think he did. As far as she knew, kings hadn't had fools for more than a hundred years, but she wasn't sure how far she knew.

And the last three Morris dancers had put on women's clothing. No, not the tents Viola and her mother and sisters had to wear whenever they went out in public. Women's clothing from the days before the Wasting. Their faces were bare, and shaved as smooth as they could get them. Two wore long blond wigs, the third a red one.

Their skirts came up halfway to their knees, showing off stockinged ankles and calves. And their blouses …. Their blouses clung to their torsos as if painted on. Whatever they'd stuffed into the front to give themselves bosoms was excessive to the point of ridiculousness.

They blew kisses to the men lining the street. The men whooped and hollered. More than a few blew kisses back, even though they had to know they were saluting other men. Sodomy was a less common sin than fornication, but no less deadly—maybe even more so.

Watching the dancers display themselves like that scandalized Viola and made her fiercely jealous at the same time. She wished she could do something like that, while also wondering where she would ever find the nerve. Part of her—too much of her—took the tent for granted.

Up Castle Road they capered, till the street bent and she lost sight of them. She still heard the shrilling flutes, though. Like the Druids, the dancers and musicians would go across most of Salisbury Plain to Stonehenge. The Druids would do whatever holy or unholy things they did at the stone circle, and the Morris men would dance all the way there. Viola expected her father to be worn out and have sore feet when he finally came home.

But the parade wasn't over yet. Excited murmurs ran through the crowd, both men and women. "The Giant!" "The Salisbury Giant!" "The Giant comes next!" In a high, thin voice, a child—whether girl or boy, Viola couldn't tell—exclaimed, "And Hob-Nob, too!"

Thump! The deep note made her bones quiver. *Thump!* There it came again, again more felt than heard. *Thump!* As the Druids' chant and the flautists' notes had before, the booms got louder and closer with each one.

"The Giant's footsteps!" another child squeaked. When you were small, you believed things like that, or you almost did. So people said, anyhow. Viola couldn't remember ever having been so silly. But then, both her father and her mother insisted she'd been born with an old head.

Along with those thumps, oohs and ahhs from the crowd marked the Salisbury Giant's path along Castle Road. As they got louder, Viola craned her old head to the left so she could see the Giant as soon as he appeared—and Hob-Nob, too, as that little child had said. They might not be real, but they were fun anyhow. Especially for women, public fun was hard to come by.

"It's the Giant!" Half a dozen people said the same thing, or something very much like it, at the same time.

Viola grinned behind her veil. She was sure most of the women around her wore the same expression. She could see those delighted grins on the faces of the men across the street.

At least twelve feet tall, the Salisbury Giant had such a swarthy complexion that she'd heard a few people call him the Moorish Giant (she wondered when last a genuine Moor had walked Salisbury's streets, and whether a genuine Moor ever had). His beard was long and thick, black and bushy. He had enormous eyes that unblinkingly stared straight ahead.

He wore robes nearly as full and flowing as the outfits women had to put on to go out in public. Under those robes walked the man who propelled the Giant along the street.

With the Salisbury Giant marched his squires: three men in mailshirts. One of them carried a lantern, as if he were Diogenes searching for an honest man. One brandished a sword, while the third swung a mace. The squires also muttered instructions to the man inside the Giant, so he didn't walk into the crowd or into a wall.

A couple of paces behind them came a man with a bass drum slung around his neck. Every so often, he smote it. *Thump!* Since the Giant had no real feet, the drum created his footsteps. *Thump!*

And behind the drummer pranced Hob-Nob, the Giant's black hobby-horse. Like the fool in the troupe of Morris dancers, he was there to stir up as much chaos as he could. He rushed from one side of the street to the other, lunging at children and chasing them. The man who made him move could work his jaws to snap at the boys and girls so they squealed in pretended terror—or sometimes, if they were young enough, in terror that wasn't pretended at all.

Viola turned to Margaret. "Hob-Nob scared you all to pieces when you were four years old. Do you remember?"

"I hope I do and I wish I didn't," Margaret said. "I had Hob-Nob nightmares for weeks after that. I still get them every once in a while."

Next came the mayor of Salisbury and half a dozen men from his council of burghers. The burghers wore somber modern suits: black trousers with white side stripes, black jackets with silver threads, black cravats over white shirts. By contrast, the mayor marched in gaudy medieval velvets and satins, with a floppy velvet hat topping it all.

"He looks like a peacock in amongst a flock of magpies," Kate said.

"He does!" Viola exclaimed. "I'll never be able to look at him and the burghers now without thinking that, and it's your fault."

"Somebody has to liven up the dull old magpies," said the middle Williams girl. "Not as if we have the bishop to brighten things with his regalia."

"No, not today," Viola agreed. The Church might tolerate the Solstice Day procession, but didn't really approve of it. If not for the

Wasting, she was sure the Church never would have put up with it. But as long as there was the off chance the Druids might touch some power proper priests couldn't find …

The Salisbury Giant and his squires, Hob-Nob, the mayor, and the burghers wouldn't go far across the plain before turning around and coming back to town. After a couple of earlier Solstice Day parades, Viola had seen them returning and trying to pretend nothing much was going on.

She'd been angry then. She wasn't any more. They had no proper place at Stonehenge. The Druids and the Morris dancers … might, anyhow.

Such a descent into magic and irrationality seemed unlike her hard-headed father. When Viola'd finally got up the nerve to ask him about it, he'd looked sheepish and said, "I don't see how it can possibly hurt anything, and I do enjoy the dancing." She couldn't quarrel with any of that, so she didn't try.

Now, though, the excitement was over. She didn't get out of the house that often—what women did? Even in her own city, she felt like a traveler from a far-off land. She gloried in the open air, even if she had to breathe it through the fabric of the veil.

She couldn't have been the only woman in the crowd who felt the same way. Most of them lingered where they were, enjoying strength in numbers. Here and there, women who recognized friends or kinfolk in spite of the outfits law and custom dictated for them talked and embraced and sometimes wept.

Someone Viola didn't recognize came up to her and spoke hesitantly: "Your pardon, but aren't you Viola Williams?"

"That's right. I'm sorry, but I'm afraid you have the advantage of me." Voice and the bit of forehead Viola could see made her think the other woman was older than she was. Could she be …?

She was. "I'm Amanda Drinkwater, Peter's mother. My daughters and I—here are Julietta and Joanna—look forward to having you in the family."

"Thank you very much! I was hoping I'd see you—all of you—here today." Viola dropped a curtsy and waved her own mother and sisters over. All the women clasped hands and exclaimed.

To Amanda Drinkwater, Jane Williams said, "Our husbands have been friends since they were boys. It's good that we're joining the families together like this."

"Yes, I think so, too," Amanda said. "Alf never fails to speak well of Richard."

"It also works the other way round," Jane said. You couldn't always tell when someone smiled behind a veil, but sometimes you could. Viola thought she could now.

One of the Drinkwater daughters—Viola wasn't sure if she was Joanna or Julietta—said, "Peter tells us you like to read."

She didn't say it as if she meant *Peter tells us you like to indulge in an unnatural vice*, which was good. Viola nodded. "That's right, especially books about travels. I can't go wandering around the world, but my mind can."

"I like to read, too," her sister-in-law-to-be said. "Mostly stories, but I do."

"Well, we'll have things to talk about, then," Viola answered, and hoped she meant it. She knew she fit into the world as it was less well than she might have. If the Drinkwaters would try to meet her halfway, that was bound to help ... wasn't it?

Her own mother and Mrs. Drinkwater were sizing each other up. Neither seemed dissatisfied with what she found in the other. Yes, everything felt promising. And then the Williams and Drinkwater women said their goodbyes. Each family headed back to its home. *Back to the familiar*, Viola said. *Back to the women's quarters. Back to our cage.*

Someone knocked on the door to the chamber Peter shared with Walter Haywood. "See who that is, will you?" Haywood said. "I'm actually trying to do some work here."

"All right." Peter knew that didn't happen as often as it might have. He got off his bed and opened the door.

The long, lean form of Ebenezer Cooke stood there. Haywood's father's tobacco factor dipped his head. "God gi' you good day, Master Drinkwater," he said, his accent as barbarous as always.

"Master Cooke," Peter said politely. He stepped aside to let Cooke in.

The man from America had to duck to keep from hitting his head on the doorjamb. "New cargo in at the docks, young Master Haywood, sir," he said, as subservient and as implacable as a dog. "Your pa needs for you to do the inspection and the estimatin'."

"Does he need me to do it right now?" Haywood asked plaintively.

"Would I be here if he din't, sir?" Ebenezer Cooke might lack rank, but he had authority.

Walter Haywood sighed. "All right, I'll come. But then, Ebenezer, I warn you—I'll have my revenge."

"What d'you mean?" The tobacco factor sounded alarmed and apprehensive, as well he might have.

"You'll find out." Haywood laughed a laugh a stage villain would have paid ten pounds to acquire. He got up from his desk, grabbed a hat and clapped it on his head, and strode toward Cooke with such determination that the larger man gave back a pace. "Let's be off, then," Peter's roommate said. And away they went.

Peter went over to glance at the essay Haywood had been writing, which lay on the desk in midsentence. Even at a glance, he could see Walter found ideas and slapped them together in a way hardly anyone else could match. He could also see Haywood didn't organize them as well as he might have.

He shook his head. He had to work much harder than his roommate did. Everything seemed simple to Walter. Then again, Peter's own essay had been finished for a day and a half. Instead of sprinting through it at the last minute tonight, he'd be able to study the laws governing what happened when someone died intestate. An examination was coming in a few days.

Study he did, till his head buzzed with relationships of the second, third, fourth, and even fifth degree. He finally gave up and went to bed. Still no sign of Walter Haywood. Either he was down at the docks grading the weed no one seemed able to do without or he'd finished that and was getting even with Ebenezer Cooke for making him do it.

Haywood reeled in some time in the middle of the night. He was singing wild snatches of wilder songs. He smelled of rum and of some strong floral scent. Sleepy as Peter was, he noticed it right away. His sisters and mother sometimes perfumed themselves, but Haywood reeked more than all three of them put together.

"Are you awake?" Walter demanded.

"I am *now*," Peter said—pointedly, he thought.

Not pointedly enough. Haywood laughed. "Want to hear how I paid Eb back?"

"No," Peter said: hard to be more pointed than that. "Tell me in the morning, if you have to tell me at all."

"You're a wet blanket." Haywood, by contrast, sounded aggrieved.

Peter didn't care. "By God and the saints, I hope so! Now shut up and go to bed."

"What happens if I don't?"

"Whatever it is, you won't like it." Peter knew he wouldn't go back to sleep if he jumped up from bed and pounded the stuffing out of his roommate. He also knew he'd likely land in trouble if he did. At the moment, he hardly cared. One more thing he knew was that he could do it if he wanted to.

Haywood must have known the same thing. "All right, all right. No need to get your pantaloons in a twist about it." He pulled off his shoes and threw his hat toward the hat tree—not onto it, because Peter heard the hat hit the floor. Haywood got into bed. "Happy now?"

"Thrilled. Shut up, why don't you?" Peter said. His roommate started snoring right away. He lay awake for some time himself, silently swearing at the ceiling. He didn't notice when he dozed off again at last.

He didn't notice anything till the Lincoln's Inn door banger shocked him awake before breakfast. Walter Haywood was either still snoring or snoring again—Peter wasn't sure which. He shook Haywood, which turned the snores to a groan. "What are you doing? Leave me alone!" Walter said.

Sweetly, Peter answered, "Breakfast time—rise and shine!" He got back some inspired profanity and obscenity. He didn't care. He'd done what he needed to do. If Haywood didn't get moving, that was *his* worry.

Walter showed up in the refectory when most of the young legal pupils were finishing. He bolted bread, gulped coffee, and hurried back upstairs to put some kind of end on the work Ebenezer Cooke had interrupted.

He turned it in at the appointed time. Whatever he'd done, it would probably be good enough to keep Master Bingham, who knew everything about precedent worth knowing, quiet if not delighted. And he was his old irrepressible self by late afternoon.

"Now—about Cooke," he said as he and Peter were swotting before supper.

"About Cooke," Peter said resignedly.

"After I finally got done with that beastly sot-weed"—Haywood rolled his eyes—"I got him drunk and took him to Madam Henderson's."

"What's Madam Henderson's?"

Walter rolled his eyes again. "You poor provincial, you. Only the biggest brothel in London—probably the biggest brothel in the world. Now he knows what it's all about, by God!"

"You are quite mad," Peter said. Haywood only laughed at him. So many people took so many chances. Some got away with them, too. Some didn't.

VI

Supper at the Williams household was chicken stewed with beans, carrots, onions, and field mushrooms. Viola had soaked the beans the night before; they were nice and soft. Kate had picked the mushrooms. She knew which ones were good and which weren't safe to eat. The chicken, one of their own, had almost stopped laying eggs. It wasn't good for anything but the stewpot any more.

Even in the pot—which bubbled above a low fire—the stringy old bird would take a deal of stewing before it got tender, if it ever did. Every so often, one of the Williams women stirred the pot so the stew didn't stick to the bottom. Viola knew there'd be hard scrubbing ahead with sand and pumice stone all the same.

A wave of fragrant steam rose to her nose when she worked a big iron spoon through the stew. She couldn't help smiling. "This will be so good!" she said.

The aroma reached her mother's nose a moment later. Jane Williams smiled, too. You could hardly help yourself when you smelled something like that. "I was thinking the same thing," she said.

"We'll probably eat most of the hen tonight," Viola said. "But I've got salt cod soaking in a bowl of water. We can put that in tomorrow, and the stew will be just about as good."

Her mother smiled again. "You have everything all figured out. Anybody'd think you were Richard's daughter."

"Oh, foosh!" Viola said. "You're the one who keeps the house going the way it should, like a water wheel turning over and over. Do you think I haven't noticed? If I get it from anybody, I get it from you."

"Thank you, but you'll make me vain if you aren't careful." Jane Williams paused for a moment, then resumed: "Wherever you get it, you have it. I only hope Peter and his womenfolk notice."

That had been on Viola's mind, too. "I'll try to fit in there. I hope I can. I hope Peter will look for a place of his own before too long."

"For things like that, you don't just hope. You nudge him in the direction you want him to go, and you keep nudging him till he falls over. If you do it right, he won't even notice he isn't still on his own pins any more." Viola's mother smiled the kind of secret smile women used among themselves when no men were around.

Viola smiled, too, nervously. "I hope I can. Have you ever done that kind of thing with Father? I shouldn't think it would be easy."

"Sometimes it isn't. Sometimes . . . . Sometimes you'd be surprised."

Viola had a notion of what her mother meant. Her father cared about a few things very much, his family, his practice, and his books chief among them. What he didn't care so much about, he hardly noticed. He might not be too hard to steer on things like that.

At supper, Father found the old hen's gizzard in his bowl. When he ate it, he grinned from ear to ear. "If this is tender enough to be easy to chew, my hat's off to the cooks!" He doffed an imaginary chapeau first at his wife and then at each daughter in turn.

The rest of the chicken was meltingly soft. The sliced carrots weren't crunchy little nuggets, either. And the beans weren't fit to be fired out of a blunderbuss. Things didn't always turn out just the way you wanted them to, but they had today.

Later, Viola remembered that thought crossing her mind no more than half a minute before somebody started pounding on the surgery door. Not knocking—pounding, hammering, beating. The door was thick oak with heavy brass hinges that couldn't rust away to fragile uselessness. A good thing, too, or it might have fallen in.

A wry smile on his face, Richard Williams stood up from the table. "Maybe I'd better go find out what that's all about," he said.

"Always at suppertime!" Viola's mother exclaimed. "And it'll turn out to be nothing, too. You wait."

"Doesn't sound like nothing. Well, we'll see." The doctor hurried away.

"Why couldn't they let him finish for a change?" Kate said. "It isn't fair. It really isn't."

"You took the words out of my mouth," Viola said.

She could hear her father talking with someone—a woman—in the surgery, but couldn't make out what they were saying. Part of her knew that was as it should be; people didn't want a doctor's family listening to what they told him. Part of her wanted to know anyhow.

A few minutes later, Viola's father stepped into the dining room again. He carried his medical satchel and looked grim. What he said next explained why: "I can't linger. That's Guinevere Worth in there."

"Oh, Lord have mercy!" Jane Williams crossed herself. Viola imitated the gesture. So did her sisters. Guinevere Worth was the finest midwife in Salisbury. She was, and deserved to be, proud of her own skill and knowledge. She wouldn't have come—have rushed—to summon the doctor unless something had gone desperately wrong.

Sure enough, Richard Williams said, "The Lord hasn't got much. Bess Radcliffe is in chidldbed over in Mill Road. Mistress Guinevere has done everything she knows how to do, and it's not enough. They'll both die unless—"

"*Kyrie eleison!*" This time, Viola's mother said it in Greek.

"That's right." The doctor's nod was as somber as his face. "She wants me to cut the baby out—a Caesarean section, it's called—and save it, at least, and maybe poor Bess, too, if I'm very lucky." He answered the next question before anyone could ask it: "She says Henry Radcliffe understands how things sit, and he's given leave for me to see his wife, and to touch her as I need to. So ... I have to try. Pray for me. It may do some good; it won't hurt anything."

Away he went. His wife and daughters flew upstairs, to look out from the women's quarters. Viola got a glimpse of her father's back heading quickly toward the bridge over the Avon. From behind, the woman who hurried along with him could have been anyone, anyone at all.

"Mother Mary, pity women!" Kate said.

"That would be well," Jane Williams said. "When I was growing up, I always feared I was a ship with too broad a beam. But thanks to that I managed to bring the three of you into the world and come through safe myself, and it was … well, no worse than it had to be, anyhow. That's good luck or God's kindness, however you care to look at things. Whichever it is, not every woman has it."

Viola had always thought that kind of talk had to do with other women, not with her. Now that she was betrothed, it suddenly seemed much less theoretical than it had before. Anything that could happen to another woman could happen to her, too, and the Wasting wasn't the only disaster lying in wait for the fair sex. Oh, no. Far from it.

"Do you know the Radcliffes, Mother?" Margaret asked. "They're only a name to me."

"I … think he's a stonemason or a bricklayer or something like that. I can't tell you what he looks like," Jane Williams said slowly. "As far as I know, I haven't had anything to do with his wife."

Near-strangers. But townsfolk. If they were in trouble, Viola knew her father would hasten to help them. What else could he do? All the same … "One more case where chances are we'll never see a penny, or even a chicken," she said.

"These things happen. Richard knew it before he went out. Of course he did. But what can you do?" her mother said.

"Nothing, not when you put it that way," Viola admitted with a sigh.

"I'm going back downstairs. The stew will be getting cold, and I was only halfway through my bowl," Margaret said. Worrying about everything that went with womanhood still lay years ahead for her.

She doesn't know how lucky she is, Viola thought. But her little sister would find out, the same way she was finding out herself.

She and Kate and their mother followed Margaret down to the dining room. The lovely chicken stew *was* getting cold. That wasn't the only reason she picked at supper, though. She was thinking about what her father was doing, and what going under the knife with so little to dull the torment might be like.

Kate and Jane Williams didn't eat much more, either. Margaret emptied her bowl and went back to the pot for more that was still steaming. No, she didn't dwell on what could happen years from now. Viola envied her.

The Williams women started cleaning up and washing up. They left Richard's bowl and spoon on the table and the stewpot above the fire, so if he cared to he could have hot food when he came home. If he didn't …. Being a doctor meant sometimes getting your evenings turned topsy-turvy. Everyone in the family understood that.

So soon after the solstice, the sun lingered long in the sky. It still shone when Richard Williams came home. Blood splashed his shirtfront and trousers. It splashed his hands, too; he'd washed them somewhere, but not very well. He had more on his cheeks and above his eyebrows, and a fleck on the end of his nose.

"How are they?" Viola and her mother asked at the same time.

"I got the baby out alive," he answered. "I hope she'll stay that way. I think she may. She's got a good screech, and she started turning pink as soon as she was breathing on her own."

"How is the poor mother?" Viola asked. "What was her name, Bess?"

"That's right." Her father didn't go on for a moment. He looked somber and weary. *The way he'll look twenty years from now*, she thought. Then he gathered himself. "I didn't kill her with the scalpel, anyway. She didn't bleed out. I sewed her up afterwards and gave her as much laudanum as she'd hold, or maybe more than that. I left another bottle with her husband, too. Lord knows she'll need it."

"What … do you think her chances are?" Jane Williams asked.

"She's in God's hands now, not mine." Richard Williams spread those capable hands of his. Looking down at them, he shook his head; he must not have realized how bloody he was. He sighed and went on, "If it were just the cutting and the stitching, she'd get over that. But when you do so much, suppuration and fever come after it the way night follows day. I have willow bark to fight the fever—I left some of that, too. But it's a straw in the wind."

She's going to die, Viola realized. *That's what he's saying, only he isn't coming right out with it. Maybe he doesn't want to admit it, even to himself.*

By her mother's face, she understood that as well as Viola did. Her younger sisters seemed more hopeful, likely because they understood less of how the world worked. Kate said, "Your poor clothes, Father!"

85

"Yes, I know. Now I know." The doctor looked down at himself again. "Then, I was just doing what I had to do. I should have put on a leather apron, the way any other butcher would have."

"Richard …" Viola's mother's voice held a warning note. "You saved one life, anyhow. You may have saved two. Go change into clean clothes now. I'll soak these in cold water. There's a chance the stains will come out." She didn't sound as if she believed it.

Richard Williams sketched a salute. "As you say, dear, so shall it be." He started to go upstairs, then turned back. "While I'm putting on something else, pour me some whiskey, will you?"

"Of course," Jane said. "Do you want it watered?"

"Not tonight. Neat, please. If I drink enough …. It won't take away the memory of what I did, but it'll put up a glass wall for a while. Heaven knows I need one." When he headed for the stairs this time, he didn't turn back.

He came down in a clean shirt and trousers. He'd washed his hands again, too, and scrubbed at his face. He gulped the whiskey like a man in the desert gulping water at an oasis, though, and he was usually moderate with beer, wine, and spirits. His eyes …. His eyes were haunted. Whatever distance the liquor could give him, it wasn't nearly enough.

Viola set a bowl of hot chicken stew in front of him. He stared at it in surprise, as if he'd forgotten he'd been eating supper when Guinevere Worth called him away. "Why, bless you, dear," he said, and began to eat. Viola got the feeling he hardly noticed what he was doing.

"Do you want more, Father?" she asked when the bowl was empty.

He seemed surprised he'd finished it, too. After a moment, he shook his head. "Thanks, sweets, but no. If you could pour me another dram, though, maybe a bit smaller than the first one? Now it's got something to land on, anyway."

After the second slug of whiskey, he went up to bed, more than a little unsteadily. Viola hoped no one fell down the stairs and broke his leg tonight, or anything like that. Her father wouldn't be much help.

Richard Williams ate cold barley porridge for breakfast the next morning, and drank more coffee than usual. "How are you, dear?" his wife asked.

86

"I've been better," he said. As soon as he finished, he made for the door. "I've got to see how Bess and the baby—Henrietta, they've named her—fare. If anyone comes for me, tell him I'll be back before too long."

"I'll do it," Viola said. When her father nodded, she went upstairs and put on the kind of clothes she wore when she left the house. If she had to talk with men from outside the family, she needed to be presentable.

She liked the smells in the surgery; the medicaments' odors put her in mind of a spice dealer's shop. She pulled a book off a shelf to look at while she waited to see if anyone came by. She thought she chose at random, but it was about female complaints and troubles. The woodcuts illustrating how to do and how to repair a Caesarean section made her flinch. She stubbornly studied them even so.

This procedure should never be undertaken if any alternative reveals itself, due to the great danger it presents, the text warned. Viola nodded to herself. Her father's bloody clothes told the same story.

No one disturbed her reading till Richard Williams came back an hour and a half later. "The baby's doing well," he said to Viola. "One of the neighbors birthed a son last week, and she's willing to let little Henrietta drink from her fountains, too. They are better off with proper milk than what you can squeeze from cows or nanny goats."

"Then why don't you seem happier?" Viola asked.

Her father's mouth twisted. "You know me too well. Bess … doesn't look right."

"After what happened to her, how could she?" Viola said—reasonably, she thought.

But the doctor shook his head. "That's not what I meant. I've seen too many patients for too many years. Some you look at and you think *he'll do fine* or *she'll get better*. Others …. Others the wrong way round. I don't know how I know, but I mostly do. Bess doesn't look as though she'll heal well. I don't know how to put it any better than that."

"You are wrong sometimes, though, aren't you?" Viola grasped at hope wherever she could find it.

"Sometimes. Not very often. I told Henry Radcliffe to rush over here if she starts feeling feverish. Willow bark and cold compresses aren't much, but they're what I have. I told him to use those, too. I'd like to be wrong, but …" Richard Williams gnawed at his lower lip as he shook his head.

Two mornings later, someone knocked at the surgery door just after the Williams family finished breakfast. Worry on his face, Richard went to see who it was. He ducked back into the dining room to say, "Cover for me, Viola. That was Henry. Bess is—burning up, he said."

Over the next four days, he did what he knew how to do. None of it was enough. He'd known ahead of time it wouldn't be. When Bess died, he came home as low as Viola'd ever seen him.

Not even whiskey blunted his misery. "I killed her," he said over and over. "With these hands, I killed her."

"She would have died anyhow. The midwife was sure of it. So were you. And you saved the baby," Viola said.

"I tell myself that. I keep telling myself that. It helps. It doesn't help nearly enough." Her father stared down at his clever, deadly hands. Yes, he'd known ahead of time this was likely to happen. He'd done it anyway. And now he was paying the price.

"Do you want to hear something funny?" Walter Haywood said.

"I'd love to hear something funny," Peter said. He was reading Viola's letter about her father's despair at losing the patient he'd had to operate on. She'd poured some of her own grief out on paper while she wrote it, too. He wondered if he'd ever be able to unburden himself to someone like that. Something funny would be a relief.

"You know how Ebenezer enjoys hauling me down to the docks so I can sneeze myself silly working out which hogshead of tobacco is which grade and what it ought to be worth," Haywood said.

"How in the world would I know that?" Peter answered, deadpan.

Walter stared at him, then snorted. "All right, all right—you know all that. And you know how much I like it every time he makes me go."

"You may have given me what I think the solicitors call a clue, yes." Peter stayed dry.

"Heh." Haywood acknowledged him with a wave. "And you know how I paid him back not so long ago."

"You got him to do something as stupid as the things you do yourself." Before, Peter had been kidding along with his roommate. He wasn't kidding any more.

"Life is for living. If you can't have fun along the way, what's the point to being alive at all?" Walter Haywood returned. "If I die tomorrow, I'll have enjoyed myself more than you do if you get as old as Methuselah."

"And you'll die tomorrow. If you were going to tell me something funny, then do it."

"I've shown him a good time twice now, not just once. And now *he's* afraid of *me*. Before, I'd flinch whenever I set eyes on the gangler. Now he tries to talk my father out of sending him after me. If that's not the best joke I've heard in a long time, I don't know what would be." Haywood's laugh said it was funny to him, anyhow.

"Hurting other people for the sport of it isn't my idea of fun," Peter said.

Walter laughed some more, a laugh that held sharp teeth. "Brothels have back rooms where you can pay extra to do just that. Not to my taste, but they wouldn't have those rooms if people didn't use them."

"That's disgusting!" Peter exclaimed. He hadn't felt so very much like a wet-behind-the-ears boy from the provinces for a long time now.

"Well, I told you it isn't my idea of a good time, either," Walter said with a shrug. "But I'm not lying to you, and they're there for one reason—they make money for the places that have 'em."

He seldom insisted he was telling the truth. When he did, Peter hadn't yet caught him out. How much that meant, Peter wasn't sure. "The chances you take—" he muttered, more to himself than to his roommate.

But Walter heard him. "Tell me you don't play at cards or dice. Have they got horse races in Salisbury? Have they even got horses? You gamble your way and I'll gamble mine."

Peter exhaled through his nose. "If I lose, I'm out a few shillings. I don't venture more. If you lose, you get the Wasting and you die so hard, they'd shoot a dog it was happening to. Didn't your dose of clap teach you anything?"

"If you don't come down with the clap, you aren't half trying. You tell me what happens if I end up on the short end, but you don't know how wonderful it is every time I win."

"My intended's a sweet girl. Our fathers have been friends longer than we've been alive. We're tying the families together."

"Oh, isn't that precious?" Haywood kissed the air.

Peter exhaled again, more slowly this time. How angry he was astonished him. He didn't let his hands tighten into fists. If he started hitting Walter, he wasn't sure he'd be able to stop. He also didn't care to try explaining to his father why he'd been sent home in disgrace.

His voice as tightly controlled as his hands, he said, "I'll be wed soon enough. Leave it there, if you know what's good for you. Till then, I've got my palm and my fingers, same as everybody else."

"Listen to the fool!" Haywood rolled his eyes in a pretty good impression of despair. "There's a banquet of cunt all around him, and what does he want? Hand hardtack, that's what."

"Live your life however you want—" Peter began.

But Walter Haywood cut him off. "You say that now, but what have you been saying since they stuck us in this chamber together? 'Don't do this!' 'Don't do that!' 'Don't do the other thing, either—especially don't do the other thing!' 'Watch out!' 'Be careful!' And now all of a sudden you're going on about 'Do what thou wilt'? Hypocrisy, thy name is Drinkwater."

Peter's cheeks and ears heated; he knew Haywood had a point. But he also knew where that last quotation came from. "Say whatever you want. Rabelais likely died of the Wasting, though, remember. They weren't careful at all for a while after it got loose amongst us. I told you that once before."

"Rabelais had bad luck. Everybody had bad luck there at the beginning. That's all catching it is—bad luck."

"It's not luck. With luck, there's nothing you can do about it one way or the other. If you don't go around sticking it into every loose woman you can find, you won't come down with the Wasting." Peter spoke as he would have to an idiot.

If Walter was an idiot, he was a damned annoying one. "It all depends," he said. "You think women don't want it, too? If some loose man back home sticks it into your girl while you're away, who knows what you'll come down with?"

Next thing Peter knew, he was on his feet and moving towards Haywood, probably with murder on his face. He didn't see things red very often, but he did now. What would happen to him afterwards, he didn't care.

Haywood must have seen he didn't, either. He jumped up, too, ready to fight or to run. "Easy, easy!" he said. "I didn't mean you in particular—I meant anybody. By God, I did!" He sounded scared. He must have known he had good reason to sound that way.

More than anything else, the fear in his voice brought Peter back to his usual self. The rage drained away like beer from a cracked pitcher, leaving him weak and almost sick. "Sweet Jesus, but you're a dingleberry on mankind's bum," he said, and made himself take a step back, and then another one.

Haywood bowed as low as he might have if he were being presented at King Michael's court. "Your obedient servant, sir!" he said, easier now that he knew it wouldn't come to blows.

If only I were easier, too, Peter thought as he lay back down on his bed. He'd hoped Walter would take his mind off Viola's letter, and instead he'd nearly wound up in a brawl. He picked the letter up again. She wrote well; she was obviously clever. That only made what she had to say strike more deeply.

When he wrote back, he said, *I share your grief—you have made me share it. Like you, I do not know the Radcliffes myself. I think the father may have done some work on the walk in front of our house a few years ago, but I am not even sure of that. Any death is always sad, a death from bringing new life into the world all the more so.* He thought for a moment, then continued, *That this mischance may—God prevent it!—lie across the future thread of your life will naturally lead it to touch your feelings even more than it is likely to affect me.*

He looked at the last sentence, wondering whether to scratch it into illegibility. In the end, he left it alone. He told Viola about his studies and some about his squabbles with Walter. He omitted the details there, judging them unsuitable for her eyes.

He did write, *By now Walter has Ebenezer as leery of him as he is of Ebenezer's sudden apparitions.* He didn't explain how Haywood had managed that—one more thing Viola didn't need to know. He did add, *Walter is not wanting in intelligence or wit, but lacks the quality my father would call having his head nailed down tight.*

After his pen left the page there, he nodded to himself. He felt certain Viola would understand what he meant there. From what he'd seen over the years, his father and hers shared a certain cast of mind. He didn't know whether that had made them friends to begin with or whether, having been friends for so long, they'd rubbed off on each other. Either way, though, the thing was real.

From the impression he'd got when he met Viola, and all the more so from her letters, Peter thought she owned that cast of mind, too. He had some of it himself; he was, after all, his father's son. He suspected she might have more—in which case, her head was nailed down very tight indeed.

The letter went into the OUTBOUND basket near the bottom of the dormitory stairs. Sometime late that afternoon, a man from the Royal Post would dump the basket into his sack. In a few days, it would get to Salisbury, and someone in the Williams household would pay the postman there threepence so Viola could break the seal and read it.

He and Clarence Starr wrote back and forth, too, but much less often. He scratched the side of his jaw; he hadn't consciously noticed that before. It was true, though. Clarence wrote less interestingly than Viola, but that had only so much to do with anything. Peter suspected Clarence's being less female than Viola had a good deal more.

Two days later, Peter was studying courtroom etiquette and proceedings—he had a mock trial coming up. He didn't know where Walter Haywood was, or care; he worked more when his roommate wasn't around. But being the only one in the chamber meant he had to get up and answer the door himself when somebody knocked on it.

There stood Cooke. He touched the brim of his hat when he saw Peter. "God gi' you good day, Master Drinkwater," he said. Then he noticed Walter wasn't there. He went from polite to scowling in the blink of an eye. "Where did the bastardly blackguard git to?" he demanded. "Off whoring again, is he?"

"I have no idea where he is," Peter answered truthfully.

"Well, I'll just set myself down outside here an' wait." Ebenezer Cooke proceeded to do exactly that. "He's got to come back some time or other."

"Would you rather come in and sit at the desk?" Peter hadn't seen Haywood's father's factor so determined or so angry before. He wondered what had gone wrong, and whether Cooke's wrath was his own or his employer's.

"Floor'll do nicely," the man from America answered. "You kin shut the door if you want to. Don't mean to bother you none. You never done nobody no wrong, not so far as I know."

Everybody had done somebody wrong at one time or another. Part of having your head nailed down at all—never mind tight— was knowing that. Peter understood as much. If Cooke didn't ... "However you please," Peter said as the factor settled his ungainly length by the door. Peter did close it, though he didn't lock it. He tried to pick up where he'd been interrupted.

He needed a little while to do that. After half an hour or so, though, he was captured by the legal manual and by the imaginary courtroom it conjured up inside his head. Then he got interrupted again, this time by Ebenezer Cooke scrambling to his feet and screeching, "God damn you to hell and gone, you stinking son of a bitch!" His reedy tenor went falsetto in fury.

Peter jumped up, too, and opened the door. Several other pupils were peering out of rooms up and down the corridor, too. Walter Haywood looked remarkably calm, all things considered. "Why don't you come inside, Eb? Whatever it is, we can talk about it in the room like reasonable people," he said.

But Cooke was not about to be reasonable. Voice louder and shriller than ever, he screeched again: "You son of a bitch, I done got me a dose of the clap on account of you!"

"Come in the damn room, Eb." Haywood manhandled the factor inside and slammed the door behind him.

"Do you want me to go?" Peter sounded dry enough to argue that his head was nailed down pretty tight after all.

"It doesn't make any difference now," Walter said. Something in his eyes told Peter his roommate didn't want him to leave, though. Who could say what would happen if Haywood found himself

93

alone with Ebenezer Cooke? Nothing good that Peter could see. He stretched out on his bed. He wouldn't get much studying done for a while, but he'd have entertainment.

"It doesn't make any difference now!" Cooke echoed, on a different note this time: more of a descending wail than anything else. "I've got me the clap, and pretty soon I'll have me the Wasting, too, and that'll be the end of the greatest rhymer the world's ever seen."

"You flatter yourself," Haywood said. Peter was thinking something along those lines, too, but he wouldn't have said it out loud, especially not then. He hoped he wouldn't have, anyhow.

Ebenezer Cooke glowered, plainly wounded. "You got your nerve."

"Well, you've got yours, too," Walter Haywood retorted. "I got clapped a while ago, it cleared up, and I'm right as rain. No fever, no night sweats, no nothing. I expect I'll get clapped a good many times again before I die, too. It's part of the price you pay for having fun. Tell me you didn't have fun, there in the house I took you to."

"The Wasting's part of the price you pay for having fun, too," his father's factor said. "The Good Book tells us, 'The wages of sin is death,' an' it knows what it's talkin' about."

"You'll be fine. In two or three weeks, you won't even remember you ever had a drippy hose," Haywood said. If he ever seriously wanted to sell tobacco or anything else, he'd probably be good at it. He sounded devilishly persuasive to Peter. He might even make a dangerous barrister if he applied himself to the work. That, though, seemed a large if.

"You drug me to that den of iniquity. I never would've lain down with that scarlet harlot, that whore of Babylon, if not for you," Cooke said.

"Why are you complaining? You should thank me. Tell me what in all the world could be finer than fucking," Walter answered.

"Not having it scorch me when I piss, for one," Ebenezer Cooke said.

"You'll get over it. I did. Everybody does. Virginity, though, virginity is always fatal." Haywood swung toward Peter. "Isn't that right, Drinkwater?"

"You can include me in your quarrels as soon as I include you in mine," Peter told him.

His roommate bowed ironically. "Just as you say, *sir*."

"What about my dick?" Cooke shouted.

"It had some exercise it needed. It was out of shape, so it's sore now." Haywood looked exasperated. He dug in his pocket. "Here's a sovereign. That's a demon of a lot more than you paid for your sport, and you bloody well know it. Take it, spend it on whatever you like—even another loose woman, once you get over the gleets—keep quiet, and go away."

The factor stared at the fat gold coin in the palm of his hand. "You reckon you kin buy me off!" he exclaimed.

"Of course I do. Isn't that what the world's about, buying and selling? Why else do you keep dragging me down to the docks to fuss over sot-weed?" Haywood studied Cooke's astonished face. "What? The price isn't good enough? Here's another one, then. Now be off with you!"

Ebenezer Cooke opened his mouth. Then he closed it again. How long did he take to earn two pounds from Walter's father? He stuck the goldpieces in his breeches pocket and walked out of the room. He even closed the door quietly.

"Buying and selling," Walter said. "Buying and selling." He sounded pleased with himself.

Peter was far from poor. He wouldn't have come to Lincoln's Inn unless his family was well-to-do ... at least as they reckoned such things in Salisbury. He also wasn't in the habit of throwing sovereigns around as if they were copper pennies.

"You really don't worry about a thing, do you?" he said. He had trouble imagining not worrying.

But Haywood nodded. "Why should I? People won't stop smoking or dipping snuff any time soon. As long as they keep at it, Papa will make money faster than I can hope to squander it. I enjoy myself trying, though."

"You're plenty trying, believe me," Peter said. Haywood only laughed.

VII

Viola walked out of Blackwell's bookshop well pleased with herself. Under her arm she carried the account of a young English naturalist's journey around the world in a Royal Navy survey ship. Albert Wallace Russell's *Voyage of the Basset* would take her to places she'd never go in person and let her mind's eye glimpse people and creatures and landscapes the eyes she saw with would never meet.

It seemed so unfair, so unjust. Because Russell was a man, he could travel wherever he pleased, and wherever his talents led people—more men!—to want him to go. The farthest from Salisbury she'd ever ventured, and the farthest she was ever likely to go, was up to Stonehenge. She'd been a girl then, too. Now, as a woman, she'd have a much harder time going there.

"God *damn* the Wasting!" she muttered under her breath. The one advantage of a veil was that it muffled her voice and kept anyone else on the street from reading her lips. She could curse as she pleased, as long as she cursed quietly.

But what would the world be like today had God not chosen to visit the Wasting upon it? She imagined a young female English naturalist—someone not too different from, say, herself—going on a round-the-world jaunt aboard a ship like the *Basset*. Would she come home to write a book with a title something on the order of *Voyage of the Beagle*?

Would women work in the fields and run bookshops and pubs? Would women be doctors and barristers and harpsichordists? Would they sit in Parliament? Would a Queen rule over England as no women had done since Mary took the throne after the Wasting had its way with Henry VIII?

She laughed at herself, but the mirth had a sour edge. However many fantasies she spun out, the world was the way it was, not the way she wished it might be (she and most of the other humans of the female persuasion in it, she was sure). The most she could do was the best she could with what she had.

Right this minute, that wasn't so bad. The day was bright and sunny, summery and warm—it had to be close to seventy, or even above that mark. A magpie snagged a grasshopper in the street and flew off with it. Somebody in a pub was playing a concertina, and not too badly.

Her mother and sisters hadn't come into the bookshop with her. They were buying tea or coffee, or perhaps calico or taffeta. Viola smiled behind her veil. By herself for a little while, she could feel free and independent even if she knew she wasn't.

A young man came toward her and then past her. He wore work clothes he'd done a lot of work in. His face carried whiskers that wanted to be a beard but weren't quite. He grinned in a way Viola didn't care for.

And, as he was going by, he reached out and pinched her backside. She jumped a foot and a half in the air and almost dropped *Voyage of the Basset*. She spun around in fury. "You shit-faced son of a whore!" she yelled.

"Pussy, pussy, pussy," he said, laughing and still grinning. "Pissy pussy, too." He started to whistle as he went down the street.

Heads popped out of shops. They all belonged to women. Those women might not have seen what happened, but they understood. The same kind of thing would have happened to most of them, if not to every one.

Three of the heads belonged to Mother, Kate, and Margaret. Viola's sisters hurried over to her. Jane Williams ducked back into the shop and came out a moment later with bundles in her hands.

"You poor dear!" she said, and hugged Viola hard.

Even in her arms, Viola was still stiff and rigid with rage. "A piece of meat," she ground out. "That's all I was to him, a piece of meat. He wanted to find out how tender I was."

"I bet his ears are still burning," Margaret said, more admiringly than not. "You don't cuss like that around the house."

"Around the house, I don't need to," Viola answered. "And he didn't care a half-farthing's worth, either. He thought it was funny."

"They never care," Kate said. "If they did, they wouldn't do it. Some men don't do it." By the way she spoke, those were the queer ducks, not the men who groped as they pleased.

"Mother Mary, pity women! It's certain sure no one else will." At that moment, Viola was angry enough to wonder whether Jesus had kept His hands to Himself in Nazareth and Jerusalem. She swallowed the blasphemy. Her sisters might have appreciated it, but her mother wouldn't.

"Let's go home," Jane Williams said, and then, a moment later, "What did you buy at Blackwell's?"

"A book," Viola said dully. All the joy had gone out of her purchase.

Her mother sighed. "I'm sorry, dear. It happens to most of us. It's happened to you before, hasn't it?"

"Of course it has." Remembering other times made her angrier again. "But I don't think it's ever been so brazen before. The way he laughed, he thought it was the funniest thing ever. And he thought I ought to think it was the funniest thing ever, too. I hope he rots in hell."

"If they thought they'd rot in hell for letting their hands rove, they wouldn't do it," Kate said. "Since they keep groping us, they have to believe God wants them to."

"Logic," Viola said tightly.

"I only wish I thought you were wrong," Jane Williams said to her middle daughter. "But I don't. I've had a monk feel me up, and a priest."

"Did you ever tell Father?" Margaret asked.

"No," Jane said. "And don't you go telling him, either, do you hear me? I'm afraid of what he might do." She resolutely turned back toward the house on the far side of the river.

"None of us will say anything, Mother," Viola said, following in her wake. She sent Margaret a stern look. By the way the youngest

Williams daughter's veil moved, Margaret stuck out her tongue behind it. But she nodded a moment later.

Viola thought—hoped—Margaret would remember that nod. Anyone who knew their father even a little had to know how much he held inside, anger emphatically included. If it got out, when it got out … Viola didn't care to think about that, or about what they'd do to him for murdering a man of God. Because she knew he would, the same as her mother did.

"We'd better not tell him about what happened just now, either," she said. Jane Williams nodded right away. A moment later, so did Kate, and then Margaret.

Jactitation! Peter had never heard of it till he learned it would be the point of dispute in the mock trial where he'd argue for the defense. He wondered whether his father ever had. He had his doubts. To say it was an obscure notion only showed how weak the power of language could be.

He asked Walter, "Could you define jactitation on an exam?"

"Could I define what?" Haywood stuck a finger in his ear, as if doubting he'd heard right.

"Jactitation," Peter repeated.

"Not if my life depended on it," his roommate said with a cheerful shrug. "What is it, anyhow? It sounds lewd." He made as if to grab his crotch.

"Everything sounds lewd to you," Peter said. If anything, that was an understatement. But Haywood'd asked him a question. "Jactitation is claiming you're married to someone when you're not."

"There! You see? I wasn't even wrong. It could be lewd," Walter said. Peter rolled his eyes. His roommate added, "Why on earth would somebody make a claim like that to begin with?"

"In case there's money in it," Peter said. "Whenever there's money in something, someone will try to do it."

"Well, you aren't wrong about that," Walter admitted.

Sweetly, Peter said, "You'd best believe I'm not. Why else would even a girl in a brothel lie down with … Ebenezer?" He'd started to say *with you*, but changed his mind at the last minute.

"Heh," Haywood said, so that pause told him what Peter'd had in mind to begin with. But it didn't show anything Haywood could prove. Walter went on, "If one of those girls said she was Eb's wife, then, he could sue her for jactitation? If he wasn't delighted, I mean?"

"That's right," Peter answered.

"And how would she defend herself against this horrible charge?" Walter sounded intrigued in spite of himself.

"There are three ways—at least that's what the lawbooks say. Showing she truly is married to him is one. Showing she never really claimed to be wed to him is another. And the third ..." He had to think to come up with the third. When he recalled it, he snapped his fingers. "Oh, that's right. If he's gone along with the idea that they're man and wife, that's also a defense."

"Ebenezer'd likely be thrilled if any woman would claim she was his wife," Walter said.

"Any woman except the one who gave him the clap," Peter said.

"Mmm, there is that," Walter Haywood admitted. Peter wondered whether the same girl had given him and Cooke their doses. Then he realized the answer to that was bound to be no. Not even Haywood would have steered the factor to the whore who'd infected him.

He went back to the notes he'd been given for the mock trial. One thing in there particularly caught his notice. He wondered whether Jack Bolton, who would be his opponent in the action, would spot the same thing he had. He also wondered if it was even there in Bolton's papers for him to spot. Someone might have made a mistake copying it out. He'd heard his father swearing about such errors.

After a moment, Peter shrugged. He had what he'd been given. If he needed to, he could show his documents to Stephen Heath, who would act as the judge. The worst that could happen would be to buy some extra time to prepare another line of defense.

In the meantime .... In the meantime, the dinner bell rang. Peter was glad for an excuse to shove the materials aside and go down and fill his belly with beef stew. As far as he was concerned, it had too many turnips, potatoes, and parsnips and not enough beef. He ate it anyhow. It could have been worse.

Pupils played whist in the lounge. They rolled dice on the carpet in front of the fireplace. A couple of young men hunched over a chessboard. Peter sat there every once in a while. He wasn't great, but he defended stoutly and could hold his own. Somebody tried to coax music from the old, battered harpsichord in a corner of the room. He didn't have much luck.

One of the cardplayers stood up from the table. Walter Haywood hurried over to take his place. "You play, don't you, Peter?" he called a moment later. "Ted says he's only going to sit in for another couple of hands."

"I've got to work," Peter answered. He did play whist, but the mock trial consumed him. He couldn't get many chances to impress the formidable Master Heath. He wasn't about to waste this one.

Naturally, everybody who heard him hooted and hissed. Admitting you worked hard at Lincoln's Inn was bad form. Your papers and arguments were supposed to spring fully formed from your forehead, the way Minerva had from Jove's. For a handful of quick, clever students, that might even have been true. Peter knew too well it wasn't for him; he was a grinder, not a floater. And if anybody else didn't care for that, too bad.

Catcalls followed him to the foot of the stairs. He looked back as he started climbing them. Haywood would surely find someone else to play in place of Ted. By the smile on his face, he planned on staying at the table for a while himself.

"Good," Peter muttered under his breath. "I'll be able to get something done in peace for a change."

He scribbled notes for ten or fifteen minutes, outlining ways to counter the lines of attack he expected Jack to use. Then someone knocked on the door. Peter's quill jerked at the unexpected sound. Ink blotted out the word he'd just written.

"Oh, bugger," he said as he stood. "I'll never get this done." He opened the door. Ebenezer Cooke stood in the hall. Peter pointed to the stairway. "Walter's not here. He's down in the lounge, playing whist."

"Beggin' your pardon, Master Drinkwater, but I don't want to say nothin' to him, not for the rest o' my born days I don't," Cooke answered. "I came over here so's I could talk to you."

"To me?" Peter said in surprise. The sot-weed factor nodded. With a shrug of his own, Peter stepped aside and waved Cooke to the chair in front of his desk. He sat on the bed himself. "What's on your mind, then?"

Eb stared down at the floorboards between his feet. In a low voice, he said, "I just wanted to tell you how sorry I am you got stuck in the middle o' that there ruction 'twixt Master Haywood and me. I was in a temper, I was, an' I didn't think to watch what I was sayin'."

"It's all right, Eb." Peter wanted Cooke to go away and leave him alone.

Whether he wanted that or not, he wouldn't get it right away. The factor shook his head, still not looking up at Peter. "No, it ain't. I was plumb humiliated on account o' what the young master done to me and on account o' you had to listen to it."

"It's all right," Peter said again. "These things happen, that's all. Are you feeling better now, anyway?"

"Mebbe a little. Don't got no signs o' the Wasting, God be praised, not yet." Ebenezer crossed himself. So did Peter. With the Wasting, what else could you do but pray? Cooke continued, "Still have me the gleets, though, dad gum it."

"I hope they go away soon," Peter said, thinking, *I hope you go away soon.* Sometimes you could learn too much about someone else's troubles. He'd done that ten times over with Walter's father's factor.

"Me, too. Damn nuisance." Cooke got to his feet. "Reckon I'll head out. Did want to apologize, though."

"You've got nothing to apologize for," Peter said. *Except for letting that fool of a Haywood tempt you into being a fool yourself.* He saw no point to telling Ebenezer Cooke that. Either the factor could figure it out for himself or he couldn't. He knew what the risks were. Everybody did. Some people thought the rewards were worth them.

Some people got the Wasting, too. Lots of people did. Were lots of people fools, then? Probably.

Cooke touched the brim of his hat once more. He gave Peter an awkward half-bow and ducked his way out of the room. Peter picked up his documents and his notes. *Where was I?* he wondered.

Viola put down *Voyage of the Basset.* She had nothing against the book itself. Russell was plainly intelligent; he wrote well enough for all ordinary purposes, and even a little better than that. But his ship had dodged icebergs. He'd seen glaciers and tramped through steaming jungles. He could do all that. People admired him when he did, in fact.

What had she done? She'd gone up to Blackwell's to buy his volume. And what had she got for it? She'd got her bum pinched, and she'd got laughed at when she had the nerve to show she didn't like it.

Tramping through the steaming jungle had to be better than that, even if afterwards you needed to light a twig and touch it to each leech's head in turn to make the bloodsuckers let go of your leg. Getting marooned atop a glacier and turning into a block of ice had to be better than that.

Her father's feet on the stairs made her try to forget such things. She could often gauge how he felt by how quickly he came up. His dragging steps now said he wasn't happy at all.

A few seconds later, he stuck his head into her room and asked, "Have you got a moment?"

"I'm sorry, Father. I was about to go catch a survey barque bound for South America and then west across the Pacific." No, Viola hadn't forgotten everything that was eating at her.

"What?" Richard Williams blinked. Then he frowned. And then he spied *Voyage of the Basset* on the table next to Viola's reading chair. His face cleared. "Oh. I see." He gave her the ghost of a smile, but a poor, sad, sorry, tattered ghost it was.

"What is it?" Viola asked. He should have liked her joke better than that.

He looked up at the ceiling, over at the bookshelf, anywhere but at her face. "Someone just came in to see me. She's got it. No doubt she's got it." He didn't name the Wasting, or need to. He kicked at the floorboards, which did duty for all the curses he wouldn't let out in front of Viola.

"Ohhh." She let the word stretch, to show she understood what he was feeling. Then she asked, "Does she know who gave it to her?"

"Yes, or she says she does. She's not a woman of the town, not a barmaid, nothing like that. If she's telling the truth—and I have no reason to think she isn't—she just got carried away one night under the moonlight, and this is what comes of that. Her lover showed no signs he had it. Now I have to report to the King's officials, and to the ecclesiastical authorities. And they'll go down to Nunton and give the lad and his family the good news."

"He'll deny it," Viola said.

"Of course he will." Her father nodded. "If he has no symptoms, I can't prove he has it. That will be up to the government and the Church. But some of the details the girl gave made me believe her. If they're true, the authorities will do what they have to do."

Some people could carry the Wasting for years without knowing they had it—and without anyone else knowing, either. That didn't mean they couldn't spread it during that time. They were dangerous to anybody who lay down with them.

"Will they brand him?" Viola asked in a low voice.

"Or send him to work in the coal mines until he shows the marks of the disease. Or both, although in their kindness and mercy they don't do both as often as they used to. They trust the W on someone's forehead will keep others from cohabiting with him … or with her." Richard Williams scuffed at the floor again. "A wonderful world we live in, isn't it, chick?"

Viola quoted Marlowe: "'Why this is hell, nor am I out of it.'"

"Yes, there is that," her father said. "Always that. But also this, from the same play: 'Was this the face that launch'd a thousand ships/ And burnt the topless towers of Ilium?' We aren't angels, my dear, only men and women. We burn hot … and we pay the price for it, God help us."

"I wish there were something to be done. The world would be a better place if there were," Viola said.

"Yes. It would. But there isn't, or nothing any wise man has found yet." Her father sighed. "The man who discovers something sovereign against the Wasting can ask for anything he wants from a grateful mankind wherever he goes for however long he may live."

What if a woman were to find it? Viola wondered. She was afraid she knew the answer there. Some man would find a way to grab the credit for it, and the poor woman wouldn't even get to take off her veil and headscarf. That was justice, as people reckoned justice these days.

Justice! Peter cared very little for justice at the moment. He wanted to win the mock trial ahead, win it however he could. He glanced across the lecture hall at Jack Bolton. Bolton was looking at him, too: sizing him up. Peter was sure the other pupil worried no more about justice than he did. Jack also wanted to win, and to make himself look clever while he did it. What else was a mock trial for?

Peter's eyes went up to the podium, where Stephen Heath sat in a sturdy chair that did duty for the judge's box in a real courtroom. To make the impression stronger, Master Heath wore a blue gown—not a judge's black one, but close enough—and an old wig he'd freshly chalked so it looked new, or at least not far from new.

He even had a gavel, which he banged on the chair's wooden arm. "Court is in session!" he declared. "I direct the honorable sergeant-at-arms to expel from the courtroom any spectator creating an unseemly racket, discord, or disturbance."

"Very good, my lord!" The pupil playing the sergeant-at-arms carried a cricket bat in place of a ceremonial mace. His grin said he was ready, even eager, to use it on anybody who got out of line.

He might get his chance, too. The lecture hall was packed. Mock trials were some of the best entertainment Lincoln's Inn offered. Peter wondered whether that was a compliment to the trials or a judgment on normal life at the legal school.

Master Heath used the gavel again. "We shall have order!" he said, and got ... some, anyhow. He inclined his head to Jack Bolton. "As the distinguished gentleman prosecuting this action, you have the floor, sir."

"Thank you, my lord," Bolton said, and bowed to the judge. His accent and his polished demeanor said he came from London, and from the upper crust at that. His family might have known Stephen Heath for years before he'd enrolled here. That was daunting, but Peter couldn't do anything about it one way or the other. The other pupil went on, "I shall show beyond reasonable doubt that my client, Countess Cudleigh, was never married to that notorious libertine and lecher, Lord Augustine Harvey"—he pointed to the empty chair next to Peter, and got a few laughs doing it—"and demands that he either prove the contrary or abandon the claim now and forevermore." *Take that*, he might have said to Peter.

Peter couldn't prove that his imaginary client had in fact wed the countess, who wasn't there, either. The documents he'd been given made that only too plain. They also made it plain he'd probably lose the trial. He had that one card up his sleeve, but whether it would prove an ace or a trey he wouldn't know till he pulled it out and tried to play it.

Meanwhile …. Meanwhile, bluster. "May it please you, my lord, Countess Cudleigh is so cuddly as to have acquired not one husband but two. Because she recently wed Duke Pierpont, she wants to expunge all her history before that."

He was drawing on the documents. What he said was true: true for the purposes of the mock trial, anyhow. Whether it was relevant was another question altogether. And, as time went on, he would look back at what he'd just told Master Heath and find whole new layers of meaning there, layers he'd never dreamt of while he spoke.

Acidly, Jack Bolton said, "If Lord Harvey claims to have been the Countess' lawful wedded husband, let him produce papers or records to that effect. If he cannot, let him hold his peace henceforward and never trouble the Countess again with his lying assertions."

He was going straight for the kill, not beating around the bush at all. With what the two pupils were given, Lord Harvey—or Peter on his behalf—could do no such thing. Peter'd expected more preliminary swordplay, but he'd have to see what his card was worth right away. "He does not need to produce any such document, my dear sir," he said.

Jack Bolton had bushy eyebrows. He raised them now, to excellent effect. "Indeed? And wherefore not, pray tell?"

"Let us approach this by easy stages, if we may," Peter said. "What is the presumed date of the suit Lady Cudleigh is bringing?" He didn't quite call her *Lady Cuddly* again, but people who heard it in the way he pronounced the name snickered.

His opponent didn't. He rolled his eyes, as if to say he was facing an idiot. Then he flourished the topmost sheet from the sheaf he'd got to prepare himself for the trial. "Why, today's date, of course. The twenty-fourth of July in the year of our Lord one thousand eight hundred and fifty-one. It's Thursday, should you also need to be apprised of that."

He got a laugh. Peter chuckled, too. "Thank you, but I was already looking forward to fish tomorrow. Now, do me the courtesy of informing the court of the date on which Lord Harvey declares that he wed Lady Cudleigh—and she him."

"One moment, if you would be so kind, sir." Bolton needed to go through the papers before he found that. He hadn't worried about it before. Peter worked to hold his face straight. He had to hope it said the same thing in his foe's papers as it did in his. "Here we are! The alleged date of this wedding that never took place is the thirteenth of January in the year of our Lord one thousand eight hundred and ... *forty-one?*" He squeaked in disbelief, staring at the sheet in his hand as if it had betrayed him.

And, as a matter of fact, it had. Relief flooded through Peter. "That is the same date my documents show. This can only mean Lady Cudleigh acquiesced in Lord Harvye's claim that they had in fact been married for upwards of ten years before deciding to contest it so her wedding to Lord Pierpont would be adjudged legal and binding. Continued acquiescence in a claim of marriage is an adequate defense against a suit of jactitation, and Lady Cudleigh is a bigamist. Not a common bigamist; a noble bigamist. But a bigamist even so."

"But— But—" Jack Bolton spluttered. He turned in appeal to Stephen Heath. "My lord!"

"One moment, if you please." Master Heath had put on his reading glasses. He was shuffling through his own set of documents. When he found the page he was looking for, he frowned. "Here the date of the alleged union between the two parties is given as the thirteenth of January in the year 1851. Let the two gentlemen approach, each with the information furnished him."

Peter and Jack both came up. They handed him their papers, one eagerly, the other apprehensively. Heath looked at the sheets. He clicked his tongue between his teeth and handed them back.

"I will be damned," he said to no one in particular. "I have been giving this case for upwards of twenty years, and I've never seen a balls-up like this. I wonder how the scribe made the same mistake twice. Perhaps he copied from the copy with the error he'd inserted, and not from the original. He shouldn't have, but that can happen. That *has* happened. Since the two of you had equal chance to note the mistake, let us continue from that point. Master Bolton, Lady

Cudleigh has not disclaimed her union with Lord Harvey from some ten and a half years. As Master Drinkwater says, acquiescence is defense against an action of jactitation. Why should I not dismiss the noble lady's suit out of hand and let the secular and churchly authorities proceed with a charge of bigamy?"

By the way Jack Bolton turned red and then white, Lady Cudleigh might have been a real person, not a figment of Master Heath's imagination. In a low voice, the pupil said, "I have no answer, my lord."

"For what it's worth to you, lad, neither do I, not on the spot," Heath said, more kindly than not. "With some sleuthing, I might come up with one, but I might not, too. As things are, with the facts the two of you had being what they are, I find myself obliged to rule in favor of Lord Harvey, Master Drinkwater's client. The jactitation suit against him is rejected. So ordered! So may it be!" He brought the gavel down smartly on the arm of the chair.

Bolton stuck out his hand. Dizzily, Peter shook it. The watching pupils burst into cheers. Peter waved once and let it go. Absent the scribe's error, he knew he'd been sure to lose.

Stephen Heath leaned toward him. "Let that be a lesson for you, son," he said. "Details matter. It isn't always how brilliant you are, or how clever. More often than not, it turns on what you see, on what you don't overlook."

"Yes, my lord. Thank you, my lord." To Peter, he was still a judge.

The legal scholar smiled. "I'm just your pestilential master again. Go out with your friends and have a good time tonight. By God, Drinkwater, you earned it."

When her father came up from the surgery looking pleased with himself, not as if he wished he could kick the whole world in the teeth, Viola counted that a win. He didn't sound like a man speaking from beyond the grave when he greeted her with, "Well, something, anyhow," either.

"What kind of something?" she asked, as she knew she was supposed to.

"Henry Radcliffe just brought in his little girl for me to look at. She's doing as well as any baby is likely to." Richard Williams rapped his knuckles against a wooden stool for luck.

"That *is* good news, Father," Viola said. "You did what you had to do."

"I killed her mother." He held up a hand. "Yes, I know they both would have died if I hadn't cut. But I wish I could have done more. No flaw with the surgery. I understood what I had to do, and I did it. Afterwards, though …. We can no more stop infections and fevers from wounds than we can treat the Wasting. We can only watch people die when those fevers come."

"They don't always," she said.

"No, not always, but too often. And when patients pull through, they pull through on their own. We have nothing to do with it." Her father sighed. "Every doctor has a graveyard in his mind, a graveyard of people he's lost. Sometimes I walk amongst the headstones. Lately, I've been pausing at Bess Radcliffe's, I suppose because the stone is so freshly carved."

"That's a morbid notion! You did everything you knew how to do. And Henrietta is living proof of it. *Living* proof." Viola bore down on the word.

Richard Williams smiled—crookedly, but he did. "You aren't wrong. I know that. Sometimes knowing it even does me some good. Sometimes not, though. This is one of *those* times. The baby makes me remember the mother." Before Viola could tell him not to do that, he held up his hand again. "I know, I know. Tell me how your world wags, why don't you?"

He felt as if he walked through a graveyard. She felt as if she lived in a prison cell. That might have been why she read so much: books let her imagine going places and doing things she couldn't in real life. Sometimes it helped. Sometimes, as with her father, it didn't.

Today, though, she had something she could tell him: "In the letter I got yesterday, Peter says he's getting ready for a mock trial. It will have happened by now, I imagine. The letter took three days to get here."

"Ah, mock trials!" Richard Williams nodded and blew cheroot smoke at the ceiling. "Alf would get all in a swivet about them back in the day. Like father, like son?"

"Peter says he's found something in the papers they gave him to prepare for the case he hopes will help him. He doesn't tell me what it is, though," Viola said.

"Knows how to keep his readers in suspense, does he?" This time, her father's grin showed real amusement.

"He taught me a new word, too," she added.

"Did he?" Now the doctor sounded surprised. "That doesn't happen every day, or every week, either. What is it?"

"Jactitation," Viola answered. "Do you know what it means?"

"As a matter of fact, I do," he said. Viola looked indignant. Quickly, he went on, "But only because Alf taught it to me when we were both pups. It was the quarrel in one of his mock trials, too. I wonder if the masters at Lincoln's Inn use the same cases over and over to train their pupils."

"A false claim of marriage doesn't seem to be something that would come up very often," she observed.

"I shouldn't think so, either," Richard Williams said. "But a lot of the point to mock trials is training you to think on your feet. So Alf says, anyhow. And it'd likely do that. When you write back to Peter, you can tell him what I told his pa: it's also a medical term."

"Oh? What does it mean for you?"

"Restless tossing and turning in bed, sometimes from a fever, sometimes from a mental disorder. It can mean general jerking and twitching, too."

Viola wrote that down so she wouldn't forget it. "I shall tell Peter. I wonder how the same word got two meanings so different from each other."

"That I can't say." Her father eyed her. "How does Peter measure up in the letter-writing department?"

"Pretty well. He writes them, which is the most important thing," she answered. "He's quite plain spoken: not much in the way of fancy talk or purple passages from him. He says what he means and then goes on and says the next thing he means."

"One—especially one studying the law—could do worse. Plenty of people do," he said. She found herself nodding.

VIII

Peter was the hero of the day. Once, in a football match on the meadows outside of Salisbury, he'd knocked a man much bigger than he was sideways and stolen the ball away from him. The way people had shouted for him then came as close to this as anything he could remember, and it wasn't very close.

Getting thumped on the back and paraded on the shoulders of his fellow pupils in front of the building was like nothing he'd ever dreamt of, much less hoped for. That Walter Haywood was one of the people who seemed happiest for him only made him feel better. He didn't enjoy quarreling with his roommate, even if they kept doing it. Haywood's grinning face said he didn't take the spats too seriously. Peter thought that was what it said, anyhow.

"Here you go!" Somebody pressed a pewter pot—a pint—into Peter's hand.

He raised it high. "His Majesty, the King!" he said. Everyone cheered. He drank. Nut-brown ale ran down his throat.

"I dub thee Sir Peter Drinkbeer!" Haywood shouted. Peter laughed himself silly. So did everyone else who heard.

In spite of his family name, he'd been Peter Drinkbeer since he was a boy. He might have had an ancestor who didn't fancy it, but he liked it fine. Most people who could afford beer preferred it to water; it was less likely to give you the galloping shits. Rich men and women drank wine, and served it to their children watered, as if they were Italians.

All through the late morning and the afternoon, people kept handing him pints. Walter Haywood gave him more than one.

"I'm going to end up on my arse tonight," Peter said. He already had to concentrate to talk clearly.

"So what? That's the idea," Walter told him. "Today, you've earned it. If this isn't the day to have yourself a grand old time, what would be?"

"By God and all the saints, you're right!" Peter exclaimed.

"You'd best believe I am. Just put yourself in Uncle Walter's hands. He'll take care of you. Oh, you bet he will," Haywood said.

His tone and his expression should have set off alarm bells in Peter's mind. Maybe they even did. But how loud could an alarm bell ring under water—or under a rising tide of beer?

Peter didn't remember walking into the refectory for supper. By then, everybody at Lincoln's Inn knew what he'd pulled off. No sooner had he slid down into his seat than everyone started singing "For He's a Jolly Good Fellow." Pupils whooped and pounded the tables and stomped their feet. "Speech! Speech!" they shouted.

Standing up was much harder than sitting down had been. "Thank you very mush!" Peter said, and then, as they laughed at him, "*Much.*" They laughed again. He went on, "You will excuse me, good friends. I've had—a bit—of beer."

This time, they laughed for him, not at him. He sat again. "What are they giving us tonight?" Haywood said. "They should've slain the fatted calf for you, is what they should've done."

They hadn't, of course. Peter's triumph at the mock trial meant nothing to the cooks. They served up what they would have offered had Jack Bolton mopped the floor with him: bowls of mutton stew, longer on turnips and beets and parsnips and whatever other vegetables they had in the rootcellars than on mutton. The stringy bits he found convinced him the sheep they came from had died of old age.

Most of the time, he would have emptied the bowl anyway, and in short order, too. Not tonight. He barely got halfway down. The foamy ocean of suds he floated on left him indifferent to food. *Beer is good for you,* he told himself.

After supper, he headed for the stairs, the way he usually did. "Where on earth do you think you're going?" Walter said.

"To the room." It seemed obvious to Peter. The stairway looked longer than usual, though, and seemed to hold more steps than it did on ordinary days. Climbing it was nothing to look forward to.

Haywood took him by the arm. "You're doing no such stupid thing, my boy," he said. "Come along with me."

"Where are we going?" Peter asked as his roommate steered him toward the door.

"Never you mind. You'll find out when you get there."

Out they went. Peter didn't fall over his own feet getting down to the sidewalk. The sun was nearing the horizon, but light would linger even after it set. Haywood looked up and down the street. A moment later, he waved. A hackman lifted his hat to show he'd seen and pulled to the kerb. "Where to?" he asked when Walter and Peter came up.

Before Haywood answered, he opened the cab's kerbside door and waved an invitation for Peter to climb in. Peter almost fell all over himself trying to, but managed in the end. Walter shut the door. He spoke a few words to the driver. They were too low for Peter to make out, not that he tried very hard anyway. He did hear the hackman laugh.

A moment later, Walter was inside with him. He extracted a silvered flask from a coat pocket, drew the cork, and handed it to Peter. "Here. Have a knock of this."

"What is it?" Peter asked. The cab began to move, and to jounce. Holding on to the flask took most of his concentration.

"Dragon's blood." Haywood took the flask back and sipped from it himself. "See, it's not poison," he added, wiping his mouth on his sleeve, and gave it to Peter again.

Peter drank. He coughed when he swallowed: West Indian rum, molasses mixed with lightning, smooth but strong, so strong. Maybe it really was dragon's blood. He stared at the wooden wall. "Why are you pouring this into me? I'm plenty sozzled already."

"Why? Because I want you to remember this night forever," his roommate said. Haywood's words made no sense to Peter then. Later they did, but that would be later.

On rattled the cab. Peter kept nipping at the rum. It was top rate, and he didn't want to seem impolite. Every so often, Walter would drink some, too.

Half an hour later, the banging and bumping stopped. The hackman hopped down from his perch and opened the door for his passengers. "Here y'are, gents. Have yourselves a time," he said. Walter Haywood set silver in his palm, enough to make the driver lift his hat. "Much obliged, guvnor."

"Any time," Walter said grandly. The driver got up to his seat and flicked a whip above his horse's back. The horse let out a very human-sounding sigh. Then it started to walk, and the cab rolled away.

"Here we are," Peter said, and then, "Where are we?" He and Haywood stood in front of a home bigger and more impressive than any in Salisbury. Whoever lived here had money to spare. They weren't too far from the Thames; he could hear the river's murmur and plash. It made him want to ease himself against a fencepost.

He didn't get the chance. Walter took him by the arm and steered him through the gate. "Where are we, my dear? Heaven on earth, or right outside it. So let's go in, shall we?"

He opened the front door. In they went. The antechamber in which they found themselves held a bench with two bruisers on it, one blond, one swarthy. Peter recognized the type no matter how drunk he was. They both stood up when the door opened. They were as tall as Ebenezer Cooke, but twice as wide through the shoulders and chest. But they were all smiles as soon as they recognized Haywood. "How they hangin', Master Wat?" the blond fellow said.

"Tolerable well, tolerable well." Haywood seemed altogether at home.

"Who's your friend?" the darker man asked. He wore a foot-long knife on his belt.

"Call him Peter, call him Dick, what difference does it make?" Haywood said.

The toughs acted as if that was the funniest thing they'd ever heard. They waved the newcomers toward the hallway that ran back from the anteroom.

Down the hall Walter Haywood went, Peter stumbling along a pace and a half behind him. Whatever this place was, it used candles

THE WAGES OF SIN

and lamps more lavishly than any home Peter'd ever visited. The hall-way seemed almost as bright as day. The framed paintings and prints on the walls …

Peter didn't pay much attention to the first couple. Then he did, and goggled. They were very well done: very educational, even. But he'd never expected to see anything like *that* in someone's front hall. "Walter, what kind of place is this?" he asked.

"I told you—heaven on earth," Haywood answered. "And see? Here comes the angel who ministers to it."

Up the hallway walked a woman dressed as any woman would be where men might see her. Her dark gray dress concealed all of her body but her hands. She wore a headscarf and a veil, the way she should have. Yet, though Peter could see only her eyes, he got the feeling she was laughing at her own outfit.

Like the bruisers out front, she knew Haywood. "God give you good even, Master Wat," she murmured, and dropped a curtsy. Her hands and her tobacco-rough voice said she was no longer young. As she straightened, she went on, "You've brought a different friend with you this time, I see."

"I have, yes." Walter Haywood half bowed in return. "What better place for them to learn, Madam Henderson?"

I've heard that name before. Peter tried to remember where. Drunk as he was, he didn't have an easy time. When the penny dropped, he gasped in horror. "I can't be here!" he exclaimed.

"Oh, yes, you can," Walter said. "This is part of your education, too. This is the best part, in fact."

"I can't be here," Peter said again, and turned to go—to flee, as a matter of fact. Haywood grabbed him by the arm and hauled him back. He told himself afterwards that he should have struggled harder. But, for one thing, he *was* drunk as a lord. And, for another, not all of him wanted to get away.

Madam Henderson watched the two young men with avidity and amusement old as time. When she saw Peter wasn't really going anywhere, she said, "You know how things go here, Master Wat. Does your friend likewise?"

"No, but it doesn't matter. I'll pay his freight, same as I did with good old Eb." Walter set coins in her palm, as he had with the hackman. These coins were fatter, though. They rang sweetly. Madam Henderson smiled and made them disappear: just how, Peter didn't notice.

"That covers it, sure enough," she said. "Won't you step into my parlor, then, and pick the companion you fancy?"

There was a rhyme about stepping into a parlor. Peter couldn't bring it to mind. He had only a moment to try. Walter Haywood took hold of his elbow and guided him forward. Madam Henderson, smiling still—and why not? she'd been paid—swept on ahead of them, opened the parlor door, and stood aside.

"Here you go," Walter said, steering Peter into the room. "Feast your eyes on *this*."

Peter's jaw dropped so hard, he heard and felt its hinges click. In the parlor sat and stood somewhere between a dozen and a score of women, most of them not far from his age. They were not dressed as a woman would be where men might see her. Most of them, in fact, weren't dressed at all. The ones who were wore transparent silks and shining satins that left them seeming more naked than mere nudity could have.

He'd seen pictures, of course, pictures like the ones on the hallway walls. They were easy to get, and inspiring when you found yourself alone with your hand. But the difference between pictures and the smiling, perfumed reality …. He thought of the difference between a picture of a roasted chicken and a perfectly done thigh on his plate. Then he thought about the girls' thighs, and what they had between them.

"Come on with me, Agnes," Walter said to one of the women. He knew them and they knew him. As he and his chosen partner headed for the back door, he added, "Go easy with him, my dears. He's only just finding out."

They all looked at Peter. A couple of them giggled. He wanted to run away again. Calm and steady as an oak tree, Madam Henderson said, "It will be just fine. Would you like me to choose somebody for you?"

"If—If you'd be so kind," Peter managed.

She nodded briskly. "Florence, why don't you show the young gentleman what he needs to know?"

"I'll do that," Florence said. Her hair was long, and somewhere near the border between blond and brown. She had everything the pictures said a woman ought to have—and she was real. Her West Country accent wasn't much different from his own. She held out her hand. "Come along with me, why don't you?"

He still could have left. Madam Henderson wouldn't have tried to stop him, not when she already had the fee. He could have, but he didn't. Florence's hand was warm and smooth in his. She led him to that door, down another hall, and into a little room with a dresser and a bed. A pitcher and a basin sat on the dresser.

Florence lay down on the bed. "Take off your clothes. I'll show you what to do," she said. Something in her voice told Peter he was far from the first to whom she'd given those instructions. She did sound more kind than otherwise, though.

Clumsily, he undressed. He'd imagined what a woman felt like in his arms, under his hands. Now he discovered what a sorry excuse for an imagination he owned. And then, a little while later ...

"Thank you," was the first thing he thought to say, his mouth no more than an inch above hers. "Oh, thank you!"

She laughed. "You're sweet. You're squashing me, too. Roll off."

He did. She got up, pulled a chamber pot out from under the bed, and squatted over it. Then she took a rag from one of the dresser drawers, wet it with water from the pitcher, and washed herself and him.

"Piss hard," she told him once she'd done that. "It may not help, but it may." He was glad to. He'd needed to ease himself for a while now.

After he got into his clothes again, he asked, "Should I give you something for yourself, above what Madam Henderson got? Is that the custom?"

"If you care to, I won't say no," Florence answered.

He extracted four shillings from his pocket and set them on the dresser. Florence took them. She hid them under a pillow before she led him back to the parlor. He realized she had to know she'd be coming back here again. That saddened him. No matter what had happened on the bed, he was nothing special to her—just another part of the night's work.

Haywood and Agnes walked in a few minutes later. Peter's roommate grinned at him. "Now you know," he said. "Ain't it grand?"

"It is." Peter could hardly say no, not with Florence sitting beside him. She laughed and nodded. Another naked woman, one whose name he never learned, came over and kissed him on the cheek. That only made him want to leave even more than he did already.

Walter was in no hurry, though. He seemed as much at home at Madam Henderson's as he did at Lincoln's Inn. *Why wouldn't he?* Peter thought. *He spends as much time here as he does there.*

At last, he and Peter went up the hall that led to the front door. An older man, pot-bellied and balding, nodded to them as he headed for the parlor. If he took Florence back to that bedroom … then he did, that was all. The bruisers in the anteroom hopped to their feet and opened the door for the departing guests as if they served a nobleman, not a bawd.

"Walter—" Peter began.

"Here." Haywood gave him the flask of rum. That wasn't what he'd wanted, but he grabbed it like a drowning man seizing a plank and gulped it dry. If he got blind, he wouldn't have to think … for a while.

They didn't have to wait long for a cab. Hackmen knew people kept coming out of Madam Henderson's. Peter almost fell asleep on the slow ride back to Lincoln's Inn. Walter had to help him up the stairs. He managed to take off his shoes when he sat down on his bed. A moment later, he slid over sideways. Whether he fell asleep or passed out was a matter of opinion.

The monster who pounded on doors to rouse pupils for break-fast woke him. He groaned; he felt exactly like death. What had he done the night before to leave him in such a horrible state?

Then he remembered exactly what he'd done. He groaned again, not in animal misery but in mortal terror. Now he understood Ebenezer Cooke.

Willows grew alongside the Avon, some of their branches leaning down over and even into the water. Gray herons stalked the shallows; night herons perched on branches, peering down hopefully for unwary fish or frogs.

The birds took no notice when Viola and her sisters stripped willow leaves from low landward branches. Their father would dry some and boil others down to a thick, sour decoction.

Though Viola could see only Margaret's eyes, she was sure the youngest Williams girl was pulling a face. No sooner had that thought crossed her mind than Margaret said, "I don't care how much sugar syrup Father mixes into his nasty willow potion. It still tastes horrible."

"It fights fever, though." Viola remembered Bess Radcliffe and wished she hadn't.

"It doesn't just taste bad," Kate said. "Whenever I have to choke some down, it makes me feel as though I've got a bonfire in my stomach."

"It does the same thing to me," Margaret said.

"To me, too," Viola admitted. "It makes the rest of me feel better, though. Father says some people can't use it at all—it makes them bleed inside."

"What a wonderful medicine, if it's liable to kill you," Margaret said.

"If it did that very often, he wouldn't use it, you goose," Viola said. "But it can happen. Come, let's fill the basket and bring it home."

"I like getting outside," Margaret said. "Only a little while ago, I could do it whenever I wanted."

"It's nice, being out in the fresh air," Kate said.

Viola opened her mouth, then closed it again. She'd always enjoyed getting out of the house, too—till that scoundrel let his hands roam free outside Blackwell's bookshop. Since then, the idea hadn't seemed nearly so appealing. She knew that might happen again any time she stuck her nose out the door.

Two men in a rowboat fished on the Avon. Viola could see them through the screening of willow; she didn't think they could see her sisters or her. That suited her fine. The less she had to do with any men except her father for a while, the happier she'd be. Richard Williams reminded her she was an intelligent human being even if she had the misfortune of being born female. She wondered whether he'd made a mistake, doing that. A lot of the time, it certainly felt as if he had.

Then one of the men in the rowboat spotted the sisters after all. He pointed their way and shouted, "Pussies, pussies, pussies!"

Viola ground her teeth hard enough to hurt, hard enough so she could hear them meet. "Let's go home," Kate said, opening her mouth just enough to let the words out.

"Do we have to?" Margaret said.

"I think it's a good idea, dearie," Kate said quietly. Viola didn't say anything. She was afraid she might start shrieking if she did.

Veils muffled a woman's facial expressions. Eyes by themselves could show only so much. Whatever Viola's eyes showed must have been enough to alarm Margaret. The youngest Williams girl was still young enough to have a good deal of hoyden left in her, but she didn't raise a fuss this time. "All right," she said, and started back to the house ahead of Kate and Viola.

Halfway there, though, she kicked a rock from the path into the field it ran through. Boys playing football would have had trouble kicking so fiercely or so straight. But that was all. She didn't complain in a way that would have let her sisters call her on it.

Kate set a hand on Viola's arm. "I'm sorry. It's ... hard sometimes, isn't it?"

"It's hard all the time. When we're locked up and shut away, and when we're not," Viola said. "'Mary, pity women!' people pray. If Mary pitied women, the world wouldn't be the way it is."

"That's—" Kate caught herself and started again: "If that isn't blasphemy, it comes too close for comfort."

"I wouldn't say it to anyone but the family. I know better," Viola said.

"Maybe you shouldn't say it even to me." Kate took the Church and its teaching more seriously than Viola did. Of the three sisters, Viola was the one most like her father. She didn't know whether he'd always been like that or whether things he'd seen and had to do as a doctor had burnt away big chunks of his faith. Bess Radcliffe floated up in her mind once more.

She knew exactly why she wanted to raise an eyebrow at so many of the things the Church required. She was a woman, after all. What she didn't know was why women all over the world failed to rise up in rebellion against the status quo.

Well, she knew part of the answer. Horrible things would happen to them if they did. Her father understood that, too. He said the right things and acted the right way in public. So did Viola. No one would ever hear her grinding her teeth when she prayed in Salisbury Cathedral. No one would know what she was thinking. And that had to be just as well.

Jane Williams was in the kitchen, plucking a chicken. Her hands worked with automatic skill. They kept going as she looked up at Viola and smiled. "You have the leaves! Good! It's nice today, isn't it?"

"Except for idiots on the river, yes," Viola answered. She'd taken off her veil and freed her hair as soon as she got inside. Her face surely showed what kind of idiots she meant.

"I'm sorry," her mother said.

"It's not *your* fault," Viola said. "Has Father anyone in the surgery, or can I give him the basket now?"

"I don't think anyone's in there. Tap on the connecting door. See what happens."

"All right."

Tap Viola did. A moment later, Richard Williams opened the door. "Oh, splendid!" he said. "Thank you—and I'll tell Kate and Margaret thanks, too, as soon as I get the chance." He took it for granted that Viola would be the one who delivered the willow leaves. So did she and her sisters. Then he snapped his fingers and handed her an envelope. "I almost forgot—this came while you were out gathering."

She recognized the hand at once. "It's from Peter," she said. One of her father's eyebrows quirked, which probably meant he'd come to know Peter Drinkwater's script, too. She went on, "I wonder how his mock trial went. He was getting ready for it last time he wrote. It will surely have happened by now."

"I'd think so, yes," Richard Williams agreed. "Been more than a week since his last letter, hasn't it? Although you never can tell with that. The postmen try, but they aren't perfect."

"Not much is," Viola said, more sharply than she'd intended to.

"What's wrong?"

"Nothing anyone can do anything about." Viola slid her thumbnail under the wax seal closing the envelope and flicked it off. The well on the seal reminded her of Peter's family name. *Before very long, it will be my name, too,* she thought. She'd practiced writing *Viola Drinkwater* a few times, always wadding up the paper afterwards and throwing it away so not even her sisters would know what she'd been doing.

She took the letter out of the envelope, unfolded it, and began to read. Peter usually opened *Dear Viola* or *My dear Viola,* as anyone starting a letter would. Not this time. He wrote *Bless me, Viola, for I have sinned;* he might have been in the confessional, with her the priest hearing what he'd done wrong.

He went on to tell her how he'd sinned—how he'd triumphed in the mock trial, how he'd drunk too much while celebrating the victory, and how he'd let Walter Haywood take him to a house of ill fame. *I shall not evade what happened in that house,* he said. *Heedless of the risks of which I, like anyone else above the age of six, am only too well aware, I had carnal congress with one of the women there.*

"Oh, sweet Mother of God!" Viola said, and crossed herself. She might have doubts about religion, but its unthinking habits and gestures were harder to shake off than the thing itself.

Her father had been sorting through the willow leaves she'd brought him. He looked up sharply. "What's wrong, dear? You're pale as a ghost."

"I believe it." Viola felt as if a horse had kicked her in the belly. After a moment, she added, "Let me finish what … what Peter has to say, and then I'll show you the letter."

"However you please, of course." But Richard Williams didn't go back to the long, narrow leaves. He kept his eyes on her, as alert as if she were a patient in a crisis. And that wasn't so far wrong, was it?

She made herself read on. *It has been three days now since I made the mistake I made,* Peter wrote. *As I set these words on paper, I show no signs of the clap or of the pox. It is still too early to be certain about either of those, of course. And it is much too early to know whether, in exchange for a momentary pleasure, the Wasting will repay me with a lifetime cut short and full of misery in that shortened span. Only time will tell.*

I could make any number of excuses for what I did. None of them matters, now that the deed is done, he continued. *I could likewise keep silent, trust to luck to keep me safe, and hope you would never learn of my mistake. But that would endanger your health as well as mine, and the health of any offspring we may have.*

I understand that telling you this may cause your family to break off its projected union with mine, Peter wrote. *I would not, I could not, blame you if that were to come to pass. But what I did is something you need to know of and to consider. If I did not set your concerns on a level equal to my own, I should not make for you a proper husband in any case.*

Should you still wish to correspond with me, I await your reply with the anticipation and apprehension you may well imagine. In the meantime, I remain your most humble and penitent servant— Peter had kept his script under tight control in the body of the letter. His signature, by contrast, was a hasty scrawl.

Viola sighed and crossed herself again. "As bad as that, chick?" her father asked.

"Worse, I think." She handed him the letter.

He held it out almost at arm's length to read it. He had spectacles to help him with small print, but didn't need to put them on his nose for this. The farther he got, the more the corners of his mouth turned down. At last, he set the letter on the tabletop next to the basket of leaves.

"I'm sorry," he said.

"So am I," Viola answered. "What should we do? What should *I* do?"

Richard Williams clicked his tongue between his teeth. "First off, whatever you want to do, we'll do. You've got good sense. No one who's known you for a minute would say anything different. And this is your *life* we're talking about."

"Thank you, Father," Viola said softly. She knew most women in Christendom—or out of it, for that matter—wouldn't have heard anything like that.

"The other thing I was going to say is, you don't have to make up your mind right away," he went on. "If he's poxed or clapped, he'll know soon enough. The Wasting, though … that's harder. It often starts with fevers and night sweats, but not always. Sometimes people can go on for a long time without having any notion they've got it."

"Like that chap in Nunton," Viola said.

"Just like him." Her father nodded. "But nothing was going to happen between you and Peter till he finished his studies. If he has it, chances are good he'll know by then."

"Is that certain?" Viola asked.

Now he shook his head. "Of course not. Next to nothing is certain with the Wasting, save only that, once you show signs of it, you will go downhill and die. But it is more likely than not, I think."

"If I say I will not wed him on account of this, it *will* make a rift between us and the Drinkwaters." Viola had no doubts on that score.

"Yes, of course it will. But I'll bear up under that, never fear," Richard Williams said. "You count for more."

Musingly, Viola said, "The only way to be sure you won't die of the Wasting is to die a virgin."

"That's so. And more than a few people choose that road. They die, too, though sometimes later and less miserably than they would have otherwise."

"If I throw Peter over and sooner or later I am matched with someone else, I have no way to know whether he's also gone a-whoring unless he tells me." Viola knew she was thinking out loud.

"True enough. And he, likewise, would have to trust that you hadn't lain down with someone you shouldn't have, the way that poor girl did with the Nunton lad." Her father held up his hand. "I mean no offense, believe me. But life's a chancy thing since the Wasting came. Chancy for everyone."

"I understood you." Viola sighed. "I'd like children one of these days. Not much point if a line ends with you, is there?"

"Well, I don't think so, but I don't know everything there is to know, either."

"You *don't*?" She sounded as astonished as if she were five years old. Part of that was play, but not all. He knew more than anybody else she was acquainted with.

He smiled crookedly. "I'm reminded every day in the surgery here how very much I don't know. But that isn't quite what we were talking about, is it? People who take vows as priests or monks or nuns would disagree. So would those who stay secular but take no partner."

"I wouldn't quarrel with anyone who wants to live that way. It's not for me, though, or I don't think it is," Viola said. "I *would* like children. I'd like healthy children, too."

"Of course. Every mother does, and every father." Richard Williams pursed his lips and blew air out through them. "Even without the Wasting, it's so hard. Lately, inoculation has made smallpox a smaller curse than it was in days gone by, but so many other sicknesses still strike, and no one knows how to stop them …. Your mother and I, we know how lucky we were to raise all three of you."

She nodded. Any churchyard had more than its share of small stones above small graves. Babies and little children seemed to fall ill and die at any excuse or none. It was dangerous to love them too much before you could be fairly sure they'd live. People did it anyhow, and too often paid for it in misery.

"It was honorable of Peter to tell you," her father went on. "That may count for something. Or it may not, depending on how you look at it."

"I think it does. If someone you're going to live with for the rest of your life isn't going to be honest with you, what's the point?" Viola answered.

"Well, I feel the same way—which may not surprise you much." He gave her that crooked smile again. He knew as well as she did that she was the daughter who most took after him. After a moment, he continued, "One more time, though, not everyone does. Some people would rather not know what their spouse does when they aren't looking."

Viola made a face. "No, thank you!" She looked down at the floorboards. "I wish I knew what to do."

"Take your time. Think it through till you're sure you've got it the way you want it in your mind and in your heart, then do that. There's no rush." Richard Williams paused. "If I tell you something, will you keep it secret even from your mother and your sisters?"

"I don't think you ever asked me anything like that before," Viola said. Her father didn't answer; he just waited. After half a minute, she said, "I promise. Tell it me."

"These mischances do happen, and more often than people care to admit. I happen to know for a fact that Alf Drinkwater sinned the same way before he married, and was lucky enough to escape the worst."

"How do you know that?" she asked.

"Because I do. I've already said too much." He gave back not another word.

The other thing that occurred to her was to wonder whether he'd done anything like that himself. She didn't want to know badly enough to ask him. Put another way, she didn't have the nerve. His news did give her one more thing to think about, as if she didn't already have enough.

IX

Every morning when Peter woke up, the first thing he did was feel his pillow and the bedclothes. One of the common ways the Wasting showed itself early on was with drenching night sweats. Every time he didn't find the linens soaked, he breathed a prayer of thanksgiving. He hadn't thought of himself as especially pious, but he prayed now even so.

Every time he pissed into a pot, he braced himself for fiery pain and for the nasty drip of pus. Every time it didn't come, he likewise prayed gratefully. He inspected his privates all the time. He didn't know just what a chancre would look like, but he thought he'd know if he had one.

Walter Haywood thought he was hilarious. "You're fine, you're fine," he said. "You see? You got away with it clean as a whistle. A devil of a lot more fun than flogging your own donkey all the time, too, ain't it?"

Peter couldn't very well deny that, since it was true. Instead of denying it, he answered, "A devil of a lot more dangerous, too."

"Ptah!" Walter laughed some more. "You tell me that, but what happened to you? Nothing happened! Except you're flogging your conscience instead of your damned donkey. If I take you back there—for God knows you'll never have the nerve to go back on your own—chances are it'll be the same way again."

Conscience? As far as Peter could see, Haywood hadn't been issued one when he was born. Since he hadn't, what point to appealing to his? Peter laughed himself, darkly. "Tell me about it, tell me *all* about it. You're the one who came back with a dripping pipe. I won't even talk about Ebenezer."

"Good. Eb's not worth talking about. Damned American semi-savage." Walter looked and sounded disgusted. "What my father sees in him, why he keeps him around, I've never figured out."

"To try to make sure you don't do anything so stupid, even you can't slither your way out of it?" Peter suggested.

He meant to wound. Instead, he made his roommate thoughtful, something that didn't happen every day. "Do you know what?" Haywood said. "You may be right. Well, he's got his work cut out for him, doesn't he?"

"He wouldn't, if you'd buckle down a little," Peter said. The trouble wasn't that Haywood was stupid. The trouble was, he'd sooner enjoy himself than use the wits he had.

Sure enough, he answered, "Where's the fun in that?"

"You're supposed to be useful to your family," Peter said.

"Maybe I will be, maybe I won't," Walter said with a shrug. "In the end, it won't matter more than tuppence either way."

Peter gave up. Walter would do what he felt like doing, and things would go on however they went on. However they went, he'd smile and laugh his way through them. Peter had no doubts on that score.

He'd learned better than to let Walter know he'd written to Viola, telling her what he'd done. Haywood would only laugh himself silly if he found out—laugh himself sillier, rather. When he wed, he'd never tell his intended he'd been clapped. That wouldn't be any of her affair, not to him.

Every day, the postman dumped envelopes into the INBOUND box by the bottom of the stairs and collected threepenny bits from the pupils picking them up. Day followed day, and no letter came back to Peter from Viola. He wondered whether he'd ever hear from her again.

He hadn't said anything to his own family, or to Clarence. They didn't need to know the way his fiancée did. But if she'd said something to the Drinkwaters, or if her father had …. When no furious letter came from his father, no horrified one from his mother or either of his sisters, he decided the Williamses were keeping their own counsel.

He thought Viola would say something, at least. He wondered whether he knew her as well as he imagined he did.

When a couple of weeks had passed since he sent her the letter, Stephen Heath took him aside after a lecture and said, "Is all well with you, young Drinkwater? Your work's slipped lately. It doesn't seem like you."

"I'm sorry, Master," Peter said. "There are some … some family matters on my mind. I'm waiting to see how they turn out."

The older man nodded. "That will weigh on anyone. I hope all goes as well as it may. Some find that throwing themselves into their studies keeps them from dwelling on troubles back home."

"Thank you for your kindness," Peter said. "I'll try that." He didn't know if he could. He also didn't think it would help if he did.

Because he prided himself on keeping his word, he did try. Sometimes, when he got interested in the details of a complicated case and weighing this against that for importance, the outer world and its worries receded for a little while. More often than not, though, he knew too well he was only trying to fool himself.

His work came back up to snuff, even if he cared much less than he would have not long before. Of course, Walter noticed he was busier than usual. "All work and no play makes Peter a dull boy," he said.

"That's my worry, not yours," Peter said shortly.

"Think so, do you?" Haywood snorted in derision. "Think again, my lad, think again. The way you are now, you're nothing but a bore to be around. I know what you need, though. You need another good bouncing at Madam Henderson's, that's what? Shall I get a doctor to write you a prescription? Will you think it's all right then?"

Part of Peter thought that was exactly what he needed. To lie down with Florence again …. He told that part he was taking no notice of it, which wasn't altogether true. When Walter next went whoring, or when Ebenezer summoned him to the wharves, Peter would give that unruly part its due. His hand wasn't the same as a woman—he knew as much now—but it was better than nothing.

"You're not answering me," Walter wheedled.

"Maybe that should tell you something," Peter said. "If you mean to live your life just as you please, kindly extend me the same privilege."

"But you don't have any fun," Haywood said.

Peter lit a fresh candle from the stub of his old one and buried his nose in the lawbooks on his desk. After a minute or so, he looked up and said, "I do enjoy driving you mad."

Walter Haywood chuckled—sourly, but he did.

Kate looked up from the harpsichord keyboard. "Have you written back to Peter yet?" she asked. The whole family knew about the letter by now.

Viola shook her head. "I haven't, no. I still haven't made up my mind what I ought to tell him."

"Whatever it is, you should tell him soon. I can see him in his little room, stewing over when he'll hear from you and what you'll say."

"After he went to the stews, he deserves to stew," Viola said. Her sister made a horrible face. Viola stuck out her tongue.

Sometimes she also imagined Peter fretting in his Lincoln's Inn chamber, and sometimes she imagined him back at the brothel, doing what men did with women when they found—or bought—women willing to do it with them. She knew the theory of what went on when men and women joined. She'd seen some of the pictures men used to inspire themselves. They didn't particularly inspire her; she found them closer to disgusting than exciting. But you could learn even from something like that.

She hoped Peter had more sense than to go there again. From his letter, from all the letters she'd got from him, she guessed he did. But what you guessed and what you knew for certain were two different things, especially when it came to men and fornication.

"You aren't really answering me," Kate said.

Viola sighed. "No, I know I'm not. And the worst of it is, you're right. I do need to tell the blockhead *something*, don't I?"

"He told you when he didn't have to," her sister observed.

"Yes, he did. It was brave, in a way. If only he hadn't been so *stupid!*" Viola sighed again. "All right. I'll go upstairs and tend to it."

"What will you say?"

"I don't know. I'll see when I start writing."

She'd sit there in front of a sheet of paper. She'd have a freshly trimmed goose quill and a bottle of ink where she could reach it without needing to move far. Pretty soon, her hand would move to the paper and words would flow out of it. As often as not, she didn't have any idea what she'd say till she saw the words.

Kate rolled her eyes when she heard Viola's answer. Her mind didn't work like that, any more than Viola could coax magic from the harpsichord the way her sister could. *Each cat her own rat*, she thought as she headed for the stairs. Behind her, the music began again.

Paper. Pen. Ink. She wrote the date and then stopped, wondering how to go on. If she said *Dear Master Drinkwater*, it would sound as if she were done with him forever. If she said *My dear Peter*, it would sound as if everything were all right. Neither of those was true.

She wrote *Peter——*, looked at it, and nodded. It was simple and stark. It would do. *Thank you for your latest, which I have received. Believe me when I tell you I am grateful for your candor*, she said. *Believe me also when I tell you how much I wish you had no need to be so candid.*

She looked at those sentences and nodded to herself. Yes, they said exactly what she wanted them to say. With a beginning like that, she could go anywhere. She hadn't been lying when she told Kate she still wasn't positive where she wanted to go. Sure enough, the only way to find out was to do it.

She wrote another couple of sentences. These, she considered more carefully. Did she really mean them? Was she being plain without needlessly wounding? The only way she wanted to pain Peter was to kick him for being stupid. He was already kicking himself. Whether that would keep him from being stupid again … she could hope, but she couldn't be sure. She just didn't know him well enough.

After a little while, she nodded again and wrote some more. Another pause for reflection. Another nod. She read it all through again, then signed her name. She'd finished it. Before she put it in an envelope and sealed it, she took it downstairs to the kitchen.

Jane Williams was cutting beef into chunks more or less bite-sized for a stew. She looked unhappy. "I should have sharpened this knife before I started out," she said.

"I'm sorry, Mother," Viola said. "Shall I hack away for a bit while you read what I've written to Peter?"

"If you'd be so kind. Let me wash my hands before I take it, though. If he sees bloody finger marks on the paper, he'll think you want to murder him—and who could blame you if you do?"

Viola set the letter on a counter and went to work on the beef. Sure enough, the knife blade didn't rival one of Dr. Williams' scalpels. She put some effort into it. Her mother rinsed off her hands, then dried them on a linen towel. She took up the letter and began to read.

When she finished, she said, "This is truly how you feel?"

"Yes, I think so. I've spent a while mulling it over. It needed a while, too."

"I can see how it would. This is serious business."

"Yes, it is." The muscles in Viola's right arm and shoulder tightened as she tried to cube the beef. "Tarnation take this worthless knife! The meat's not as tender as it might be, either."

"I know. That's why it's going into the pot." Her mother paused. "Has your father seen this?"

"Not yet. I wanted you to look at it first. You're a woman, too. And it has more to do with how I feel than with how I think."

Her mother smiled thinly. "Nobody would ever claim you don't know the man who sired you. If you want to know what I think, you've spelled out what's in your heart and in your mind as well as anyone is ever likely to. Your father will very likely say the same thing."

"I hope so. I don't want to cause quarrels in the family," Viola said.

"I don't think you will. He and I both know you're old enough and sensible enough to decide what you want to do and then to do it."

"Father said something like that when I showed him what Peter wrote to me. I thanked him then. I thank you now. Not everybody would have said anything of the kind. This is the kind of business they write romances and stage plays about."

"I trust we can steer clear of anything like that." Jane Williams made a small motion that said she wanted nothing to do with such dramas. Viola wanted nothing to do with them, either, which had less to do with what she got than she wished it would. Her mother continued, "Now wash *your* hands before you take him the letter."

With clean hands, Viola carried the letter to the door connecting the rest of the house to the surgery. Her father didn't open when she tapped. She put her ear to the door. He was talking with another man in there. She took her head away. He'd trained the Williams girls not to snoop, and they … mostly … didn't.

A three-legged stool sat by the door. She sat down and waited ten or fifteen minutes before her father opened up. "I thought I heard you," he said, and then, "What have you got there?"

"My letter to Peter. I've done it at last. Would you care to see it?"

"Oh, I might," Richard Williams said dryly. "I'd like to know where we'll be going, and whether we need to take in sail and brace for stormy weather."

"Here." Viola gave him the letter.

He read it as he'd read Peter Drinkwater's: nearly at arm's length. When he finished, he nodded. "If that's how you want it, that's how it will be."

"Is that all you've got to say?"

"What else do I need? You write well, but I know you know that. You can probably write books people would read, if you care to."

"What I'd like to write is accounts of my voyages to faraway places, and of the strange people and stranger beasts and plants I found there. But I'm not likely ever to have the chance to do that, am I?" Viola didn't bother trying to hide her bitterness. It wasn't as if her father didn't know she felt it.

His mouth thinned and tightened. "No, I'm afraid you're not. The world isn't the way we wish it were, it's the way—"

"The way our grandfathers, and their grandfathers, and *their* grandfathers made it," Viola broke in. "And our grandmothers, and theirs, and *theirs*, didn't get to say one word about it, or it wouldn't be this way."

"Ah, chick, you're bound to be right about that. But if you want to write about strange people, you'd have a devil of a time finding any stranger than the ones right here in Salisbury," Richard Williams said. He startled Viola into laughing. She hadn't dreamt he could do that just then, and loved him for it.

Peter thought one of the envelopes the postman threw into the box by the stairs was the kind Viola commonly used. Sure enough, when he snatched it out he saw it was addressed to him. His heart leaped and his stomach sank at the same time: hope warring with fear.

"That will be threepence, young sir," the postman said.

"Here you are, Master Nelson." Peter dug in his pocket. He handed the postman a small silver coin with the king's image in profile on one side and a three surmounted by a crown on the other. Nelson touched a finger to the bill of his cap, then went back to putting mail into the box.

Up the stairs Peter went, taking them two at a time. When he opened the door to his room, Walter Haywood wasn't there to ask him why he'd impersonated a charging rhinoceros on the staircase. He breathed a sigh of relief. He didn't want his roommate watching if he burst into tears, and he knew too well he was liable to.

He could have blamed Haywood for putting him in the predicament that made him liable to weep. Every so often, he tried to—in his own mind, anyhow. But Walter hadn't shoved a blunderbuss into his back and marched him down the hallway with naked Florence. No one had made him mount her, either. He'd done it all by himself, and right eagerly, too. And he'd thanked her afterwards. He remembered that, even if it embarrassed him.

He broke the seal affixed to the envelope and took out the letter. *Do I want to unfold it?* he wondered. Whether he wanted to or not, he needed to. He knew as much, knew it only too well.

Peter— Viola began. No *Dear*. No *My dear*. He'd taken them for granted till they weren't there any more. Well, he had nobody but himself to blame because they weren't.

She went on, *Thank you for your letter, which I have received. Believe me when I tell you I am grateful for your candor. Believe me also when I tell you how much I wish you had no need to be so candid.*

He bit down on the inside of his lower lip till he tasted blood. Again, it wasn't as if he didn't have that coming. He might have wished she'd been less forthright about it. But he'd already seen she was in the habit of saying what she meant, and saying it as clearly as she could.

You will understand that your mistake gives me a dreadful problem, she wrote. *That you lay down with another woman before we wed is bad enough. That you lay down with a whore, a woman who had lain down with so many before you, is far worse. You risked not only your life and health but also mine and that of any children the two of us might*

134

conceive. You will understand this, I am sure, as well as I do. I hope the momentary pleasure was worth the throw of the dice.

Peter's ears burned though he was reading the letter, not hearing it. His father had often noted how Richard Williams owned a sardonic cast of mind. If Viola hadn't got hers from her sire, she'd acquired it somewhere else. Wherever it came from, she had it.

My first thought was to bid you farewell, or perhaps to hope that you suffered the torments of damned souls in hell forevermore, she continued. No, she left him in no doubt about what she felt. *But then it occurred to me that, having discarded you, I should likely some day join some other man in marriage. You showed uncommon honesty in telling me of your foolishness. This would not mean a different fiancé would not have been foolish, only that his honesty was more apt to be of the common sort: which is to say, no better than it has to be.*

When we met, I found no great flaw in you, Viola wrote. *Nor can I deny enjoying the correspondence between us since you removed to London. Whether I could easily do better is a hard question ... so long as the Wasting does not touch you with its bony fingers.*

Peter flinched. The woman to whom his family had yoked him seemed to be able to read his mind. Every morning he woke without having soaked his bed in sweat, he still breathed a quick prayer of thanks.

Let us hope this is not the case, Viola went on. *You were foolish in a way that young men—yes, and young women as well—are only too apt to be foolish. If you have learnt from your mistake, and if you do not go back to it like a dog returning to its vomit, I remain willing to wed you after you finish your studies, so long as you remain healthy. If that is agreeable to you, let me know, and likewise if not. I hope you are and continue well.* Her signature followed.

"Oh, God be praised!" Peter exclaimed. No, he hadn't been in the habit of calling on the Lord before he called on Madam Henderson's. He also hadn't been in such danger before he visited her establishment.

He knew he couldn't have asked for anything more from his intended. He was lucky she offered so much. She and her family might easily have decided to break all ties with the Drinkwaters, now and forevermore. That would have been his fault, no one else's.

When Walter Haywood came in a few minutes later, Peter was already sitting at his desk writing Viola a grateful reply. "You're scribbling away like a recording secretary there," Haywood noted. "If you went at it any harder, you'd set your paper afire. What's so important? Did you forget you have a brief due tomorrow?"

"No, that's more your style," Peter said, which made his roommate scowl because it was true. "I'm just answering a letter I got today from my fiancée in Salisbury."

"Salisbury." The way Walter said it, it might have been some nasty skin disease, the kind you treated with a stinking sulfuretted ointment. With a leer, Walter went on, "Are you going to tell her everything you did with—what was her name?—Florence, that was it?"

I already did, Peter thought. But that was the last thing he wanted to tell Haywood. "As a matter of fact, no," he replied. When—and if—he got around to confessing his fornication to a priest, he could confess the lie, too.

Haywood's laugh told him the flat way he'd come out with it made it more believable, not less. "That's the way! What they don't know never hurts them."

Unless it kills them—and me, Peter thought.

That was one more thing he didn't care to tell Walter. Then Walter said to him, "I expect I'll go over there again tonight. More fun than sticking my nose in a damned book, that's certain sure. Feel like coming along?"

"No, thanks," Peter said shortly.

Haywood laughed again. "Silly lad! There's no difference between once and twice, save that you'll be hung for a sheep, not a little bleating lamb."

"No, thanks," Peter said again, and made a point of going back to the letter. Walter Haywood thought he was hilarious.

Viola's father tapped his fingernail against her open door, then tossed an envelope on her bed. "You and that bloke in London are going to make me run out of threepences to give the postman," he mock-grumbled.

"That stupid bloke in London," Viola said.

"These things can happen. You hope they don't, but sometimes they do anyway." Richard Williams pointed to the envelope. "Are you going to find out whether he's properly grateful you're more generous than he deserves? Or do you want me to go away before you look?"

"No, it's all right," she answered. "I'm the one this most involves, but it takes in the whole family." She broke the seal—the familiar seal, now—took out the letter, and quickly read through it. "He *is* properly grateful. Not quite blubbering, but close."

"Good. He had better be. Does he make any promises he may not be able to keep?"

"No. I was looking for those, too. He says he'll do his best to be worthy of me, but that's as far as he goes."

"Probably just as well," her father said. "The bigger the promise, the bigger the lie. That's how it usually goes, anyhow. If I had a threepence for every patient who promised me he'd never touch rum or whiskey again—"

"You'd have plenty to give the postman?" Viola broke in.

"Never mind the postman!" he said. "I'd be so rich, they'd call me Earl Williams. Maybe Duke Williams, lord of Salisbury. Of course, I'd be richer yet if everyone who swore he'd pay me next week actually brought in the brass."

He was joking, and then again he wasn't. Along with money, he'd got paid in livestock and vegetables, in loaves of bread, and, once, in a gallon jug of rutabaga wine and a quart jug of rutabaga brandy. Viola'd had sips of the wine; she remembered it as being less horrible than she'd expected. Richard Williams drank the brandy himself, over the course of a couple of years. He'd said he didn't know anyone he disliked enough to give it to.

"Now I spend the next however long it is praying the Wasting does not show itself in Peter," Viola said as she put the letter back in its envelope.

"Yes, there's always that. If it should, the arrangement between the Drinkwaters and us falls down. You wouldn't need to worry about it any more," her father said.

"I understand that I wouldn't. But I wouldn't wish the Wasting on Peter. I wouldn't wish it on … well, on very many people." Viola'd started to say she wouldn't wish it on anyone, but that wasn't quite true. She knew she wouldn't shed a tear if it took the lout who'd felt her up outside Master Blackwell's bookshop. Not wanting to remember him, she continued, "Until all this happened, I'd rather come to like him through his letters—and the other way round, too, I think."

"Ah," her father said, and then, "Well, that's not necessarily a bad thing between husbands and wives."

She opened her mouth to say something sharp, but didn't. With anyone else, she would have. But she'd had a lifetime to learn how he talked, when he expected to be taken seriously, and when he didn't. Instead of snapping at him, she asked, "Did you and Mother like each other when you were first joined together?"

He looked surprised, as if he hadn't thought about that for a long time. He probably hadn't. With a small laugh, he answered, "Like each other? We barely knew each other. I'd seen her without her veil once, when I went with my father to decide whether she'd suit me."

"I'm glad you thought she would. Of course, I'm selfish about that—I shouldn't be here if you hadn't," Viola said.

"There is that, yes," her father agreed. "And, after all these years, we get along about as well as a married couple are likely to. We're a couple of river pebbles, knocking together in the stream of time. By now, we've rubbed most of the corners and rough places off each other."

"That's a pretty figure!" Viola silently clapped her hands together.

"Is it? I don't know anything about such fripperies. I leave them to the folk who're good at them, like you."

She stuck out her tongue at him. "You're putting your candle under a bushel. What's more, you know it, too."

"I'm a doctor, which means I don't know anything. How many times have I told you that? Most days, I don't even suspect anything."

"You help people."

"Here and there. Now and then. I am a decent bonesetter, sure enough, but that isn't something I do very often. I can fight pain—a little. Also fever—a little, again. Past that, like as not I make my patients worse, not better. I don't say that to them, though. Sometimes thinking they'll get better helps them do it." Richard Williams scowled. "Sometimes it doesn't, too."

"Henrietta Radcliffe is in the world today, thanks to you," Viola said.

Her father's scowl only darkened. "And her mother isn't, also thanks to me."

"They both would have died if you hadn't gone. Mistress Worth said as much. Will you tell me she doesn't know her business?"

"She knows it was well as anyone can. By the same token, I know mine as well as anyone can, too. Too often, that boils down to not well enough. If I knew how to keep Bess Radcliffe free of fever after I cut her, they'd both still be with us. But I don't. Nobody does, any more than anybody knows what to do about the Wasting. We're children, with the understanding of children."

"Sooner or later, we'll learn more. Doctors will do better."

"And they'll think people like me were nothing but stupid butchers. Like as not, they'll be right."

Viola scowled back. When he drifted into one of these black moods, he had to get himself out of it. If anyone else tried, he dug in his heels and stayed gloomy longer.

"However you please. Things *do* change, though. Didn't you tell me we've known of laudanum for less than a hundred years? Who knows what we'll learn in the next hundred?" she said.

"Whatever it is, I won't be here to see it," he replied.

No, he wasn't going to stop enjoying his unhappiness. At the door, she waved. He gave back a small answering wave that was a quarter of the way toward being a salute and walked out of her room. Would Peter prove so stiff-necked? She hoped not.

Carrying the letter, she walked down to the kitchen. Her mother spotted it right away. "Is that from Peter Drinkwater?" she asked.

"Oh, yes." Viola nodded.

"What does he say? Is he properly grateful to you? He'd better be."

"He is. He's a decent fellow, I think—except for that one little while when he was an indecent fellow. If he got off lucky then, I dare hope he's learnt his lesson. And if he didn't ... I also dare hope that will show itself before he comes back to Salisbury and we wed."

Jane Williams exhaled through her nose. "Men are stupid—especially men his age and yours, but men in general, too. And they make us cover up and hide ourselves away so they can try to protect themselves from their own stupidity. They're the ones who shouldn't be let out unless they're on a lead, like so many dogs."

"I'd like that!" Viola exclaimed. "A ruddy short lead, too."

"Don't hold your breath," her mother said. "As long as you're here, will you chop up a couple of onions for me?"

"Of course. How fine do you want them?" Viola set Peter's letter on top of a canister full of flour so nothing would happen to it and got to work.

Somebody knocked on the door to the room Peter shared with Walter Haywood. For a wonder, Walter was working at his desk, not downstairs playing cards or out visiting Madam Henderson and her lovelies. "If that's Eb Cooke, I'll scream," he said. "I've got to finish this, damn it all."

If he'd started working on it a few days earlier, he probably would have had it done by now. Peter was making some small last-minute improvements on his own pleading. Since his desk was closer to the door, he stood up. "Only one way to find out," he said.

Ebenezer Cooke touched a bony finger to the brim of his hat. "God gi' you good evenin', Master Drinkwater," he said. "Is Master Haywood—? Oh, yes, I see him." He raised his voice a little: "Master Haywood, there's a schooner in from Maryland full to the scuppers with baccy that wants grading and pricing."

Walter threw back his head and shrieked as if someone had dropped a boulder on his foot. Peter jumped. The sot-weed factor gave back a pace in alarm. "The tobacco can go hang, for all I care," Haywood said.

"Shall I tell your father you said that?" Cooke asked.

Not many things made Walter wince. Invoking his father was one of them. Swearing under his breath, he blew out the candle on his desk and set down his quill. "I'll come," he said with a martyred sigh. "If I get a rotten mark on this, you can tell my old man he's to blame."

"You've got to learn the business, too." Cooke pronounced *learn* as if it were spelled *larn*. Peter sometimes thought he hardly seemed to speak English at all.

With a martyred sigh, Walter put on his hat and followed the factor away. Peter closed the door behind him. Then he went over to his roommate's desk and looked at what he'd done so far. On a small scrap of foolscap, he scribbled a couple of citations Walter had missed and a few suggestions on how to wrap it up. Haywood *was* working; if he had a few hours carved out of the time he needed to get done, helping him to the finishing line didn't seem too wicked.

Peter'd gone to bed long before Walter came in again. "D'you mind if I light the candle and get back to it?" he asked.

"No—go ahead," Peter said muzzily. A moment later, he added, "It's bloody late. Did you drag him to the joyhouse again to pay him back?"

"You'd best believe I did. And I wanted some fun myself, after what he put me through." Walter fumbled with flint and steel before he managed to get the candle going. When he saw Peter's note next to his work, he whistled softly. "God bless you, Drinkwater! You're a lifesaver!"

I'm a sleepy lifesaver, Peter thought. He listened to the quill pen scraping across paper for a minute or two, but no longer than that. Next thing he knew, the early-morning door knocker woke him up, and Haywood with him. Walter must have come to bed at some point, but Peter hadn't roused when he did.

"Thanks again," Walter said as they pulled off their nightshirts and donned daytime clothes. "I bet I'd still be at it if you hadn't given me some signposts to speed me along."

"It's all right," Peter said, taking care not to tack on *any time.* Instead, he asked, "And how was the baccy?" He imitated Eb Cooke's way of talking with malice aforethought.

"It was brown. It smelled like sot-weed. Lucille, now, Lucille was pink and smelled of lavender, and her cunt was tighter than tight." Walter went on in lewd detail. Peter threw the door open and hurried down to breakfast.

X

Viola had doubts. Oh, so did everyone else—she understood that. But they seemed to burden her mother and her sisters much less than they did her. She knew how she came by them, sure enough. Of the three children in the family, she was the one who took after her father.

And so it was to him that she wondered out loud, "Do you think I did the right thing with Peter?"

"You did … what you did. If you change your mind about it, you can still tell him so," Richard Williams answered. "He is not guaranteed to be healthy—we both know that. But, men being what they are, no one is guaranteed to be healthy. You understand that as well as I do, I think."

"Oh, yes. It would be simpler if we could go on peopling the world without any need for men at all." Viola paused, eyeing her father. "I mean no offense, of course."

"Of course." His tone, commonly dry, now might have blown up from the Sahara on the wings of a sirocco. Siroccos didn't reach England; Viola knew about them from books. The doctor continued, "We're the simple ones, though. The world holds more complications than we've even begun to imagine."

"Doesn't it!" she said. "If only Peter hadn't got himself in one—and me along with him."

"Yes, if only," her father said. "But people aren't perfect, however much we wish they could be. The only perfect man was our Lord and Savior, Jesus Christ. Being God's Son, He had a bit of a head start on that."

"Just a bit." Viola looked at him in surprise. He seldom came even so close to speaking of religious matters.

He hadn't finished, either: "And our Lord and Savior, living when He did, had no need to worry about the Wasting."

They were alone in the surgery. No one else in the house could hear them. Viola looked out the front window. No one was passing by out in the street. All the same, she wanted to shiver. "The Church would not think well of your coming out with things like that."

"No, eh? I never should have guessed." Richard Williams chuckled harshly. "I wouldn't come out with them to anyone but you—oh, maybe to Alf, if we were both good and pickled. I wouldn't say them to your mother. She knows what I think, but I have the good manners not to rub her nose in it. Your sisters—"

"They may suspect," Viola observed.

"Think so, do you?" Her father sighed. "I'm not the dissembler I wish I were, then. Anyone would think they knew me."

"Hard to credit, isn't it?" she said, and he laughed. She went on, "Since we're skating on thin ice here, may I ask you another question?"

"You can always ask. I may pretend not to have any idea what you're talking about."

"I'll be as plain as I may, in that case." Viola took a deep breath. She needed it to steady herself. "If …. If I turn out to have made a mistake and the Wasting lays hold of me, have you got medicines to give me a quiet, peaceful ending in place of the awful one I'd have from the disease?"

His eyebrows came down and together. Two sharp vertical creases appeared between them. At the same time, the lines around his mouth deepened and filled with shadow. He looked all at once twenty years older.

Slowly, he said, "Suicide and homicide are both mortal sins in the eyes of the Church. When I became a doctor, I swore Hippocrates' Oath. One part of it goes, 'I shall not give anyone any deadly drug, even if asked to do so.'"

"None of that answers what I asked you," Viola replied.

Richard Williams smiled the smile a condemned man might have smiled on the gallows in the instant before the hangman dropped the trap. He sighed. "I hoped you wouldn't notice," he said.

"Now you've offended me," she said.

"I daresay. You're a great many things, but stupid is none of them." He sighed again. "Yes, of course I have those potions. I've used them now and again—less often than you'd guess, though. Most folk cling to life as long as they may. There. Are you answered now?"

"Yes, Father. Thank you."

"You have a secret sin from me no confessor has ever heard. What penance will you give me?"

"It doesn't seem a sin to me," Viola said. "And it's good to know, in case things go wrong."

"That strikes me as absolution enough," he said. "Now it's my turn to thank you. I do, from the bottom of my heart."

Curious still, Viola asked, "Does Mother know you have those medicines?"

"We've never talked about it, not in so many words," he said. "She's less straight-ahead than you are—she'd sooner go around troubles than through them. But I should be astounded if she didn't."

"'Sooner go around than through.'" Having weighed the words, Viola found herself nodding. "Yes, I think that sounds like her."

"And what of 'sooner go through than around'?" Her father's voice was sly. "Does that remind you of yourself?"

"It might. I do seem to work that way ... as much as any woman can work that way. A woman who bared her face in public these days—just her face, mind, nothing more—would earn more scorn and hatred than Lady Godiva got for riding through Coventry stark naked. Or will you tell me I'm wrong?"

"I only wish I could," Richard Williams said.

Somebody brought down one of Peter's teammates with a tackle savage enough to leave him crumpled on the grass clutching at his knee. Nobody paid any attention to him. The ball squirted free. Footballers from both sides dove after it.

Peter got one hand on it for a moment. Then somebody—he thought it was somebody on his own team, not a foe—dug an elbow into his ribs. "Oof!" he said, and let go. He tried to give as good as he got. Football didn't have many rules anyhow, and not everyone agreed about which rules it did have. One thing everyone did agree about was that, in a pileup of this sort, all the rules flew out the window.

A player on the other team came away with the ball and started running toward the goal line. He passed it to a friend just before a tackle flattened him. A moment later, Peter brought the friend down from behind.

"You bugger!" the other Lincoln's Inn pupil shouted.

"That's what your mother said," Peter answered cheerfully. The other player kicked him. Peter grabbed his ankle and twisted it in ways it wasn't meant to go. They wrestled and punched each other. Nobody tried to separate them. The game went on.

When the sun slid below the horizon and Lincoln's Inn Fields got too dark to play on any longer, Peter's side were declared the winners. He thought the score at the end was 35-18, but he wasn't sure. For one thing, he'd lost track of how many times the two teams had scored. For another, people from different parts of England argued about how many points you got when you touched the ball down beyond the goal line and how many you got for kicking it over the goalposts' crossbar.

He limped toward the refectory. He had a sore knee—someone had kicked him, probably by accident—those aching ribs, a bruise under his left eye, and an ear the fellow who'd grabbed it hadn't quite managed to tear off. "Good match!" he said to the warrior closest to him, who happened to have played for the opposing side.

"Grand match!" the other pupil said. He'd got his nose bloodied; both his face and his shirt showed it. He also kept wiggling his left shoulder, as if something in there didn't work the way it should have. But, like Peter, he was smiling. "All swotting and no play makes Johnny a dull bloke!"

"There you go! Not much further removed from inheritances and contracts than football, is there?" Peter said.

"I should say not. Who was the Greek chap who said you could tell a philosopher because he'd go on living the same way if all laws were done away with?"

"Pyrrho of Elis." Peter had run across that very line in his reading not long before. He chuckled. "Only goes to show old Pyrrho never saw a football match, wouldn't you say?"

His recent foe laughed and stuck out his hand. "You're right, by God! I know your face but not your name. I'm Bob Wright."

"Peter Drinkwater, at your service." Peter clasped with him.

"You're Drinkwater? The fellow who turned his mock trial inside out because the scribe made a mistake?" Wright shook hands with him all over again. "Anybody who could make Master Heath stop and consider is aces in my deck."

"I got lucky. If the mistake hadn't been there, I didn't have a prayer," Peter said.

"But you saw it, you ran with it, and nobody could tackle you till you got over the line, not even the master," Wright replied.

"You give me too much credit," Peter said.

"Just the opposite—you're too modest."

"I'm a modest man with plenty to be modest about, believe me."

Bob Wright laughed again. "That's nicely put. Not true, I'm sure, but nicely put. Is it yours or did you hear it somewhere?"

"My father says it. I don't know if he made it up or heard it from someone else," Peter answered. "If he heard it, it's likely from his particular friend, a doctor whose daughter I'm going to marry when I finish here." *I pray I'm going to marry Viola*, Peter added, but only to himself.

"I've got a girl waiting for me, too. A lot of us do," Wright said, nodding. "Is your pa another doctor?"

"No, he also practices law. I'm a chip off the old block. He calls me a chip off the old blockhead."

Bob Wright grinned. "By God, I like your old man! Where does he hang out his shingle? Somewhere in the West Country, by the way you speak." In the last sentence, he buzzed his s's so they sounded like z's, as people from places like Cornwall and Devon and Wiltshire had a way of doing.

"That's right. Salisbury," Peter said.

"All I know about it is, it's got a grand cathedral and Stonehenge is somewhere close by." Wright talked like a Londoner. He seemed to think like a Londoner, too. To folk from the capital, from the great metropolis, the rest of the kingdom was nothing but a blur of unimportant places. To them, if you weren't from London, you were as much a barbarian as a trousered Gaul gawking on the streets of ancient Rome would have been.

Most of the Londoners at Lincoln's Inn had that attitude. Walter Haywood certainly did. Bob Wright was more polite about it than Walter was. Maybe Bob didn't come from quite so much money.

As if thinking of Walter were enough to conjure him up out of thin air, he waved to Peter. "Hail the conquering hero!" he called.

"I didn't see *you* out there," Peter said pointedly.

"No, and you won't, either," Haywood answered. "I've had too much football, and I don't consider bleeding all over myself to be a sport, unlike some people I could name." He sent Wright a sidelong glance.

Wright gave back the horns, which made Walter snort. "You two plainly know each other," Bob remarked.

"I'm afraid we do, yes," Walter said in lugubrious tones. "Peter also infests the room they gave me."

"That 'also' says you infest it, too," Peter observed.

"I wouldn't begin to tell you anything different," Walter said. "I'm as squalid a bedbug as ever drew blood at any of the Inns of Court. Well, with one possible exception." As he mimed scratching a bug bite, he kept his eyes on Bob Wright.

"You can call me a bedbug if you care to, old chap, but if you call me a squalid bedbug you've gone over the line," Wright said with dignity.

He and Peter and Walter were all laughing as they climbed the stairs. Peter's knee didn't care to go up steps, but he ignored it. In the refectory, they got bowls of stew and mugs of beer no better than it had to be. "This is sorry stuff," Haywood said, which hadn't kept him from draining his mug faster than either Peter or Bob. "We should head for a tavern and find something worth drinking."

"I'll pass," Peter said quickly. He wasn't about to let Walter get him drunk again.

"Spoilsport." Walter turned to Bob Wright. "Are you game? All kinds of fun we can find after a few pints."

"Thanks, but I don't think so. You take more chances than I feel easy with," Wright said. Did everybody in Lincoln's Inn know about Walter's habits? It seemed that way to Peter.

Haywood himself was neither offended nor abashed. "I have more fun than you do, you mean. I've fucked myself silly—"

"Sillier," Peter broke in.

"Sillier. Thank you. Yes. I've fucked myself sillier, I should say, ever since I first had hair down there, and I'm right as rain. You don't know what you're missing, I'll tell you that."

Right as rain? How many times had he wound up with a dose of clap? More than once: that was as much as Peter knew. As for the other, though …. Drunk as Peter'd been, now he did understand how much more marvelous a woman was than his hand ever could be. He stayed in the refectory even so, while Walter went out to play the game he loved best: the dance with death.

Viola peered out from the windows that didn't let prying eyes peer in. "They're here!" she said.

"Remember, everyone," her mother warned, "they don't know we know about Peter's worries. They may not know about those themselves. Father says Alf Drinkwater doesn't show any signs of knowing."

"We won't forget," Kate said.

"That's right." Margaret nodded. She was the one Viola worried about, both because she was the youngest and because she had the habit—unfortunate in one who'd been born a woman—of saying what she thought. Short of gagging her and tying her up in a closet, though, Viola didn't see what she could do about it.

"I'll go let them in." Jane Williams hurried for the stairs.

Like Portuguese men o' war scudding across the ocean on the breeze, the Drinkwater women came to the front door. When that simile crossed Viola's mind, she realized she'd read more travel narratives than were good for her. But that was what the shapeless masses of their street costumes put her in mind of.

Someone down below knocked on the door. Viola's mother opened it. She and the Drinkwaters exclaimed about how glad they were to see one another. Then they all came upstairs.

"It's very nice here," Amanda Drinkwater said when they'd entered the house's women's quarters. She went on, "Nobody here but us hens now, so we don't need to worry about masks for a while." She unveiled and took off her headscarf. Her two daughters followed her lead.

Viola dropped a curtsy. "Good morning, Missus Drinkwater. Good morning, Julietta, Joanna," she said, and presented her own sisters, reminding the visitors of who was who.

"I hope no one gave you trouble on the way over here," Kate said. If that wasn't one of the most common things women said to one another all around the world, Viola couldn't imagine what would be. Men, after all, remained men all around the world.

"Only the usual hoots," Julietta said. With her square face and dark hair, she looked more like Peter than Joanna did.

Joanna said, "No, that one fellow on the riverbank grabbed himself." She made as if to clutch her crotch.

"I didn't see him," Julietta said.

"Neither did I." Amanda Drinkwater added, "I would've given the filthy scut a piece of my mind if I had."

"I did that when somebody pinched my bum not long ago," Viola said. "It made me feel better, but it didn't really help. Not as if men care about anything like that."

"Not as if men care about anything. Leave it right there," Julietta said. Nobody else tried to tell her she was wrong.

Staying with the thought that had crossed her mind before, Viola said, "All over the world, women who get together with other women are bound to talk like this."

Amanda Drinkwater smiled at her. "Well, of course they are, my dear." By her expression, she was only just realizing her daugher-in-law-to-be had a working brain. She seemed to like the idea, anyhow, which made Viola feel a bit better. And, after a moment, she continued, "After all, where in the world are men anything but beasts?"

No, you don't know about Peter, Viola thought. *You wouldn't talk that way if you did. And I'm twice as sure you don't know what Father told me about your husband.*

"Excuse me a moment," her own mother said, and went downstairs.

Viola hardly noticed. Another notion had crossed her mind, one she didn't want to lose. To make sure she wouldn't, she inked a pen and scribbled herself a note. As casually as she could, she turned it upside down to keep anyone else from reading it—though her quick scrawl might have taken care of that.

"What were you writing?" Joanna asked, reasonably enough.

"Just something to remind me of what I need to do." Viola tried to sound casual, too. "Things fall into my head from one side and fall out the other." She touched first her left ear, then her right.

Joanna, Julietta, and their mother all smiled and chuckled. But Julietta said, "Really? Peter's letters make you sound clever as a Jesuit."

"He does me too much credit!" Viola exclaimed. She hoped she wasn't doing Peter too much credit by thinking him unlikely to be taken by the Wasting at his first taste of sin.

Before Julietta could answer, Jane Williams came back to the women's quarters with a tray that held a teapot, a small pitcher of milk, a sugar loaf, and plates of biscuits and scones. Drinkwaters and Williamses fell on the snacks with glad cries. "I must get your recipe!" Mrs. Drinkwater said.

"Viola knows them. She's a better baker than I am," Jane Williams answered.

"I am not!" Viola denied it most sincerely.

The women from the two families chatted and gossiped for an hour, or a bit more. Viola got on well with the Drinkwaters. They seemed willing to let her be what she was, even once part of what she was was Peter's wife. More than that, she could hardly ask for.

And she made sure she rescued the note she'd turned face down. She had no idea whether she could manage what she'd thought of, but she wanted to find out. If she could, she might be someone people noticed and remembered even if she was a woman. If she tried and failed, on the other hand, how would she be worse off? She wouldn't, not so far as she could tell.

Walter Haywood slammed his fat lawbook shut. It made a noise like a gunshot, and also made Peter jump. "What did you do that for?" Peter asked. "You scared me out of a year's growth."

"Sorry, old man." For once, Walter sounded as if he meant it. After answering, he yawned till the hinges of his jaws creaked loud enough for Peter to hear. They creaked again when he closed his mouth. "I'm going to curl up and fall asleep. I'm too fagged out to swot any more."

"Maybe you wouldn't be if you didn't burn the candle at both ends every chance you get," Peter remarked, less kindly than he might have.

His roommate gave back a filthy gesture, but his heart didn't seem in it. "Not like that. I know what that's like—sure as the devil I do," Haywood said. "But I always get over that in a hurry. This feels different, like I'm walking around with a load of lead in my pockets so I weigh half again as much as I ought to." He yawned once more, not quite so widely this time.

"What are you reading there?" Peter pointed at the leather-bound volume on Haywood's lap.

"Sanford and Merton, *On Torts*," Walter replied.

"Well, there you are!" Peter said. "I plowed through that last week. It'll send you to Slumberland quick as if you'd been coshed—it's poppy juice in print, nothing else but. You'll be better in the morning."

"I hope so. I feel like a cooked sausage that's been sitting on the counter for a couple of days after it came out of the pan, know what I mean? You pick it up and you sniff it, and you can't make out whether it's off or not. Maybe nothing will happen if you eat it, or maybe you'll spend the next two days puking your guts up."

"There's a cheery picture!" Peter had done things like that—who hadn't? He'd paid for it a few times, too. Again, who hadn't?

"Isn't it, though?" With what looked like a real effort, Haywood picked up the tome and set it on his nightstand. Sanford and Merton made heavy going, whether metaphorically or literally. "A solid night's sleep won't do me any harm, that's certain."

"Now you're making good sense. You should try it more often," Peter said.

"Such a funny fellow. See? I'm laughing." Walter bared his teeth in a ghastly grin.

Then he unbuttoned his shirt and pulled it off over his head. "No wonder you feel off! You've got a rash on your chest—on your back, too." Peter pointed. "Didn't you have chickenpox and the measles when you were a little fellow?"

"Of course I did. Everybody did, near enough," Walter answered. "I hated the measles. I was sick as a hound, and my mother kept the curtains in my room closed for ten days so the light wouldn't hurt my eyes. Christ, I was bored—as bored as I've ever been till I opened up Sanford and Merton here."

"That sounds familiar—my mother did the same thing with me," Peter said. "All right, you don't have those. You can only get those once. But you've got *something*."

Haywood peered down at himself. "Damned if I don't. I never even noticed. I wonder if all this just popped up today out of nowhere."

"Does it itch?" Peter asked.

"Not really. It's just—there. I daresay I would've paid attention to it if it itched." Peter let his trousers fall. "It's on my legs, too, or some of it is. A cousin of mine gets all red and blotchy if he eats strawberries, and he loves 'em, too, poor bugger. I wonder if it's like that."

"Don't ask me. I'm not a doctor." Peter wondered what Viola's father would make of the rash. He turned the subject: "Will it bother you if I go on reading for a while?"

"Not a chance," his roommate answered, donning his nightshirt. "Right now, I think I could sleep through the noisiest verses in Revelations." He pulled back the bedspread and got under the blankets and sheets, then tugged the spread up again for extra warmth. "Good night." He blew out his candle.

"I hope you feel better tomorrow," Peter said.

"That would be good. Don't want the lovely ladies of London missing me for too very long, do we?" Haywood said.

In spite of himself, Peter snorted. If ever the word *incorrigible* had been invented to fit anybody in particular, his roommate was the one. Before long, Walter started snoring. Peter read a while longer. Legal prose set in small print eventually started gluing his eyelids together, too. He didn't stay awake longer than a minute after snuffing out his own fat candle.

Next thing he knew, the villain who banged on pupils' doors to summon them to breakfast was performing his evil office. Bounced out of bed, Peter started getting dressed. "Time to rise and shine," he said.

Walter didn't answer him; he was still snoring away, now on a slightly lower note than the one he'd used on falling asleep the night before. Peter stared at him, genuinely impressed. Anyone who could sleep through the Door Pounder's loving ministrations could sleep through the end of the world.

Peter went over and shook Haywood. That broke the rhythm of his roommate's snores. "What is it?" Walter asked blearily.

"Rise and shine, sweetheart. It's breakfast time," Peter said. "You were sleeping so hard, you might as well have been a wintertime dormouse. If you hadn't been making a horrible racket, I should've guessed you were dead."

"Not yet, old man. Not yet." Walter Haywood stood up, yawned, stretched, and twisted till the joints in his spine cracked like knuckles. He pulled off his nightshirt. "Well, I'm still bumpy," he said, and yawned again. "I'm still sleepy, too. That's why God created coffee and tea, isn't it?"

"You'd need to ask a priest or a monk about natural law. I have enough trouble with the ones people hammered together." Peter ran a comb through his hair. He rubbed his chin. His beard wasn't very dark or very thick yet; he decided he could get away without shaving this morning.

He glanced over at Walter, who was still putting on his own clothes. *At least he's moving*, Peter thought.

Down the stairs they went. By the racket coming from the refectory, they were late to the feast. Bob Wright waved to Peter. "I thought you'd decided to hibernate," he called, and patted the bench beside him.

"Walter was the one who didn't want to wake up." Peter blamed Haywood without hesitation. Why not? He'd earned it.

Even though they could have got there sooner, there were still enough fried potatoes and blood pudding to go around. Peter strewed salt from a pewter saltcellar onto his potatoes; they were insipid this morning. He drank tea. Sure enough, Walter poured down several cups of coffee.

"You'll be pissing like a racehorse," Peter predicted.

"Probably. I don't care, as long as I don't feel like curling up in bed any more—by myself, you understand, not with a pretty girl."

"Braggart." Bob Wright's grin said not to take him too seriously.

"It could be." Haywood grinned back. "I am a boastful man with plenty to be boastful about." He'd not only remembered Peter's line from a little while, he'd adapted it to suit his purpose.

"Oh, nicely put!" Wright made as if to clap his hands.

"I have a way of listening to people I hang around with." Walter nodded toward Peter, which knocked any thought of plagiarism over the head.

"You're giving me credit? You *must* not be feeling well," Peter said.

"Citing my sources, as a proper solicitor should," Haywood answered. "You see? I've learnt something here after all."

"Have you learned to pass the potatoes? I could use some more," Peter said.

Pass them Haywood did. "You're a bottomless pit, is what you are."

"Bottomless? My thundermug tells me otherwise," Peter replied. Haywood and Wright both made horrible faces. Disgusting his roommate pleased Peter.

"Are you writing again?" Margaret asked.

"No, dearie." Viola shook her head and answered with the relentless precision that marked her as her father's daughter: "I'm writing still."

"That's going to be the longest letter in the history of letters," her sister said.

"It's not going to be a letter. It's going to be a book, or I hope it will," Viola said.

"A book? What kind of book?"

"A book about travel to far places. One far place in particular."

Margaret looked at her as if she were a common lunatic. A lunatic, Viola was willing to believe herself to be, but not a common one. Margaret pointed out the obvious: "How can you write about far places when you're a woman and you haven't been anywhere?"

"Because they're imaginary far places. An island off the west coast of North America that isn't really there, in particular," Viola answered.

Her sister screwed up her face. "Who'd want to read about places that aren't really there?"

"Well, you need to have imaginary far places to have imaginary people on them, and the people who live on this island that isn't really there aren't real, either." Listening to herself, Viola was uneasily aware that she sounded like a lunatic trying to convince an ordinary person she wasn't in fact daft.

The way Margaret looked at her warned her she sounded that way to her sister, too. "What's so special about these imaginary people? Why are you writing about them? It sounds like a waste of time, if you ask me."

"I didn't ask you," Viola said sweetly. She was convinced little sisters were the biggest nuisances in the world. She knew some people claimed little brothers held that title, but there she lacked standards of comparison. After a moment, she went on, "What's so special about these people is, they're as civilized as we are, only they've never, ever heard of the Wasting."

"Ohhh." The word came out of Margaret's mouth as a soft sigh. Little sister she might be, and big nuisance, too. But even she understood what a gigantic change that would make. "What are they like? Can I read it?"

"Now you're interested, are you?" Viola said.

"Of course I am. Who wouldn't be?"

Viola smiled at how eager Margaret sounded. "You can read it when it's all finished, if it ever is. Or when I say you can. Not till then, you hear me? If you try sneaking peeks, I'll make you sorry. And I'm going to tell Father what I just told you. He'll make you even sorrier, I promise."

She knew Margaret didn't worry about her. Little sisters never worried about big sisters, except when it came to how to get around them. But all of the Williams girls took their father seriously. So did everyone else who'd met him, as best Viola could judge.

"All right, all right, I won't bother your stupid papers until you say," Margaret replied. Viola heard the unspoken *unless I'm sure I can get away with it*. She would have been more annoyed if she'd expected anything else.

Later that afternoon, she put her ear to the door that connected the surgery to the rest of the house. Not hearing anything, she tapped at the door. A moment later, Richard Williams opened it. "Hello, dear," he said. "Does someone need me? Did something go wrong?"

"No, or I hope not, anyhow," Viola said. "Do you remember how, after you saw my letter to Peter, you told me I wrote well enough to write a book people might want to read?"

"I'm not likely to forget that. I meant it. Why?"

"Because I'm trying to write one." Telling her sister had been easy. Telling her father felt weightier, *realer*, to Viola.

His left eyebrow, the quizzical one, jumped a little. "Are you? Have you got a name for it yet?"

"I'm calling it *A Voyage to the Island of the Temeculans*." Giving him the title felt weightier, too.

"There are several atlases in the house. If I were to look for this island in them, would I find it?"

"I'd be surprised if you did."

He cupped his chin in his hand. "Where do you imagine it to lie?"

"Off the west coast of North America," Viola said, as she had to Margaret.

Her father nodded. "That is a good place for it, I think. Those seas still are not so well known as they might be."

"The same thought occurred to me," Viola said. Not for nothing had she read all those accounts of voyages to the back of beyond— and every single one, every damned one, written by a man!

"And what are the Temeculans, that you are mindful of them?" He trusted her enough to tease her with a bit of the Psalms, casting her in the role of God.

She smiled, but gave back a serious answer: "A civilized folk who've never met the Wasting."

"You have my attention," he said at once. "When you've got some of it into a shape someone else might see, I'd love to take a look."

"When I do, you'll see it." That reminded Viola to pass on the warning or threat or whatever it was she'd made to Margaret.

He laughed. "I don't think you need to worry about that. But if you do, I'll take care of it." He was more optimistic than she was, but she didn't tell him so.

XI

"How are you feeling this morning?" Peter asked Walter Haywood as they got ready for breakfast.

"I'm getting better. You haven't had to shake me awake in the morning for more than a week now, have you?" Walter said.

"I shouldn't have to shake you awake at all. The bugger who bangs on doors would rouse the dead," Peter replied.

Haywood went on as if he hadn't spoken: "This bloody rash is going away, too." He pulled up his shirt so Peter could see his torso. He told the truth, too; he wasn't nearly so blotchy and bumpy as he had been when he first came down with whatever he'd caught. He also had a theory about that: "Must have been the grippe, or something like it."

"You're studying medicine and law at the same time?" Peter suggested. Walter made a face at him. If he was studying medicine, Peter didn't think he was studying very hard. Well, he didn't always study law very hard, either. But who came down with the grippe all by his lonesome? When you got the grippe, half the people you know commonly caught it at the same time.

Peter didn't argue. He didn't see the point, especially when doctors couldn't do much about disease anyhow (Viola's letters talked about how much that irked and frustrated her father). He didn't want to imagine any other possibilities. Neither did Walter, no doubt. He buckled on his shoes and said, "Let's go feed our faces."

"Yes, let's." Walter nodded. "I've got an appetite. First time in a while, it feels like. I've got a couple of appetites, in fact. Been a while now since I lay down with a pretty girl."

"Maybe you should wait till your bumps are all gone, or you won't find a girl who wants to lie down with you," Peter said.

"Maybe. Or maybe a few extra shillings on the nightstand will convince her I'm as handsome as I always was." Haywood was one of those people dead sure money could make everything right. Peter had never lacked for it, but he'd also never had enough to give him an attitude like that. Then again, his roommate was also much more enamored of himself than he was. Walter didn't have sisters or brothers to take him down a peg when he needed it.

At the refectory table, Walter shoveled in barley mush and greasy sausages as if afraid they'd outlaw food at a minute past noon. He hadn't done that lately. He hadn't ever really done it; he was one of the many who complained the food at Lincoln's Inn didn't measure up to what they got at home. Peter felt the same way, but ate it without grumbling. If they set food in front of him, he'd make it disappear. With Haywood now, he took gluttony as a good sign.

Along with several others, he gave a mock peroration before Master Heath. The legal scholar scribbled notes as each pupil spoke and critiqued each one after he finished. With Peter, he was short and to the point: "Everything is in its place. Each point follows logically from the one before it. Were that the only requisite, you'd never lose a case. But you must also make a judge—and, even more, a jury—*listen* to you, not merely hear you. There, you still have more work to do."

"How do I go about it, Master?" Peter asked. He'd also worried that he needed more fire than he knew how to bring to bear.

Stephen Heath only shrugged. "You may find it within yourself. It is possible, though far from sure, that study with an orator or an actor would give you what you need. Or you may never find it, in which case you will make a splendid solicitor or a capable barrister but not an inspired one. Many worse things have happened, believe me."

Peter's own father was a solicitor. He'd never stopped to wonder why the man who'd begot him wasn't a barrister, let alone an inspired one. Wouldn't an inspired barrister have come to London to show off his talents on the biggest, most brightly lit stage in

England? If Master Heath thought he might make a capable barrister, he had to agree—many worse things had happened. And he liked Salisbury fine.

He and Walter were studying in their rooms that night when someone knocked on the door. "Oh, sweet Jesus!" Haywood said. "If that's dear Eb, tell him I'm molting."

"Tell him what?" Peter said. Haywood threw his hands in the air. Peter went to the door and opened it. "Good evening, Master Cooke. I hope you're well."

"God be praised, I am, thankee." The tall, scrawny American ducked into the room. "And God gi' you good evenin', young Master Haywood. There's some baccy down to the piers as wants gradin' an' pricin'."

"There would be," Walter said darkly. "Does my father want me to learn the law or to learn too much about tobacco?"

"Why, both, o' course. If you're to run the business after him—though may he live a hundred an' twenty years, like Moses in the good book—you cain't have but one string for your bow." Ebenezer Cooke took that as much for granted as he did Moses' long lifespan.

"Trying to do both of them at once is a confounded nuisance, though," Haywood said with great feeling.

"Reckon it ain't no worse'n dodging wild red men an' bars an' catamounts," Cooke replied. Peter needed a moment to realize he meant *bears*; he didn't seem to realize how barbarous his accent was. Peter knew catamounts lived in America and were smaller than lions but bigger than pussycats. Past that, his knowledge of them failed. He wasn't even sure whether the London Zoological Gardens displayed any.

"All right. All *right*. I'll look at the God-damned tobacco, God damn it. And then, when we're through on the docks, we'll go and do what *I* want to do." Walter eyed his father's factor with an unmistakable glint in his eye.

Cooke flinched. "You just took the name o' the Lord in vain. Twice. How many more commandments d'you aim to break tonight?"

"As many as I can!" Walter said. Ebenezer Cooke flinched again, less, Peter judged, at the blasphemy than at the gaiety with which Haywood answered.

The room was quiet and peaceful with Walter out of it. Peter sighed as he got down to work again. He wished he had one all to himself. Some second-year pupils did. The privilege of privacy cost extra, of course. Till now, he hadn't thought about bearding his father for anything beyond the basics. But if he could persuade him a room of his own was a necessity, not a luxury …

He imagined himself delivering a peroration not to Master Heath but to his pater. He would be logical. He would be organized. And he would be fiery! If anything could inspire him to grand flights of rhetoric, it was the thought of not having to cope with a roommate again.

Walter Haywood came back some time in the middle of the night. He was singing under his breath, but not far enough under. "Keep it down to a low roar, can you?" Peter knew he sounded annoyed. He was.

"Sorry, old man." Haywood sounded not the least bit sorry. "What a night! Rose had tits like pillows and a cunt tight as a flea's arsehole. Oh, didn't she just!" He sighed rapturously. Peter could smell wine coming off him, too.

"Shut up and go to bed," he said.

"Have to towel myself off first. Rain's coming down in buckets out there. Summer is over, it truly is."

He kept on singing as he dried himself. Peter rolled away from the noise and buried his head under his pillow. It didn't help enough.

Haywood threw himself onto the mattress. The bedframe squeaked. *He must have made the bedframe at Madam Henderson's squeak, too,* Peter thought irritably. Either this Rose hadn't worried about his rash or he'd paid her enough so she'd pretended she didn't.

No more than two minutes later, Walter started to snore. That irritated Peter, too. He stayed awake quite a while himself. Not having a clock whose hands he could see, he didn't know just how long. Longer than he cared to—he knew that. Some of the curses he aimed at Walter deserved remembering, though no typesetter would have dared immoralize them in print. His own eyes slid shut at last.

Who felt gloomier and more ill-used the next morning was anyone's guess. Neither Peter nor Walter Haywood had much to say as they dressed and shambled downstairs to the refectory.

Walter bolted his food, then headed back up to the room. "Have to make up the swotting I didn't do last night," he said to Peter over his shoulder as he left.

"Have fun," Peter told him. Haywood gave back an answer imperfectly amused. Peter … smiled.

Viola soon discovered you couldn't, or at least she couldn't, write a book every waking moment of the day. Her first bright flash of inspirations faded after a day and a half. Not only that, she had work to do around the house: washing, sewing, cleaning, cooking, and everything else that added up to ordinary life. Sometimes she even enjoyed talking with her family or reading a book she wasn't working on herself.

But she stuck to it. She found that, if she could steal an hour or two a day, she would get a page or two done. It was less than she'd imagined she'd turn out every day, but enough to keep her moving forward.

"Where inspiration fails, perspiration can pull you through," she said after finishing a session.

"Perspiration? Where?" Kate answered. It wasn't cold yet, but it was chilly, and it had rained on and off through the past week. Most of the birds had flown south for the winter. The trees were losing their leaves.

"Even if it's nasty outside, what I'm doing makes me sweat." After a moment, Viola added, "It's harder than I thought it would be."

"Which probably explains why more people don't write books," Kate said.

"I suppose it might," Viola said in some surprise. "We'd be up to our eyebrows in them if everybody did, wouldn't we?"

"Deeper than that, I'd say." Her sister fixed her with a speculative stare. "When do the rest of us get to see what you've been up to? What are your Temeculans like?"

"Let me get more done, so what you do see makes some sense," Viola replied uncomfortably. She'd shown their father what she was doing as she was doing it, but hadn't told anyone else about that. She'd asked him not to say anything, either. And he hadn't. If a doctor needed to know how to do anything, it was keep his mouth shut. Father, she was sure, would have been good at that no matter what line of work he found himself in.

"What will you do when you finish it?" Kate asked.

"Why, try to publish it, of course," Viola said. "There are lady authors, you know. It's one of the things we can do without letting any men get a glimpse of us." She didn't try to hide her bitterness at how unfair the world was. Some of that—quite a lot of it, in fact—came out in the book, too.

"Yes, of course. I only wish music worked the same way." Kate sounded wistful—no, sad. You had to be close to the people who were playing for you to hear them. Music couldn't be trapped forever, the way words could. When Homer smote his ancient lyre, his poetry would have been every bit as evanescent.

Of course, when Homer smote his ancient lyre, it wouldn't have mattered so much, because the Wasting lay thousands of years in his future.

"I'm sorry, dear." Viola knew how well her sister played the harpsichord. Were she a man, she might have made a good living doing it. A man she was not, nor any kind of musician who could make a living with flashing fingers.

Kate sighed. "So am I. Nothing to be done about it, though, not the way things are." She hesitated, then asked, "What do you suppose your intended will think of being yoked to a lady author?"

Viola ran into that question headlong, as if it were a stone wall in her path she somehow hadn't seen. "I don't know," she said slowly. "I'll have to find out, won't I?"

"Her mother and sisters are nice enough. And his father and Father have been particular friends since they were boys. You have some hope, anyhow."

"Hope of not being cast out of the nest to starve under the tree? Huzzah!" Viola wondered what Peter would make, not so much of her being a lady author, but of the book she was writing. She said, "Do you really want to hear about the Temeculans? You've already heard what you need to know. They are as wise as we are. They are as pious as we are. And they have never met the Wasting."

163

"Yes, that's what Margaret told me," Kate said. "Now I can't wait until you let me see some of it. I can't wait for you to write more, either."

"I'm working on it. I'm not as fast as I hoped I would be, but I'm working on it. Oh! Do something for me?"

"What is it?"

"Remind Margaret I'll know if she tries sneaking a peek at what I'm up to. I said that once, but would you tell her again, please? And tell her I'll make her sorry if she does."

"You aren't saying that to me," Kate remarked.

"With you, I didn't imagine I needed to. Was I wrong?"

"You never can tell." But Kate sounded mischievous, not like someone who aimed to go manuscript-hunting.

Viola stuck out her tongue at her. "You really never can tell with the little one, though." There, if anything, she understated. Margaret was a law unto herself.

"Think so, do you?" Instead of sticking out her tongue, Kate stuck it in her cheek. Viola burst out laughing. Kate knew the youngest Williams as well as she did, and went on, "If you want to keep it safe, maybe you ought to find out whether Father has a lockbox of the right size he'd let you use."

"That's a grand idea!" After a moment, Viola added, "If Margaret doesn't know how to pick locks, I mean."

"I've never seen her try," Kate answered, which was as much as anyone could safely say about Margaret.

Richard Williams did indeed have a spare lockbox. He needed to try several keys before he found the one that made it an unlocked box. "Here you are, dear. Hoping to hold snoopers at bay?"

"One, anyhow," Viola said.

Her father chuckled. "It would be more than one if you weren't already letting me see what you're up to."

"Do you think it will ever come to anything?"

His grin disappeared; he recognized a serious question. "I think it may," he said slowly. "It is as good a jape on travelers' tales as any I've ever seen. It will amuse people. It will make them think, too. We've lived the way we've lived for a great many years now. We take it for granted. No one remembers when we lived any other way. No old man's grandfather would have remembered when we did. No one stops to wonder, *What would things be like if we didn't need to do this?*"

Viola found her father an admirable man. At this moment, though, she found him just a man. "Forgive me for contradicting you, Papa," she said, "but women stop to wonder that every hour of every day of every week of every month of every year."

"A hit! A palpable hit!" he exclaimed, and clapped his hands to his chest as if struck square by a musket ball. "Well, you're bound to be right there, I'm sure. I cry your pardon for not realizing it myself."

"Not many men would say even so much." Viola wondered what Peter would say if and when he saw the manuscript—or perhaps even a copy of the finished book.

Her father's mind ran in a different direction. "If a publisher should want to put it into print, I do hope he'll be able to get a *nihil obstat* and the *imprimatur* from the Church."

"Aii!" Viola wanted to scream louder than she did. She hadn't worried about that one bit. "I hope it won't be too hard. The Temeculans aren't shown as Christians, after all."

"True, but the way they do things is shown to have the author's approval. A *censor librorum* may frown on men and women strolling the city streets together, none of them wearing any more than they did when they came into the world to begin with."

"I show them as nude, not naked. They don't do it to arouse one another, but because they take nudity for granted. They can do that, lacking the dreadful knowledge of the Wasting we have."

"They can, but would they? Our ancestors didn't before the disease afflicted us."

"Temecula has a better climate than England does. Than anywhere in Europe does. I've already said that in the story. I'll say it again, more strongly. I'll make it so, if you were choosing only for the weather, you'd leave heaven to go to Temecula."

Her father laughed. "That might do it. And you can hope to find a censor who won't even blink. As long as you don't come right out and attack doctrine, your chances aren't bad. They don't go after dirty stories and pictures the way they did in bygone times."

"They'd better not! Those stories and pictures are what people use instead of—" Viola stopped, unsure how to go on.

"Instead of one another," her father finished for her. She nodded, admiring his precision. He continued, "It may be nothing. Or a publisher may know of an easygoing censor, or one whose palm he can grease to make sure he's easygoing."

"That would do it." Viola knew priests were as corruptible as any other mortals. As corruptible in every way; it wasn't as if priests didn't die of the Wasting.

"I hope that would do it," Richard Williams said. "If you just had a dirty story here, I'm sure it would. But making people want to play with themselves is one thing. Making them think about how the world works, and how it *should* work, is something else again, something more dangerous."

"I'm not going to change my point," Viola said. "If not for that, why would I write the book to begin with?"

"I understand you. I can think of a place or two where you may not care to beat your reader over the head with it, though," he replied. "Isn't it like salt in a stew? Some makes it better, but too much makes you want to stop eating."

She started to get angry. Then she stopped. She could think of a place or two herself where she'd let rage flow through her pen. "Point them out to me," she said. "If I can soften them without losing my meaning, I will."

"All right. I'm sorry. I don't want to upset you or wound you."

"You aren't, or not for long. I'm learning how to do this. It isn't like writing a letter. That teaches you how to write smoothly, but not how to tell a long, complicated story. And having someone else look at it helps me know where I've gone off my trail."

"I hope so. Oh—one other thing. Make sure you keep the lockbox key where … nobody else can get her hands on it."

He knew perfectly well she was protecting the manuscript from Margaret. Neither Kate nor Jane Williams was likely to snoop without permission. Viola might have herself, had one of them been working on a book. *But I'd only be curious. I wouldn't do it to be a nuisance*, she thought virtuously.

Aloud, she said, "I'll wear it on a string around my neck, even when I'm sleeping."

"That ... may do it," her father said. He and Viola smiled at each other.

The fall rains went on and on. It rained a lot in England, of course, at any season of the year. Some of what fell from the sky seemed genial, some harsh. These were the kind of rains Viola could have done without—hard, cold, lashed on by the wind so they scoured the last leaves off the trees and beat at your face if you had to go outside.

They didn't seem to want to let up, either. The Avon filled its banks and slopped over. The Williams home lay only a few blocks south of the river, and, to Viola's way of thinking, not far enough above it. How far could the waters spread?

Gamely, Jane Williams said, "We've never flooded yet, not in all the years I've lived here."

"There's always a first time," Margaret said. Viola would have put up with that better had her sister not sounded so cheerful about it. Thinking that made her notice the lockbox key between her breasts, which by now she mostly didn't. Margaret's tone and the need to stow that key there somehow went together.

"I don't think this will be it," Richard Williams said. "I do worry about the bridges, though. The river's running as hard as I ever remember. If a pier or two goes down and they fall into the water ... I shouldn't want to have to row across, or get rowed, when we need to visit the shops and markets in the middle of town." After a beat, he added, "I shouldn't care to be cut off from the cathedral, either."

"Of course not. Neither should I," his wife said.

They were sitting at the table, finishing up a supper of stewed chicken, all pretty much at the sopping-up-gravy-with-a-piece-of-bread stage. Viola looked down at her plate so she wouldn't say what she was thinking. The family went to church on Sundays, took communion, and regularly confessed their sins (or some of them) and did penance for them.

Nothing unusual about that. Almost everyone in England did: everyone but the handful who followed Luther's schismatic doctrine or Calvin's and the even smaller handful of Jews. Looking at them from the outside, nobody would have thought the Williamses at all unusual. From the inside ...

Viola wasn't sure when she'd realized her parents were mostly go-ing through the motions of religion to keep the authorities in the wider world from troubling the family. It had been a while now; she hadn't been shut up in the women's quarters yet. She hadn't talked about it with Mother or Father. They kept quiet about it, so she did, too.

After a while, she decided it was a comfortable way to live. They rendered unto Caesar the things that were Caesar's, and unto God the things that were God's. And if, in private, they didn't render so very much unto God, well, whose business was that but theirs?

She wondered how the Drinkwaters felt about such things. *Have to ask Father*, she thought. She didn't suppose he would have stayed particular friends with Alfred Drinkwater if Peter's father clung to all the conventional pieties. And he practiced law. If that wasn't corrosive of piety and of taking things for granted, she had trouble imagining what would be.

After supper, she scoured the iron forks and knives and spoons with sand to scrub away any tiny flecks of rust. They weren't rich enough to eat with silver all the time. Silver was easier to care for than iron, but even it tarnished.

"Is the book going well?" Unlike Margaret, Kate didn't sound as if she was prying. If she was, she was doing it in a pleasant tone of voice.

"It's going, anyhow," Viola answered. "I don't like how short the days are getting, though. You can write by candlelight or lamplight, but I don't want to do it any more than I have to."

"Even when we can see the sun, it just scurries across the sky from rising to setting," Kate agreed. "And we've hardly seen it at all the past fortnight."

"I know. I always get gloomy this time of year. Everything else in the world seems to—why shouldn't I?" Viola said.

"Because we have to put up with you," her mother put in. Jane Williams was scrubbing the pot the stew had cooked in.

Margaret would have added *or try to*. She was doing something upstairs, though. Viola heard the gibe even so.

"Think about getting it printed and selling lots of copies," Kate said. "If that doesn't cheer you up, what would?"

"It doesn't seem real," Viola said.

"It doesn't have to, does it? You're writing fiction, after all." Kate winked at her.

Viola winked back, but she answered, "Well, that depends. It isn't true, but I want it to seem as if it were. If I wave a flag under my reader's nose and shout 'This is all made up!' it loses most of the effect I want it to have."

More than anything else, Viola wished Temecula were real. She wanted it to be real. She thought it might have become real by now if the Wasting hadn't blighted the world. She had no way to prove that, of course, but it seemed reasonable to her. Why did men subjugate and hide women? Because of the Wasting, of course. Without it, the two sexes could live together in something more like equality.

Kate said, "I shan't quarrel with you, especially when I haven't seen it."

"Neither have I," Jane Williams said, a certain edge in her voice.

"It won't be too much longer, honestly," Viola said. "Let me get a little further along, and then I'll show you both." She crossed her heart to show she meant it.

"And Margaret?" Kate asked with another wink.

That made Viola think for a moment. Sighing, she nodded. "And Margaret. She'd hate me if everybody else in the family got to look at it and she didn't."

"You're a good sister, dear," her mother said.

"I know." Viola sounded so glum, her mother and Kate both started laughing.

Peter eagerly opened Viola's latest letter. She began it with *My dear Peter*, which made him smile. She'd gone away from that and similar friendly beginnings after he told her about his visit to Madam Henderson's, preferring for a while the dour simplicity of his given name alone. He wanted her to feel friendly toward him. *Till death do us part* could seem forever and a day without friendship.

I hope you continue well, and that you may continue so for many years, she wrote. She hadn't forgotten that visit, then. He knew he could hardly blame her for remembering it. He could blame Walter for pushing him headlong into stupidity, but that didn't mean he hadn't been stupid.

The next few paragraphs talked about the recent rains, the way the Avon had risen till its waters neared the Williams house but didn't quite come in, and other bits of Salisbury news and gossip. He'd heard of or knew most of the people she mentioned; one of them was a longtime client of his father's. And her jaundiced view of that fellow matched his father's, too.

Then she got down to what he took to be the meat of the letter. *As you had a confession for me, so I now have one for you*, she said. *I am writing, or trying to write, a book. It is an account of a voyage to a distant land that—alas!—exists only in my imagination. My father feels it may have some hope of publication should I finish it, and I hope he is right. His judgment in such matters, I think, is better than fair, and likewise his impartiality.*

So it is at least possible, if not yet likely, that you may find yourself yoked for the rest of your life or hers to one of the strangest creatures this poor sorrowing old globe yet knows, the lady author, Viola continued. *Should this prospect alarm you, or indeed any member of your august and eminently respectable family, you might do well to speak now or forever hold your peace.*

She wasn't sardonic just about acquaintances. Peter'd already noticed that. Her cynical perspective included those closer to her as well. He could see why his father'd said her father also had that cast of mind. It seemed to run in the family, sure enough.

Peter scratched his head. He didn't mind the idea of an author as a wife. He did wonder what would happen if she became a highly successful author and drew more notice to herself than a woman was supposed to garner. After a few seconds, he shrugged. As long as no one tried to break down the door to the house—and as long as Viola didn't try to break out from the inside—he didn't imagine it would grow into a problem bigger than he could manage.

Inside his head, he ran that thought back. He never would have even dreamt his sisters or his mother might break out of the house. If not always perfectly content with the way the world worked, they were used to it. Viola's letters told him she was more complicated, more difficult, than that.

He shrugged again. As far as he was concerned, pepper and horseradish perked up a meal. He wished his mother used more of them when she cooked. He suspected a wife with a mind of her own would perk up a marriage.

Walter Haywood walked into the room they shared. "What have you got there?" he asked, and then answered his own question: "A letter from your sweetheart, I'll bet."

"What if I do?" Peter didn't quite growl, but he came close.

"Nothing. Nothing at all. If you want to go back to Salisbury, I'm sure the two of you will be happy as can be there." *If you want to disappear and bury yourself under a flat rock* ... were the words behind the words.

"I like Salisbury," Peter said.

"I know." Had Haywood been a judge condemning Peter to the gallows, the words could have seemed no more damning.

Peter started to get angry. Then he realized his roommate was poking him on purpose. Londoners scorned provincials as naturally as they breathed. Outside the capital, provincials laughed at Londoners just as hard. But that wasn't so easy for a provincial in London. Not only was he vastly outnumbered, but the city was large enough and grand enough to overawe anyone used to a smaller town.

When Peter didn't snarl and bristle, Walter wagged a half-reproachful finger at him. "You're learning, Salisbury boy. One tiny step at a time, you're learning," he said. "Harder to get a rise out of you than it used to be."

"So sorry to disappoint you." Peter thought Viola, and even her father, would have liked the way he delivered his line.

Unabashed, Walter chuckled. "Don't fret yourself. Chances are it'll work next time I try."

"Is that what you said right before you got clapped?" Peter asked innocently.

Haywood bared his teeth for a moment; that got home. But only for a moment. Then the snarl turned into a grin. "Oh, it worked fine then. If it hadn't, I wouldn't have. But I'm done with that now, God be praised."

Would Richard Williams have agreed? Not being a doctor himself, Peter didn't know. He said, "You're not all over red blotches and bumps any more, either."

"I'm not sorry they're gone, let me tell you," Walter replied. "They didn't itch the way chickenpox does, but I don't miss them a bit."

"I can't blame you," Peter said. So many things went wrong with people, and doctors could do so little about so few of them. Peter didn't doubt his prospective father-in-law was as good at his trade as any man could hope to be, but did wonder how he coped with what had to be his many failures.

"Now I'm my magnificent self once more." Walter struck a pose.

"At the very least," Peter said, drier than dry.

Haywood mimed deflating like a popped pig's bladder. They both laughed a little. Then Walter sat down on his bed and pulled out a text full of dogeared pages. "Let's see how much I can get done here before that whoreson Cooke drags me down to the docks again."

"Why do you think he'll come tonight?" Peter asked.

"Because I really need to do … some of this contract, anyhow," Walter said, "and he always shows up when I most need to finish something."

As if to spite him, Ebenezer Cooke didn't appear. Peter also wrestled with the contract. He needed to be concise, if he could. He also needed to be clear, always. *Ambiguity is your enemy*, Master Heath had declared, again and again. And he needed to leave no loopholes. Meeting all the goals at once seemed at least difficult, more likely impossible.

After a while, Walter set down his pen. He was quicker in the attack than Peter, but less dogged and persistent. "Now I almost wish Eb would have pounded on the door, the way he does," he said. "It's not far from the docks to the brothels."

"Do you *always* think with your prong?" Peter said.

"Of course. Why don't you?" Walter answered.

To Peter, the worrying part was that he sounded as if he meant it. He and his roommate eyed each other in perfect mutual incomprehension. At last, Peter said, "We're each of us as God made him. I suppose we may as well leave it there."

"However you please. I have no idea how God made you. He made me to enjoy myself, and I'm going to do it … if I ever get this bloody piece of work done."

"Why do you even care?"

"If I annoy Father *too* much, there's always the worry he'll cut me off without a penny. I'm sure as sure can be I shouldn't enjoy that one bit. So I have to look busy enough to keep him quiet."

Peter would have said *to keep him happy*. As far as he could tell, though, the only person whose happiness worried Walter was Walter.

He sighed and went back to work. He wouldn't let himself worry about Haywood's self-absorption, any more than he did about his clap or his odd rash and lassitude. *They're his affair, and nothing to do with me*, he thought. He had trouble making himself listen. His parents might have raised a Christian after all.

He'd nearly finished when Walter said, "I'm turning in. I've done enough so I can crank out the rest between breakfast and when I've got to give it to Master Heath." He started getting into his nightshirt.

"Do you mind if I keep going?" Peter intended to keep going whether Walter minded or not.

And Walter understood that full well. "Not a bit, not that you'd care if I did. Good night." He blew out his candle. Peter wrote on.

XII

Fog from the Avon shrouded Salisbury. Viola could barely see the henhouse from the back door. She shivered when she closed it behind her; it was chilly inside more than a few feet away from the stove and the fireplace, but it was downright cold out here.

Her feet crunched on the crust that had formed over the snow blanketing the ground. Even through her veil, her breath smoked. She might have left it off. She didn't think anyone from the street could spy her here. But the more she outraged custom in her book, the tighter she clung to it in real life. No one would be able to claim the lady author was a genuine eccentric. She knew what she wrote was fiction.

"Of course I do," she muttered. Her breath smoked more when she spoke. She wasn't surprised. She imagined it wasn't just vapor that showed, but real smoke from the fire of her fury at the way things were.

Then she stopped in her tracks—a fox trit-trotted past. It wasn't carrying a fat chicken in its mouth, anyhow, so it probably hadn't got into the henhouse. It suddenly froze, its sharp ears quirking forward. It crouched, then sprang nosefirst into a snowdrift. When it drew back, a mouse or a vole kicked between its teeth. Off it strutted, seeming as pleased with itself as a cat that had caught a cockroach.

Viola went on to the henhouse. No, the fox hadn't beaten the latch or got in through the windows. Her father had set thick wires across them, vertically and horizontally, and secured those with horseshoe-shaped nails driven into the planking. So far, they'd done what he hoped they would. They let in light and air, but held raiders at bay.

The hens clucked sleepily. She put grain in the feeding trough and poured fresh water into their bowls. What they'd had in there hadn't frozen overnight, which was good. Food and drink got them off their nests. She scooped up three eggs and closed the henhouse again.

"Here you are, Mother," she said when she got back to the house and set the eggs on the kitchen counter.

"Thank you, dear," Jane Williams said, and then, "Only three? I'd hoped for one or two more."

"These are what I found," Viola answered. "The hens aren't as young as they used to be."

"Nobody is," her mother answered.

"Maybe we should enjoy chicken stews and chicken soup for a while and get ourselves some younger birds that make better layers." Barley and parsnips and onions and potatoes danced in Viola's head. "Have we got any leeks? We could pretend to be Scots and make cock-a-leekie."

"Cock-a-leekie is good. I shouldn't care to pretend to be a Scot, though," Mother said.

"Well, neither should I," Viola admitted. Like most English folk, she thought the northern kingdom nothing but a nuisance. Every generation or two, England and Scotland fought a silly little war over the Debatable Lands, which centuries had proved were not worth owning. Every century or so, the Scots allied with France to cause England serious trouble. All the same, Viola continued, "Cock-a-leekie is very good."

"I don't think there are any leeks in the larder. Maybe I can find some in town. If I can't, I know we have plenty of onions."

Viola considered. "It wouldn't be quite the same, would it? But it would still be tasty."

"I was thinking the same thing." Jane Williams smiled.

"Good. We have enough stored away to make it through till spring, I think, even if we don't massacre the hens," Viola said.

"I think so, too, God be praised. We've always managed." Her mother smiled again, this time less pleasantly. "And, of course, half the people your papa takes care of will pay him with bread or bacon or honey from their beehives or rutabaga wine instead of silver."

"I remember the last time he got a jug of rutabaga wine. It was better than I expected it to be."

"Yes, I thought the same thing. That isn't praise, though, or not very much," her mother said.

"I've heard people say it can be tasty if it's made right."

"I've heard the same thing. If it's true, I don't recall our ever getting a jug that was made right."

"Hmm. Neither do I," Viola said.

Jane Williams turned the subject: "I like what you've written. You make your Temecula sound like a real place. And anyone would think you'd sailed around the world three or four times yourself, the way you talk about ships."

"Thank you!" Viola exclaimed; writers soaked in praise the way flowers and trees soaked in sunlight. After a moment, she felt she had to add, "You wait, though. Some man who's really gone to sea will notice something I've done wrong. He'll write my publisher a rude letter, my publisher will forward it on to me, and we'll have to give the postman threepence for the privilege of reading his detailed explanation of how I'm not merely an imbecile but a female imbecile at that, one who's got no business pretending she knows anything at all."

"Whereupon you can write a rude letter back, and make him pay threepence to read your telling him where to head in." Her mother's eyes twinkled.

"A capital idea," Viola said. "I should quite enjoy that."

"You could even work it into the next story you do. A lady author receives a letter of correction. She writes back rebuking and correcting the corrector, a correspondence develops, and romance follows from it."

"That's ... not the worst notion I ever heard." Viola had started to say it was foolish, but the more she thought about it, the more she realized it wasn't. She didn't know whether it could make a book, but she was sure it could make one thread in the skein.

"I know Kate likes what you're doing," Jane Williams said. "Margaret hasn't said anything to me. Has she to you?"

"She did like the idea that women could keep going out in public after becoming women, but she said I had too many naked people running around. The adventure interested her, though."

"What did you tell her?" Mother sounded amused.

"The same thing I told Father: they're nude people, not naked people. You're nude if you don't wear clothes. You're only naked if your being without clothes"—Viola paused to find a way to phrase what she wanted to say—"if it heats up the people who see you that way. I don't think Margaret paid much attention to the ideas behind the adventures."

"She's only thirteen, dear," her mother said gently.

"I know." Viola nodded. "And I've been trying not to lay things on too thick—I don't want people to think I'm in the pulpit preaching to them. But don't *you* think men and women would be closer to equals if they didn't have to fear the Wasting?"

"Probably. You need to remember, though, they weren't equals before the Wasting came along."

Viola nodded again. "That's true, of course. Back then, though, women didn't have to put on tents before they left the house. They showed off their shapes—they didn't hide them. They didn't cover everything but their eyes and their foreheads, either. They were *scandalous!*" The way she said it made it sound like praise.

"If your book is published, some people will call you scandalous," her mother pointed out.

"I know. I've told Peter some of what I'm up to, and asked him if he and the rest of the Drinkwaters could put up with having a writer in the family. He seems less alarmed than I worried he would."

"Good. That's good. I hoped it would be so. I thought it would—your father never would have stayed friends with Alf all these years if Alf were narrow-minded—but I didn't know for certain."

"Neither did I. Peter seems nice enough—better than nice enough—in his letters." Viola sighed. "If only he hadn't gone and been stupid."

"If only," her mother agreed, and sighed on the same note. "Original Sin isn't very original these days, but it's still sin. Dangerous sin." Viola nodded one more time.

Lincoln's Inn got cold as winter drew near. The most prized pupils' rooms were the ones just over the kitchens. Heat rising from ovens and open fires kept them comfortable even when most of the building wasn't. The chamber Peter shared with Walter Haywood, alas, lay nowhere near those lucky rooms.

They had no fireplace of their own. They were allowed a brazier apiece. Each had to rest on an iron tray with legs, to keep it from igniting a nightstand or dresser. Peter wondered whether Walter would follow that rule, since he seemed to enjoy flouting so many others. But follow it he did; he seemed disinclined toward possibly starting a fire and making an ash of himself.

When it snowed outside, though, braziers weren't even sending a boy to do a man's job. They were more like sending a cat to do a man's job, and a poor, thin, starving cat at that. If you held your hands over a brazier, they would eventually—very eventually—warm a little. More than two feet away, the heat the braziers put out was imperceptible.

"I wonder how many bright young lads were found frozen stiff in their rooms after somebody finally noticed they weren't handing in work," Walter said one bitter night.

"Quite a few, I'm sure," Peter said. He had a couple of thick wool blankets on his bed. He knew cold was liable to wake him in the middle of the night anyway.

"If I'm one of the victims of frigidity, tell Ebenezer my last thoughts were of sot-weed." Haywood sketched a salute, as a soldier might before going out on an attack he knew he wouldn't come back from. Then he blew out his candle. Snorting, Peter did the same. The room plunged into blackness.

Peter slept through the night in spite of his grumblings and forebodings. Next thing he knew, the door demon was making sure Lincoln's Inn would have no pupils sleeping late. He jerked, swore under his breath, and started to get out of bed.

He stopped short with only one foot on the floor. It wasn't the chill; he'd automatically braced for that. For a couple of heartbeats, he had no idea just what it was. Then he realized he was sniffing like a hound on a red deer's trail.

His own nose wasn't nearly so keen as a hound's. It didn't need to be, though. The room stank of sweat, stank as if soaked in it. He'd been smelly when he came back from the latest football match. Everyone who'd played in it had. He didn't think all the footballers put together would have reeked like this, though.

Ice ran up his back, ice that had nothing to do with the winter weather. This was the ice of fear—not to put too fine a point on it, the ice of panic. He ran a hand through his hair, then along his cheek. Whiskers rasped under his fingers, but his skin was dry. He felt of his nightshirt. It was dry, too.

He didn't dare believe his luck, not at first. He felt the fading warmth that marked where he'd slept. The blankets weren't damp. The sheets weren't soaked.

It was still dark; the sun came late these days. Peter fumbled for flint and steel. His fingers shook so much, he had trouble using them. He finally got the candle going.

Walter was shoving the chamber pot under his bed. His hair looked as wet as if he'd been out in a driving rain. His clammy nightshirt clung to his flesh. Ice ran through Peter again. He hadn't had the dreaded night sweats after he went to bed. *He* hadn't, no, but...

As gently as he could, he asked, "Do you feel all right?"

"Of course I do, old man. Why shouldn't I?" Haywood made a good game try at sounding as if everything were fine.

"Because the only way you could be any wetter is if you put on your shirt while you were in the bathtub," Peter said.

"It's nothing." Walter laughed. It sounded almost like a natural laugh, but not quite. He knew, too. He could hardly not know, not the way he was drenched, but he didn't want to admit it. Chances were he didn't want to admit it to himself most of all.

"You should see a doctor," Peter said.

"It's nothing," his roommate repeated, more sharply this time. "Just sleeping under too many blankets, that's all. Let's get dressed and go have something to eat."

Before he blew out the candle the night before, he'd joked about freezing to death. But if Peter'd ever heard anyone who wasn't going

179

to listen, Walter Haywood was the man. "*Kyrie eleison,*" he murmured, and made the sign of the cross, something he seldom did.

Walter pulled off his nightshirt. Since it stuck to him, that wasn't easy. He ran a towel over his torso and through his hair. That was as big a concession as he made to what had happened in the nighttime. Even in his shirt and trousers, he stank of salty sweat.

As they went down the stairs to the refectory, earnest Peter tried again: "You know, you really ought to—"

"Bugger off!" Walter snarled, his face as savage as a cornered rat's. A moment later, he added, "Doctors can't do damn all anyhow, and you know it as well as I do."

He didn't say what they couldn't do damn all for. Doctors couldn't do damn all for so many things. He didn't name any one in particular. Peter didn't think he named it even to himself. But that didn't mean he didn't know what it was. Oh, no. It didn't mean anything like that.

Peter gave it up. His roommate wasn't about to hear anything he had to say, not this morning. And it wasn't as if Haywood were wrong. Doctors couldn't do anything for him. The only way anyone knew not to die was not to get what he knew he had.

Walter ate like a pig. Peter had much less appetite. *It could have been me,* he thought. *It still could be me.* He had no guarantee. No one who took chances had any guarantee. He remembered his mother warning him about laundresses before he came to London. That seemed funny now. She'd meant well, as mothers do, but what an innocent she'd been!

He'd been an innocent himself. He wished he still were. He knew more of the world now than he had back in Salisbury. He could never unlearn what he'd discovered since. He might put it to good use one of these days. He would, if he was lucky in his learning. Or it might rise up one of these years and kill him and others who mattered to him. No way to tell, not till it happened or it didn't.

Walter, now … Peter didn't care for any of the thoughts he had about Walter. If you kept shooting dice, sooner or later you were bound to lose. Haywood must have thought it could never happen to him. Young men who burned hot often thought that way … till it did.

Something must have happened in the lecture halls and discussion chambers that day. Whatever it was, Peter never remembered it. Afterwards, he did remember hoping it didn't come up when he sat the examinations for the bar.

At supper, Haywood seemed his usual cheery, raucous self. He went into the lounge to play whist when he finished. Peter went up to the room to study. He told himself he might have been imagining things when they got up. People tell themselves such things even when they know better—especially when they know better, sometimes.

His roommate seemed pleased with himself when he came upstairs a couple of hours later. "I won nine shillings," he said, grinning cockily. "Plenty for a good time at a good joyhouse. A small slam at clubs did the trick."

"Walter—" Peter stopped. He was imagining a W branded on Haywood's forehead, one that had nothing to do with his first initial. No brothel would welcome him once he wore that warning.

"Don't start again! Bugger off, d'you hear me? Just bugger off!" Walter went from pleased to furious in a heartbeat.

"I may as well. You never listen to me anyhow." Peter was astounded at how sad he sounded.

"You're God-damned right I don't, not when you keep talking out your arsehole."

Before Peter could answer, there was a knock at the door. It couldn't have been timed better in a stage-play. Walter clutched his head with both hands. Not without a certain amount of wry pleasure at his roommate's annoyance, Peter stood up and threw the door wide. "Good evening, Master Cooke."

"God gi' you good evenin' as well, young Master Drinkwater," Ebenezer Cooke replied. After ducking into the room, he turned his attention to his master's son. "And good evenin' t'you as well, young Master Haywood. The *Phlox* is just in from Baltimore harbor, across the stormy winter seas. Her cargo'll want your attention."

Walter Haywood turned and looked him full in the face. He spoke one word: "No."

He'd said no before, of course, a good many times. He'd always yielded in the end. Peter didn't think he would now. The single harsh, flat word hung in the air as if it were carved from a block of adamant.

Cooke must have felt the same way. His muddy brown eyes widened. He didn't take a backward step, but shifted his weight in a way that suggested he had to catch himself to make sure he wouldn't. "Come, come, young master," he said, as coaxingly as he knew how. "Am I to tell your father you refused me?"

"Tell him whatever you bloody well please. I don't care, not to the extent of a fart in a thunderstorm." Walter's tone matched his words. He could have illustrated absolute indifference.

"He'll not be happy if I tell him you told me nay." The senior Haywood's factor had no quit in him. He trotted out his big cannon: "Should you anger him enough, you know you'll see no more silver from him." He pronounced it *siller*.

Walter only shrugged again. "I don't care about that, either."

"You say so now. Will you say so again once you're busted?" Coke said. *Once* came out as *oncet*; Peter needed a moment to realize *busted* had to mean *skint*.

"I'll worry about that then. For now, go away. If I never see you again, it'll be too soon." Walter still didn't raise his voice, or need to. He made himself more than clear enough in soft, reasonable tones.

Ebenezer turned to Peter. "Kin you talk sense into him, young sir?"

"I'm not about to try. Sorry, but I'm not. This is between the two of you," Peter answered.

"Thank you," Walter said, still quietly.

Peter didn't think his roommate had ever sounded more serious or more sincere, not to him. "You're welcome," he replied, very much the same way.

"Young Master Haywood, I'll take your pa what you said. Don't reckon he's going to be pleased with you," Cooke said.

"I don't care if he is or he isn't. I'm not wasting any more of my life on tobacco, and that's flat," Walter said.

Ebenezer Cooke turned and walked out of the room with the lean, awkward, angular gait of a mantis or a walkingstick. "Your pa ain't going t'fancy this," he threw over his shoulder as he started toward the stairs.

"You already told me that. I already told you I don't give a rap," Haywood answered. To Peter, he said, "Close the damned door."

Peter did. "You never told him off like that before," he remarked.

"I should have, by God, and long since, too. Tobacco doesn't matter. Nothing matters any more."

Was he tacitly admitting what he couldn't or didn't dare come right out and say? Peter thought about asking. In the end, he held his peace. Whether Walter came out and said it or not was one of the things that didn't matter any more.

They passed the rest of the night in near silence. Neither of them seemed to want to break it. They went to bed within a few minutes of each other, with no more than muttered good-nights. *Maybe this is all a bad dream*, Peter thought before sleep overwhelmed him. *Maybe everything will be fine in the morning.*

Next thing he knew, the usual bang on the door woke him. The room wasn't frozen, but it was cold. Cold or not, the air stank horribly of sweat. As he had the day before, Peter checked to make sure he wasn't the one it had poured from. He was less surprised and relieved than he had been then to find it wasn't. Less surprised and relieved, but still some.

"That miserable bugger of a door-pounder," Haywood said from the other bed.

Instead of answering, Peter lit the candle on his nightstand. He needed a little light to dress by. And, as casually as he could, he glanced over to his roommate. Walter's hair and nightshirt were as drenched as they had been the morning before. Candlelight reflected greasily from his face. For a moment, Peter imagined he could see the skull beneath the taut skin. Then the vision, if that was what it was, passed.

But it hadn't been a bad dream. It might be a nightmare, but it hadn't been a bad dream.

Shaking his head, he put on his day clothes. He didn't say anything to Haywood till he asked, "Are you ready to go down?"

"Just about." Walter ran a comb through his wet hair. Drops of sweat flew from it. Haywood pretended not to notice. So did Peter, though the effort to go on as if nothing were wrong filled him with sorrow sharper and more bitter than any he'd ever known.

He managed to tamp down his feelings and get through the day almost normally. *This*, he realized, *is what adults do most of the time*. For the life of him, he had no idea whether it was admirable or reprehensible. *Some of both, probably*, was as close to an answer as he could come.

After supper, Walter went upstairs with him. "I'll get more work done if Eb truly does stay away," he said.

"So you will." Peter didn't want to touch off a quarrel.

The knock on the door came less than half an hour after they'd closed it. Haywood jerked as if stung by a hornet. "God damn him to hell!" he said.

"I don't think that's his knock," Peter answered. He opened the door. Ebenezer Cooke didn't stand there. Stephen Heath did. "Uh, good evening, Master," Peter said in surprise.

"Good evening, Drinkwater. Is Haywood here?" Heath said. He answered his own question: "Ah, I see he is. Haywood, I need to speak with you."

"I'll leave if you like," Peter said quickly.

Heath nodded, but Walter said, "It's all right. Stay if you care to. Why not? A witness may be useful—isn't that right, Master?"

"It is … possible," Heath replied after a moment. He stepped into the chamber. Peter closed the door. He would have liked to flee, but Walter wanted him there. Stephen Heath sniffed once, twice. The room had aired out somewhat during the day, but that sour, salty sweat stink still lingered. The corners of the master's mouth turned down. He looked suddenly older. He must have hoped against hope, too.

When he didn't speak right away, Walter did: "Say your say, sir, if you'd be so kind." His voice was rough as shagreen.

"As you wish," Heath replied. "Several people—pupils, masters, servers—have noted your … your haggard aspect these past two days. I have smelled the reek this chamber holds too many times before to have much doubt as to its meaning. I fear, young Haywood, you are afflicted with the Wasting."

"That's ridiculous," Walter said, though even he didn't sound as if he believed his own words.

"Given what is common knowledge about your habits, I doubt it," Heath said. "If you play with fire long enough, you must expect you will get burned. Please believe me, I speak far more in sorrow than in anger."

"You can't prove I've got the Wasting!" Haywood said furiously.

"No one can be proved to have it until he or she passes it on to someone else, at which point formal proof comes too late," Stephen Heath replied. "But certain signs warn of the disease before it is full-blown. You have displayed more than one of them, or will you deny the rash and lassitude that afflicted you earlier this year?"

Walter looked as though he wanted to, but the glance he threw Peter's way suggested he knew he'd be given the lie if he tried. Staring down at the floor between his feet, he shook his head.

"Both Church and state have procedures to be followed in these cases," the master went on inexorably. "We shall require of you a list of as many of the people with whom you've lain whose names and whereabouts you can recall. If your sweats pass as the tiredness and rash did, you will also need to be marked as a warning to others."

They're going to brand him, Peter thought sickly.

"No! You can't! My father won't let you!" Walter said. By the sad, determined look on Master Heath's face, he was sure the senior Haywood wouldn't be able to stop them.

Richard Williams tapped the latest manuscript papers into a neat stack. "This all reads very well," he said, "but I have a question for you."

"What is it, Father?" Viola tried not to sound apprehensive. His questions often had barbs as sharp as a porcupine's quills.

"As things stand, your Temeculans have lived for years uncounted in their version of the earthly paradise. But when the *Ad Astra* anchors by their island and Englishmen come ashore, has not the serpent entered Eden?"

"What do you mean?" Viola feared she already knew.

Sure enough, her father went on, "They know nothing of the Wasting. That, to us, is largely what makes them interesting. Having no need for rules against congress between the sexes, they have none."

"Well, not very many," Viola said. "Rules against congress by force, and rules against relations within the prohibited degrees."

"Not very many." He accepted the correction. "They lack the ones they will need most. Sailors are men like any others. They will want female companions, especially after a long time at sea. The Temeculans will not know what a W on a man's forehead signifies."

"The captain can warn them," she said quickly.

"True. He can," Richard Williams said. "How much good will it do, though? Some can carry the Wasting for years without showing any signs or even knowing they have it. That poor bloke in Nunton did. The Temeculans may have to learn in a great hurry what people here painfully pieced together over a century and a half."

Viola thought about that for a little while. It struck her as horribly likely—likely enough to make her hang her head. "Maybe I should just throw the whole silly thing in the fire."

"Don't do that!" He held up a hand. "It's a fine story. It amuses and provokes thought at the same time. As long as you can keep them safe till the *Ad Astra* sails away, you will have done your duty to the reader. The way you suggested can serve well enough for that without twisting Lady Plausibility's arm too hard, I think. But you had better show the question has crossed your mind."

"I suppose so." She still didn't want to look him in the face. "In the long run, though, my lovely Temeculans are doomed, aren't they?"

Her father shook his head. "Doomed? I shouldn't say so. We still go on, after all."

"Doomed," Viola repeated. She spelled it out as plainly as she knew how: "Their freedom is doomed. The equality of their women. They'll go on—locked up inside houses, wearing tents and scarves and veils when they have to come out. Their kinsmen will arrange their marriages for them—they'll have no chance to choose for themselves." She stopped then. Her own rage threatened to choke her.

She felt ashamed of herself. Of the three girls, she'd always been the calm one, the sensible one—the one, as she knew, created in her father's image. She always had been. She wasn't any more. Not for this.

"Is it … as bad as that?" he asked softly.

"No," Viola said. "It's a hundred times worse, a thousand, a million …. There are no numbers big enough for how bad it is. It's every moment of our lives, from the time we're women till the time we're dead. And men don't know one *damned* thing about it."

She was sure she'd never cursed with such concentrated venom before, not even at the man who'd let his hand run free outside the bookseller's. "Men don't care. Why should they? The shoe doesn't pinch them. The women's quarters and the tents and the veils don't hide them. You may have some tiny idea. If you do, that puts you ahead of almost every other man in the world."

"The Wasting is a horrible way to die. I know too well—I've seen too much of it. We have no cure, nor hope of one," her father said. "We built the world we have today with the best intentions, chief among them to make its spread as rare as possible."

"Which road do they say is paved with good intentions?" Viola returned. "Women are on that road, and may not escape it save in dreams and fancies." She reached out and touched her manuscript to leave him in no possible doubt of what she meant.

"And how would it be if in the real world we had the license your Temeculans enjoy because they need fear no consequences?" he asked.

That was a serious question. "I don't know," Viola admitted. "I only know what I have, what women have had—have been forced into—all these years. And I know from the inside out it is not a fit way for a human being to live."

Richard Williams sighed. "If we did not love fornication so dearly, things might be different. But not even the fear of death will keep us from it. Fornication, after all, laughs in the face of death."

"What we have now *is* the face of death. If you are a woman, it is. If you are a man, you can pretend not to see the bones under the skin." Viola gathered up the pages he'd just read. "I'll make the changes the story needs. I do thank you for pointing them out to me. For the book's sake, I do."

He smiled that lopsided smile of his. "For yourself, you'd sooner send me to the Devil."

"You made me see things I hadn't before. I'm glad you did." She left the surgery as fast as she could.

Some of the changes had to go into the early part of the story, to make what came afterwards seem sensible. Those early changes meant more had to go in later, to take them into account. The revisions cost Viola more than a week. She hoped they didn't mar the manuscript too much. She wrote a neat hand; she thought a pub-lisher would be able to set type from what she was doing. If she had to make a fair copy before submitting it, she would, that was all.

She was about to go on from where she'd paused to revise when she got a letter from Peter. That gave her an excuse to stopper the bottle of ink and not write for a little while, an excuse she gratefully seized. She'd been hard at work on the book for some time now. The letter, though, the letter was new.

My dear Viola, he wrote, *I hope you and yours are well. By the grace of God, I still seem to be. And I know indeed that it is by God's grace, since Walter Haywood has unmistakably been taken by the Wasting.*

"*Christe eleison!*" Viola exclaimed when she read that. She crossed herself.

"What's wrong?" Kate asked.

"I'll tell you later," Viola said, and kept reading. Haywood's father, as she'd gathered, was rich enough to be a man of some importance in London. He'd thought he was important enough to get Lincoln's Inn, the secular authorities, and those of the Church to go on as if nothing were wrong with his son. Peter said, *I do not know if he tried to use some of his money to that end, but if he did, he failed. Men may not always be treated equally under the law, but when it comes to this dreadful disease I should say they are.*

Viola read that several times. *Men may not always be treated equally under the law ...* Peter didn't even notice how women were treated under the law. He was a man himself, of course. Why would he?

He went on to talk about how Haywood had left Lincoln's Inn, and how he himself now had their room by his lonesome. *This is a privilege usually reserved for pupils about to sit their examinations, so I am reckoned uncommon lucky. If I could, though, I should give it up in a heartbeat, if only that would make poor Walter well again*, he wrote.

He was a decent fellow ... except for that one time when he hadn't been. He'd been lucky then—lucky so far, anyhow. Haywood, who seemed to have been indecent whenever he got the chance, hadn't.

When Viola started downstairs, her sister said, "You're going to tell whatever it is to Father before you tell me, aren't you?"

Since she'd been about to do just that, Viola couldn't even deny it. She summarized the letter in a couple of sentences. Kate's eyes went big and round. She also made the sign of the cross. "Now you know," Viola said.

Richard Williams' face got longer and longer as he read through Peter's letter. "There are people like that, men and women," he said at last, sadly, handing it back to Viola. "Precious few old people like that, though."

"I should think not," she answered.

"We'll all pray for poor Haywood, and for Peter," he went on. "I don't know how much it will help, but it can't hurt." Viola nodded. She was grateful he didn't compare Peter's roommate to her Temeculans. Then again, he surely knew she'd do that for herself.

XIII

Peter found life much more peaceful without his cockproud roommate. That was not to say he was glad Walter had come down with the Wasting; a man would have to have a heart harder than Herod's to wish it on anyone. He hoped Haywood would live a good many years before it came down on him full force.

And he hoped that, while Walter waited and the sickness lay low, he would take his pleasure from his hand, not from whores or from other women he sweet-talked into bed with him. Otherwise, he wouldn't just carry the Wasting; he'd likely spread it.

That was why people who had it wore the W on their foreheads: to warn others against lying down with them in love. Peter sighed when he thought of that. If anyone would want to get around the telltale mark, Haywood was the man. He might also be ingenious enough to manage it somehow.

Even though he had the room to himself now, Peter didn't stay in it all the time. Along with a swarm of other pupils, he fought in a savage snowball war on Lincoln's Inn Fields. Snowball fights had even fewer rules than football matches. A couple of lads lost teeth when they got caught with snowballs built around rocks. In the confusion, no one was even sure who threw them.

As the fight wound down, Peter and Bob Wright pelted each other with snow till they both looked like snowmen. One of the pupils who'd got hurt stood close by, both mittened hands clutched to his face. "That's a dirty business, if you care to know what I think," Peter said, nodding toward him.

"No arguments from me," Bob answered.

"Either somebody held a grudge or it was one of those buggers who hurt people for the fun of it," Peter went on.

"There are people like that, sure as the devil," Wright said. "You try to steer clear of them or you make sure they know they'll get worse than they give if they try it on you."

"That's about the size of it," Peter agreed. Low in the south-west, the late-afternoon sun came out from behind the clouds. Peter smiled; he hadn't seen much of old Sol lately. None of London had. "Feels warmer," he said. "I'd looked for it to stay freezing all the way through Christmas."

"If it stays like this tomorrow, the snow will melt and the Fields'll be mud deep enough to drown in," Bob said.

"Good job we got our war in, then," said Peter, who'd been think-ing the same thing. Quickly, though, he added, "Good for most of us, I mean."

"That's the way things go." Wright shook himself like a wet dog. Like drops of water flying off the dog, snow fell from his hair and his wool jacket. Peter did the same thing. Then he headed back to the dormitory. He wanted to stand in front of the blazing fireplace in the lounge. Standing and talking instead of running around made him realize how chilled he was.

After supper, he was studying without much enthusiasm and thinking about going to sleep early when someone knocked on the door. Feeling an odd sense of *déjà vu*, he got off the bed and opened it. He wasn't even surprised to see Ebenezer Cooke standing in the hallway. "Good evening, Master Cooke. Come in, come in," he said, and stood aside. As he did, he glanced back at the other bed. No, Walter wasn't lying in it, or sitting at his desk.

"I thank ye, young Master Drinkwater. God gi' you good evenin' as well." Cooke ducked into the room. He too looked toward where Walter would have been.

When he didn't say anything more, Peter asked, "And what can I do for you tonight?"

"Well, young sir, I came to cry your grace, I did. For you always been kind to me, a stranger of no account. And you was always kind t' young Master Haywood, too, even when he weren't worthy of no kindness. I do thank you for that, very much. I want you to know I seen it."

"Oh." Peter's cheeks heated. "You're welcome, I'm sure. I don't think I did anything special."

"I reckon you done did. You was always tryin' t'save the young master from hisself, too, only it couldn't be done on account o' the bounce in his trouser snake." Cooke paused. "I hope *you're* well?"

"So far I seem to be, *Deo gratias*," Peter said. "I hope you are, too."

"I am over the clap, and it don't trouble me no more," the sot-weed factor replied. "Been long enough so I don't reckon I came away with anything worse. You don't never know for sure, but I don't reckon so."

"The same with me." Peter wondered how long he'd go on wondering. Every time he felt odd for the next five or ten or twenty years, he'd wonder if he was showing the first signs of the Wasting and be afraid till the feeling went away ... if it did. The Wasting was a fearsome disease in every sense of the word.

"That is good. That is mighty good." Ebenezer Cooke spoke with even more grave solemnity than he commonly used. "I cannot begin to tell you how awful I'd feel if young Master Haywood's leading you into temptation led you into the same misfortunate fate he landed in his own self."

"I shouldn't be thrilled about that, either," Peter said. "It'd also be sad if it happened to you."

Cooke nodded. "I thank ye for the sympathy. It's more'n I'd ever get from him or his pa, you'd best believe that."

"Why do you keep working for his father if you feel that way?" Peter asked.

"On account of bein' a poet don't pay beans," Ebenezer answered bleakly. Peter didn't think he was wrong.

They called the celebration at Salisbury Cathedral a Christmas Ale, even if it took place the day before the anniversary of the Lord's birth. As usual, Viola was glad for any excuse to get out of the house.

192

If her headscarf was of wool rather than linen, if she wore not only a heavy dress but a thick cloak on top of it, so what?

Her sisters and her mother were just as excited. Her father took it all in stride. "You don't care because you get to go out whenever you want to," Viola told him.

"I don't care because people will get drunk and stupid, and the food won't be as good as what we eat here," he answered. He was bound to be right about all that, but Viola thought his rightness beside the point.

And her mother said, "I don't care a cranberry. We won't have to cook today, and we won't have to clean up afterwards, either." Kate and Margaret both clapped their hands.

Richard Williams mimed pulling a knife out of his chest. "*Et tu, Brute?*" he murmured.

"I am for liberty—from the tyranny of pots and pans and dishes—for a day, anyhow," Mother answered.

Laughing, the doctor put a tall black hat on at a man-about-town angle and nodded toward the door. "Shall we be off, then?"

Off they went. The sun shone, but low in the south. The sky was more nearly the color of steel than the blue it should have been. There wasn't any snow underfoot, or any mud. Were it warmer, there would have been mud, but the ground had frozen hard. The cold nipped at Viola's forehead and fingers. Her mother and sisters wore gloves, but she thought she was covered enough.

How Temeculan of you, she gibed at herself. The Temeculans, of course, never had to worry about weather like this. Lucky them, even if they were fictitious.

Her footfalls and those of her family echoed on the planks of the bridge over the Avon. The river flowed along, ducks and a goose bobbing in it. It was cold, yes, but not cold enough to cover the stream in ice.

The cathedral lay only a little north of the Avon. People were filing up the stairs. Viola smiled behind her veil at how many were women. Her mother and she weren't the only ones who didn't want to cook and did want to get out. Nowhere near.

At the top of the stairs stood a table with an offering bowl. Father dropped silver into it. A deacon behind the table nodded to him. The fellow was there, Viola knew, to make sure none of the offerings walked with Jesus on Christmas Eve.

Cloth stretched on poles divided the cathedral in two. Women went to the left, men to the right. "See you later. Enjoy yourselves," Richard Williams said as he separated from his wife and daughters.

Once past the curtains that gated the women's half, Viola took off her veil. Tables with ham and chicken and bread and candied fruit awaited. They were the reason for the screening; veiled, you couldn't eat. You also couldn't drink. A couple of grannies with arms like a blacksmith's stood behind barrels of beer, cider, and rum punch. As women took cups, the servers plied dippers with might and main.

Women were waving to one another and exclaiming, even embracing. *Liberty*, Viola thought. Parsimoniously served out, of course, but as much as women ever saw. Most of them might not even notice the parsimony because any break in routine made them so happy.

Then Viola, a cup of beer in one hand and a ham sandwich in the other, spotted Peter's sisters. Since she couldn't very well wave, she exclaimed. Joanna and Julietta did wave—they hadn't loaded up yet. They pushed their way through the crowd and hugged her. She hugged back, carefully.

"Are you really writing a book, the way Peter says you are?" Joanna Drinkwater asked.

"That's right." Viola wondered if she should admit it in public.

"How exciting!" Julietta exclaimed.

Viola took a bite from her sandwich so the Drinkwaters couldn't tell what she was thinking. Writing a book—the sheer physical process of it—was about the least exciting thing she'd ever done. She sat there, the paper in front of her. When she thought of a sentence, or two or three, she set them down. In between bursts of writing, she looked at the blankness she still needed to fill. Sometimes she got the feeling the blankness was looking back at her.

"When do we get to read it?" Joanna asked.

"When it's properly in print, if it ever is. Otherwise, I'll be one of those people who tried to write a book and didn't have any luck at it." From things Viola had heard, she knew there had to be a lot of people like that. Some of the books she'd read argued there should have been more of them.

That was one big reason she'd made herself sit down to write to begin with. She knew she was unlikely to match a towering genius like Marlowe or Tavisham. But some of the authors who got their names on title pages were a long way from that lofty level. If they could do it, so could she.

Of course, most of the authors like that she'd noticed were men. Whether a man—and it would be a man—at a publishing house wanted to let the world see her words might be a different question. But publishers did put out books by writers who'd suffered the misfortune of being born female. Sometimes. When they felt like it. So she kept her hopes up.

Joanna Drinkwater said, "I hope a publisher *does* want it. I'd enjoy having someone clever enough to write a book in the family."

"Me, too. Mother's said the same thing," Julietta added.

"I'm glad to hear you say so." Viola meant that. Being a white crow in her husband's family wasn't something she'd looked forward to.

She looked around to see where Amanda Drinkwater was, and spotted her over by the barrel of rum punch, talking animatedly with her own mother and a couple of other women who had grown children. *Old women*, Viola thought. They seemed that way to her.

Then she noticed Kate trying to eavesdrop and trying even harder to pretend she wasn't doing any such thing. It occurred to Viola that Lucy Anderson and May Muncy had boys who were just about men. Was Mother talking about a match with either one of them, or with them both? On the other side of the barrier, was Father doing anything like that with Ralph Anderson or Morris Muncy? Viola hadn't wondered about it till now; negotiations for her were over and done with. But her sister had to wonder what the future held, and whether she'd be able to bear it.

When that thought crossed Viola's mind, she saw Christmas Ales in a new and more sinister light. They weren't just gatherings where people could get together; they were places where people could do business together. Yes, this was a Christmas Eve celebration. It was also a livestock market.

In her Temecula, people married people *they* chose, not spouses their families picked for them. She hadn't thought about what that would do to occasions like this, occasions when they came together. *I'm going to have to change a few more things in the manuscript*, she thought resignedly.

Joanna said, "I wonder how many weddings will come out of this Ale."

"I was thinking the same thing!" Viola exclaimed. So you didn't have to be a writer to have ideas like that cross your mind. All you had to do was pay attention to the world around you.

Then there were angry shouts on the men's side of the divide, and the unmistakable sound of a fist smacking flesh. "Christmas cheer," Julietta said, and rolled her eyes.

"Too much Christmas cheer," Viola agreed.

Her Temeculans had grapes and made wine. She wouldn't need to make any changes there. When you had things like wine, sometimes you'd have too much of them.

"What was the fight about?" she asked her father on the way home.

"I didn't see it start," he answered. "A couple of fools who got crocked, I suppose. One of them will wear a fine shiner for the next week or two."

"I was hoping for better than that," she said.

"Sorry, my dear. Even in the cathedral, I haven't got all the answers," he said. She wondered how to take that. Knowing her father, he'd meant her to.

No one pounded on the doors at Lincoln's Inn on Christmas Day. There were no lectures. No one had to turn in any work. The pupils could sleep as late as they pleased. Peter tried to sleep late. He couldn't do it. He was used to hopping out of bed with the sun—or before it, at this season.

The refectory clock said he walked in a few minutes past seven. The dining hall was less crowded than on an ordinary day, but not so much less as he'd expected. He wasn't the only pupil who'd got used to bouncing out of bed at a heathen hour.

He sat down next to Bob Wright. "Happy Christmas!" he said.

"Happy Christmas!" Wright echoed. "Mine would be happier if I were still asleep."

"So would mine. See what creatures of habit they've turned us into?" Peter said. He eyed his friend's plate. "What's on the bill of fare today?"

"Same old swill, only there's bacon, too. Or there was when I got some." There was none on the plate; Bob had made it disappear in a hurry.

Peter got his own barley mush, hard-fried eggs, stewed prunes, blood pudding, and bacon. He liked his grilled better than boiled, but still … bacon! Lincoln's Inn didn't serve it up every day, or every week, either. Full plate in one hand and coffee mug in the other, Peter came back to the table. He started disposing of his food the same way Bob Wright had.

"Know what I heard?" Wright said.

"Tell me," Peter urged—nothing went with breakfast like gossip.

"They say there'll be a Jew coming in when the new mob joins us this spring," Bob told him.

"A Jew? Really? Training for the law?"

Wright nodded. "That's what they say."

"'They say' isn't evidentiary," Peter observed. There were a few Jews in Salisbury, as there were in most English towns: a money-lender, some shopkeepers, a tailor. They hadn't had to practice their faith in secret for a couple of hundred years now, not since it became plain to even the dullest dullard that they couldn't spread the Wasting without sickening of it themselves. These days, they weren't even baited … too often.

"It may not be evidentiary, but I think it's true. He's supposed to be an apothecary's son—an apothecary with connections at court," his friend said.

"Really?" Peter hadn't dreamt a Jew could get court connections. But this was London. Strange things happened here. After a moment, he went on, "Well, he won't try to filch our bacon next Christmas morning. Or our blood pudding any old time."

Bob Wright laughed. "I hadn't thought about the bacon. Ham, either, and regular sausages. But the blood pudding slipped my mind. You're right, though, aren't you?"

"I think so." Peter didn't want to show he knew all that much about being a Jew, especially when he didn't. He'd heard or read that somewhere, and it had got stuck in his memory. To change the subject, he said, "I wonder what Walter's having for breakfast."

"Whatever it is, it's bound to be better than this." Wright's face clouded. "Of course, he'd sooner be here and shoveling in the slop we get than whatever dainties his father's been feeding him since he came down sick."

"There is that," Peter said.

"Just thinking about him makes my hair want to stand on end," Bob said. "It's as though I can hear the goose walking over my grave. Almost as though I can feel it—know what I mean?"

"Oh, too right I do!" Peter replied with great feeling. "But he had—has—a demon in him, a cock-demon. And his hand wouldn't make it lie down. He had to have women, any he could find or buy. And it caught up to him."

"You'd know more about that than I do," Wright said.

"More than I ever wanted to," Peter agreed. "If enough musket balls fly your way, sooner or later one will knock you over."

"Everybody gets the urge. That's why God gave us hands," Bob said. "Did you know that, back before the Wasting, you used to have to confess that kind of impurity no matter who you were, not just if you were a priest or a monk or a nun who has to stay chaste?"

Peter laughed. "Weren't the priests too busy ever to leave the confessional, then? If that's a sin ..." He shook his head. He had trouble imagining it.

"It's true, though." Bob Wright crossed himself to show he meant it. Then he stood up. He came back with his mug full again—and with more bacon on his plate.

"Now there's a good idea!" Peter jumped to his feet. He also got more coffee and more bacon. "Maybe I can eat myself sleepy and go back to bed."

"They should give lectures today. Then we'd all be yawning in nothing flat," Bob said.

"Will you go home to see your family later on today?" Peter asked. Ninety miles from Salisbury, he couldn't do that. He missed them.

"If I don't get into a card game, I may. I can go home any time I care to, though. It takes the thrill off."

"I can see how it might, yes," Peter said dryly. Walter hadn't cared to go home much, but then Walter's father had been trying to force him into a mold where he didn't fit. Into a couple of molds where he didn't fit, in fact: he wasn't cut out to be either a lawyer or a sot-weed magnate. His only ambition was rake.

The career struck Peter as enjoyable but not profitable. It also came with risks neither the legal profession nor the tobacco business shared. Walter'd fallen afoul of them, too. Peter wondered what he'd do now.

Half the sheet of paper in front of Viola was still blank. She looked down at it for a long time—a time that seemed long to her, anyhow. Then, in the middle of the blank space, she wrote *The End*, and drew a heavy line under the words. Below the line, in a smaller hand, she added, *13th March, 1852.*

"Dear God," she said, more to herself than to the Lord, "I did it. I really did it."

No sooner did the words escape her mouth than the sun came out from behind a cloud. If that wasn't a token of good fortune and heavenly favor ... it was one of the many vagaries of English weather. Half the time, it wanted to be spring. But it had poured rain for two days straight just the week before. A few days before that, it had snowed. Viola knew the fields might still get another white mantle, too.

"Make haste while the sun shines," she murmured. If that wasn't the most English maxim in the world, she had no idea what would be. Englishmen—Englishwomen, too—knew you couldn't count on Old Sol's shining for long.

Her Temeculans, who enjoyed warmer, steadier weather (how else could they wander around nude all the time?), never would have made, or needed, a proverb like that. Her Temeculans .... She took her last half-dozen pages downstairs. She didn't believe her father would think she should change much, but you never could tell. And she wanted him to know she'd finished.

When she tapped on the door between the rest of the house and the surgery, though, he tapped back a moment later. Someone was in there with him. Sure enough, when she put her ear to the door she heard two men's voices. After a few seconds, one of them sounded very unhappy. She pulled her head away in a hurry; that was none of her business. She sat down and composed herself to wait.

After twenty minutes or so, Richard Williams opened the connecting door. "Hello, my dear," he said. "That was Fred Oliver."

"The miller?" Viola said.

"That's right. He had an ingrown toenail that'd got inflamed and full of pus. I cut it down for him—"

"Is that why he made so much noise?"

"Only at the very end. He bore it bravely till then—hardly even wiggled. I cleaned the wound as best I could, and bandaged it, and gave him Epsom salts to mix into warm water and soak his foot in every night for the next week. With luck, the wound will heal clean."

"And will he pay you in white flour or brown?" Viola asked, half joking—but only half.

Her father gave her a severe look. "I'll have you know I got four shillings from him: real silver, with King Michael's head, God bless him, on every coin. Two and sixpence for carving on him, the rest for the salts."

"Well, good! That doesn't happen every time." She held out her pages to him. "And here it is—the last of the beast!"

"Huzzah!" He clapped his hands together. While doing that, he noticed he still had blood on his right thumb and index finger. He went back into the surgery. Viola heard him splashing his hands in a bowl or basin. He came out again, drying them on a rag. "I shouldn't leave any unfortunate stains on your work. People would wonder about you if I did, not about me."

Viola snorted. "Tell me what you think."

Richard Williams read through to the end of the book. They teased each other about lots of things, but not about that; it was serious business. He handed back the sheets and nodded. "Congratulations! You not only started it, you got all the way through to the end. You told a good story, too."

"Thank you," she said in a low voice. "It means a lot to me that you should think so."

"Have you decided where you'll send it in hopes that the wider world will be able to admire it, too?"

"I have," Viola answered. "I've looked on the shelves at Blackwell's to see which publishers have the gall to put out tales from lady authors. The ones who most stands out is Thomas Egerton, in Whitehall in London. So I shall send it to him first, and see what happens."

"Very good. And may you have the best of luck with it!" Father paused. "Something else occurs to me. Fallible human beings run the post. Should your manuscript go missing on the way between Salisbury and London, or—heaven forbid!—on the way from London and Salisbury after a rejection, could you write it again out of your head?"

"Oh!" Viola bit down on that as if it were an unexpected pit in a cherry pie. "Not word for word, certainly. Not scene for scene, either. If I did have to try to do it over, it would be a different book on the same theme."

"Is that all right with you, or would you sooner make a copy before you send it off?"

"It would be a lot of work. Buying so much paper and so many quills over again wouldn't be cheap, either," she said fretfully.

"I don't begrudge the money. We aren't rich, but we have enough—and the reward from a printed book would more than repay what we spend," her father said. "And many hands make work light. If your mother and your sisters and I were also to copy parts, the thing would be done much sooner. Should your original disappear, you'd likely need to make a fair copy in your own hand before you tried again with some other firm, but you'd have the pages to make it from."

"If you'd do that, it would be wonderful," Viola said. "If I could read it once you'd done it, I mean." She eyed him. "You have a doctor's hand."

He made a face, as if she'd cursed him. "I'll try to stay legible, and I'll leave out as many Latin abbreviations as I can remember to."

"I know what most of those mean," she answered. "I was more worried about your ordinary hen scratches."

Richard Williams snorted. "I never should have taught you to read, much less to write."

"Too late to whine about that now." She stuck out her tongue at him.

Recopying the manuscript took longer than she wished it would have, even with five scribes rather than one. Moments for writing got sandwiched in between things that had to be done and things people wanted to do more. Every now and then—more often than Viola expected—a sister or parent would ask her to decipher what she'd written.

"Perhaps, being a doctor's daughter, you've got something of a doctor's hand yourself," her father said, his voice sly.

"Piffle!" she answered, which made him grin.

But everything got done. Easter fell on the eleventh of April that year. By then, it was officially spring, not that God had told the weather. Rain poured down on the Williamses as they squelched to the cathedral. During the service, it occurred to Viola that her manuscript had just about been resurrected by now, too. She knew the thought was blasphemous, which didn't stop her from having it.

It was still raining three days later. Richard Williams carried the manuscript to the post office in a leather sack that kept it dry. "I saw them put it in the bin that says 'London' on the side," he told Viola. "It will go out tonight, and it should get there in a few days."

"Thank you, Father," she said, and then, "I wonder how long Master Egerton will take to let me know what he thinks of what I've done. I wonder if I want to hear what he thinks of it."

"It's in that bin, so you're going to hear whether you want to or not," he said.

"But what if he doesn't like it?" Viola said—the cry of the worried writer down through the ages.

"Then you offer it somewhere else, and you keep on doing that till somebody takes it. You told me so yourself."

"Yes, but—" Viola didn't go on. He wouldn't understand, any more than she really understood how not being able to help a patient gnawed at him. It didn't matter anyway. The Temeculans were out of her hands, out of the house, out into the big, cruel world. A cold-hearted stranger would judge them. All things considered, Viola thought she'd sooner be a patient.

The sun was going to bed later by the day, and getting up earlier. Even in London, the smell of green things burgeoning warred with the year-round city stink. Birdsong was everywhere. Every tree in Lincoln's Inn Fields seemed to have a nest or two in it.

Peter noticed all that, but only peripherally. He paid much more attention to the fine print in the books from which he studied. He couldn't afford to take things easy. If he didn't work hard, he wouldn't do well. It was that simple, and he understood as much.

He sat in what had been Walter Haywood's desk chair to work while daylight lasted. It sat closer to the window than his, and the sun didn't set now till well after supper. He didn't find divisions of property after an annulment especially interesting, but he still had to know about them. Annulments themselves, of course, lay in the hands of canon lawyers, but secular folk like him had a say in who got what once the annulment was an accomplished fact.

He would have welcomed a knock on the door. It would have given him an excuse to do something interesting instead of slogging through dry legal prose. So he told himself, anyhow, till somebody *did* knock. Then he said, "Damnation!" and slammed the law book shut. No, once he got going, he didn't like having to stop.

He threw the door open ... and stood there gaping like a fool. "What? Aren't you going to kiss me?" Walter Haywood said. He strode past Peter into the room that had been half his.

"I didn't think I'd see you back here," Peter said, staring still.

"Why? I'm not dead yet. As a matter of fact, I feel happy." Walter struck a pose. He looked the same as he always had. Almost the same, Peter realized after a moment. Walter's hat seemed half a size too big, so it dropped low on his forehead. It nearly covered the now-healed brand there: nearly, but not quite. The red spots that marked the bottom of the W still showed.

"How are you besides happy?" Peter asked.

"I could be worse. I still have the night sweats, but not as often as I did when I was here," Haywood answered. "No purple spots all over me, no thrush in my mouth, none of the other delights I've got to look forward to. I'm just the way I always was, only I don't have to paw through those stinking books any more."

"Some things you can buy at too high a price."

"Yes, Mother," Walter said.

He's trying to get you angry, Peter told himself. He was doing a good job of it, too. Working his best to keep his voice expressionless, Peter said, "If you're so glad to be free of this place, why did you come back? Just for the sake of annoying me?"

"That's part of it, heaven knows." Haywood blew him a kiss. Peter snorted; his ex-roommate couldn't have been much better at playing the scamp, either. Walter went on, "The bigger reason was to remind myself of everything I'm not missing. What were you rotting your brain with just now?"

"Property settlements after annulments," Peter answered automatically.

"We hadn't got to that by the time I had to leave, *Deo gratias.* Boredom will kill you faster than the Wasting can."

Peter had been bored while he studied. Now he was irked. "Are you bored with your hand yet?" he asked, a gibe nastier than he usually came out with.

"I've always been bored with my hand, old son. I'd use it when I didn't have anything else, that's all. Why do you think I went after the cunt instead? But I'm no more bored than I ever was, if that's what you mean."

"I don't believe you," Peter said. "Do you leave the hat on when you visit Madam Henderson's? What do the girls think of that?"

"You're a silly child, Drinkwater. You're a silly child from Salisbury. D'you think there are no women with the W on their foreheads? How d'you think they got it? Because they like cock the same way I like cunt, that's how. There are places where people like this can find more people like this. Why not? We can't do anything worse to each other now. What do they say? Misery loves company, sure enough."

"That's—" Peter broke off. For a moment, he felt like a silly child from Salisbury. He hadn't imagined anything like what Haywood was talking about. But that wasn't necessarily a failing. "Call me whatever you please. As far as I know, I'm still healthy."

"As far as you know," Haywood said mockingly. Everyone knew the Wasting didn't always show itself at once.

"Whose fault is that?" Peter said.

"I didn't go into the room with you. I didn't stick it in for you, either. I did my own sinning down the hall, and a devil of a lot of fun it was, too."

"You got me drunk."

"You were already drunk. I got you drunker."

"I wouldn't have gone there if you hadn't taken me."

"The more fool you."

They glared at each other. "Maybe you'd better go," Peter said. To make sure Walter understood what he meant, he added, "Maybe you'd better go before I knock your block off."

Another blown kiss and Haywood strode out the door. Peter hoped he never saw him again.

XIV

A month went by, and another one. The solstice celebration lay around the corner. "When shall I hear?" Viola asked her mother. "How do I even know the book ever got to London?" She was slicing onions while she worried. That gave her an excuse for having tears in her eyes.

Jane Williams was cutting potatoes into cubes. She paused a moment. "You'll hear when you hear. It will take as long as it takes, but you *will* hear. If you wanted to know the manuscript arrived, you should have put in a letter with our name on it so they could send it back."

"You're as bad as Father!" Viola exclaimed. She didn't worry out loud to Richard Williams any more. He'd lost patience with her, at least as far as that went. And she'd realized she should have included a letter acknowledging receipt of the package the day after it went into the post, which was, of course, too late to do her any good.

Her mother went back to her knifework. By the sound of it, she was bearing down extra hard. "I'm not magical, dear. I can't make things happen. I expect they will, though."

"But *when*?"

"When they do, of course. I don't know how long it takes for a publisher to get around to reading something by a writer whose name he doesn't already know. Do you?"

"Of course not!" Viola wasn't used to talking to her mother as if she were an idiot, but she did then. "Whom do I know who might tell me? No one!"

"In that case, all you can do is wait," Jane Williams said placidly. "While you're waiting, will you cut those onions a little finer, please? Then throw them into the stewpot."

As her mother had with the potatoes, Viola took out her frustration on the onions. Into the pot they went. The stars of the upcoming stew, three rabbits who'd got trapped raiding the back garden, lay on the counter, skinned, cleaned, and jointed. When it came to blood, Mother was at least as cool as Father ... though the blood she dealt with wasn't of the human variety.

"Thank you, dear," her mother said, and not another word. She added the potatoes. Carrots had gone in earlier; they took longer to get tender. Jane Williams started slicing mushrooms.

Viola pointed at a pale one. "Are you sure that isn't the bad kind?"

Her mother picked it up and studied it, then set it aside. "No, I'm not sure, and it isn't worth taking a chance on. You can take it out to the midden with the peelings and scraps."

"Right now?" Viola didn't feel like muffling herself in outside clothes.

Jane Williams understood that; any woman would have. "No, it can keep," she said.

The rabbit stew turned out tasty. After supper, Viola did take out the waste. Flies still buzzed around the midden. The sun slid slowly down toward the northwestern horizon, but at this season of the year it would be a while getting there. No one was walking or riding along the street in front of the house. Viola could have got away without coming out without veil and headscarf, or even nude as a Temeculan. She hadn't known that ahead of time, though.

A few days later, she watched the start of the procession from the town up to Stonehenge with her mother and sisters. The Salisbury Giant, Hob-Nob, the Druids in their white robes, all the rest of the mummery .... The ceremony wasn't something that happened every day, so it did hold some interest. Just the same, she understood that the Druids' prayers to the old gods wouldn't do any more to cure the Wasting than the priests' prayers to the Father, Son, and Holy Spirit.

207

Zero equaled zero. Could prayers have halted the illness, it would have vanished centuries before.

She wouldn't say that out loud, even to her family, though she was pretty sure they could see what she saw. The only one she held the slightest doubt about was Kate, who was young enough and sweet-natured enough to fan the fires of hope as long as she could.

Naturally, men hooted at the women as they left the area set aside for them. That was as much a part of the solstice ceremony as the parade was. It was if you were a man, anyhow. Viola wanted to swear at the louts the way she'd sworn at the bastard who pinched her. She wanted to, but she didn't.

As she and her sisters and mother headed home, she wondered why she hadn't given the men what they deserved. *They train us*, she thought. *From the time we're tiny, they train us the way they train dogs and horses. And when we act the way they want us to, they're a little nicer to us. Not much, but a little. It's like giving a horse half an apple or a dog a scrap of meat.*

She wished she'd had that clear realization sooner. She would have put it in the book. She knew just where, too; it would have fit perfectly. She sighed, loud enough so Margaret noticed and sent her a curious look. *Nothing I can do about it now*, Viola thought.

But that wasn't true, was it? One of these days, she'd probably write another book. She didn't know yet what it would be. A new account of a voyage to a land that never was? Something closer to home? Whatever it was, it would touch on how men and women got along, and on how they didn't. Her insight would find a home there. *Have to note it down on paper so I don't lose it*, she told herself.

Would she still be working on it after she married? She'd know things then that she was only imagining now. *Marriage: its utility to the scribbler* went through her mind. It made her laugh. Margaret looked at her again. She paid no attention to her little sister.

The powers that be at Lincoln's Inn decided to let Peter keep the room he had, though they took out the second bed, desk, and nightstand. He persuaded them to leave the second chair, a bit of impromptu pleading that left him hoping he might make a barrister after all.

208

"You can do it," Bob Wright told him. "If I can get up there at a mock trial without making too big a fool of myself, anybody can, believe me."

"Heh," was all Peter said. Bob had an easy confidence he lacked himself. It made a difference, a big one. And, like Walter, Bob was a Londoner, and a rich one to boot. That also made a difference.

"You'll be fine," Wright said. "And you won't have to worry about the examinations, where I'll be biting my nails down to the quick till they let me know whether I'm allowed to take the orals."

"Won't have to worry?" Peter let out a raucous laugh—indeed, one that sounded slightly cracked.

"You study. You remember things. You can even apply them. D'you think the masters haven't noticed?"

"They've noticed how much I *need* to study. I'm sure of that," Peter dreaded the thought of failing, all the more so because his father had succeeded. How could he show his face in Salisbury if he came home after a disaster like that?

"You'll do fine," Bob said easily. "The only other pupil I've seen who swots the way you do is Katz. And he studies so hard, I mostly *don't* see him, if you know what I mean."

"He's a grinder, that one," Peter agreed. Mordechai Katz, the apothecary's son, worked like a man possessed. It occurred to Peter, more slowly than it might have, that a Jew at Lincoln's Inn bore a heavier weight on his shoulders than a lad from the provinces did. Young Katz was skinny and looked as if a strong breeze would blow him away, but his burden was such that he might have been able to hold up the heavens had Atlas given them to him. If he didn't make good, how many years would it be before another coreligionist of his got the chance to try?

Wright nodded. "That he is. But make sure you count how much money you've got in your pockets before you come within arm's length of him." He laughed, punched Peter in the shoulder, and went on his way, comfortably Christian.

He was too smooth and too friendly to say anything like that to Katz's long, somber face. Peter had better manners, too. But not all the pupils did—not all the masters, either.

Peter saw it in the refectory and the lounge more than in the classroom and the lecture hall; he was senior to the new lad, after all. Katz didn't fire back. He let insults pour off him like rain from a steeply pitched roof. Sometimes he eyed the man who was baiting him as if the fellow had suddenly started spouting Polish or some other language no civilized person could be expected to understand.

He got his revenge in his work. It soon became clear he was the sharpest knife among the new pupils. Peter watched him perform at a mock trial. Had it been a boxing match, Katz would have knocked his foe out of the ring. He hardly even raised his voice. That made him more devastating, not less.

The pupil opposing him was one of those who enjoyed making sport of him. If Katz was especially pleased to eviscerate him on account of that, he didn't let on. Not letting on also left its mark on the young men in the gallery.

Most pupils would have been cheered till the welkin rang after such a victory. Only a handful of people came up to congratulate Mordechai Katz. There he stood, a stranger in his own country.

Yes, he's got a harder road to travel than the one that took me from Salisbury to London, Peter thought as he approached the Jew. He held out his hand, "That was brilliantly done! Brilliantly!"

Katz's grip said he was stronger than he seemed. As he shook hands, he replied, "I thank you very much, sir." The two of them hadn't had much to do with each other till then. But Peter was one of the senior pupils now, so the new lad acted properly deferential.

"If you can do something like that any time you choose, you'll go a long way. As far as—" Peter remembered his thought of a moment before and changed what he'd been about to say: "As far as other people let you."

Till then, Katz had been merely polite, as he would have been towards any near-stranger. His searching stare said he all at once found Peter worthy of more serious attention. His eyes, Peter saw, weren't brown, as he'd thought, but hazel. He had long eyelashes, too. On a woman, when they were as much of her as a man could see, those eyes would have been bewitching.

"You aren't one of us," Katz said. It wasn't a question. He might have been a stranger in England, but to him everybody in the outside world, the gentile world, was a stranger.

"No, I'm not." Peter nodded, acknowledging the obvious.

"But you understand at a glance what most people—most people who don't live it every moment of their lives, I should say—never see. How do you do that?"

"I don't know," Peter said. Maybe he did, though. "The woman I'll marry when I go back to Salisbury speaks—speaks most eloquently—on the plight her sex faces. It isn't the same as yours, but it's of the same kind."

"Of exclusion, you mean?" Mordechai Katz said.

Peter nodded again. He hadn't realized that was what he meant, but the Jew had unerringly put his finger on the right word.

"How interesting!" Katz murmured. "I can see how the comparison applies, but I never should have thought to make it myself."

"Viola—Viola Williams is her name—says men aren't in the habit of thinking about what women go through because they're women. I'd guess the same holds true with ordinary people and Jews."

"With Christians and Jews." Again, Katz spoke with relentless precision.

"That's right," Peter said.

"Well, well. You've given me something new to think about. You have, and your fiancée has. The two of you will write back and forth, I suppose? Next time you send her a letter, please be so kind as to thank her for me."

"I'll do that." *Unless I don't*, Peter thought. He was glad his family and the Williamses had arranged the marriage that would link them. He was also glad Viola was unlikely ever to meet Mordechai Katz. The two of them might like each other much too well.

As luck would have it, a letter from Viola came that afternoon. She talked about the parade up to Stonehenge, about the way some men had annoyed the women of Salisbury as they were going home, and about how she remained in suspense over her book.

I don't imagine you can visit Whitehall and light a fire under Master Thomas Egerton, she wrote. *A metaphorical fire, I mean, of course, not one of the arsonous kind. I'm sure I mean that. For the time being, I'm sure.*

Peter smiled. He knew she was joking—for the time being, as she said. He enjoyed her darting thought. His own didn't dart; it plodded. But it got where it was going. That hadn't seemed like a lack, only a difference, till he watched someone else whose thought did dart in action.

In spite of muttering to himself as he wrote, he mentioned Mordechai Katz and the conversation about how women were treated and how Jews were he'd had with him. *You will know there are places where Jews are made to stay inside one small quarter of a town,* he added. *In them, the comparison becomes more pointed still.*

When he finished the letter, he put it in the OUTBOUND box for posting to Salisbury. He wished he were going home, too. *It won't be long. After I sit the bar examinations.* That time seemed simultaneously far away and rushing ever closer.

Viola kept waiting for a letter from a man she'd never met. Instead, she got one from a man with whom she grew ever more familiar. Some of the ideas in Peter's letter were new to her, though.

"He has a point, doesn't he?" she said to her father. "The way the world treats women isn't so very different from the way it treats Jews."

Richard Williams rubbed his chin. "It's even closer in countries that hold more Jews than England does. A lot of them make their Jews stay in sections of towns walled off from everyone else. Ghettos, they call them."

"Yes, Peter mentioned them, too. I know what ghettos are. I've read about them. I never thought to make the connection, though," Viola said, half angry at herself because she hadn't.

"One of the reasons I talked with Alf about a match between you and Peter was that I knew he wasn't stupid. Heaven help you if you were yoked to a fool—and heaven help a fool yoked to you," her father said.

Viola smiled, but not so widely as she might have. "I thank you for that. Plainly, you could have done much worse. I'll never have the chance to find out if I might have done better, will I?"

"One of the things I've noticed is, the gap between bad and worse is far wider than the one between good and better," he answered. "The older I get, the truer that seems."

Like most of the things her father said, that sounded sensible. But how much did sense matter in marriage? Wasn't what went on between men and women more an affair of the heart than one of the head? She'd thought so when writing about her imaginary Temeculans.

But she understood Temecula *was* imaginary. England was real. So was the Wasting. She understood that, too, however little she cared for it. "I'd like to see women's plight cross the gap up to bad," she said, and then, as an afterthought, "I suppose people should treat Jews better, too."

Her father cocked his head to one side, studying her. "Are you thinking of that Katz fellow in young Drinkwater's letter?"

Her cheeks heated. Her father knew her as well as … as well as a father was likely to know a daughter, or maybe even a little better than that. "Some," she admitted. "Not to do anything about, even if I could. But to think about, why not?" She was nearly as sensible as he was. She hoped he knew that, too.

By his nod, he did. "No reason at all. If he's as clever as Peter makes him out to be, of course he'd interest you. Intrigue you, I should say. Peter's the known quantity, though."

"I understand that," she said. "Known except for whether he carries the seeds of the Wasting in him, anyhow."

"That's true. It's also true for any man you might end up with, men being what they are—what *we* are," Richard Williams said. "We've already gone round this barn, haven't we?"

"We have. We need to keep going round it, don't we? I'll likely be going round it inside my head ten or twenty years from now."

"By twenty years from now, I don't think you'll need to worry any more. The Wasting hardly ever lies fallow that long."

If Peter should pass it on to her ten years into their marriage, though, it might be another ten years before it showed itself in her. She thought about mentioning that to her father, but at the last moment held back. What point? To show how clever she was? To quibble for the sake of quibbling? She did that every now and then, but didn't feel like it this afternoon.

Belatedly, she noticed Father hadn't warned her away from Mordechai Katz because he was a Jew. That was interesting. A priest or a monk would have found some other words for it. Most Easter seasons, there was at least one sermon on the Christ-killing Jews.

She also noticed she'd let Katz intrigue her even if he wasn't Christian. She laughed quietly. As if she'd had any doubts, she knew now how she'd come to think the way she did.

When she wrote back to Peter, she praised him for drawing the comparison between women and Jews. *It was there under my nose all this time, and I never once saw it,* she said. *I am in your debt for pointing it out to me.* Past that, she kept quiet about Mordechai Katz. If she was going to marry Peter, which she expected she was, no point giving him the vapors even before they became man and wife.

She did sound out her mother about what *she* thought of Jews. Jane Williams looked at her in some surprise. "I haven't had much to do with them," she said slowly. "I've bought a few things at Ben Reuben's shop. His prices are all right. He never tries to cheat me when he makes change. He's a shopkeeper, a man. He's never thrown filthy talk at me, I will say that. I wouldn't have gone back if he had."

"Sad when 'he's never thrown filthy talk at me' marks a pretty good man," Viola said.

"It is, isn't it? But you know it's true as well as I do," her mother replied.

"Too right, I do," Viola said. "Do you think Jews will go to hell because they don't believe Jesus Christ is the Son of God?"

"I've heard people say that. I've heard a priest or two say it. But if you ask me, most of the folks who talk that way don't have any idea what getting into heaven takes themselves."

Viola laughed in delighted surprise. "I love you, Mother!"

"I love you, too," Jane Williams said. "The way it looks to me is, we have enough trouble coping with the world we're in to waste a lot of time worrying about the one to come. Plenty of people think otherwise, and that's fine—for them."

"No wonder you and Father get on well," Viola said.

Her mother nodded. "No wonder at all."

Peter didn't spend much time in the lounge. The card games and the play at dice were usually for stakes higher than he cared to risk. And when he was playing, he wasn't working. Gossip spread in the lounge, of course, but it also spread in the refectory, so he didn't miss much.

Every once in a while, though, he would play chess with Bob Wright. Neither of them was especially gifted, but they were evenly matched. However much Peter wished he could, he found himself unable to keep his nose in his lawbooks all the time. And you could enjoy chess without gambling on it.

One evening, Mordechai Katz watched them go at it. He didn't offer suggestions, the way some pupils would. Peter wanted to hit people who did that. Katz just stood behind him, eyeing the board over his left shoulder. Peter almost forgot he was there till he said, "May I have the honor of playing whoever wins?" As usual, he sounded polite, quiet, deferential.

"Why not?" Peter said.

"Fine by me," Bob agreed. "I'm tired of shredding this bloke all the time, anyhow."

"Perjury is right out," Peter said sweetly. Bob winked at him. Peter twisted his head a little so he could see Katz's face. The Jew looked amused and patient at the same time, like a grown man listening to a couple of little boys.

As things worked out, Peter managed to promote a pawn. When he put the queen on the board in its place, Bob tipped over his king. "You've got me," he said. He got to his feet, waving Katz into the chair in his place.

"Now we'll see how smart I really am," Peter said. He took a white pawn and a black, stirred them around behind his back, and held out closed fists to Katz. The Jew tapped the left one. Peter opened that hand. It held the black pawn. Peter started setting up the white pieces. He had the feeling he'd need the small edge moving first gave him, and any other help he could find.

Sure enough, inside ten moves he knew he was in far over his head. Mordechai Katz moved swiftly and certainly; he didn't seem to need to pause to think. How many moves ahead was he seeing? *More than I am*, Peter thought with glum certainty.

Several exchanges followed, all but one of them forced by Katz. When the dust cleared, as it were, Peter found himself down a bishop and a pawn, with most of what he had left trapped in one corner of the board. As Bob Wright had before him, he resigned.

"I'm afraid I'm punching out of my weight," he said, nodding to his foe.

"You have a notion of what you're about. If you play steadily, you won't be half bad," Katz said, which told Peter he wasn't half good now, not by whatever standards the Jew used to judge.

"Can I have a go at you?" Bob asked the victor.

When Mordechai Katz nodded, Peter all but jumped out of his seat. "Let's see if you last any longer than I did," he said.

His friend didn't. In a real fight, Katz wouldn't have broken a sweat. He forked Wright's queen and a rook with his knight. The queen died a few moves later, pinned and then killed in front of Bob's king by a marauding bishop. Shaking his head, Bob said, "Smile for me," to Katz.

"I beg your pardon?" the Jew said.

"Smile for me," Wright repeated. Warily, Katz did. Bob whistled: a long, low, sad note. "I will be damned. You've got a man's teeth in there after all. The way you chewed me up, I thought sure you'd have a shark's chompers instead."

"Oh." Katz didn't seem certain whether that was an insult or praise. Peter wasn't, either.

"My hat's off to you." Bob made as if to doff the one he wasn't wearing. "I didn't watch your mock trial, but Peter told me about it. Now I see what he must have meant: if you argue the way you play, Lord help anybody on the other side."

Mordechai Katz looked down at the chessboard. "You're much too kind," he murmured, modest as a child.

"I don't think so," Bob said.

"I don't, either," Peter said. "Just how well do you play, really? You didn't need to work to mop the floor with us—I could see that."

The young Jew hesitated, plainly deciding what he wanted to say. Peter readied himself for some polite lie. But when Katz replied, "I came in seventh at the royal tournament last year," Peter believed him, all the more so because he added, "My game isn't so good now—I've got rusty because I need to study more than I'd been in the habit of doing."

"Seventh! How do you feel about that?" Bob Wright asked him.

"I didn't expect to win. I know there are people better than I am. I was hoping for third, but I traded a bishop for a knight early in one game, and it cost me in the ending." Katz made a sour face, still annoyed at himself a year later.

He said his goodbyes a few minutes later. Staring at his back, Peter said, "When he's chosen his Majesty's Solicitor General thirty years from now, we can say, 'Mordechai Katz? I knew him! He used to thrash me at chess.'"

"He'd make a good one, I expect, if he weren't a Jew," Bob said.

"Mm, there is that," Peter admitted. "He's so clever, though, they might pick him even if he were a Parsee from Bombay." That wasn't altogether fantastical—just mostly. Bombay was the biggest English trading station on the coast of India; France and Portugal and Holland held similar outposts.

"Cleverness gets you only so far. What really matters in how high you go is who your friends are," Bob said. Peter couldn't decide whether that was the most cynical thing he'd ever heard or simple realism. His friend continued, "He's liable to fall short there. Who'd want a Jew for a particular friend? Except another Jew, I mean."

"He's here at Lincoln's Inn." Peter didn't want to believe the cynical and the realistic could be such close allies. "Things are looser than they were a hundred years ago. They'll get looser yet as our lot takes hold of the reins."

Bob eyed him. "Would *you* want Katz for a particular friend?"

"One could do plenty worse," Peter said.

"That's not a responsive answer," Bob snapped, as a barrister might.

"I honestly don't know," Peter said. "Till Katz got here, it never once crossed my mind. The Jews in Salisbury don't move in the same circles I do. But …. You may have the question backwards, you know. Shouldn't it be, Would Katz care to have me for his particular friend? Didn't you tell me his father was court apothecary? That gives him the ball for such choices, eh?"

Bob Wright shook his head. "You don't know how things go. People—regular people, I mean; Christian people—use Jews for what they can do. They admire them for their brains and their money, or they're jealous of them. But like them? It hardly ever happens."

"That's a pity," Peter said. "Maybe we'll outgrow such foolishness one day."

"Maybe we will, but don't hold your breath waiting. It would kill you as quick—and as dead—as the hangman putting a noose around your neck. If you want to tell me it should be different, I shan't argue with you. If you want to tell me it will be any time soon, I shan't believe you. I've lived in London my whole life. I know better, by God."

Shut your gob, you silly provincial hayseed. That wasn't what Bob Wright said, but it was what he meant. Living his whole life in London left him sure he always knew how things worked. Walter Haywood had had some of that in him, too, though the things he most cared about weren't the same as Bob's. To his ruin, he hadn't been as smart as he thought he was. Bob might not be, either.

Or he might. Years would go by before either of them could decide how things had turned out and what that meant. Even then, they might disagree. Life was complicated. The older Peter got, the more complicated it looked to him. He wondered whether everybody felt the same way.

Viola hardly noticed her father's footsteps on the stairs leading up to the women's quarters. She heard that small sound every day. And she was scribbling notes from travelers' tales—*male* travelers' tales—of journeys along the Amazon. They could name the great South American river after a warrior woman, but no women had explored it.

Then her father tapped at her door. That made her look up. "What is it?" she asked. If she sounded a little annoyed, she felt that way, too. She'd come across some things that looked useful to her.

He held up an envelope. "Letter for you," he said, and set it on the table next to her notes.

"Who sent it?" Viola asked. Then she saw the return address. "Oh!" she said. In a spidery hand, it read, *Thomas Egerton, Whitehall near the Military Library, London.*

Her own hand shook as she opened the envelope. "Would you like me to step out?" her father asked.

She thought for a moment before shaking her head. "No, never mind. One way or the other, you'd find out soon enough."

"All right," he said equably. He leaned against the wall while she pulled out and unfolded the letter.

It was in the same script as the address. "'My dear Miss Williams,'" she read in a voice that trembled more than she wished it would have, "'I thank you very much for sending my firm your manuscript entitled *A Voyage to the Island of the Temeculans*. It is admirable in a great many ways, and we should like to undertake its publication.'"

"By God!" Richard Williams said, and smacked his right fist into his thigh. "You did it, girl! You really did it! What will he pay you? Not bacon or barley, I hope."

"I was just getting to that." Viola went back to reading: "'For the privilege of seeing it into print, we propose a fee of a hundred fifty pounds gross, deduction to be made for expenses necessary in obtaining from the relevant authorities the *nihil obstat* and *imprimatur*. Experience has shown that these expenses are likely to amount to approximately ten per cent of the gross.' He'll bribe the church officials, he means."

Her father chuckled. "He certainly does."

"'If this is acceptable to you, let me know soonest so that we may set things in motion. Once more, my thanks for an enjoyable and thought-provoking few hours' reading. I look forward to a long and profitable association with you. Yours most sincerely, Thomas Egerton.'" She turned to the doctor. "What do you think?"

"The money's not bad. We could live for a year on a hundred fifty pounds—maybe for more than a year. What do *you* think? It's your book."

"I wouldn't get all of it. He'd keep that share for his bribery," Viola said. "A hundred fifty pounds is a nice, round number. Let him pay the priests out of his own pocket instead of taking money out of mine."

"If that's how you feel, write and tell him so. Politely, of course, but you know how to do that," her father said.

"What if he tells me no? What if he says he won't print it if I insist?" she asked nervously.

"See how he answers. You can always climb down from your high horse if you have to," he answered. "I have the feeling fifteen quid matter more to you than to him, though."

"All right," she said, praying it would be.

"Before you write your letter, tell your mother and your sisters. You didn't shriek when you got the news, so they won't know yet." Her father winked at her.

"You are a monstrous man," she said, which made him laugh. Then she went to do as he'd suggested. Plenty of shrieks followed, and squeals, and excited noises of every other sort under the sun, and hugs. Viola got hugged till she could hardly breathe, in fact. Though she'd had only small beer with breakfast and lunch, she felt as drunk as if she'd poured down whole big glasses of brandy.

She wrote the letter asking for a hundred fifty pounds net, not a hundred fifty pounds gross. Before she stuck it in the envelope, she had both her father and her mother read it. Though they hadn't taken holy orders, they both gave it their *nihil obstat* and *imprimatur*. She put it in the post the next day, which was a Tuesday.

About a week, she told herself. That was how long a letter commonly needed to go from Salisbury to London and a reply to come back. When the following Tuesday brought no answer from Thomas Egerton, she began to worry. When Wednesday likewise proved silent, she worried in earnest.

Thursday brought the envelope she hoped for and dreaded at the same time. She thrust it back at her father when he handed it to her. "You read it," she said. "I can't bear to."

"All right." He set his cheroot in an ashtray and popped off the seal with his thumbnail. "'My dear Miss Williams, Your amendment is acceptable: a hundred fifty pounds net, not gross. You confirm my experience that women are apt to bargain harder than men, perhaps because they have fewer ways to come by money than men do, and so depend on writing more. Your charming romance captivatingly pictures a land where this does not hold true, which greatly enhances the interest it arouses. Yours most sincerely—'"

"He said yes." Viola had trouble believing it.

"He did," Richard Williams agreed. "Do you know what that means? It means he thinks he can sell enough copies so what he pays in bribes will look like pocket change by comparison."

"I hope you're right. I hope he's right," Viola said. She still felt amazed and dazed and awed, as new authors have a way of doing.

XV

When summer came, Peter would sit the examinations that determined whether he could join the bar. He studied every waking moment he could. When he complained to Stephen Heath that his head felt ready to explode, the master smiled and said, "If I had a penny for every pupil who told me something like that, I'd live in a grand castle with fields and meadows and pastures out as far as the eye could see, and all of them mine. But I'll tell you something in return: you will never know as much about the law as you do when you sit down with your papers and your questions. Never."

"I hope you're right, Master Heath," Peter said, most sincerely. *I hope it will be enough*, he thought.

"Your father said the same thing, lad," the master replied. "He's turned out all right, eh? I expect you will, too."

Peter wished he expected something like that. He also soon discovered he couldn't study *every* waking moment. Life kept getting in the way. An excited letter from Viola told him her romance of the Temeculans would be published. When he wrote her, he likewise had to sound excited, and congratulatory as well.

He worked hard on his letter back, not least because he hadn't really thought she could find a home for the book. That she'd succeeded, and at the first crack of the bat, told him he'd be wedding a woman of parts. It behooved him to show he was also possessed of some parts himself.

Try as he would, he couldn't make himself stay in his room all the time. After a while, the fine print and the numbing legal prose made him flee to the lounge. Sometimes he sat and talked; sometimes he scowled over a chessboard at Bob Wright, Mordechai Katz, or one of the other handful of pupils who enjoyed the game.

Katz trounced him with monotonous regularity. He felt his own game improving on account of exercise, but had no wins to show for it. After one more thumping, the Jew looked across the board and asked, "Don't you get tired or angry, losing all the time?"

"Why should I?" Peter asked in real surprise. "Chess is an honest game. I'm doing the best I can."

"I only wish more players thought that way." Mordechai's crooked grin reminded Peter of Richard Williams. "I only wish I thought that way more myself. You *are* getting better, for whatever it may be worth to you."

"Coming from someone who plays like you, it's worth a lot," Peter said.

Katz looked around. Not seeing Bob Wright, he said, "Your friend has more pride than you do, and cares less about the game." After taking his lumps a few times, Bob didn't square off against him any more.

"I'm stubborn," Peter said.

"One needs to be," Mordechai agreed. Was he speaking as a chessplayer? As a pupil? As a Jew? Peter didn't care to guess.

A couple of weeks later, they fought each other down to a king and a single pawn apiece. The pawns were in the same file, so they blocked each other's paths forward. "Is that a draw?" Peter asked, hardly daring to believe it.

"Nothing else." Katz stuck out his hand. "Good game. You held your concentration all the way through. You didn't do anything wrong. Not quite enough things really right for a win, but nothing wrong."

Peter clasped with him. "Thank you!" In musing tones, he went on, "Held my concentration? I hadn't thought of it like that, but I suppose I did."

"That's what it is, the same as it is with our studies," Katz said. "You have to take notice of every detail. If you let your attention slip, you're ruined."

"Yes." Peter remembered his triumph in the mock trial when he'd spotted the misdated document Jack Bolton missed. Encouraged by that memory, he asked, "Have you got time for another go?"

"Why not?" Mordechai Katz said. Peter soon rued his own request. Try as he would, he couldn't consistently concentrate the way Mordechai did. He found himself down a knight in short order. He fought on for a while, as one can while losing, but Katz made no mistakes. Peter knocked over his own king.

"I should have kept my mouth shut," he said.

"You took your mind off the game for a moment," Katz said. "You pay for that, in chess and anywhere else."

"Don't you, though?" This time, Peter recalled what he could of the night following his mock-trial success. He hadn't exactly taken his mind off the game; he'd got too drunk to have much of a mind to take off. He'd learned some things he'd never known before, and paid with worry that never left him.

As far as he knew, he was healthy. He hadn't shown any of the marks of the Wasting Walter Haywood had. But, with the Wasting, one never knew how far one knew. He might have it in him, waiting to burst forth and blight his life, Viola's, and those of any children they had.

He didn't want to worry about that, so he cast about for something, anything, else. What came out of his mouth was, "Do you mind if I ask you a question?"

"That ... probably depends on what the question is." Katz chose his words with obvious care. After a moment, he waved in invitation. "Go ahead and ask. I don't promise to answer, you understand."

"Oh, yes. Of course." Instead of asking his question, Peter all but blurted it: "What's it like, being a Jew?"

"What's it *like*? Isn't that interesting? I'm not sure I ever asked myself that, at least not that way." Mordechai Katz paused in thought for close to half a minute. "Have you ever been someplace where you're on the outside looking in? Things are going on all around you, but you aren't part of them, you can't be part of them."

Peter thought Viola would understand that better than he did. He said, "When I first came to Lincoln's Inn, I felt that way all the time. I don't so much now. I'm part of the crowd, and I more or less know how things go."

"Fair enough. I may know some of that, too, after I've been here a year. I'm not sure it will do me any good, though. Being a Jew is like being on the outside looking in your whole life long. Everything that happens, happens without you. Most of the time, people don't even notice you're out beyond the touch line, watching. If they do, like as not they'll chuck a stone at you to remind you not to get too close."

That was more of an answer than Peter'd looked to get. Maybe Mordechai trusted him a little, anyhow. Or maybe he'd just taken him by surprise. "How do you live like that, with your nose pressed up against a window, so to speak, but one you can't open or go through?" Peter thought of women's quarters. Yes, Viola would appreciate that.

"There's another good figure of speech." Katz was a year or two younger than Peter, but far more sophisticated, enough so that Peter felt like a child pestering an adult. "We have our own room with that window in it, you see. It's a small room, but when we're together with our own kind, we can make as if the big room on the other side of the glass isn't there at all."

"You're in the big room now," Peter said. "How do you like it here?"

"Some people are decent enough—people like you and Bob." Mordechai held up a hand. "I know what you're thinking. Bob doesn't stay away from me because I'm a Jew. He stays away from me because I beat him like a drum. He'd stay away from me the same way if I were the Cardinal of London."

Peter laughed. "I daresay he would. How likely are you to wear a red hat?"

"Not very," Katz said. "Even if I accepted Catholicism and studied its theology the way I've studied chess, to too many I'd still be that damned Jew convert. Some of the things I hear here ..." He broke off, shaking his head.

"I'm sorry." Peter wouldn't have wanted to be a Jew for all the money in the world. Even so .... Some people in Salisbury baited bulls with dogs. He'd never been able to see the sport in it. The bull, tied to an iron pole driven into the ground, could hardly fight back.

No more could a lone Jew against a swarm of tormentors. It hardly seemed fair.

"I knew it would be like this. I looked for it to be worse, to tell you the truth. I expected the louts and the ones who think they're wits. I hadn't been sure anyone would treat me like a human being. I've read *The Jew of Malta* too many times, I suppose."

Peter'd read it, too. Most people who read English would have; Marlowe was one of the touchstones of style to this day. He'd read it thinking Barabas the Jew deserved everything he got in the play. His schoolmaster taught it that way—of course he did. Peter'd never wondered how it might look to someone from the other side of that imaginary window he'd talked about a few minutes earlier. If he ever taught anyone *The Jew of Malta*, he wouldn't do it the way his schoolmaster had.

Till now, he hadn't realized the window had two sides.

Richard Williams traveled to London, something Viola could hardly do on her own. In Temecula, she might have; not in England. Her father came back with a black-painted wooden lockbox. When he unlocked it, everyone in the family oohed and ahhed.

"I've never seen so much gold in one place at the same time," Viola said.

"It's yours, chick. You earned it," he said.

"I'm going to write a book and get rich," Margaret said. "If Vi can do it, I can, too."

"Go ahead," her mother said. "If you can, more power to you."

"When will it be a book?" Kate asked. "A real book, I mean, bound and with pages and everything else that goes into one?"

"Not for a while yet," Viola said. "I still have to see what kinds of little changes the publisher wants me to make, and whether I want them made. Some other things have to happen, too." She would have gone into more detail, but she didn't know any more. She was learning as she went along.

"You're still earning your money," her father said. "If you'd known it would be so much work, would you ever have started?"

"Of course I would. I'm not so sure I would have finished, though," Viola answered. Richard Williams chuckled and sketched a salute.

225

The next day, Viola went into town with her sisters and her mother. She made a point of popping into Blackwell's bookshop and telling the proprietor about her sale of *A Voyage to the Island of the Temeculans.*

Blackwell beamed at her. "There's splendid news!" he exclaimed. "I confess I'm less surprised than I might be that someone who reads so many books would come to write one—from all I've heard, it often works that way. Thomas Egerton, you said? A good house! You may be sure I shall order copies for the shop."

"Thank you, Master Blackwell," she said, grinning behind her veil. That was just what she'd hoped to hear.

In due course, the manuscript she'd sent to London came back to her. It was marked with comments and queries between the lines and in the margins, with occasional changed words, and with symbols some of whose meanings she could puzzle out—some, but not all. Far from all. An accompanying letter from Thomas Egerton said he wanted the manuscript returned within a month.

"How can I return it if I don't know what it's talking about half the time?" she said the next day, in something close to despair.

"Have you looked to see if we have any books that might explain your strange squiggles?" her father asked.

"I have. We don't," she answered gloomily.

"All right." He seemed much less upset than she felt. *Of course he does!* she thought. *It's not his book!* He went on, "Do the things you can do. I'll see what I can find out about the whatever-they-ares."

He left the house early the next morning, taking with him a manuscript page leprous with incomprehensibilities. He came back an hour and a half later with the page and with a smaller sheet of paper. Someone had written PRINTING MARKS at the top and then gone on to set down symbols and what they stood for.

Viola squeezed him. "Where did you *get* these?"

"Well, I went to Mort Blackwell, thinking someone in the book trade would know how manuscripts turned into volumes. He did know some, but not enough to make either one of us happy. So he sent me on to Henry Whyte, the printer. I don't know him at all well, but he was kind enough to help me anyhow."

"Please thank him for me, from the bottom of my heart!"

"I already did."

"Thank you, in that case," Viola said, and then, a moment later, "He doesn't come to you for doctoring, does he?"

"No, he sees old Osbert French, on the north side of town," her father answered. "He told me so. He also told me to congratulate you."

"Something else to thank him for."

"I took care of it, believe me." Richard Williams smiled his crooked smile. "When Osbert finally stops working or, God forbid, dies, I expect I'll inherit a good many people who've been seeing him for years."

"They won't pay you any better than your own regulars do," Viola predicted.

"I'm sure you're right. Over pints in a pub, Osbert will talk about the chap who gave him squirrel skins for lancing a boil, and the one who wanted to give him a pair of old boots for cutting off a big wart on his cheek." Her father chuckled. "He's likely been telling those stories as long as I've been alive."

"He didn't take the boots?"

"He would have, but they were too small. He got a couple of shillings out of that one. A couple of shillings! And here you are with all your shiny gold."

"If you don't think I'm as surprised as you are, you'd better think again."

"I'm very proud to have a lady author in the family. I hope Peter will be, too."

"From what he says in his letters, he seems to be." Viola worried about it, too. "His sisters like the idea. He told them about it; I didn't."

"That's a good sign." Her father pointed to the manuscript. "Do you think you'll be able to get it back to Egerton now soon enough to keep him happy?"

She nodded. "I should, yes."

She sent it off to London with a week to spare, which gave it plenty of time to get to her publisher. Thomas Egerton wrote back, *My dear Miss Williams, This is to acknowledge receipt of the edited manuscript for your book. I thank you for returning it in so timely a fashion. Women seem more apt to do that than men; men, however, invent far more fanciful excuses for their tardiness. When the typesetting is complete, I shall send you galleys for your examination. Ahead of them, I send best wishes and the hope that you may prove as punctual with them as you have thus far. Yours most sincerely—* Egerton's signature was even more cramped than the rest of his hand.

The galleys got there a month later. Seeing her name on the title page, and her words in print rather than her own script, made the book seem real to her in a way it hadn't before. When it was between boards, it would look like this—except for as many typographical errors as she could root out beforehand. She went through the pages with what she hoped was an eagle eye—and with Henry Whyte's list of marks close at hand.

"Now I know why they call it galley slavery!" she exclaimed one day in the kitchen when she was nearly done, and mimed pulling a heavy oar.

"That's not the same thing," Margaret said with a sneer that made Viola want to give her hair a good yank.

Nobly restraining herself, she answered, "It feels as though it is."

"How do you know? You never rowed in a galley," Margaret said.

"I don't think anyone in England who's still alive ever has, unless it was some traders who got captured by the Sharif of Casablanca or the Bey of Tunis," Viola said. "The Venetians and some other Italians still have a few slave galleys, but not many. Almost all sails these days in Christendom."

"How do you know all that?" This time, the youngest Williams sister sounded suspicious.

"How do you think? I read things. Not as if a woman from Salisbury can sail down to the Mediterranean herself and see what it's like. I wish I could—the weather is a lot nicer than it is here." Viola gave Margaret her best dirty look. "And if I did, you'd be out of my hair for a while."

"If you could go, I could, too," Margaret retorted, which was bound to be true. Then she aimed an accusing forefinger at Viola. "*That's* how come you wrote your Temeculans the way you did—so they could go and really do all the things you only wish you could."

"You just now figured that out, Mistress Ninny? You aren't half as smart as you wish you were," Viola said.

"If you call people names like 'Mistress Ninny,' *you* aren't half as smart as you think you are, either," her mother said.

Viola didn't think that was fair. Margaret got away with provoking her unbearably, while she couldn't hit back even a little? She knew better than to complain, though. Mother would just tell her she was the eldest, she was twenty now, and she needed to behave in proper ladylike fashion. She could hear the words inside her own head in Jane Williams' voice. She didn't need her actual ears for that.

Margaret stuck out her tongue at her. "That will be enough from you, too, my dear," Mother said. Viola didn't think she'd ever heard *my dear* sound less endearing.

Margaret deflated. "Sorry, Mother," she muttered, and even sounded as if she halfway meant it.

"That's better," Jane Williams said serenely. She turned to Viola. "If your arms aren't *too* worn from rowing, do you suppose you could peel some potatoes?"

"I might be just about able to do that," Viola answered. "Just about."

Her mother looked at her. "The only way you could sound more like your father would be to come out with that in a baritone."

"Even by Temeculan standards, that would take the equality of the sexes too far," Viola said with dignity. Margaret made a horrible face.

Viola attacked the potatoes with a paring knife. If she had a little extra gusto when she went after the first few … then she did, that was all. The potatoes plopped into a big wooden bowl with a cracked bottom. It was older than Viola, probably older than her mother. It wouldn't hold liquids any more—the crack went all the way through. But for something like this, or for chopping meat or vegetables in it, it was fine. The Williamses weren't rich enough or vain enough to throw things away when they could still get some use out of them.

The peelings went onto the midden. In due course, they'd help nourish plants in the garden. When the family kept a pig, it would have eaten the refuse instead. Right now, they didn't.

After the potatoes boiled till they were soft, they went back into the bowl for mashing. Margaret did that, stirring in butter and cream all the while. She grumbled about how much work it was.

Viola looked on with a superior air—but made sure she kept her back to Mother so she wouldn't get caught at it.

She finished the galleys the next day. Back to Whitehall they went. Again, Thomas Egerton sent a letter letting her know they'd made it there. *As I noted with the copy-edited manuscript, I greatly appreciate your prompt attention to the minutiae involved in seeing a book through production. It makes things far easier here, believe me,* he wrote.

You are kind enough not only to print it but to pay me for the privilege of so doing, she replied. *If I can make your task easier, I am happy to do so.*

A week later, she heard from him again. *If only all authors viewed things from this perspective, a publisher's life would be a happier one. When your writing becomes as well known as it assuredly deserves to be, I pray you will remember and cling to the principles you espouse today.*

She showed her father that letter. "Why shouldn't I act the same way after my ... oh, I don't know, say my tenth book as I do with the first?"

Richard Williams rubbed his chin. "Master Egerton is a Londoner. In Salisbury, people don't get famous enough to think the rules are for everyone but them. People who want to be that famous mostly move to London; it's the only place where they can."

"Oh." Viola chewed on that. "I have my vanity, heaven knows. Everybody does. But the idea of a woman's being able to put it on display is just ... silly, even if I wanted to."

"You know that, and so do I, but your estimable publisher doesn't," her father said. "And lady authors break the rules for their sex. Excuse me: for your sex. They don't become famous for themselves, but for their words. They don't have to put themselves on display, either, only those words."

"It would be different in Temecula. That's why I wrote what I wrote—to show that it might be better to live so," Viola said.

"I know. It probably would be, if not for the Wasting."

"Yes. If not for ... Is *Timor mortis conturbat me* to ruin the whole world until the end of time?"

She got no help from Richard Williams. "Probably," he said. "Very little is stronger than the urge to go on living and not to die. I've seen folk dying in torment from the Wasting or from cancers beg me for potions to give them an extra day, an extra week, an extra month. Not to relieve them of their agony—they're past that, long past it. Only for more time."

"Even with the hope of heaven before them? Even after they've had the last rites to ease their going?"

"Even then. Everyone is sure of this world. It's all we know ourselves. I hope the priests are right about the one to come. I pray they are. I even believe they are—on good days I do, anyhow. But I don't *know* they are, nor does anyone else." Viola's father held up a hasty hand. "I say this to *you*, you understand. I say such things to your mother now and then. To no one else. I should not wish others to hear them."

"You wouldn't say them to me if you thought I gossiped," Viola replied. "You would have to be a fool to do that, and—"

"I am a great fool, many kinds of a great fool, as any man is," he broke in. "But you're right. I'm not that kind, or I'd better not be. Still and all, better to say without needing than to need without saying."

"Fair enough." Viola nodded.

Somewhere in London, men would be making small changes in the type they'd set, changes based on the squiggles she'd sent to Thomas Egerton. Would they pay close attention? Or would it be just part of their everyday work, something for them to get through as fast as they could so they'd be able to move on to the next manuscript or set of corrections?

She hoped for the first while suspecting the second was more likely. She imagined her typesetter puffing on a pipe and swapping jokes with the fellow who worked beside him. His hand would reach for the proper piece of type from the case the way hers reached for the right knife from the right drawer in the kitchen. He wouldn't need to think about it to do it. Thinking about it might get in the way.

Pages. Pages sewn in signatures. Signatures bound between buckram-covered boards. Her title and her name—*her* name!—stamped on the front cover and on the spine. Stamped perhaps even in gold leaf that would stay shiny forever.

What could be grander than that?

The next time she went to confession, she told the priest about the pride she felt when she thought of the finished book that was coming, along with a representative but incomplete sample of her other sins of word and deed, omission and commission. She worked her rosary beads as she knelt and recited Our Fathers and Hail Marys for her act of contrition.

She felt better after she left Salisbury Cathedral. Confessing sins didn't mean she wouldn't go right on sinning. She was a human being, and human beings sinned. Sinning was part of what made people human. She believed that. She also believed she was better for letting the sins out rather than holding them inside her to fester.

(And she believed the Church was more apt to see sin in women than in men. After all, the Serpent had tempted Eve, not Adam. She believed the Church was more apt to think women sparked sin in men than the other way round, too. She also knew better than to admit having such beliefs to anyone but her parents and possibly Kate. Not even Margaret—Margaret's tongue sometimes ran ahead of her brain.)

Viola wondered whether she'd be able to admit holding such beliefs to Peter. She hoped so. She wondered if he had such beliefs himself, and how he'd feel about admitting them to her.

Things to find out, she thought.

A day or so later, she wondered—again!—whether he carried the silent seeds of the Wasting inside him, and whether their wedding would be followed in too short an order by sickness and death.

Things to find out echoed in her mind once more.

"What am I going to do?" she asked her mother.

"Will you be happier if you put the marriage aside?" Jane Williams asked. "If you will, then do that. None of us will say a word against you. Would you rather have children of your mind than of your body?"

"I'd rather have both," Viola said. "But I'm afraid."

"The Wasting came more than three hundred years ago," her mother said. "Everyone since then has been afraid. One of these days, if God is kind, that curse will be lifted from us, but it hasn't happened yet and it doesn't look like happening any time soon. Till then, we go on as best we know how."

"Not even so much that the Wasting is the curse. The fear of it is, I think," Viola said. "The fear ruins everything."

"I know. Not many families it hasn't touched, and it's a slow, horrible way to die. God made us want to do the things that replenish the world, and He made the illness that slaughters us when we do. If I should ever see Him face to face, I want to ask Him some questions about that."

"You sound like Father!" Viola said.

"Do I?" Jane Williams looked amused. "That's one more thing that happens when you're married a long time. You'll find out … or else you won't. It's up to you."

Afterwards, Peter remembered very little of the last six weeks before his examinations for the bar. There probably wasn't much to remember. You remembered things that were different. Everything in those six weeks was the same. He stayed in his room all the time, coming out only to eat. He was desperately trying to soak up as much knowledge as he could.

Master Heath had told him he'd never know so much as he did the day he sat his examinations. He hadn't believed that then. He almost did now. He'd proved a more capacious sponge than he'd dreamt he could.

When examination day drew near, many of the second-year pupils looked as harried as he felt. Even rich, smooth, confident Bob Wright showed the strain. One evening at supper, he sent Peter a ghastly grin. "Remind me again why we ever wanted to do this," he said.

"Ask somebody else. I've got no idea," Peter replied.

"You aren't playing chess, either," Bob noted.

"Chess? What's that?" Peter said, and his friend laughed. Peter went on, "I haven't the time for it, and I haven't the brains for it, either."

"Well, I know what you mean, and that's the Lord's truth. You're making Katz sad, though. He's stuck playing the new lads, and not a one of them has the staying power you do."

"Not a one of them's such a glutton for punishment as I am, you mean," Peter answered.

"You said it. I didn't." Bob picked up his plate and silverware—everyone called it that, although of course it was cheap pewter. Rolling his eyes, he said, "Back to the swotting."

"I'm only a couple of minutes behind you," Peter said.

When the appointed day and time rolled around, Peter approached the examination room assigned to him with the same dragging steps a convicted murderer surely used on his way to the gibbet. As required, he carried three quills, a pen knife, and a bottle of ink. He knew he would spill a lot of it before he staggered forth.

The room held half a dozen widely separated tables, each with a hard chair behind it. On each lay a stack of paper. At the front of the room, a master sat in a more comfortable chair. "Good day, Master Drinkwater," he said, and made a tickmark on a list.

"Good day, Master Brentford," Peter said in a voice even he could barely hear.

Two other pupils were already sitting at the frontmost tables. Peter slid behind one in the second row. He was ten minutes early. The remaining places filled before anyone was tardy.

Brentford stood. "Is everybody in?" he asked rhetorically. "The ceremony is about to begin. I shall serve as your proctor. If I see any sign of cheating, your head will roll. It really is that simple. Do you understand me?"

Peter nodded. The master waited a moment, presumably so everyone else could nod, too. Then he resumed: "This of course includes copying off any other examination you may be able to read. So that you shall not be led into temptation, know that each of you will have either different questions or questions posed in different orders. Again, do you understand me?"

All the pupils nodded once more. *They've done this a great many times* ran through Peter's mind. *They know the tricks pupils can play. And they know how to make sure pupils don't play them.* Master Brentford walked down the aisle between the three rows of tables. On each table he set a sheet of paper, face down.

Once he'd given out all the examinations, the master strode back to his chair. Before sitting down, he declared, "You may turn over your sheets and begin work. Make sure you set your name on each page you write. You have six hours. Use your time wisely."

Peter looked at his questions. When he saw the second one, a smile stretched across his face. He'd had to answer one almost identical to it only a few months earlier, and he'd reviewed the text on the relation between secular and canon law just a few days ago. He knew he'd make hay on that one. The others …

Quills were already scratching across paper as his comrades in misery got to work. He paused for half a minute before starting to write himself; he wanted to have his ideas in order first. Then his pen also began to race. He hoped the masters would be able to puzzle out his hasty scrawl. Well, it wasn't as if they'd have no practice at reading bad handwriting.

A clock on the wall near Master Brentford ticked away the minutes. Peter noticed the noise only when he looked up to see how he was doing for time. He finished the first question just before the hour-and-a-half mark. The second had to do with the King's power to legislate, Parliament's, and the Papacy's.

As he had on the earlier examination, he started with the principle stated in the *Digest* of Justinian: *Quod principi placuit, legis habet vigorem.* What pleases the ruler has the force of law. He traced the modifications to that rule up through time to the present, inclining more to secular power than to ecclesiastical. He wasn't trying to become a canon lawyer, after all.

His biggest problem with that one was not to spend three hours on it and slight the last two. Realizing he knew more than he had time to set down helped ease his mind. He did overwrite, but only by a few minutes.

He was slogging through the last question when Master Brentford said, "Half an hour to go." Then it was "Fifteen minutes." Then "Five minutes." And then "Set down your pens at once. This examination is over."

Peter'd finished half a minute before. His wrist ached. His hand was sore. He shook it to try to bring back some life. He wasn't the only one doing that: nowhere near. He realized how badly he needed to piss.

Brentford took the examinations. Once he had them all, he said, "Those who pass will be informed tomorrow of the time and room for their oral questioning. You are dismissed. Oh"—an afterthought—"good luck."

All the second-year pupils looked wrung out at supper that evening. "I know I enjoyed that," Bob Wright said with a smile from beyond the grave. Peter's answering grin was perfect gallows.

Someone knocked on his door the next morning soon after break-fast. He opened it. There stood Stephen Heath. "We shall see you in the Harnham Room at nine tomorrow morning," the master said.

"Thank you, Master," Peter answered, but Heath was already on his way down the hall.

One more day to try to pickle himself in legal lore. Some of the pupils played football instead, to relax themselves. Peter stayed in and tried to ignore the shouts and the occasional wail of pain that floated in through his window.

He reported to the appointed room at the appointed time. Master Heath, Master Brentford, and two more equally stern men awaited him there. Heath did smile when he asked, "Are you ready, Master Drinkwater?"

"As ready as I'll ever be, Master," Peter said, not sure how ready that was.

It seemed to satisfy Stephen Heath. "Very well," he said, and closed the door behind Peter. The click of the latch sounded dreadfully final. Heath waved Peter to a chair. "Take your seat, take your seat."

He took his seat. It began. Afterwards, he recalled next to nothing of what happened in there. It was as if Viola's father had used a scalpel to slice three hours out of his life; try as he would, he never got most of them back. The masters asked him things. He answered, or tried to answer. They asked him more. It went on and on.

Then, not quite knowing how he'd got there, he stood in the hallway outside the door, with it closed against him. Inside the Harnham Room, the masters debated his fate. He could only wait for what they decided. If they didn't think he'd shown well enough, he'd have to do his second year over again. He wondered whether he could bear that, and whether his father would pay for it.

The door opened. Stephen Heath looked at him, stone faced … for a moment. Then the master grinned. "Congratulations!" he said. "Welcome to the club!" He stuck out his right hand. Dazedly, Peter shook it. In his left hand, Heath held a shot glass of whiskey. "Here. Drink this. You look as though you could use it, by heaven!"

Peter believed that. Choking a little, he got the whiskey down. It burned, then warmed. He leaned against the wall; his legs didn't want to hold him up. "Dear God!" he breathed. "I made it."

XVI

"**V**iola!" Richard Williams called from the foot of the stairs. "Come down here a moment, will you?"

"What is it?" she asked in some annoyance—she was taking more notes for the book she meant to write next. "Can it wait?"

"However you please, of course," he said, "but the postman's brought you a parcel from London."

"Oh!" She dropped the pen and all but flew down the staircase. No matter how fast she was, Margaret beat her to the ground floor. Kate and Jane Williams were no more than a step behind her.

Her father held the parcel on the palm of his right hand. It was of a goodish size, securely wrapped in heavy brown paper, and tied with twine. By the script, Thomas Egerton himself had addressed it to her.

"What do you suppose it could be?" Father wondered aloud, his voice full of knowing innocence.

"Take it into the kitchen and open it on the table," Mother said.

He nodded. "That's an excellent notion." Into the kitchen he went, the women of the family parading after him. He had his pick of knives and scissors in there, but disdained them all, instead taking a little leather case from his pocket and extracting a scalpel. The small blade cut the twine and slit the paper protecting whatever lurked inside. Then he bowed to Viola, as if at court. "It's your parcel. Care to do the rest of the honors yourself?"

She didn't answer with words, but made short work of the wrapping paper. "It's real," she breathed, staring at the books. The publisher had sent her a dozen: four stacks of three. They were bound in light blue buckram. *A Voyage to the Island of the Temeculans* and her name were printed on the cover in black ink, but, she saw, in gold leaf on the spine. Not exactly the way she'd envisioned it, but close enough, close enough.

As if in a dream, she picked one up. It was so new, it still smelled of printer's ink. She opened it. There on the title page were her chosen title and her name again, along with the name and address of Thomas Egerton's firm. The next page bore the *nihil obstat* and the *imprimatur*. The one was given by a certain Edward J. Rivers, S.J., *Censor Librorum*. The other came from the Bishop of Watford, Terence Johnson, and bore a small cross.

"I don't ever remember seeing these names on an approval page before," Viola said. She was the kind of person who noticed and remembered such things.

Richard Williams chuckled. "You were smart to ask for a hundred fifty pounds net, not gross. What will you bet Egerton had to cast his net wider and spend more coin than he expected to find men who'd give him the go-ahead?"

"I don't think I want to touch that," Viola replied. Under Bishop Johnson's name lay the standard text: *The* nihil obstat *and* imprimatur *are official declarations that a book or pamphlet is free of doctrinal or moral error. No implication is contained therein that those who have granted the* nihil obstat *and* imprimatur *agree with the contents or statements expressed.*

She usually took that for granted. Now .... Now she imagined two or three *Censores Librorum* reading, frowning, and shaking their heads. Once Egerton had found a friendly or worldly or venal Jesuit to give the *nihil obstat*, she imagined him going from bishop to bishop around London till one of them consented to the *imprimatur*.

"It doesn't matter," her mother said firmly. "However it happened, it happened. That's what matters. And your book is there for the whole world to see. That matters, too." She hugged Viola. Viola squeezed back, hard.

When they separated, Viola picked up that first copy again. She turned to the first page of the actual story. There they were: her words, as she'd written them, in print for the whole world to see, as her mother had said. The thought was dizzying—dizzying enough so she set her free hand on the tabletop to steady herself.

Margaret asked, "How soon do you think you'll find a mistake you missed when you were going through it before?"

"Oh, hush! What a thing to say!" Kate told her.

She sounded angrier than Viola felt. Viola only laughed. "It will probably happen. By the time I went over the galleys, I'd been through the story so often, I'm sure I missed something. Nobody's perfect but God." *And even He gave us the Wasting*, she thought, though she knew better than to say that out loud.

Margaret nodded, even if she looked disappointed. She'd hoped to get a rise out of her older sister, and she hadn't done it. *A soft answer turneth away pests*, went through Viola's mind. *Sometimes*.

"Now that it really is a book, will you read it again?" Kate asked—she could find sly questions, too.

"Probably," Viola admitted with another laugh. She picked up a different copy and held it out to her father. "Will you give this to Alf Drinkwater, please, with my compliments? He may as well know the worst about his to-be-daughter-in-law as soon as he can."

"I was going to ask for one if you hadn't beaten me to it," he answered. "I'll do that tomorrow morning, in fact. He can read it, and his wife and daughters can read it, and once they have we'll go on from there."

"I'm sure it will be all right," Jane Williams said, though she sounded less sure than she might have, as anyone who said something like that was apt to.

"If it's not all right, better we find out before the wedding than afterwards," Father said.

Viola nodded; the same thought had crossed her mind. "It isn't so very scandalous," she said. "It just wonders what the world would look like without the Wasting. I can't be the only one who's thought about that."

"No, eh?" Richard Williams said.

More sharply than she usually spoke, Viola's mother said, "Every woman ever born these past however many years, whether in Christendom or amongst the Turks or the heathen Chinese, has thought about that."

"I'm sure you're right," Viola said.

Father looked from one of them to the other. "Since you started the book, Viola, I've come to realize how very unhappy women are."

"Better late than never," Viola snapped. Her mother and sisters stared at her; even inside the family, women didn't commonly show how fed up with the world they were. She sighed. "At least you have realized it. Most men never have the slightest idea." She sighed again. "I wonder whether Alf and Peter Drinkwater know, or even suspect."

"If they don't, they'll find out as soon as their womenfolk start going through your book," Kate said.

"That would be good." Viola hoped Julietta and Joanna and their mother would react the way Kate expected. If they didn't—if they turned out to be the kind of submissive women priests so often preached about—living with the Drinkwaters seemed more likely to prove hell on earth than heaven.

"I think it will work out. I hope it will. I pray it will," Richard Williams said. "Alf and I wouldn't have made the match if we hadn't thought you and Peter could get along, and that the rest of the family would like you."

"I understand that," Viola said. "It is strange, though, to be bought and sold like a pound of mutton, or like a slave on the auction block in America."

"That goes too far. A slave can't say no when he changes hands. You could have, and no one would have said a word about it," her father answered with some irritation of his own.

"Because you and the Drinkwaters would have allowed it. Plenty of women never get that chance. No one *must* give it to them," Viola said. Yes, things went differently on the island of the Temeculans. Marriage there was by choice of both parties. So was divorce. That might have been part of the reason Thomas Egerton had had to look hither and yon to find clergymen who would let her book sneak into print.

He let out a sigh of his own. "This is the world that cursèd disease has given us. I don't know what else to tell you."

"This is the world men made because of that cursèd disease. I don't recall hearing of their ever asking women what *they* thought of it," Viola retorted. His mouth twisted. She guessed he wanted to tell her she was wrong, but couldn't without lying—and, worse, obviously lying. She respected him for not doing that, anyhow.

A few days later, she went up to the bookshop with Kate and Margaret and their mother. Mortimer Blackwell had been as good as his word. He'd not only got half a dozen copies of her romance, he'd set them on the counter in front of his own place with a little sign by them: *The new book by a woman of Salisbury.*

He smiled when he recognized the Williamses, smiled and held up *A Voyage to the Island of the Temeculans.* "Hello! May I interest you in a new book, Mistress Viola? You've always enjoyed travelers' tales, and this one's excellent. I've been through it, so I know what I'm talking about."

Viola smiled, too, even if he couldn't see her do so. "Thank you, Master Blackwell. Thank you very much indeed, but I fear I've already read it." Everybody laughed.

Peter got down from the diligence in front of the King's Arms in Salisbury. A moment later, the driver handed his trunk down from the roof. He set it between his feet and stretched till his joints creaked and cracked. Then he picked up the trunk, grunting at the weight.

A few seconds after that, his father and Clarence Starr folded him into bear hugs. "Welcome home, lad! Welcome home!" Alfred Drinkwater said. "And congratulations!"

"Thank you, Father." Peter squeezed the older man and his friend in return. "Have the two of you been waiting long?"

"Not too," his father answered. He was puffing on his pipe; Peter suddenly wondered whether Walter Haywood had graded and priced the tobacco in it. "The coach was supposed to come in an hour ago. I knew better than to believe that, so I got here half an hour ago. I didn't expect it that soon, you understand, but it could've happened."

"What does Salisbury look like after two years in London?" Clarence asked.

"It's smaller than I remembered. Till I saw London, I thought this was a real city. Now? I shouldn't need an hour to walk across it."

His father laughed at that, then stopped all at once. "The reason it's funny is, I said almost the same thing when I got home. But Salisbury's big enough for me."

"I think it will be big enough for me, too," Peter said. "Let's head home."

Toward home they went. Everything seemed familiar to Peter, familiar enough so a couple of buildings with fresh coats of paint and one with new brickwork startled him.

They were about halfway there when Clarence peeled off. "My old man's got work for me," he said. "I'll see you soon."

"You're right. You will," Peter said, and waved a good-bye. Clarence might wed Joanna or Julietta one day, the way he himself was going to marry Viola, but it would be highly improper for him to go into the Drinkwater house and see them before that time came, if it did.

Then Peter's father spoke in casual tones that really weren't: "Doctor Williams will want to see you in his surgery when you have the chance."

"He will? Why?" Peter said.

"To make as sure as he can that you're all right before you yoke yourself to Viola, that's why," his father answered.

"Oh. I should have thought. Yes, I can pay him a call," Peter said. "Um, do Mother and my sisters know about that?" Viola must have let her father know, though, and he would have told Peter's father. He couldn't blame her, not when it was so important and when Richard Williams was a doctor.

Alfred Drinkwater shook his head. "No. I didn't, either, not till I got the news from Dick." He scowled for a moment, but no longer. "I can see why you clammed up about it in your letters home. I'm just surprised you told Viola."

"I thought she needed to know. I … I wasn't exactly proud of myself when I wrote to her, right after it happened," Peter said. "I was afraid, too." With Walter Haywood for a roommate, he'd learned more about that fear than he'd ever dreamt he might.

"Oh. Well, Lord knows I can understand that." They walked on for a few paces before his father resumed: "I was stupid that way once myself, when I was at Lincoln's Inn. I told Dick about it, but not another soul, not till now. Your mother and sisters have no idea. I was lucky. I'll burn candles that you are, too."

Peter didn't know what to say to that, so he didn't say anything. His father had always struck him as a stuffy, somewhat overstuffed man of conspicuous virtue. Imagining him at twenty or so and wild for life? The effort was too much for Peter. He gave it up as a bad job.

He wondered whether Richard Williams had told Viola about his father's fall from chastity. He suspected the doctor might have; that would show her one didn't necessarily catch the Wasting from sinning once. Of course, one didn't necessarily *not* catch it, either. One never knew.

After a few more steps, his father turned the subject a little. "She's quite the author, that fiancée of yours. Dick gave me a copy of her book, and we've all been through it by now."

"Everyone but me," Peter said mournfully. "The last letter I had from her before I left London, she told me Egerton had sent her copies. I'll have to catch up to everybody else."

"It's better than I looked for it to be. It reads so much like a real traveler's tale, you don't realize what she's driving at straight away. When you do—" Alfred Drinkwater whistled, a long, low note. "I'm gobsmacked her publisher found churchmen to sign off on it. Of course, the bloke who gave her the *nihil obstat* is a Jesuit."

"Ah," Peter said. Ever since its foundation, the Society of Jesus had had a name for cleverness, and a name for worldliness. Jesuits fiercely fought heresy and misbelief wherever they found them, but they didn't always find them where ordinary people would. Like a lot of Englishmen, Peter was a little suspicious of the Soldiers of the Pope.

Then he stopped caring about the Jesuits or anything else, because they turned on to the street where his family lived. Coming up the walk to the front door, he felt as if he were moving in a dream. His father threw the door wide and shouted, "Look what fell off the diligence!"

Squeals came from the kitchen, where Peter's female kin could gather without fear of being seen from outside. He gladly set down the trunk and hurried in there. Everything looked the way it had when he left; he might have stepped out of the house an hour earlier, not two years. He might have, except for the way his mother and sisters burst into tears as they hugged him. He felt like bursting into tears himself, but, though his eyes stung, he didn't.

"You've grown!" his mother said. Julietta and Joanna both nodded.

Peter shrugged. "Have I? Not much. Not even enough for me to notice."

"You have," his mother insisted. "A good inch, I'd say. And your beard is so much thicker than it was."

He rubbed his chin and nodded himself. He agreed with that. "I've thought about letting it grow. Quite a few men do."

"Maybe you should wait to see what your bride thinks about that," his father said.

"Oh." That hadn't occurred to Peter. He realized it should have. "Yes, you're bound to be right." He sniffed. "What smells so good?"

"They've killed the fatted calf for you, prodigal," his father replied with a chuckle.

"We have not! That's a goose roasting in a pot over the fire. Anyone with a nose should be able to tell," Julietta said.

Alfred Drinkwater rubbed his. "It's big enough and to spare, heaven knows. I might almost make a Jew." He chuckled.

Peter's mother and sister laughed, too. He didn't. He was sure he would have before he traveled to London and got to know Mordechai Katz. The clever first-year pupil might be bound for hell because he didn't believe in the divinity of Jesus Christ, but here on earth he was a pretty good fellow. Peter knew he never would have thought anything like that about a Jew before he went to Lincoln's Inn. He'd learned things there that had nothing to do with the law.

He kept quiet about that. He didn't want to touch off a quarrel as soon as he got home. Instead, he said, "Has everybody here finished Viola's book? I want to look at it as soon as I can."

"It's … not what I expected it to be," Joanna said. "It's good—don't mistake me. It makes you wonder why things are the way they are. But how does she write about faraway places as though she's seen them with her own eyes?"

"She likes reading travelers' accounts. I suppose some of what she reads goes into what she writes."

"She's always had a passion for those," his father agreed. "Dick would talk about it when she was only this high." He held his hand at the level where his chest and belly joined. "He thought it was funny then. If she can make a book out of it, if she can make money out of it, it's not so funny after all."

"Some of the things in there … I don't know how the church let it go into print," Peter's mother said. "It isn't, mm, nasty, but it's frank. That's the word—frank."

His father nodded. "I said the same thing when we were walking back here."

"Well, you people aren't making me want to read it *less*," Peter said. His mother and father and sisters laughed.

Then his father picked up a large wooden bucket. "I'm going to the Swan and Leopard around the corner, to bring back some beer."

"Do you want me to come along and carry the full bucket back?" Peter asked.

"No, I'll be fine. Sit down, relax. You're just home, and you've come a long way." Out the door Alfred Drinkwater went.

Peter didn't feel like sitting down. He felt as if he'd been sitting forever; ninety miles *was* a long way. He stood there and talked with Joanna and Julietta and his mother.

His father came back soon, red faced and listing a little to the right, the hand in which he held the bucket. With a grunt, he lifted it up onto the table. Amanda Drinkwwater put in a dipper. Joanna got mugs for them all. Peter's father filled them.

He lifted his on high. "To the prodigal's return!" he said. "And return as a passed member of the bar!" The mugs clinked together. Peter made sure each touched all the others—that was important. Everybody drank.

"Ahh!" Peter said. "This is better stuff than they gave us in the refectory."

"Isn't it, though?" his father said. "They dished out whatever was cheapest there. At the Swan and Leopard, they want you to like it, or you'll go somewhere else."

A couple of mugs remarkably improved Peter's attitude. So did a goose thigh, dark meat juicy and dripping with fat, the skin all golden and crackling under his teeth. "This is wonderful!" he said when he got too full to eat any more (which took a while). "It's so good to be home!"

"You're only telling us that because we've fed you," Julietta teased.

"Not *only*," Peter said, which got another laugh. He washed his hands in the basin that would soon be full of dishes and silverware, and dried them on a dish towel. "I don't want to leave greasy finger marks on the pages of Viola's book."

"I'll get it for you." Julietta went upstairs and came back with it. Seeing Viola's name on the cover made it feel real for Peter. It also intimidated him more than he cared to admit, even to himself. He'd known he was going to marry a clever woman; that had been plain from the start. Viola'd been clever back in the days when they were small enough to play together, too. Being clever, though, was one thing. Being clever enough to write a book and get money for it? That was something else again.

He took the book out to the parlor and started reading while his mother and sisters cleaned up. Before long, he saw what Joanna meant; Viola wrote about a storm in the South Pacific as if one had almost pitched her overboard. Then the *Ad Astra* found Temecula, and he got to the heart of things.

The Temeculans were at least equal to their discoverers in the mechanic arts, but their society was very different. Men and women were as near equals as made no difference, and educated the same way. Men took the risks of warfare, women the risks of childbed. Peter hadn't looked at it that way before, but decided Viola had a point.

Yes, the Temeculans went nude most of the time. Their kind climate encouraged the habit, and without the Wasting they didn't worry about stirring up desire. *If one must be a heathen, there are worse ways to live*, Viola's English narrator declared.

What the Temeculans' fate would be now that the wider world had found them, Peter's intended left undefined. But if they were hospitable to visitors, as they were with the *Ad Astra*, wouldn't the Wasting silently, swiftly, and surely establish itself amongst them, as it had everywhere else? Wouldn't it end their days of easygoing commerce between the sexes?

And wouldn't that be a tragedy?

So Peter read it, anyhow. He finished the book by lamplight, having got up to set two burning when it grew too dark for him to read without them. As his family did, he wondered how Viola and her publisher had got her story past the Church. The *Censor Librorum* and the bishop who'd given the *imprimatur* were both celibate, of course; maybe they hadn't read the book the way the Drinkwaters had.

Peter snorted. Of course they had. Men—and women—who were supposed to be celibate weren't always, any more than other people were. (*Any more than I was myself,* he thought uneasily.) He knew all kinds of dirty jokes about priests and monks and nuns. Everybody did. That kind of joke went back hundreds of years, back to the days before the Wasting cast its shadow across the world.

His father stepped into the parlor just as he closed Viola's book. "What do you think?" Alfred Drinkwater asked.

"She writes very well. I knew that from her letters," Peter said. "The story …. You're bound to be right. Her publisher must have paid off the clerics who let it through. Otherwise, it never would have seen print."

"It will stir up a ruction amongst the women who read it. You can count on that," his father answered. "Let me tell you, it stirred up a ruction in this house. In the Williams house, too, as she was working on it, from what Dick tells me."

"I'm not surprised. Maybe we need some of that. Viola certainly seems to think we do," Peter said.

"Just a bit!" his father said. "Marriage may make her look at things differently. Or it may not. D'you want a spitfire like that on your hands?"

"I've been thinking about that for a while now. She's taking a bigger chance on me than I am on her," Peter said.

The older man grunted. "A point. Fair enough. We'll go forward, then. I did want to be sure you were clear in your own mind."

"Thank you, but I am. We'll go forward if the doctor says we'll go forward, anyhow," Peter said.

"Mm. Indeed." His father sounded like a rival pupil when he scored a point in a mock trial. "Go see him tomorrow. When we have his *imprimatur*, we'll know where we stand."

Peter'd got used to the bed in his room at Lincoln's Inn. By comparison, the one in his own bedroom seemed uncommonly soft and thick. He wondered how he'd do in it. Travel left him tired enough to sleep an hour after sunrise.

After breakfast—again, better than what he'd got at the refectory—he went to the house on the south side of the Avon where his fiancée and her family lived. He knew which door opened on to the living quarters and which to the surgery; he knocked on the latter.

When Richard Williams opened it, his smile seemed friendly enough. "Welcome home!" he said as they shook hands. "It's good to have you back. Come in!"

"Thank you, sir. It's good to be back," Peter said.

His prospective father-in-law closed the door behind him. "Now," he said briskly, "shuck out of your clothes and we'll see what we've got here."

"I'm no Temeculan," Peter said as he stripped. "This doesn't seem natural to me."

"You've read it, then?" Williams asked.

"Last night, yes. Give your daughter my compliments, please. It's even better than I looked for."

"I like the way you put that. I'll tell her, first chance I get. Lift your arms up toward the ceiling, if you would."

As Peter obeyed, he asked, "What are you looking for?"

"I'm going to poke you and prod you and inspect you like a side of beef, trying to judge whether you've got the Wasting in you." Richard Williams proved as good, or as bad, as his word. He felt and prodded at Peter's armpits, hard enough to hurt, and at his groin the same way. He kept talking while he did: "The disease is a trickster, and hides in plain sight like a chameleon. I won't know anything certain here, mind you—nothing's sure with the Wasting. But your lymph nodes don't seem swollen or tender, which is a good sign. Now push back your foreskin, if you'd be so kind."

"Why?" Peter asked as he did.

Richard Williams bent to examine his penis. "Because I want to see if I can judge whether you have the pox or the clap. Neither one of them is as dreadful as the Wasting, but I don't want you passing them on to Viola, either."

Humiliated, Peter said, "I never had a chancre. It never hurt to piss, and I never had the gleets." He'd learned all kinds of things from Walter Haywood, most of them things he would rather not have known. Most, but not all.

"Good. That's good," Viola's father said, not looking up. When he did straighten, he went on, "Well, as far as I can tell, you were a lucky fellow and got away with enjoying yourself. That's *as far as I can tell*, you understand. With the Wasting, I can never tell far enough, not ahead of time. But I'm pretty sure you missed the other two, and that means there's a good chance you haven't got it."

"I'm glad to hear it," Peter said.

"I'm glad to be able to say it. Viola wants to go ahead with this. She understands she'd be taking the same chance with any other randy young man, only she might not know it beforehand. She likes you. So do I, from what I've seen. Put your clothes back on. We'll go forward as if nothing happened, and we'll all pray we're doing the right thing."

"Thank you, sir. Thank you," Peter said with his shirt still over his head.

Viola let a piece of paper flutter down to her writing table. "The nerve!" she snarled. "The brass!" She hadn't been so furious since that lout pinched her bum outside the bookshop.

Kate peered in from the doorway. "What is it? You sound ready to bite nails in two."

Answering meant Viola had to pick up the offending piece of print again, even if touching it made her want to wash her hands. "Master Egerton sent me a magazine cutting from the *Fortnightly Examiner*. It's a notice of my book."

"What's wrong with that? Aren't you pleased to get notices?" her sister asked.

"I should be delighted to get notices not written by a cretinous imbecile," Viola ground out. "This one, though …" She wanted to spit on it, in hope the ink would run.

"Why? What does it say?"

That meant Viola either had to show it to Kate or to read it out loud herself. She chose the latter course: "It is not to be believed that *A Voyage to the Island of the Temeculans* could in fact have been penned by a woman. The author's name given, Viola Williams, assuredly must be a pseudonym affected by a satirist or reformer in the hope of making the ideas he presents appear more palatable.' "*He!*" She laced the word with scorn.

"Oh, dear," Kate said.

"Wait. It gets worse," Viola said grimly. "'No woman born could write of the sea, and of the storms thereon, with such verisimilitude, such depth of detail, and such awe and terror. And the fair sex, the sequestered sex, is bound to be far too delicate, too sheltered, and too innocent to imagine such lewd individuals as the Temeculans show themselves to be.'"

"Oh, dear," Kate said again. "No wonder you aren't happy with this—" She paused.

"His name is Atkinson, George Atkinson, and I am not unhappy with him," Viola said. "I want to cut his heart, assuming he has one, out of his chest with a knife made from volcanic glass and devour it whilst it still beats, in the manner of the Aztec priests when the Spaniards found them."

"You want to do *what?*" That wasn't Kate. It was Margaret, who'd caught only the tail end of Viola's wrath. She sounded more admiring than anything else.

"Never mind," Viola said. She couldn't bear to repeat herself, or to read out the rest of the notice. It was all in the same vein, anyhow.

"Since you can't cut out his heart and eat it"—Kate seemed to hope Viola couldn't, at any rate—"what will you do?"

"Master Egerton asked me the same thing in his covering letter," Viola said. "He tells me it's bad form to respond to notices except to point out egregious errors of fact, but notes that thinking me a man falls into that category. He does warn me to be brief, which may cramp my style. But if I can't tear out his heart with both hands, I hope I do manage to make it skip a few beats."

Margaret looked at her as if she'd never seen her before. "You're nastier than I thought you were," she said: by her tone, highest praise.

"Dearie, I put up with a lot. Women have to. If you don't know that yet, you'll find out sooner than you want to. But I will be damned if I put up with a halfwit sharpening his claws on my arse!"

Margaret and Kate both burst out laughing, more from surprise than from amusement. "Show Father the letter before you send it," Kate urged. "If any one of us besides you can spice it up, he can."

"That is a capital notion, and I'll do it," Viola said. "Even if he doesn't improve it, he'll like it."

She sat down and started to work. After a couple of hours, she began cutting instead of writing. Eventually, she found herself with three quarters of a page of concentrated venom. Then she took it and the cutting down to the surgery and tapped on the connecting door. Her father tapped back, so he was with somebody. Viola sat down to wait for him to finish. She was still so angry, her stomach hurt. She stewed till the door opened at last.

"What's gone wrong?" Richard Williams asked as soon as he saw her face. "Something must have."

She showed him the notice from the *Fortnightly Examiner* and her response. "Can you think of anything else I should say to this, this ... Atkinson personage?" she asked while he read.

He looked up when he'd finished. "Mm, no, I think he's quite scorched enough with what you've done to him here," he said. "I shouldn't change a word. May I add a bit to it, though?—on a separate sheet, of course. You can throw it out if you don't care to use it."

"Please," Viola said.

He went back into the surgery, sat down, and wrote quickly, then handed her what he'd done. *I am Richard Williams, a doctor in Salisbury*, she read. *I have the privilege of being Miss Viola Williams' father. I can and do attest from personal knowledge that* A Voyage to the Island of the Temeculans *is entirely her own work, from idea to execution and from beginning to end. Anyone presuming to doubt this*

251

has no knowledge of the woman in question. Yours most sincerely— And he scrawled his name.

Viola kissed him on the cheek. "That's perfect. Thank you!"

"My pleasure, chick," he said. "If there's anything left of Atkinson after he reads your little love letter, we can take him on together. About the only thing you didn't tell him was that he suffers from paresis."

Thanks to his medical tomes, she knew what that was. "I'd never say such a thing to a gentleman," she replied, as if she were the shrinking violet the reviewer imagined all women to be. "Why, it would be indelicate."

Her father guffawed. "It would, wouldn't it? Even if he does suffer from it, I mean. Perhaps especially if he does."

On that note, Viola sent her response, and her father's, to Thomas Egerton, asking him to forward them to the *Fortnightly Examiner*. A week later, a letter came back from the publisher. *My dear Miss Williams,* he wrote, *I shall walk them over myself, the* Examiner's *office lying only three blocks or so from my own. I want to see the look on Frank Holiday's face when he reads them; he is the editor there. I knew you had fangs from the way you dickered with me. Now the world will know as well.*

That made Viola grin. Margaret was less impressed. "Your Master Egerton doesn't know anything about *me*," she said.

"Write him your book, then, the way you said you would, so he can find out."

Viola's sister lost some of her starchiness. "I tried to, but after a while I put it away," she answered. "It wasn't as easy as I thought it'd be, and after a while I didn't know what I should say next."

"You can always go back to it when you get more ideas," Viola said.

"Maybe," Margaret said. "Will *you* be able to keep writing books once you get married and start having babies?"

"I don't know," Viola said uncomfortably. That thought had been on her mind more than usual now that Peter had passed her father's inspection and got his *nihil obstat*, as it were. "I'll just have to find out, that's all."

"When do they read the banns the first time, Sunday after next?"

"That's right." Part of Viola was eager to find out what marriage would be like. Part of her was scared green. Which part she paid more heed to varied from day to day.

On the Tuesday after the priest had read the banns in the cathedral for the third and last time, she got from Thomas Egerton a cutting of her reply, and her father's, in the *Fortnightly Examiner*. He wrote, *Now we see how Atkinson responds, if he has the gall to do so. Myself, I doubt he will, for you have divided all of his gall* in partes tres. He added, *In any case, the foofaraw he stirred up is helping your book. I am printing more copies.*

Although Viola smiled at first to see that, she frowned a moment later. He'd paid her a flat fee for the right to print *A Voyage to the Land of the Temeculans*. No matter how many more copies he sold, she'd never see another copper from it. That hardly seemed fair. She consoled herself as best she could, thinking, *If this one does well, he may pay me more for the next.* May. She noticed the word as soon as it crossed her mind. What if Egerton didn't care to? What then?

She could worry about that later. She hadn't even started writing her second story yet. She also worried about George Atkinson. Did she want to embed herself in a feud by letter? She turned out not to need to fret over that. Atkinson didn't rise to the challenge.

Which meant all she had to worry about was the wedding. The closer the day got, the more it seemed like a boulder rumbling downhill to crush her flat.

XVII

Peter squeezed into silk breeches so tight, he feared for his manhood. "This is a ridiculous costume," he grumbled, not for the first time. His shirt was all over ruffles, his bright green velvet jacket extravagantly baggy. He thought he looked like a fool.

"I feel the same way," Clarence Starr said. Peter's particular friend was acting as his best man. The only difference between his outfit and Peter's was that his jacket was a more somber green.

Peter's father took everything in stride. "It's what men of a certain station wear to get married in," Alfred Drinkwater said. "I put on the same kind of getup, only my jacket was blue. A hundred and fifty years ago, men with a little money dressed like this all the time, you know."

"I'm sorry for them," Peter said. "If I'd got a scar on my bum playing football on Lincoln's Inn's Fields, everyone who sees me today would know about it."

"You may be wearing it on your wedding day, but you won't be wearing it on your wedding night," Clarence said with a grin.

"Yes, why don't you think about that for a while and quit your fussing? You've fussed more since you came home than you did after you stopped cutting baby teeth," Peter's father agreed.

"I'm sorry, sir," Peter said, which was not altogether true. His father had put him to work drawing up papers and filling legal forms, labor he thought better suited to a clerk—or a half-witted donkey—than to a man who'd passed the bar.

Alfred Drinkwater tugged at Peter's gaudy green neck scarf, then at his own plain cravat. "A couple of peacocks, we are." He set a hand on his son's shoulder. "Nothing to it, lad. You walk up the aisle. You listen to the priest say the Latin over you. You say 'Yes' or 'I do' when you're supposed to. Easy as you please. My pa told me the exact same thing."

"Did you believe him?" Peter asked.

His father snorted. "Of course not. Nobody ever does. It's true anyhow, though. Now—head up, shoulders back, and we'll parade to the cathedral."

They'd hired two carriages: one for Peter and his father and Clarence; the other, enclosed, for his mother and sisters. The day had threatened rain, but didn't look like making good on the threat. The sun was trying to come out. People stared at Peter's getup, and his friend's, as he rattled along. Some of the men bawled out bawdy suggestions. Peter did his best to hold his face straight. It wasn't easy.

"Here y'are, guvnor," the driver said, pulling to a stop in front of the low, broad stairs that led up into the cathedral.

"Obliged," Peter's father answered, and tipped him two bob. He gave two more to the driver of the women's carriage. You were supposed to be generous on a wedding day.

The Williamses had already arrived. They—all of them but Viola—greeted Peter and his family and his best man in the narthex. Peter didn't know where the bride-to-be was. Someplace where he couldn't see her. It was said to be bad luck for a groom to do that on his wedding day till his intended came up the aisle on her father's arm.

Richard Williams was dressed much like Peter's father: as a tolerably prosperous gentleman, in other words. The doctor's cravat was bright red, not black, perhaps to liven up an otherwise dull outfit, perhaps because he spilled blood in his line of work every now and then. The Williams women wore their best shapeless dresses, scarves, and veils, as Peter's sisters and mother did.

Viola's father shook Peter by the hand. "Welcome to the family," he said, with that crooked smile of his. "Now you'll have more people to squabble with."

"So will Viola," Peter answered. Richard Williams' smile got wider and straighter. He let his palm rest on Peter's arm for a moment, then dropped it to his side.

Peter's father peered into the cathedral's long, narrow nave. "We've beaten the guests here, anyhow," he said. "We'd best make ourselves scarce till the hour of doom is upon us."

"Alf!" Peter's mother said reproachfully. Peter didn't think his father was talking about his brush with the Wasting. He also didn't think his mother knew of that. He wasn't sure about either of those things, though. Right at that moment, he wasn't sure of anything at all.

A deacon led his family into one of the little side rooms whose purpose he'd always wondered about. Another deacon took the Williamses into a different room. Peter heard people starting to come in: friends and relatives of the two families. There weren't many relatives; neither clan was large, or particularly close to people related to it by blood.

Then the clock in a bell tower chimed three. It dated back to the fourteenth century, and was said to be the oldest working clock in England. No one in London had pointed to an older one, which made Peter think the claim was true.

The wedding procession formed in the narthex. Peter got his first glimpse of Viola. She wore white from headscarf to shoes. Her veil was so thin, he could see her smile at him through it. At any other time, that would have been shocking. So would the way her wedding dress made her look like a woman, not a walking turnip. Weddings, by the nature of things, were out of the ordinary.

The organ began to play. As if in a dream, Peter walked up the aisle toward the altar. Clarence followed a couple of steps behind him. Men sat to his right, women to his left. The priest stood waiting. After coming up on her father's arm, Viola took her place beside him.

As with his exams, he remembered little of the ceremony. The Latin just rolled over him. He did recall the priest's saying he and Viola were conferring the sacrament of marriage on each other. And he remembered slipping the slim gold band Clarence's father had made onto the fourth finger of her left hand.

Then she turned to face the crowd. Slowly and deliberately, she let her veil fall—the only time she was ever likely to do that in public as a grown woman. She smiled out at everyone (Peter wondered if she was thinking of her Temeculans as she did it). Having done that, she turned back to him. She was still smiling, which he hoped was a good sign.

He bent to her. He didn't have to bend far; he was only three or four inches taller than she was. Their lips touched. Peter barely heard the soft, pleased sounds that rose from the crowd. *What therefore God hath joined together, let not man put asunder* ran through his head. They were joined together. Married. For the rest of their lives. Forever, as people measured forever.

As the carriage stopped in front of the Drinkwaters' house—her house now—Viola tried not to show her sigh. She'd ridden barefaced through the streets of Salisbury. She hadn't been barefaced in public since she was a girl. She probably never would be again. *Too bad*, she thought. *Oh, too bad!*

"Well, guvnor, we're back," the driver said, turning around to grin at Alfred Drinkwater. His eyes met Viola's for a moment, and the smile turned to a leer. Her cheeks heated. She made herself pretend she didn't notice him.

Her father-in-law (what a strange thing to have all of a sudden!) gave the man money. Then he went back and gave more to the man driving the closed carriage with his wife and daughters (*My mother-in-law! My sisters-in-law!*) inside.

Peter handed Viola down from the carriage. As Clarence Starr got out of it, he told her, "Oh, I nearly forgot to say—I bought your book at Master Blackwell's. I quite enjoyed it. My father and mother are reading it now."

"Thank you so much!" she exclaimed in delighted surprise.

The carriages rattled away. Clarence said his farewells and headed back to his own house. The Drinkwaters (*I'm a Drinkwater now, not a Williams ever again*) and Viola went up the walk to the front door (*my front door, till Peter finds somewhere of his own to live*).

Peter opened the door. Then he put his arms around Viola's waist, picked her up, and carried her over the threshold. The rest of his family (*my family now*) laughed and clapped their hands. One more ritual completed. Another still remained ahead. It wouldn't wait much longer. The sun was setting soon.

"I have a bottle of Madeira I've been saving for a special day," Peter's father said when they were all inside. "If this isn't a special day, hang me if I know what would be."

The wine was strong and sweet. It made Viola worry less about how she'd fit into this strange new place, how she'd fit in with these people who were still too close to strangers, and particularly how she'd fit together with her new husband (*With my what?* part of her asked in astonishment). If her father-in-law had opened it for that very reason .... Well, he was her own father's particular friend, and her father, whatever his many virtues, had never suffered fools gladly.

Amanda Drinkwater bustled about lighting candles and lamps. Yes, it was getting dark. Peter caught Viola's eyes. "Shall we ...?" he asked.

She nodded. "I think we shall," she answered. The Madeira definitely made that easier to say.

"See you in the morning—late in the morning, I expect," Alf Drinkwater said. His wife laughed. A beat later, so did Peter's sisters. They'd likely be going through this in some other houses before too long.

Peter led her to his room. "Do you want a lamp or not?" he asked.

She was glad he'd thought to ask her. "I suppose so, but however you please," she said.

He got one, which answered that. Then he closed the door behind them, and they were alone together. The room was not large, and crowded. As she was wondering where she'd put her things, he said, "The bed's new. It's big enough for the both of us."

"It had better be, don't you think?" This time, Viola was the one who said, "Shall we ...?" *Another ritual*, she thought again.

She'd never undressed in front of a man before. Peter would be ahead of her there: ahead of her in some other things, too. *As long as he's well. Please, God, let him be well.* Prayer didn't come easily to her, but she meant that one.

He was grunting his way out of the tight wedding breeches, shedding shirt and jacket. He seemed distracted by what she was doing. "You're beautiful," he breathed.

"Thank you," Viola whispered. No one had ever said that to her before. It hadn't even occurred to her before. As far as she was concerned, Kate was the prettiest Williams sister.

He took her in his arms. Bare skin against bare skin was new, too. This kiss was real, unlike the polite one in the cathedral. Neither of them had much practice, but they learned fast.

Viola didn't remember afterwards how they got from there to the bed, but they did. Explorations continued. She'd known in theory what went on at such times, but theory, here as many places, had only so much to do with reality. Theory didn't say anything about how much fun it was, either, or how surprising. When she pleased herself, she knew what would happen before it did.

Theory also didn't say anything about there being another person on the bed with her, someone who cared enough about her to do his best to give her that pleasure. If his best was awkward, so was hers. She tried to please him anyhow, to turn theory into practice.

"Are you ready?" he asked after a while.

"I ... think so," Viola said. Theory said it would hurt the first time. Not only that, there was still the fear he might carry the Wasting. She made herself not think of that. Because of the other, she added, "Go slowly, if you can."

"All right." He moved forward, stopped when he met resistance, then moved forward again. It did hurt, but less than she'd been braced for. Peter said, "Can I go on?"

"I ... think so," she answered, as she had before. Then she nodded. Here, theory was right; this was what happened when a woman lost her maidenhead.

Go on her husband did. It still hurt, but not so much. It wasn't the rapture theory talked about, not for her. But she was pleased that she was pleasing him. He grunted, quivered, gasped, and spent himself.

"You're squashing me," Viola said a moment later. The mattress was soft, but not soft enough to keep her from feeling his weight on her.

"Oh. I'm sorry." He slid out of her and rolled off her. "I'm sorry, Missus Drinkwater," he amended.

"Don't worry about it, Master Drinkwater," Viola said. That last ritual was complete, too. Any way you looked at it, they were man and wife now. She was wetter and sloppier down there than she cared to be. "Can you give me a wet rag to clean myself with? We probably should have put a towel under my bum."

Peter did. She felt shy wiping herself in front of him, but told herself she'd get used to that. Blood wouldn't be mixed with his seed after this, either. He did watch what she was doing. As she finished, he said, "The stain on the coverlet's not bad. I've heard there are places where we'd go out and show it off."

"That's true. There are." Viola had read of such things herself. She felt obscurely glad Peter knew of them, too. She went on, "I'm glad we don't have that custom here. I think it's barbarous."

"You're telling me the Temeculans would never do such a thing?" he said, and poked her in the ribs.

She squeaked, in surprise and because it tickled. Then she said, "You're teasing me!"

"What if I am?"

He went on teasing her, only not with words. She reached down once, to move his hand a tiny bit higher. She hoped that wouldn't make him angry. It didn't seem to. Then she stopped caring about that, or anything else.

After her heartbeat slowed again, she said, "We don't know much about each other yet, Master Drinkwater, but we know how to make each other happy." She laughed again, at how prim she sounded.

"We'll find out the other things as we go along. That one, though, that one's important," Peter said. "Do you want to, uh, try again?" He plainly did.

"I think I'd be raw if we did it again so soon." Viola saw he looked disappointed. "I could do this, though." She took him in hand: one more thing she knew from theory.

After a few seconds, he said, "Spit in your palm, why don't you? It'll help." He knew about that business, and not just from theory. She did what he asked. Before very long, he was the one who needed a wet rag. She used it after he did.

He squeezed her. "Here we are."

"Here we are," she agreed. *For better or worse*, as the wedding ceremony said. He seemed kind enough, and also gentle enough. He wasn't stupid. *I could have done worse*, Viola thought, wondering whether she could have done better and whether the same thing was going through his mind.

It might well have been. "One way or another, we'll figure it out," he said. "You were right—we don't know much about each other yet. This"—he ran his hand along her—"it's not much like writing letters, is it?"

"What ever could you mean?" This time, Viola poked Peter. He squeaked, too. They both laughed. It might not have been exactly what theory said a wedding night should be, but it wasn't so bad.

Peter discovered he liked being married. He indulged himself in the most obvious reason for a young man to like being married as often as Viola would put up with him. Unlike his hand, she wasn't ready and willing whenever he was. That sparked some friction for a while. But she didn't say no all that often, and when she did, she said it in a way that made him understand she wasn't angry or uninterested, just busy or tired. That helped.

He'd known about the family connections in the match before-hand, of course. Viola and he would go over to the Williams house for supper two or three times a month. The better he got to know them, the more he liked them. He very quickly came to see why her father was his father's particular friend.

And he got along with her. She had her own fair share—or even a little more than that—of Richard Williams' sardonic wit. There were a couple of times when she visibly didn't say something she was thinking.

"I won't burst into tears if you tell me what's on your mind," he remarked.

"When it matters, I will," she said, and he believed that. She continued, "But I don't want to hurt you just because I have the habit of letting fly. And I really don't want to wound your mother or your sisters. They're apt to be slower to forgive me than you would."

She cocked her head to one side, the way her father did, waiting to see whether he got what she was driving at. After a moment, he did. It boiled down to *They aren't going to bed with me.*

"They like you," he said, which was true. "They're glad you do your share of the housework without, uh—"

"Without their needing to nag me about it," Viola finished for him, which was also true. "You can let them know I'm glad they let me have a little time to myself to set words down on paper."

"You made money with a book. They know that. They hope you'll make more money with another one. I hope you will, too," Peter said. "No one in this house has ever thought anything was wrong with making honest money."

His wife—the thought still startled him whenever it crossed his mind—stuck out her tongue at him. "Assuming writing *is* making honest money."

"So stipulated, yes," Peter said, almost as dryly as Viola's father might have. She laughed. He was happy he hadn't married someone to whom he would have had to explain what *stipulated* meant. She was more likely to need to explain things to him; he'd seen that from her letters when he was studying in London.

Her grin faded. "I hope the stew I made last night wasn't too spicy for everybody," she said.

"I liked it. Pa did, too—he told me so," Peter assured her. "Everybody took seconds, I think. Don't worry about it. Eating with your family's shown me you all like spicing your food a bit more than we do."

"Bland isn't interesting, or it isn't to me," Viola said. "But I'll go easy if I'm the only one who feels that way."

"Mother was talking about getting more of that yellow powder that comes from India—or is it Ceylon?" Peter aid. "It's easy to find in London. Even the refectory cooks put some in sometimes, to liven up dull porridges and such."

"Curry powder."

"That's the stuff. But you can't always find it here." Peter sighed. "We really are a provincial town. I got teased once or twice because of my accent, and people thought I was daft for wanting to go back home after I passed my examinations. To somebody from London, it's the only place that counts."

"I like it here. I'm glad you do, too," Viola said.

"Living in London might be an advantage for you. That's where the publishers and printers are," Peter said.

"I've thought about it. But I do like it here," Viola said again, more firmly this time.

Though still new at marriage, Peter recognized a warning not to push it, so he didn't. Instead, he asked, "How is the new one coming?" She hadn't shown him anything yet, whether because she hadn't got it into a shape that satisfied her or because she didn't trust his judgment. He hadn't pushed that, either.

Her mouth twisted. "It's harder than it was the first time. I want to say what I want to say, but I don't want to repeat myself. I'd sound like a trumpeter who could only play one note."

"Whatever you say, what you feel about what you say will come through, won't it?"

She looked startled. Then she kissed him. "Thanks!" she said. "I hadn't looked at it that way, but you're bound to be right."

Peter knew little about how books came to be. Till Viola wrote and published hers, he'd never dreamt that could be important to him. Now he said, "I hope it helps a little."

"Oh, it does!" she said. "Anything that makes me find reasons to want to go on writing helps right now, believe me." That kiss and her smile made Peter feel suffused in a warm glow of virtue for the rest of the day.

Viola'd feared all along that writing a second book wouldn't be as easy as the first one had been. For one thing, she was doing it here, not back at the house where she'd grown up. Everything that had to do with marrying, changing homes, and getting used to new people militated against sitting down and scribbling.

And, for another, the story she'd decided to tell next wasn't set on an island that existed only in her imagination. The town in which it took place was a lot like Salisbury. The characters were based on people she knew or people she knew about. She changed them enough so—she hoped—they wouldn't recognize themselves or hate her too much for the way she portrayed them if they did. If she wasn't going to be extravagantly inventive, she had to stick close to home. So things moved slowly when they moved at all.

Close to home .... She had to learn to get along with the Drinkwaters. Their family had its own rules and customs, often different from the ones she'd taken for granted. One afternoon, she said something moderately sharp to Julietta—the next day, she couldn't even remember what. It was the kind of thing she might have said to Kate or Margaret, the kind of thing to which they would have responded with something just as sassy. Then life would have gone on.

But Julietta stopped what she'd been doing—chopping celery—and stared at Viola as if she'd slapped her. Her eyes filled with tears. Viola felt mortified. "I'm sorry, dear," she said quickly. "I won't do that again." She hoped she wouldn't, anyhow.

"It's all right," her sister-in-law said, but Viola knew it wasn't, and wouldn't be for a while. She tried not to make the same mistake twice.

She could be a little more pointed with Peter; she had ways of sweetening him that she couldn't use on the rest of the Drinkwaters. She enjoyed those ways, too. He did try hard to please her, and succeeded more often than not, if not quite so often as she let on. Things there could have been worse.

That was what she thought during the day, anyhow. When she went to bed very tired, she would wake up in the middle of the night, afraid the tiredness had nothing to do with cooking and cleaning and washing. If she had too many covers piled on her and her husband rolled up against her so she got sweaty in bed, sometimes she couldn't go back to sleep for hours. Sometimes, she couldn't at all.

Timor mortis conturbat me ran through her mind again on some of those long, dark nights. But it wasn't fear of death that held her in thrall, or not exactly. It was fear of the Wasting, of the long, horrid miseries the Wasting brought to dying. Every time she lay with Peter in love, she knew too well the chance she took.

Because she had no way to tell, no way at all. No one did, anywhere in the world. A man or a woman might stay perfectly healthy, at least on the outside, and then die over years in ways that made the torments of the damned look merciful by comparison. Someone who seemed healthy might pass the Wasting on to someone else, whom it seized more quickly. That was what all those branded W's meant.

And a mother might give it to her baby. Viola tried very hard not to think about that. Every time she lay with Peter, she took the chance of conceiving, too.

She'd been married not quite six months when her courses didn't come. She wasn't perfectly regular in them, so she didn't think anything of it for a week or ten days. After two weeks went by, though, she told Peter, "I'm late."

She wasn't sure he would even know what she was talking about, but he nodded with no show of surprise at all. "Yes, I thought so, but it wasn't my place to say anything about it," he answered. He'd learned to keep track of her body's rhythms, too, then. She couldn't decide whether that pleased her or annoyed her.

"I don't think it means anything yet, not for certain," Viola said. "If another fortnight goes by, though ..."

"In that case, chances are you'll be a mother and I'll be a father," Peter said. "My pa will bust his buttons, he'll be so proud. Yours, too."

"I know." Viola also knew her father would be worried for the same reasons she was. She hadn't really talked about that with Peter. Did he also have nights where he woke up frightened? If he did, she didn't think he'd had them on nights where she lay awake and scared. Which, of course, might not mean anything.

He said, "Whatever happens, we'll get through it the best way we can find." She made herself nod. That didn't seem enough. She reached out and squeezed his hand. Yes, it was on his mind as well as hers.

"*Kyrie eleison!*" she said, though the Lord seemed to talk about mercy more often than He chose to dole it out.

"*Christe eleison!*" Peter added. Viola nodded. Jesus took mercy more seriously than His Father did.

Two more weeks went by, and then a bit longer. By that time, Viola had no doubt she was in a delicate condition. She was constantly sleepy, and she'd lost her breakfast a couple of times. Once, she'd been unable to eat two lovely eggs fried sunny side up. They seemed to be looking up at her in mute reproach. She made some excuse or another for fleeing the table.

So the other women in the Drinkwater family weren't astonished when she and Peter made the news official. "I've wondered for a while now," Viola's mother-in-law said. Joanna and Julietta nodded.

"Why?" Peter sounded quite humanly—quite masculinely—astonished.

"Women have their ways," Amanda Drinkwater said. She and Viola shared an amused look. It wasn't just how Viola needed pegs to prop her eyelids open and had the beginnings of morning sickness. It was also that lately she hadn't had any rags for soaking in cold water to get the stains out.

Alfred Drinkwater hadn't suspected anything—or, if his wife and daughters had whispered in his ear, he didn't let on. Viola guessed they'd kept quiet. He seemed too far over the moon for pretense. "A grandfather! I'm going to be a grandfather!" he exclaimed. "Whether you have a boy or a girl, I aim to spoil the little brat rotten."

Peter looked at him. "You never said anything like that when you were raising us."

"That's right!" Joanna and Julietta agreed, almost in chorus.

"Of course not," their father said. "You were my children. I had to keep you in line—and it wasn't always easy, either, believe me. But a grandbaby! I don't have to worry about a grandbaby! Keeping a grandbaby in line is your job, Peter, yours and Viola's. I can just have fun with the tyke."

The next Sunday, Viola and Peter went over to the Williams house for supper, and to give her family the news. Snow lay on the ground: not much, but enough so she wore boots and thick wool stockings under them. The air was crisp and cold, and smelled of woodsmoke and coal smoke. Every hearth in Salisbury was doing its best to keep homes, if not warm, then warm enough. Here and there, soot streaked the white carpet.

"We've got something to tell you," Peter said as soon as Richard Williams let him and Viola in.

"Do you?" Viola's father looked from Peter to her and back again. His left eyebrow quirked. "Is this something we should all hear?"

"I think it may be," Viola said.

"Well, then …" Her father closed the curtains before he called her mother and sisters out of the kitchen and into the parlor. They were unveiled, as Viola was around Alf Drinkwater, but it wouldn't do to let anyone going by on the street peer in at them. Richard Williams went on, "I think we're about to hear an announcement."

Viola made it as short and to the point as she could: "I'm going to have a baby."

All the Williamses except her father squealed. He grinned from ear to ear and pumped Peter's hand. Everybody hugged Viola; her mother kissed Peter on the cheek, then blushed prettily at having done it. Her father poured whiskey for Peter and himself. They clinked glasses and drank a toast. Kate got mugs of beer for the women.

As Viola sipped hers, she wished she could talk with her father about her fears. Even more than Peter, he would understand what she worried about, and why. He might understand all that better than she did. How many babies born with the Wasting from their mothers had he seen? She didn't remember his ever talking about that. Of course, it wasn't something made for casual mealtime conversation.

Certainly, no one said a word about it over mutton stew. The talk was all excitement over becoming grandparents and aunts, of what name to give the child if it was a boy or if a girl, of everybody's hopes and dreams for the little one. Hopes and dreams went with good food and drink. They also went with the word that a new generation would be rising. But so did fear, even if not a word was said about it.

Every so often, Peter noticed his father's eye on him in a particular way. The older man never said anything when he measured Peter like that. Then again, he didn't need to. Peter understood well enough what was on his mind. When Mother was carrying him, Father would have tormented himself the way Peter was now. Alfred Drinkwater had also sinned before he married, and must have wondered whether he'd pay in full the price for his brief moment of joy in London.

It might even have been worse for him. Peter didn't think his mother knew his father'd indulged his lust before they married. One could write stories about situations like that. For all Peter knew, Viola was writing one of those stories. He still hadn't seen much of the new manuscript. She kept working at it when she could, but that wasn't much these days.

Meanwhile, he practiced law with his father. To say the work was less than exciting gave it too much credit. "This hasn't got much to do with what I studied at Lincoln's Inn," he remarked one day.

"You do need to pull out the fancy stuff once in a while, but only once in a while," Alf Drinkwater said. "Most of what happens, it's wills and deeds and contracts for goods and services and property settlements after annulments. Everything else is just a candied cherry on top of your cake."

"How do you go on doing the same things over and over without wanting to bash your head against your desk?" Peter asked; he'd certainly felt temptations along those lines.

"Well, for one thing, it keeps food on the table and a roof over our heads," his father answered with relentless middle-aged practicality. "And for another, less than half the job's in the papers. The rest is getting to know the fellows you make up the papers for. That's not so dull, is it?"

"I suppose not," Peter said, more from duty than because he believed it. He'd gone along with his father to meet clients at their homes, which were generally grander than the one he lived in. Those people had to know their needs would still be met if something happened to Alfred Drinkwater. At the moment, though, Peter felt like a spare wheel on a wagon. He was there for a reason, but nobody had much use for him.

Sometimes his father didn't go to clients' homes. Sometimes he met them in one pub or another, laying papers down on the bar or on a table ringed with the marks of countless pint mugs. Pipe smoke and the smell of beer filled the air, as they did at the London pubs near Lincoln's Inn.

Beer did help lubricate Peter's tongue, which wasn't as forward as it might have been. But, had he drunk enough beer to let him forget that the clients he was drinking with were almost all his father's age or older, he would have quietly slid under one of those stained and battered tables.

They wanted to pretend they were still young, or young again. They didn't fool him; he doubted they fooled themselves. They asked him how he liked being married with a leer in their voices. He smiled and said things like, "Pretty well, thanks." He knew his father wouldn't be happy with him if he punched one of the old lechers in the teeth.

Instead, he vented his spleen with Viola. "They're disgusting creatures," he fumed one night, behind the closed door to the room they shared.

"They're men," she said, as if that explained everything. To her, it seemed to.

"I'm a man, too. I hope I won't act like that when I'm fifty or sixty," he said.

"So do I," she told him. "But men have a way of taking the world the way it is for granted. Why shouldn't they? They set it up, and it's set up for them."

He wanted to tell her that wasn't true. He wanted to, but he couldn't. The most he could say was, "Maybe it will change one day."

"Maybe. If they ever learn how to cure the Wasting, that may do it. Or it may not—when people have power over others, how often do they ever want to give it up?" Viola looked thoughtful. She scribbled a note on a scrap of foolscap. "Something I may be able to use in the new one," she explained.

"All right." Peter nodded. He did say, "You have a harsh way of looking at things."

"I have a woman's way of looking at things," she retorted. "Do you think your mother and your sisters feel any differently? If you do, you haven't paid much attention."

"They don't complain," he said.

"The way I do, you mean?" she said—it wasn't really a question. "The women men don't see don't talk the way we do when we're around you. We're safer amongst ourselves."

"You're talking now," Peter pointed out.

"But I'm already a scandal. I've written books about these things, books even men can read if they care to." Viola paused, considering. "And I'm coming to think I can trust you. You and my father—that's about as far as that goes."

He might have asked her about his own father. He might have, but he didn't. He didn't fancy the man his father turned into at pub meetings himself—not for the same reasons Viola was wary of him, but for related ones. After a moment, he said, "The company is good. Thank you for the compliment."

"Thank you for being someone I could pay it to," she answered. "I know I'm difficult. You're trying to put up with me. The least I can do is try back."

"I have my reasons for liking you around. Some of them have to do with my being a man, but not all," Peter said.

She wrinkled her nose at him. "I ought to put that in the book, too."

"Go ahead, as long as you don't call the person who says it Peter."

Viola laughed. "I wouldn't. I'm trying *not* to make my characters too recognizable."

"Good. That's good," Peter said.

XVIII

After a while, Viola didn't feel as if she needed to fall asleep every waking moment. Morning sickness left her, too, though more slowly. She began to think carrying a baby wasn't so bad after all. For a little while, with fresh energy filling her, she forged ahead on the new book.

One evening, lazy after making love with Peter, she looked down at herself. "For heaven's sake!" she exclaimed. She knew what she was supposed to look like, but she didn't look like that any more. "I'm starting to show!"

Peter ran his hand along her belly and nodded. "Yes, I can feel the little bulge." His palm rested just below her navel. "Has the baby started to move yet?"

"No," she answered, setting her hand on top of his. "All the rumblings and stirrings have just been me. So far."

Not very much later, she wasn't sure of that any more. And, shortly afterwards, the baby left her no more room for doubt. "I've got company in there," she told her husband.

"Do you suppose I could feel it, too?" he asked, and put his hand on her belly—clothed this time—once more. Viola didn't know whether he'd notice any internal squirmings, or whether there would be any for him to notice. A few seconds later, though, the baby gave a wriggle stronger than any she'd felt before. The look of awe that spread across Peter's face told her she wasn't the only one who'd felt it. "Was that—?" he said.

"It certainly was."

"You *are* quickening!" he said.

"I'd better be," she said, but then apologized for sounding cross. He was watching from the outside. It was happening to her. She couldn't have escaped it even had she wanted to (and there were times when she rather thought she did—she and Peter wouldn't be moving out and setting up their own household soon, for instance, not when they'd want help with the baby).

Peter's father and his sisters were as excited when they heard the news the next day. His mother, though, looked at Viola and said, "Wait another couple of months. You'll think he's playing football in there." She was the weary voice of experience. She'd carried four babies, though one of them had died only a few months after coming into the world. The Wasting was far from the only worry infants faced; so many never lived to grow up.

"I think we should lay eggs like birds," Viola said. "Sitting on a nest would be easy and convenient."

"Ha! There's your book to follow on this one!" Alfred Drinkwater said.

Everybody laughed, Viola included. As she dried dishes after breakfast, though, she tried the idea on for size. She wondered if she could make it plausible. If she could, could she make it interesting? Would she ever have time to write anything anyway after the baby came?

Those were all interesting questions. She couldn't answer any of them, especially the last. When she got the chance, though, she wrote the notion down so she wouldn't lose it. One of these days …

The next time Viola and Peter went to the Williams house for supper, her father said, "I've told Guinevere Worth about your condition."

"Oh, good! Thank you," she said. "I was going to get around to letting her know myself, but I haven't yet."

Peter looked from one of them to the other, confusion on his face. "Who's Guinevere Worth?" he asked.

Viola eyed him in surprise. Then she realized he wasn't a doctor's child, and he would have been only a little boy when his sisters were born. No reason the name should be familiar to him. Patiently, she explained, "Mistress Worth is Salisbury's best midwife."

"She's the only one who knows what she's about, if you ask me," Richard Williams said. "The others, I wouldn't call them to help a dog have pups."

"Oh," Peter said in a small voice. "That's ... important."

"A bit," Viola's father said. She nodded and changed the subject. She didn't want to dwell on it till the time came. She'd have no choice then. Babies weren't the only ones in danger at and around birthing time. Mothers died during and after, too.

"Everything will be fine," Jane Williams said, understanding what was in Viola's mind.

"Of course it will!" Peter said loudly. Viola reached under the tablecloth and tapped wood with her forefinger. She knew that was superstition. Most of her understood it wouldn't do any good. She didn't see how it could hurt, though, so she tapped wood anyhow.

After a couple of mugs of beer, Peter visited the privy. "He seems to be shaping tolerably well," Viola's father said.

"Everything is all right," she agreed.

"I'm glad. I hoped it would be," he said. Peter's returning footsteps cut short that thread of talk.

She looked at her husband sidelong as they walked back to the Drinkwater house. *Is he really the best I could have done?* she wondered. Only knowing that everyone surely had such thoughts now and again kept her from running away to wherever she might run ... that and a kick or an elbow from the baby she was carrying.

Peter might not be the best, but he was what she had, and he wasn't half bad. Viola knew she wasn't the best, either. He put up with her.

A few seconds later, he turned to her and said, "I always enjoy visiting your family. They're more—more interesting than my kin."

Viola thought so, too, but she never would have said so. Had those words come out of her mouth, he would have been offended. Since they'd come out of his, she answered, "Do you think so?" and smiled. She was getting good at sounding surprised.

Another meeting and gabfest at a pub with one of Alf Drinkwater's clients. Peter drank beer till his back teeth floated. He nibbled smoked sardines and salty little hard crackers. The air was so thick with tobacco fumes, they might have smoked those sardines right there.

On the way home, his father said, "That went well—better than I hoped. You put in a couple of good notions on how Ted can get the best rents for his properties."

"I'm glad you think so, sir." Peter couldn't remember what he'd said. He'd spent most of the afternoon wishing he were somewhere, anywhere, else. He'd spent too many afternoons, or sometimes mornings, wishing things like that.

He didn't tell his father. He might be a married man with a child—with any luck at all, with a son—on the way, but he was emphatically the junior Drinkwater. The idea of saying no to his father about anything that mattered scared him spitless.

That evening, though, in the safety of his room, he exploded to Viola: "I don't think I can bear the law—what passes for the law here in Salisbury—another minute! I hate it. It makes me hate myself."

Had he said that to Joanna or Julietta, he knew they would have told him to get used to it and to buckle down till he did. Viola didn't tell him anything for a bit. She studied him, perhaps deciding if he was serious. She must have thought he was, for she said, "What else might you do?"

"Starve," he said at once. "Pa would throw me out on my ear, and you and the baby with me."

"My family wouldn't let us go hungry or without a roof over our heads," she said.

"I don't want anything to do with charity," he said with a stubborn, hopeless pride—a young man's foolish pride.

"It might not be needed," Viola said. "If Master Egerton likes the new book once I finish it—if I ever finish it, I mean—he might be persuaded to give me more than he did for the dear Temeculans. He's written more than once that they've done far better than he looked for."

"What did you get for your first one?" She'd sold it to Thomas Egerton while Peter was still in London. She hadn't talked about how much he'd paid her, which made him assume it wasn't much. Had he made a mistake?

He had. Viola answered, "A hundred fifty pounds."

THE WAGES OF SIN

He stared at her. "That's—a lot of money," he said slowly. "Where is it?"

"My father's holding it for me, if I should require it," she said. "But I was thinking that, if I could write a book each year, we should have a chance of making a tolerable living."

She wasn't wrong, either. All the same, Peter's stiff-necked pride rose up in him once more. "What sort of man lives off his wife's earnings?"

"A man who's poor?" she suggested. "A man whose wife has the wit to earn enough to live on? And I don't suppose you'd spend all your time sitting at home or sitting in a pub?"

"Not sitting in a pub, Lord knows!" At that moment, Peter never wanted to see—or smell—the inside of a pub again as long as he lived.

"All right, then. If you don't care to practice law, what do you want to do?"

"You'll think I'm foolish," Peter said.

By the look in her eye, Viola already thought he was foolish. But she said no more than, "You've got something in mind, then."

"If I were to do something worthwhile with my time, I could do worse than teach boys—and girls, up to the point you'd expect—to read and write and cipher. A teacher, though, too often lives a hungry life."

"'Up to the point you'd expect,'" Viola echoed. "The only reason my sisters and I, and your sisters, too, learned as much as we did was that we had parents who taught us. Too many women haven't got mothers and fathers like that."

"Of course. But—" Peter spread his hands. "I'd not be able to keep company with them, you know."

"There are women who teach other women. Not as many of them as there should be, but there are." Viola paused. "I wonder if Kate would care to do that one of these days. Not just for the harpsichord, I mean, but other things as well."

"Your sister is clever," Peter said, and then, a beat later, "It must run in the family."

"It does us less good than I wish it did," Viola said.

"I was thinking the same thing about teaching. If I took it up, we wouldn't live as well as we would if I went on working with my father and gradually began to get a practice of my own. I don't want to let you—you and the baby—down when it comes to comfort," Peter said. That was an understatement. He wanted nothing less than to lose Viola's good opinion of him.

She rubbed her chin—a gesture, Peter remembered, her father also used when he was thinking. "How would this be?" she said. "Suppose we wait and see whether Master Egerton wants to buy the book I'm working on now, or whether someone else will if he does not. Suppose we see what he or some other publisher would pay for it. If we add that to what you bring in, don't you think we could live tolerably well?"

Peter suspected she might end up earning a good deal more money than he did. No one outside the Drinkwater and Williams families needed to know that, of course. But he would know it. He wondered how much it would gnaw at his own sense of self-worth. He didn't care to come right out with that. Instead, he said, "It would be an irregular way of doing things."

"Has it not occurred to you that I am an irregular person?" Viola said.

It had occurred to him. He'd tried not to dwell on it when it did. His father was a pillar of the community, and expected him to be one, too. Pillars of the community were not irregular. But pillars of the community, by the nature of things, bore a lot of weight. If he didn't care to have that burden pressing down on his shoulders, he could do worse than having someone like Viola at his side. Much worse.

"I love you, you know!" he exclaimed.

Viola looked startled, or possibly astonished. "You never said that before."

"I guess I didn't." Peter was a little surprised, or more than a little, himself. "Neither did you." He waited nervously.

She sighed. "We aren't the Temeculans. They get to know each other before they marry. We do it blind, and only find out what we have after we have it." *After we're stuck with it* were the words Peter heard under the ones she said. She went on, "You're a good man. You've borne with me, and I know I can be strange and difficult. I think I love you just for that."

He took a deep breath. "You bear with me when I may be carrying the sickness that will kill us both, and our child with us."

"I suspect I'd take the same chance with most other men, too. Men are what they are," Viola answered. "I'm hoping luck is on our side. You never showed any signs of the Wasting you didn't tell me of, did you?"

"No. By God, no!" Peter crossed himself to show how much he meant it.

"Good. I didn't think you had. I still don't," she said. "So shall we go on for a while? We'll see what the roads ahead look like, and we'll try to decide which one we should take, and we'll find out how that works. What else can we do? What else can anyone do?"

Peter suspected most people bounced from one thing to another with no more control over what happened next than a twig bouncing from one rock to another in a swift-flowing stream. They might think they had it, but did they really? Accidents, illness, quarrels ....
.How could you know ahead of time?

Money helped pad those rocks and soften the blows, though. He was sure of that. He was also sure teachers didn't make much. Richard Williams told of getting paid in food and homemade wine. He laughed about it. It wasn't so funny to Peter, not if he was going to throw away the sure living the law promised. Could Viola keep writing books and make money from them?

Could she do it whilst raising a baby? Whilst raising several small children?

If anybody could, she was probably the one. "If you're game to try, let's," he said.

"You should let your father know what's in your mind." Viola's voice suggested she'd been thinking it through while he stewed. "It wouldn't do to ambush him when he isn't expecting it."

"I suppose not," Peter replied with no great enthusiasm. Giving his father news the older man didn't care to hear was nothing he looked forward to. But Viola was right. He needed to do it ... if he could find the nerve.

Viola's belly bulged more. Walking turned uncomfortable, sleeping even more so. Even in the shapeless clothes women wore, no one could have doubted her time was drawing near. The baby kicked and squirmed more and more and harder and harder. "He doesn't know it's the middle of the night," she grumbled. "Or she. Either way."

"It's always dark in there," Peter observed.

"You're right. It is." Viola laughed—she hadn't looked at it that way before. "I need a womb with a view, so the baby can see it isn't always dark out here."

"A womb with a—" Peter broke off and sent her a reproachful look. She stuck out her tongue at him. The more she played with words on paper, the more she played with them when she talked.

Viewless or not, her womb soon started talking to her, giving small squeezes that foretold the bigger ones yet to come. Sometimes they would go on for a while, making her wonder whether her labor was beginning. She wished it would; she'd been carrying all that extra, awkward, kicking weight now for what felt like forever. But the little pangs kept subsiding and leaving her disappointed.

Then one morning, right around sunup, she woke suddenly. Something had gone *snap!* inside her. She'd felt it, and she thought she'd heard it, too. And liquid was streaming out of her—it was as if she were wetting herself, only there was more and she had no control over it.

She shook Peter awake. "You'd better go fetch the midwife," she told him. "My waters just broke." Then she grunted in pain. Her womb had just squeezed her again, and this time it meant business.

"Oh, dear God!" Her husband sprang out of bed and started throwing on clothes. Viola got out of bed, too, more slowly and clumsily. She squatted over the chamber pot. Better to put the waters there than to soak the bed any more than she already had.

Peter hurried out of their room. Before he left the house, he woke his mother and father. Then he was gone, slamming the front door behind him. That would probably rouse his sisters. In case it didn't, Viola was sure Amanda Drinkwater would.

Instead, her mother-in-law came in to see her. "How are you, dear?" she asked.

"It isn't playing games … any more." Viola had to pause before the last two words. Yes, these contractions were in earnest.

"Walk around. Walk around as long as you can. It helps a little."
The older woman smiled wryly. "Nothing helps much. After a while,
nothing helps at all." She would know what she was talking about.

Viola walked around. Every five minutes or so, she gritted her
teeth through another contraction. Peter came back with Guinevere
Worth. The midwife nodded to see Viola on her feet. "How strong
are the pangs?" she asked.

"Strong enough!" Viola said.

Guinevere Worth's smile showed little mirth. "That's what you
think now. When the time comes, you'll feel like you're trying to shit
out a watermelon, excuse the bad language." By the way Amanda
Drinkwater laughed and cut it off short, the midwife's phrase might
have been foul but was also on point.

Viola walked and walked and walked. Peter went into his parents' bedroom and stayed there with his father. The women had the
rest of the house to themselves. Every so often, Guinevere Worth
would feel Viola's belly. "How much longer, do you think?" Viola
asked after a while.

"You're coming along fine. The baby's head is dropping down the
way it should. Another two or three hours, I'd say."

"So soon?" Julietta said.

"So long?" Viola said. Anyone, even a man from the moon, would
have known which of them was having the baby.

Viola's mother-in-law put an old sheet and a lot of old rags on the
bed. Pretty soon, Viola waddled in there and lay down. Guinevere
Worth closed the door. "Make as much noise as you need to," she
said. "No one will care." Viola would have anyway. The contractions
were in charge now. She wasn't.

She gasped. She swore at Peter for putting her in the fix she was
in. She groaned. Once, when the midwife reached inside her to check
the baby's position, she shrieked. Then she made a sound of enormous,
supreme effort as she pushed. *Shitting out a watermelon* summed it up,
yes. She really did empty her bowels at the same time. St. Augustine
had been right when he wrote *We are born between shit and piss*.

"One more!" Guinevere Worth said urgently. Viola didn't think
she had one more left. She must have, though, because a second

later a shrill cry filled the bedroom. The midwife let out a happy sigh. "You've got a son!"

"Let me see him!" Viola said.

"Wait a moment. I'm tying off the cord … and now I'm cutting it." Guinevere Worth held up the blood-streaked baby in bloody hands.

"Is he supposed to look like that?" Viola asked anxiously. He was as much purple as pink. His little face was all screwed up, while his head seemed more a cone than a sphere.

"He's just fine. He's perfect. He got squashed pushing through, that's all. And he's getting pinker, just the way he should. What will you call him?"

"Call him?" Viola said blankly. Thinking about anything came hard. She felt as if she'd just run twenty miles with a harpsichord strapped to her back. Slowly, she found an answer. "Alfred. He's Alfred Richard Drinkwater." She and Peter had decided they would have named the baby for their mothers had it been a girl. "Put him on me, will you?"

"Of course, dear." The midwife laid Viola's son on her breast, his cheek against her flesh. The baby rooted, searching for a nipple. He might not know much, but he knew how to do that straight out of the womb. He found what he was looking for and started to suck. Just for a moment, his eyes opened and stared at Viola. Then they closed again. He tended to what he was doing. Gently, Guinevere Worth said, "Let him do that for as long as he cares to. I'll go out and give your family the news."

She closed the door behind her. Viola heard cheers from outside the room. Some of them, she thought, came from her own blood kin. Someone must have gone over and told the Williamses her labor had begun. That was good, and not just because her father was a doctor.

She secured Alfred Richard Drinkwater in the crook of her elbow. He nursed noisily till he fell asleep all at once. Viola dabbed at the corner of his mouth with a rag. That made him root again, but didn't wake him. She began to doze herself. If she'd ever earned sleep, this was the time.

With a cradle in it, Peter's room was more crowded than ever. He found he enjoyed being a father, even if he didn't like it when Little

Alf—which was what everybody started calling the baby—woke up wailing two or three times a night. Viola would get out of bed, clean him off, give him her breast, and then return him to the cradle. Peter was tired all the time. So were his father and mother and sisters. Little Alf's racket woke them, too.

If he and his blood relations were tired, Viola was exhausted. She changed the baby most of the time and fed him all the time. She ran a fever for a week or so after he was born. Peter worried. "It's common. She's been through a lot," Richard Williams told him. "If it gets high, or if it doesn't fade fairly soon, then …" His father-in-law's voice trailed away, which made Peter guess the doctor worried, too. Everyone knew mothers could die of childbed fever.

But Viola got better, not worse. She slept whenever she could, whether it was dark outside or light. She ate enough to startle Peter, but not his mother. "She's feeding Little Alf along with herself. She needs the extra victuals. I know I did," Amanda Drinkwater said.

When Viola was awake, she focused on the baby to the exclusion of everything else, Peter included. He understood that with the part of his mind that had made him quick on his mental feet at Lincoln's Inn. The part that had got used to a wife who put him first resented it. He tried not to complain too much. He had the feeling Viola tried not to snap at him too much when he did.

A month or so after Little Alf was born, Viola felt strong enough to go to the cathedral with the Drinkwaters and join the Williamses for his baptism. A priest dipped him in the font and, above his squawks, baptized him in the name of the Father and the Son and the Holy Spirit. The Latin washed over him as the water did.

"I'm glad that's done," Peter said as he carried the baby home.

"Yes, it's good to take care of it," Viola said. He wondered exactly how she meant that. He'd long guessed she and her family took the faith and the Church even less seriously than he and his relatives did. She didn't flaunt that or make a fuss about it; she was always polite and outwardly observant. But he would have been surprised if she cared much.

Three or four weeks later, Peter was holding Little Alf when the baby looked up at him and smiled. He felt himself turn to gelatin, so much so that he almost dropped his son. He exclaimed about it.

"Did he?" Viola said. "I've thought he was trying to a couple of times, but I haven't seen him really do it."

"Come look," Peter said.

She did. Little Alf's eyes swung her way. They were darker than they had been when he was born; Peter guessed they'd end up green or hazel. As soon as the baby recognized his mother, his face creased and his mouth opened wide in a bigger smile than Peter'd got.

"You're right!" Viola sounded as entranced as he'd felt a moment earlier. "That's … the most wonderful thing I ever saw."

"It's marvelous," Peter agreed. "But the most wonderful thing I ever saw was you holding him on the bed after the midwife told us you were both all right."

His wife set a hand on his shoulder for a moment, though she said, "I must have looked as if a teamster wagon had run me over. I felt that way!"

"I was so glad everything went the way it should, I'm sure I didn't notice. Besides, you always look good to me," Peter said.

"You're sweet," Viola told him. "I'm sure you're lying through your teeth, but you're sweet."

"I have passed the bar. I am pledged to fidelity to truth," Peter said with dignity. Viola laughed at him, which rather spoiled the effect.

When Little Alf was about three months old, he figured out how to roll over. Joanna was almost five years younger than Peter; he remembered her doing that when she was a baby. She'd wiggled and squirmed till she managed it. His son found a different way. He used the weight and momentum of his head—which, like any baby's, was large and heavy in proportion to the rest of him—to flip over from his stomach to his back. He seemed very proud of himself afterwards, too.

"We'll have to be careful watching him from now on, or else he'll throw himself down off the bed and onto the floor," Viola said. "Margaret did that once or twice, no matter how hard we kept an eye on her."

"By what I've seen of Margaret, it doesn't surprise me a bit," Peter replied.

Viola laughed and nodded. A moment later, though, she grew more serious. "Little Alf is doing everything a baby ought to do.

He's putting on weight—he's a big, husky boy. He's smiling at us. He's making silly noises. And now he's rolling over."

"He should be. You said it yourself—he's doing what he ought to."

"I know. I'm so glad. It's the surest, purest sign he hasn't got the Wasting. Babies who are born with it don't thrive. They don't do things as fast as healthy children do. God spared us that, anyhow."

"Oh." Peter hugged her. She clung to him. *Even unto the fourth generation* rang in his mind. But that, at least, hadn't happened here. "I can dare hope I haven't got the taint inside me," he said.

"We can both dare hope," she answered. "I've always hoped. You've shown no signs of it, *Deo gratias.* Nor have I. The baby might have told us otherwise, but he seems well, too."

"Yes," Peter breathed. "He does." The fear had been in his mind, too. It still was. He wondered whether he'd ever get out from under it and come out into the pure, clean light of confidence. He wasn't there yet, but he thought he could see some of that light off in the metaphorical distance.

"We're on this path together," Viola said. "All we can do is go forward along it."

"And hope everything works out all right," Peter said.

"And hope," his wife agreed.

Bit by bit, Little Alf's habits grew more regular. He slept through most nights, which meant his harried parents also got more sleep. In the morning and afternoon, his naps got more reliable. Peter started doing more to help in his father's practice. He had no trouble taking care of what the older man required of him, though he enjoyed it no better than he had before.

Viola began helping with the women's work in the household once more, too. She also began to write again when she could snatch ten minutes or fifteen or sometimes even half an hour from all the other things she needed to take care of.

"I used to think any stretch less than half an hour long wasn't long enough," she told Peter, and laughed at her own naïveté. "If I can get a couple of sentences down now, I do, and pick up again three hours later for another paragraph or two. It isn't a pretty way to write, but it's better than not writing at all."

"Good." Peter knew he sounded distracted. He lay closer to Little Alf than Viola did; if the baby tried to dive off the bed, he'd have to catch him.

"I'll have to change some scenes I wrote a while ago," Viola said. "I know things now that I didn't before." She reached out and touched his cheek. "I have a better notion what love's all about, for instance."

"Well, so do I," Peter said. "You think about it beforehand, but you don't think about it with some particular person. Hello, particular person."

"Hello," she answered. Then Peter did have to grab for the baby, who was also very much a particular person, and getting more so by the day.

Stolen minutes. Stolen quarter-hours. A few words. A few sentences. A few paragraphs. A few pages. A few chapters. Everything took longer than Viola wished it would. Episodes that looked grand and sweeping in the story she was trying to tell got put together in dribs and drabs, bits and pieces, like a picture puzzle assembled from dozens of tiny, oddly shaped wooden pieces.

The writing. The housework. Her husband. The baby. Above all, the baby. Peter was pretty good at understanding she couldn't pay as much attention to what he wanted as she had before—pretty good, but a long way from perfect. Every once in a while, she snapped at him. She supposed she was lucky he didn't hit her.

Her husband had his own frustrations. She thought they were smaller than hers, but knew he wouldn't agree with her. "When will you finish your book?" he asked one evening after Little Alf had gone to sleep. "If I never have to draft another bill of sale for real property, it will make me the happiest man on earth."

Viola didn't quite snap at him then, but it was a damned near-run thing. As calmly as she could, she answered, "I would write more if I had more time to write in. With the baby, the work around the house, and you, I have a good deal less than I wish I did. This shouldn't be news to you."

By Peter's expression, it wasn't. "Bugger the housework!" he exclaimed.

"When I hear that from your mother, I shall take it seriously. From you? I fear not," Viola said. "I also ought to remind you I have no guarantee Master Egerton will pay me even a farthing for the new book, let alone enough so we can live comfortably on that payment allied to whatever you bring in by teaching. Writing is a chancy business." He looked more unhappy yet, but held his peace.

A couple of days later, when it was just the two of them in the kitchen, Amanda Drinkwater said, "Peter tells me you wish you had more time to write."

"Yes, that's true." Viola nodded.

"He says you wish you didn't need to do so much housework, so you could use that time—or as much of it as the baby gives you—to put words on paper," her mother-in-law continued.

Now Viola shook her head. "I have never said that! He asked why the new one wasn't moving faster, and I told him—there aren't enough hours in the day for me to work on it as much as I'd like. So I work on it as I can, and it does move forward. Slowly, but it does. The world is the way it is, not the way we wish it were." Viola's mouth twisted. "Any woman who doesn't live in Temecula would say the same."

"Heaven knows *that's* true." Amanda Drinkwater paused. "You made more money from your Temeculans than I thought you had. Would the new one bring in as much, or perhaps even more?"

"I can't tell you that. I hope so, but I don't know. I can't even guess."

"You're in the habit of saying what you mean. Anyone who knows you for even a moment will understand that. As far as I've been able to judge, you're also an honest person."

"Thank you, Mother Drinkwater. I do my best," Viola said.

As if she hadn't spoken, the older woman went on, "You've never shirked the work here, either."

To that, Viola just shrugged. "It's the same kind of thing I was doing at my family's house before I married Peter. I know how. The ways I learned aren't just the same as yours, but most of them are close enough."

"Your mother can manage a house. No doubt of that." Amanda Drinkwater smiled, at first thinly and then more as if she meant it. "I've talked with Julietta and Joanna. They wouldn't mind, and I shouldn't, either, if you took half an hour or an hour every day to work on your story. If Little Alf lets you get away with that, I mean."

"Yes, if!" Viola exclaimed. "And thank you very much! I never wanted to make a nuisance of myself by asking for anything special. That was the fastest way I could think of to wear out my welcome here."

"It's work, the same way lacemaking or embroidery would be. I gather it pays better—or it can pay better—than either of those. Since that's true, I'd be a fool to try to keep you from doing it. I hope I'm not a fool, or not that kind of fool, anyhow."

"No one would ever call you a fool." Viola meant that. Her mother-in-law might not be the most interesting person in the world, but she was far from stupid.

"My turn to thank you," Amanda Drinkwater said. "One other thing, by the way—Peter thinks the sun, the moon, and the stars all spin around you."

Viola's cheeks heated. She hoped the older woman wouldn't notice. "I think I've made a lucky marriage. I'm glad he does, too."

Little Alf chose that moment to wake up from his nap with a yowl. Viola was relieved to escape her mother-in-law. She cleaned off the baby's backside, put a fresh clout around him, and took him out to the parlor so she could sit in the rocking chair there while she nursed him. He gulped milk as if he thought he wouldn't get any more after this.

She looked down at his small, intent face. He stared up at her. He knew who she was now. *I'm the milk wagon, that's who*, she thought. But she knew there was more to it. She was his mother. She liked that, and so did her son.

Her words were her children, too. They were the only children writers who were men could bear. For some lady writers, they were enough. If the child of her flesh slowed the birthing of the next child of her mind … she shrugged, which made Little Alf smile. The life she had wasn't what she dreamt of, but it wasn't bad, either.

If Peter stayed well. If she did. If any babies she had later did. The Wasting hadn't gone away. It wouldn't, not while she lived. If her children stayed healthy when they were young, she'd worry about them again when they grew up. What else could she possibly do? With things as they were, few triumphs seemed grander than managing to live a full life. The sickness had made everyone afraid since it broke out across the world. As far as she could see, it always would.